Polly Crosby lives in Norfolk with her husband, son and rescue cat. To find out more about Polly's writing, please visit pollycrosby.com. Polly can also be found on Twitter as @WriterPolly.

Also by Polly Crosby

The Illustrated Child

'Like a surreal cabinet of curiosities – haunting, eerie, evocative.'
Bridget Collins, *Sunday Times* bestselling author of *The Binding*

...sh, mythical world...
this dream-like novel set on a small island . . .
But what's so impressive is the layered richness of
Crosby's imagination, realised beautifully in vivid writing.'
Eve Chase, *Sunday Times* bestselling author of *The Glass House*

'Like a butterfly emerging from a chrysalis, the story emerges
slowly, allowing you to immerse yourself in its wonders.'
Heat

'A luminous and beautiful novel that gently lures the
reader into a captivating story with a mystery at its
heart. The slow unravelling of secrets throughout the
novel was utterly absorbing and emotional.'
Jennifer Saint, *Sunday Times* bestselling author of *Ariadne*

'A beautifully written tale of butterflies, secrets and silk.'
Sonia Velton, author of *Blackberry* and *Wild Rose*

'Rich and evocative storytelling is at the heart of this
beautifully atmospheric book.'
My Weekly

'Immersive, atmospheric and so very imaginative.'
Kate Sawyer, author of *The Stranding*

The
Unravelling

POLLY CROSBY

ONE PLACE. MANY STORIES

HQ
An imprint of HarperCollins*Publishers* Ltd
1 London Bridge Street
London SE1 9GF

www.harpercollins.co.uk

HarperCollins*Publishers*
1st Floor, Watermarque Building, Ringsend Road
Dublin 4, Ireland

This edition 2022

1

First published in Australia and New Zealand as *The Women of Pearl Island* by
HQ, an imprint of HarperCollins*Publishers* Ltd 2021

First published in Great Britain by
HQ, an imprint of HarperCollins*Publishers* Ltd 2022

MIX
Paper from
responsible sources
FSC™ C007454

This book is produced from independently certified FSC™ paper
to ensure responsible forest management.

For more information visit: www.harpercollins.co.uk/green

This book is set in 11/15.5 pt. Centaur by Type-it AS, Norway

Printed and Bound in the UK using 100% Renewable Electricity at
CPI Group (UK) Ltd, Croydon, CR0 4YY

To Mum and Dad

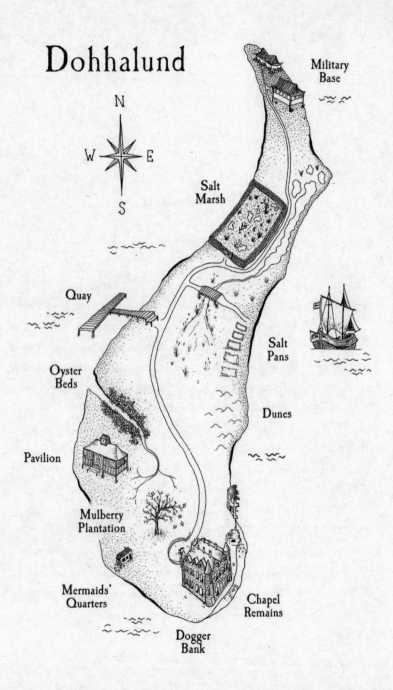

Dohhalund

Military Base

Salt Marsh

Quay

Salt Pans

Oyster Beds

Dunes

Pavilion

Mulberry Plantation

Mermaids' Quarters

Chapel Remains

Dogger Bank

Prologue

Marianne
1955

Marianne bent over the ragged remains of the poor butterfly's broken wing. The insect held still, as if it knew she was only trying to help.

The wing was damaged beyond repair, and she gripped the tweezers in her left hand and, with great care, lifted the replacement silken waxed wing she had made, stopping to consider it in mid-air. It was a perfect match to the quaking peacock butterfly's remaining wing, even down to the glittering dust that coated its surface.

She painted a fine dab of clear glue onto its edge and brought it fluidly in to the broken wing, holding it in place with motionless hands. Four shimmering blue eyes aligned on the wings and gazed up at her, and she allowed herself a small smile.

Carefully, she opened the tweezers, and the butterfly lay pulsing on the desk, unaware it was free.

'Go,' she said, wishing it upwards.

Slowly, delicately, it lifted its wings, both the real and the manufactured, until they closed above it. Marianne frowned as the silk wing lagged slightly, but then, with sudden weightlessness, the butterfly took off.

It flew around the great panelled room, and Marianne sat back in her chair, following its path with her eyes, a surge of joy bursting through her as she watched it in its jagged, miraculous flight.

Turning back to her desk, she began to clear away her work. The remains of the damaged wing lay like a spent husk on the leather surface. It had been torn away, almost down to the core, the pattern of the two eyes smeared and disfigured and, for a brief moment, she had the feeling that it was looking at her, the eyes penetrating her in a way that she didn't understand.

Above her, the repaired butterfly danced high in the air, unaware that anything was wrong.

Chapter One

Tartelin

Summer 2018

'I do not require nappy changing, I do not require spoon-feeding, I do not require my ego massaging. What I do require is someone with a deft pair of hands. I asked for someone with experience in dealing with little things, delicate things. A scientist, perhaps. Is that you?'

I nod.

'Show me your hands then, child.'

I hold them out, palm side downwards, and she wheels herself over and inspects them. Her own hands, I see now, have a tremor.

'You're a pretty girl,' she says, her eyes drifting over my face, glancing off my cheek, and I feel my skin redden. 'Not very robust though. Are you sure this is the right job for you?' I open my mouth to speak, but she cuts me off. 'What did you do, before you came here? How is it that you are suited to this vacancy?'

I frown. We went over all this in our letters, back and forth, back and forth. Written on paper, not sent by email, each one signed 'Miss Marianne Stourbridge' in her regimented, barbed-wire scrawl. My life back home was the reason she chose me. But then she is old, and she can't be expected to remember everything.

'I grew up around my mother's artwork, helping her out in her studio,' I say, more loudly than I mean to. 'And then I went to art school myself. Mum's work was focused on found objects ... making art from bits of nature: feathers, leaves and twigs—'

'Lepidoptera aren't "bits of nature", Miss Brown.'

'She also made sculptures out of grains of rice in her spare time. I helped her.'

'Why on earth would anyone do that?' She leaves the question hanging in the air and turns her chair abruptly, wheeling herself back to her desk.

The chair is made from cane. It looks like an antique, and I'm surprised it still works. It must be exhausting to propel.

'It's a shame you don't have a scientific background, but now you're here, you'll have to do. Here, hold this.' She lifts a pair of gold tweezers into the air and I hasten forward and take them. 'No, not like that. Pinch. Gently. That's it.'

I adjust my hold, and feel how the spring of the tines is like an extension of my fingers and I'm back with my mother and she's saying, 'Careful, Tartelin, don't squeeze too hard, feather barbs bruise easily.' But before I can use this new-found body part, the tweezers are whisked away from me, and she's turning again to the desk and bending over her work. I stand by her side and wait, wondering if I'm allowed to go. The clock on the mantel chimes loudly. I count eight. I look at my watch. It's ten past two.

'Miss Stourbridge? Shall I adjust your clock?'

'No point. It'll only go back to eight o'clock.'

I look over at it, frowning. The second hand is juddering in jerky movements. It makes me dizzy to look at it, as if it's measuring a different kind of time. I turn back to my employer.

Miss Stourbridge is so still as she works. I can see her teasing the

4

body of a dead moth from a cocoon, her fingers moving infinitesimally slowly. I look around the room. It is lined in dark panels of wood, and every surface has frames and frames of butterflies and moths, glinting pins plunged into husked bodies.

'Did you catch all these butterflies?'

She is silent, and at first I think she hasn't heard me. But then I see she's holding her breath so as not to disturb the moth's delicate wings. I watch closely, the clock ticking behind us. I'm looking, not at her work, but at her ribs, waiting for them to inflate, waiting for her nostrils to swell, anything that shows air is passing into her chest. My eyes sting from the pain of staring. She is so still that she has become a part of the chair she sits in. Only her finger and thumb move achingly slowly, and the minutes tick by.

When I was young, I used to try to be as still as she is now. My mother would sit me on her knee and tell me stories, and I would hold myself as still as a statue, bewitched by her tales.

'Long ago,' she always began, in a voice that was reserved only for when the moon was rising, 'I was a tiny jellied spawn, no bigger than a pearl, floating in the earth's great oceans. The fish nibbled and swallowed my brothers and sisters up, snap, snap, snap, and I was left, coming at last to rest on the pebbled shore of a beach. And that is how I came to have these,' she would say, waving her hands in front of my face, so close that they skimmed my eyelashes and all I could see was the thin layer of webbed skin between each finger. To my unprejudiced four-year-old eyes, the webs were not a deformity: they were beautiful, useful, magical, and I wished with all my heart that I could be like her, could be from the sea.

I take my eyes from the poor moth on the desk, and look over Miss Stourbridge's head to the picture window that frames the sea beyond, and I remember anew that the sea surrounds us here, like a comforting arm holding the world at bay. A feeling of calm settles over me. However strange this woman is, whatever my job might entail, it was the right decision to come here, I can feel it.

I had seen the advertisement in one of Mum's ornithological magazines. Mum bought them for the photographs. She particularly liked the close-ups of the birds' eyes and feathers. The magazines were littered throughout our house, spattered with drops of paint, pages ripped out and twisted together into the vague forms of gulls and robins, so that every surface was covered in paper birds made of paper birds.

But the latest magazine had landed on the doormat, pristine and untouched, and when I shook it from its clear plastic covering, it had fallen open on the advert.

PA required to assist lepidopterist. Must be able to start immediately. Must not be squeamish.

When I had written to ask for more information, the return address had intrigued me.

Dogger Bank House, Dohhalund.

Dohhalund. An unusual word, not English-sounding at all. A bit of research showed me that it was a tiny island off the East Anglian coast, the long thin shape of it reminiscent of a fish leaping out of the water. Its heritage was a mixture of English and Dutch. Looking at it on a map on my phone, it had looked so small that I imagined you could walk its circumference in only a few hours. I had tried to picture what kind of an island it would be: a cold, hard rock grizzled with the droppings of thousands of seabirds, or a flat stretch of white sand, waiting for my footprints? Whatever it turned out to be, the isolation of it appealed to me.

Miss Stourbridge's letters had been vague about the position she was offering, but she did tell me, rather proudly, that the island had belonged to her family for hundreds of years. While I wait, I look about the room, searching for photographs, evidence of other people. Where is her family now?

I shift my weight carefully from foot to foot and I glance at my watch. Two twenty-three. Thirteen minutes. I wonder if I'm being paid to stand and do nothing. I look around the room. Next to the desk is a large clear glass box. Inside hang rows and rows of cocoons of all different shapes and sizes. One or two are twitching. I turn away with a sting of shame, feeling somehow as if I've looked at something I shouldn't have.

Over by the window, there is a huge black telescope on a stand. Unlike everything else in this place, it looks very modern. Next to it on the windowsill sits a battered pair of binoculars on a worn leather strap.

Quietly I back towards the chaise longue in the corner and lower myself onto its tattered silk cover. It's the first time I've sat down in hours, and my body sings with relief. I edge my hand into my pocket and pull out my phone. It's switched off: the battery ran low somewhere off the coast of Norfolk at around the same time that the signal disappeared. The lack of signal hadn't worried me: I'd been looking forward to charging my phone when I arrived, tapping in Miss Stourbridge's Wi-Fi code, the friendly glow of my phone's screen a comfort in this new place.

I look around for a socket in the room, and with a sudden slick shiver I find I can't see any. There must be electricity here, surely. But if not … realisation runs through me like a thrill: if there's no electricity in this house, there won't be any Wi-Fi either. And with no signal, there's no way of contacting the outside world. No way for the outside world to contact me. The roar of the sea appears to amplify through the thin glass of the window, rough and crashing, as if it is rushing towards me like a tsunami. Suddenly England seems very far away.

I look down at my phone and contemplate turning it on. I have a desperate need to open the photos app, to gaze at a familiar face in order to find an anchor in this strange new world. I touch my finger to the button, trying to remember how much battery I have left. Two per cent? Eight? My finger rests lightly on the button, undecided, the screen black and glaring.

Across the room, Miss Stourbridge sits back against her chair, and I tuck my phone away and approach the desk. I can feel it pressing against my skin, pulsing against me like the beat of a heart that isn't mine.

Miss Stourbridge sighs, her breath ruffling the damp wings of the newly hatched moth in front of her.

'Dusky brocade,' she says, nodding at the tiny brown body, 'they have such beautiful names, moths. They may not be as pretty as butterflies, but the names we have given them over the centuries means even Shakespeare was a fan. Beauty isn't everything, it turns out.'

I see her looking at my cheek as she says it, and for a moment I'm disappointed. Surely here, on an island in the middle of the North Sea, I am away from prejudice? It had been part of the reason the job appealed to me: to be able to stride across this island without the worry of others' stares. Or perhaps I'm naïve, and intolerance breeds in isolated outcrops like this, running within its very seams.

She sets down the delicate tweezers at last and, turning awkwardly in her chair, looks me in the eye for the first time since I got here. Her eyes are a deep grey-brown, not dissimilar to the moth on the desk. They are full of a cataclysmic wisdom, as if a fuse has been lit but the spark is not rushing along as intended.

'So, Tartelin, do you understand what I am doing, here on this island?'

'You're a lepidopterist.' I say, remembering the word from the advert. 'You catch and study butterflies and moths.'

'Yes and no. I think that's probably the closest term for what I'm trying to do. Dohhalund is a good place for finding the butterflies that get lost, the ones that get blown over from the Netherlands and Denmark. They rest on the ships, you see – and on the trawlers and Dogger boats the island is named after. But in the last few years I've dedicated my life to mutations. Do you understand what that word means?'

'Yes.' I bite my tongue. Who doesn't know what a mutation is, living as we are in a world where viruses mutate in our bodies and on our screens every day? I think of my mother's webbed hands. I go to touch my face, but stop myself just in time.

'Take me over to the window,' she orders.

I push her across the uneven floorboards and she wobbles in her chair like a marionette. The room is large. It might once have been an upstairs sitting room, but now it is a workroom: a vast empty space of floorboards and wooden panelling. The desk, a huge, unfashionable mahogany lump inset with green leather, sits in front of the window facing the sea. A small Chinese cabinet on ornate legs has pride of place beneath a wall of pinned butterflies. There is an upright piano near the door, and the tattered chaise I sat on looks as if it's been pushed unceremoniously into a corner, as if to get it out of the way. Other than that, the room is empty, as long as you don't count the hundreds of pairs of butterflies' eyes watching you from the walls.

'What could cause mutation, Tartelin?'

'I ... I'm not a scientist, Miss Stourbridge.' Panic begins to set in. This feels like an interview, but surely I already have the job? I've come all this way. With a prickle of tension, I wonder if she'll send me back on the next available boat.

'When I came back to the island two months ago,' she says, leaning forward and indicating I should open the large bay window, 'I saw a little white bird over the sea. Just there.' She points with a shaking, liver-spotted hand.

Struggling to follow the darting direction of her thoughts, I edge past the telescope and unlatch the window. Immediately, the wet breeze skims off the North Sea and bursts into the room. A pile of papers ripples on the desk, barely held down by a lump of unpolished amber the size of a human skull.

'Swallows always return to the same nest, year after year,' she says. 'I remember the swallows nesting here when I was a girl. Their descendants are there now, just above the window. Have a look.'

I sit on the edge of the window, careful not to knock the binoculars off, and lean out, looking up. Immediately the wind wails in my ears. Just above the window frame a line of mud nests are glued to the eaves. Tiny voices can be heard from within.

'You've seen swallows before, I take it? You know what they look like?'

I lean back in. 'Of course.' I'm getting used to her short, sharp way of talking, like a schoolteacher to a child. It must just be uneasiness at having someone new in her house, a way of setting boundaries. I hope it will mellow with time.

'Tell me then.'

I think back to Mum's magazines. 'They're quite small, dark birds with a long, forked tail.'

'Good girl. Keep watching.'

I lean out again. The baby swallows are poking their heads out now. Three little navy blue and pale peach faces. With a faint whoosh the mother swoops in, narrowly missing the top of my head. Her body is white from head to toe. The fledgling swallows' mouths open, gaping wide. A fourth baby pops its head out, squealing for food. It, too, is white. I've never seen anything like it before.

'The term for an abnormally white bird is "leucistic",' Miss Stourbridge says. 'It's strange that she was able to find a mate. Most leucistic birds never manage it. They are considered freaks, and freaks are rarely accepted, even in the avian world.'

I watch the mother ignore the tiny white dot in the nest, shovelling dead insects into its three siblings' beaks instead. I have a feeling Miss Stourbridge is studying my cheek again. I stay on the windowsill, looking up, avoiding her gaze.

'I suspect there have been changes to a few species on this island since I was last here. Notably the winged ones. This is why I need you to catch some butterflies for me: so that I can know for sure.'

A movement out of the window catches my eye, and I stiffen.

'Is that your dog?' I point to the ground below the window, where a thin, swollen-nippled bitch is trotting across Miss Stourbridge's garden, her five puppies straggling behind.

Miss Stourbridge leans forward to look. 'No. The dogs here are wild. Presumably some were pets once.' She lifts the binoculars and peers more closely at the dog. 'There's something rather wolfish about her, isn't there? It's funny, humans have bred dogs for thousands of years, turning them into sick caricatures of themselves, but leave them to their own devices and they flourish. We don't always get it right, playing God.'

The mother dog sits suddenly and scratches her ear with a hind leg, the puppies pouncing on her floppy belly and suckling voraciously. Behind her, the garden ends abruptly at the edge of the cliff. A house this size would surely have had a much bigger garden. I look at the cliff edge, at an oak tree that grows precariously out from it, gnarled roots reaching into empty space. The garden must have eroded over time. How long until the rest of it disappears, devoured by the sea?

I lean further out of the window and look to the left, along the length of the island. There are more wild dogs in the distance, packs in groups of three or four, lithe and skinny, trotting over the brambled ground.

'In order to explore, you'll need to understand the layout of the island,' Miss Stourbridge continues. 'This house is situated on the most south-easterly point, the highest part of Dohhalund. On a clear day you can just make out the coast of Holland from here. To the north,' she points to the left, 'on that long spit of shingle, is the military base.'

I look in the direction she's pointing. Far away I can see what look like buildings, hazy on the horizon. I'd like to look through the binoculars, to get a better view, but they are still in her lap, her hand on them protectively.

'To the west of us of course,' she says, gesturing loosely behind us with a wave of her hand, 'is England.'

I think of the map I saw of the island, of the way it looked like a leaping fish, long and thin, a sharp spit of land at the north like a flicking tail and a soft curve of beach at the south like a head. I look down into the garden again. The mother dog is still there, stretched out in the sun.

'Are they dangerous?' I say, nodding at it.

'The dogs? Oh, I shouldn't think so. Only when protecting their pups. They might follow you if they think you have food, but I'm sure they'll do you no harm.'

'And am I right in thinking there's no electricity on the island?'

'That is correct. There used to be a generator at the military base, as I recall, but I doubt it works now.'

'And is there a phone signal anywhere?'

She regards me with those sharp, wise eyes. 'I have no idea, having never owned a mobile telephone.'

I look out at the island again, scanning the land. She hadn't warned me about the dogs before I came, or the lack of electricity. She'd hardly filled me in on the nature of my job at all, as if she wanted to trap me here so that I had no choice but to give it a go. As I stepped off the fishing boat earlier, gripping the handlebars of the ancient bicycle she had left for me at the station, I realised with a sense of queasiness left over from the boat ride that this wasn't an ordinary island, not a holiday destination certainly. Not really beautiful at all in the traditional sense of the word. It was a land covered in pebble and concrete, sewn together by weeds that twisted like rough stitches across its surface.

The fisherman had silently pointed a weatherworn finger when I asked where Dogger Bank House was. I couldn't read his expression, his heavy-lidded eyes drawn like a shutter to repel years of salt water. He hadn't wanted to stay around and help me with my bags to the house. I got the sense that he rarely brought his boat into these waters, that he avoided stepping foot on the island as much as he could.

'It's been sixty-three years since I left Dohhalund for the mainland,' Miss Stourbridge says, bringing me back to the darkness of the room, 'and still this island is changing.' Her voice softens as she says this, and I pull myself in from the lure of the sea to hear her properly, latching the glass closed against the spray.

'As well as finding butterflies, you will help me with menial tasks in the house: light the lamps for me, run my baths, cook my meals. You will also wind the clock each day.' She nods towards the mantel clock as it ticks erratically.

'But I thought it—'

'The key is in place. Twelve clockwise turns. No more, or you will break it.'

But it's already broken, I think.

'Above all else, Miss Brown, your job is to observe. Observe the island. Observe what I do. You are my eyes and ears, and you cannot begin to help me until you have submerged yourself here. Island life is very different to mainland living, this island more so than others. Now, do you have any questions?'

'Why did you leave the island?'

Miss Stourbridge looks at me as if I have said the wrong thing.

'We were told we must,' she says simply, her hands gripping the bony wheels of the chair so that her knuckles whiten unpleasantly. 'Do you have any questions about your role here?'

I flush, realising my mistake. 'Why did you choose me?' I say, grabbing onto the first question that offers itself.

'Honestly? Because you could come immediately.'

I am affronted by this answer. That's it? My timing? Not my CV, or my artwork, or the care I have given my own family?

'From our correspondence, I also suspected you would be a good fit. You have something of the islander about you, I can sense it. You're astute, and you keep your emotions closed in. I like those qualities.'

Are they qualities? To me, they sound like faults.

'I don't want an emotional snip of a thing that flees at the first sign of my scalpel. I've had two like that already. Third time lucky, I think the saying goes.'

She glides back over to her desk, and leans over the glass box containing the cocoons. Lifting the lid, she reaches inside, and carefully detaches a chrysalis from its delicate fastening. It pulses as if it knows what she is going to do. She settles back at her desk, sitting the cocoon on the scratched leather surface, and picks up a scalpel. I realise the conversation is over.

'Is it safe?' I blurt out, thinking of the rough sea and the barren landscape and the isolation of it all.

Miss Stourbridge pauses, looking up. 'Safe?'

'Out there.' I point to the window, to the evening sun slanting across what remains of the garden.

'Yes, on the whole. Make sure to avoid the areas of inland shingle, we don't know what's beneath it. And don't get too close to the military base on the spit. Remember, we are, to all intents and purposes, alone on this island, Tartelin. There are no hospitals here. No police. Even the safest places can be dangerous for one who is *too* carefree.'

In the brief moment before she turns back to the moth, I see something else in her eyes, a darkness like ink spreading in water. Then she hunches over the insect, and I realise I'm dismissed.

I cross the room, taking one last look at the frail, bent woman in the wheelchair, before going out through the door onto the landing. As I begin my descent of the stairs, her voice drifts down, following me where her body cannot. The authority of it ties me to the stair.

'You'll find your rooms and the kitchen on the ground floor. I take my evening meal at seven o'clock – there is a whole sea bass in the ice box. You can gut a fish, can't you?'

I clutch the polished banister in my hand as I descend.

Chapter Two

Marianne
October 1927

The blindfold rustled against her eyelids. She reached up to smooth the material, conscious, even when unsighted, of how she looked.

'Is it a horse?' She had wanted a pony for an age. Papa's excuse had always been that there were no boats big enough to transport one, but perhaps now she was fifteen?

'No, it's not a horse.'

Marianne wrinkled her nose, feeling the silk of the blindfold bunch between her eyes. 'A new croquet set, then?'

'No, but it *is* made of wood.'

Close by, Ebisu struck up his cry, and Marianne jumped slightly at the sound. She could tell it was him, because none of the other peacocks were as bloodcurdlingly loud or as bold. He had a habit of following her, however much she tried to shoo him away, and she put a hand out and felt the rustle of his feathers as he strutted past.

She heard Papa sigh quietly to himself, and she applied herself to the puzzle in hand, wanting to please him. A sudden thought struck her.

'Is it a new butterfly net? A folding one like yours?' She swung round wildly towards her father, forgetting she couldn't see him. 'Am I to be allowed to go catching alone?' Perhaps her father had finally given in. Perhaps her surprise was the gift of freedom: a perfect birthday present.

Her father's hands, resting on her shoulders as he steered her across the garden, squeezed painfully for a moment. 'You're getting closer. Keep guessing.'

She could hear the tremble in his voice. She wondered if the surprise was really for him.

'The clue is in the blindfold,' he whispered, close to her ear.

She reached up again and touched the cloth over her eyes. How could a clue be in something that was stopping her from looking? She ran her fingers over the material. It was one of her mother's scarves, the cool silk slick as water.

'I haven't any idea, Papa, please let me look.'

His hands left her shoulders and pulled gently at the knot at the nape of her neck. The silk scarf fell away and she blinked in the blue light that misted up from the sea.

They were standing in a secluded corner of the gardens, a square space bordered by boxwood and yew, a small fountain at its centre. It was indeed where Marianne had envisioned her croquet game to be played, but instead of colourful mallets and hoops, she saw before her rows and rows of saplings. They had been dug into the manicured grass with no thought to the prettiness of the place. Marianne stepped delicately over a pile of earth littering the walkway. Mama would be furious; this garden had been sown by her great-grandfather.

'Do you know what they are?' Papa was standing very still, his hands bunching in and out as if he were trying to contain his excitement.

She took one of the leaves between her fingers. It was large and papery, the dull green of an overgrown nettle.

'Is it ... is it mulberry?'

'It is!' Her father stamped his foot in excitement. He marched forward and plucked a great fistful of leaves, looking at them with such rapture that Marianne couldn't help but smile.

'I take it this is only part of my surprise?'

'You're right, you're right, darling girl, this is just the start. I am expecting a delivery of silkworms and eggs later this very week. And not just that. I have got you your very own silk-girl. She'll teach you everything you need to know. You will learn the job of empresses! Of queens!'

'Wherever did you find a silk-girl?'

'An acquaintance of mine had adventures out in France during the war, resulting in a child. Her mother died a few years ago and he brought the girl to England and secured the finest schooling for her, so she will be a good intellectual match for you, *mijn parelmoer*. She must be eleven or twelve now. She grew up in a *magnanerie* – a silk farm – so she is educated in the art of silkworm rearing. She'll teach you everything you need to know, I'm sure.'

Marianne was momentarily swayed by the image of a foreign servant-girl following her around, dressed head to toe in silk. What did French people look like? She had only ever met one French person before: an old Onion Johnny who had stopped off at Dohhalund on his way back home. She remembered him knocking at the kitchen door whilst she was watching Cook bake a cake. His bicycle had been piled high with strings of globular, pink onions, and he'd had a pinched face and watery eyes, no doubt from the constant astringent waft rising from his wares. Marianne wondered if the new girl would smell of onions too. She wrinkled her nose at the thought.

'But …' She saw how the single word brought her father back to the ground, and guilt prickled at her skin, but she continued anyway, resolute. 'But, I want to hunt butterflies, Papa. Wild lepidoptera. Out there.' She gestured at the island. 'Not take care of caterpillars inside.'

'Marianne,' the way he said her name, exhaling it so that it seemed as if it had three times as many vowels as usual, she knew she had lost the fight. 'My dear Marianne, we will continue to hunt butterflies. And the silkworms will form part of your scientific education. *Bombyx mori* are very close to many of our own native moths, you will learn a great deal. It is a fascinating hobby. And a lucrative one,' he added. 'I'm sure you would prefer that to gutting herring?'

'We aren't *that* poor, surely Papa?'

Her father raised his eyebrows. 'Not yet, *mijn lief*, but we'll be far richer once the Dohhalund silk worms rival those of the continent!'

Chapter Three

Tartelin

Summer 2018

I find my bedroom halfway along a dimly lit corridor off the kitchen. It is a small, high-ceilinged space, with barely enough room to slip in beside the single bed. A thin, arched window fills almost all of the exterior wall.

I open my suitcase on the bed and survey its meagre contents. On top is a large, faded book, its spine long since fallen away. On the front in gold lettering it reads, '*L'histoire de la nature des oyseaux.*'

I hold it in my hands for a moment, the familiar weight a comfort, my mind running through the strange illustrations within: bones and feathers, beaks and gleaming eyes. My mother's most successful pieces, her collection of birds, were made with the help of this book.

I have a hazy memory of seeing it for the first time when I was young. Back then, the spine was still intact, and I remember tracing my small finger over the words, complex and important like golden hieroglyphs, no idea that they were in French, not English.

I remember, the book was so heavy that I had to climb onto the table to pull it open. It settled on a diagram of two skeletons. At first glance I thought it was two people, but then I noticed one had a sharp beak where a nose should be. There was an elongated thinness to its arms, and I realised that it was a bird. I remember staring at the two images, thinking how close we must be to birds under our skin, how similar human arms were to wings. I turned the page and found images of ruffled feathers, so like the ruffle of skin on my cheek that I gasped.

'What are you looking at?' My new mother, bending over me to see, her long hair tickling my face.

'The bird's skin,' I said, my hand going to my cheek, touching the soft fray of scales there. 'It's like mine.'

She gave a laugh. 'They're feathers, Tartelin. Perhaps you're part bird.' She pulled my hand from my cheek. I had got into the habit of rubbing at the mark there until it was raw and red. 'Does it hurt?' she asked.

I shook my head.

'May I touch it?'

I drew back, glaring at her.

'You can touch my hands in return.' She held her hands out in front of me and stretched her fingers wide, revealing the soft web of skin between each one. I hesitated, wanting to touch but knowing very well what it was like when a stranger poked and prodded you.

'Go on,' she said, 'it's OK. I trust you.'

I lifted my hand and touched the skin that stretched taut between her finger and thumb, feeling how smooth and thin it was.

'May I?' she said again, her hand hovering close to my cheek, and I nodded. Her fingers stretched out and delicately brushed the strange patch of skin that had always been a part of me, and was the reason – so my foster brother often reminded me – that no one had wanted to adopt me before Mum came along.

'Webs and scales,' my new mother said, hugging me. 'We are alike, Tartelin. So very alike. You were meant to come to me.'

My mind still in the memory, I put the book aside and pull from the case a thick woollen jumper. I unwrap it slowly. Inside is a Quality Street tin, and I hug it to my chest for a moment, enjoying the coldness of the metal on my hot skin. I open the bedside cabinet and place it inside, closing the door on the tin and the memory at the same time.

I turn my attention back to the case, lifting out a small pile of clothes one by one and placing them in a drawer. My phone charger is at the bottom. I look around again for a socket, knowing before I do that there will be none. I put the charger in the drawer, feeling a sense of unease at the separation from the outside world.

There is only one thing left in my suitcase now. It is so small that I might have missed it if I hadn't known to look. I reach into the corner of the case and lift it out carefully, smoothing the tiny feathers. It is a little bird, one of the first of Mum's avian collection, from a series she made when I was very small. Its feathers are woven individually from threads she found out on walks: sheep's wool, discarded clothing, scraps of cloth blown about in the wind. There was a nest, Mum told me once, found in a church, that was made completely of wedding confetti. It is what she held in her mind as she worked on this bird. In the fading light of my little island bedroom, I hold the bird up to my cheek, brushing its soft feathers against the ruffle of skin there. I wish, for a moment, that it would come to life, to keep me company on this strange, lonely isle. Its eyes are black glass, staring into mine like dark pearls, and I place it on the windowsill, its face turned away so that it can look out over the sea.

A bell tolls somewhere outside, and I take my phone and put it on the bedside table, its blank face staring up at the ceiling. My stomach lurches again at the thought that there is no connection to the world across the water, no link tethering me to England. I have an urge to turn the phone on, to scroll through and drink in the last face that I took a photo of. I have a feeling that she has left me a message too, that it's waiting for me inside the phone if only I could pick up enough signal to see it. But I know I must conserve the battery.

I wonder why Miss Stourbridge didn't tell me about the lack of electricity. Perhaps she thought that if I had known, then I would not have come. She may have been right. It is enough for now to know the photo is tucked away inside my phone, hidden from view. For the first time I wish I had brought a real photograph, something I could look at as I lay, eyes half closed, contemplating sleep. But nobody has real photos any more, glossy prints to tuck under glass or inside a wallet. The idea feels like it's from another age.

The sea bass is overcooked, but Miss Stourbridge doesn't make comment. She is silent as we eat, the clink of fish knives against splintery bones the only sound as we sit in the small upstairs dining room and shave off mouthfuls of fish.

After dinner there is yet more work to be done. Miss Stourbridge shows me how to light the gas lamps in the panelled room, the ghosts of long-dead butterflies flickering into life all around us. For a moment I can feel them brushing against my face and catching in my hair, and I go to swipe them away in panic. But then I see her face in the shadows, watching me. I drop my hands and smooth down my skirt instead, and she nods in approval.

'I shall have my bath tonight,' Miss Stourbridge announces, pushing herself across the room, and I shudder at the thought of helping this woman lower herself into her bath: the slap of soap on aged skin, the thin, unsightly bones and drooping, flattened breasts. I swallow, feeling a half-melted sea-bass bone lodge in my throat.

There is a small washroom downstairs next to my bedroom, but Miss Stourbridge leads me instead to a door off the panelled room that I hadn't noticed before. It's set into the wood without a frame, and made of panelling like the walls surrounding it. Inside lies the largest bathtub I have ever seen. It's made of copper, and sunk so deep into the floor that I wonder what the ceiling below must look like. It has two taps, as most baths do, but a third, larger tap sticks proudly out from the wall as well. The floor-length windows face the same way as the ones in the panelled room, providing a magnificent view of the sea, presumably even when the bather is submerged.

'Use the smaller taps. They need a good hard twist.' She gestures to a damp bookcase against the wall, stuffed with inflated, mouldy paperbacks. 'Find a book – I want it deep, and it takes a while to fill.'

She reverses her chair from the room, pulling the door to, and I glimpse her as she settles by the picture window, her eye to the telescope, before the door closes completely. And then I am alone next to this strange burnished tank. I give the closest tap a twist. It is encrusted with green that flakes off as I turn it. Hot water immediately flares out, and I realise too late that I haven't put the plug in. I scrabble around, burning my hand in the flow of water, and place the stopper in its hole. Then I straighten up and stand at the window, staring out to sea, aware as I do it of the symmetry between my own stance and that of my employer, beyond the bathroom wall.

The wind has dropped, and the sea is calm and grey. Here and there, tiny waves pick up the light from the setting sun and throw it across the water. I blink. There are circles on the surface of the sea, four or five. Large enough that I could stretch out in them, I estimate. As the water washes over them they appear and disappear. A cloud shifts away from the sun and the whole of the sea sparkles copper, and the circles are gone.

I remember the bath behind me, and jump to see it is nearly full. I twist the taps closed and wait for the swirl of water to slow. Steam rises in plumes, filling the room, and I try not to think of Miss Stourbridge lying in there, naked as a mussel.

'It's ready,' I call, and she wheels herself into the room as if she were waiting just the other side of the door. I am unsure how to go about preparing her for her bath. Miss Stourbridge doesn't help. She stares wistfully out of the window, as if waiting for something. Perhaps she can see the circles too. I try to pluck up the courage to ask her, but it seems childish somehow, what do I imagine they are? Fairy rings? I push them from my mind and stand for a moment, gathering the courage to undress her, and then I drop down and begin to unlace one of her shoes that pokes out beneath the blanket on her lap, but she kicks me away.

'That is all for tonight,' she says, and before I know what has happened, I find myself outside the steamy bathroom, the door closed behind me.

I stand alone in the panelled room, pulling down my rolled-up sleeves, the unbuttoned cuffs damp. The Chinese cabinet flashes in the sinking light, and I notice one of the doors is slightly ajar. I take a step towards it, and run my finger over the design on the front, feeling the shine of the lacquer. Mother-of-pearl birds are inlaid into the base of the doors: birds of paradise or peacocks. Their long tails are like great curlicues flowing behind them, swirling up towards the top of the doors, where pearlescent butterflies flit as if they wish to take off and go flying about the room. I pull open the doors, safe in the knowledge that Miss Stourbridge is ensconced in her bath.

Inside are wooden trays. I pull the topmost one out, and am presented with a frame of pinned butterflies. They are all the same shape, but some are smaller, their wings a pale white-green, while the larger ones' wings are the bright yellow of early autumn leaves. They are shaped like leaves, too, and dotted with brown as if they are about to drop from the tree. Each butterfly has a pin pushed through its body, white tape holding its wings flat. A few have an empty chrysalis next to them, papery and fragile.

I pull the next tray out, but it is just more of the same type of butterfly.

The middle tray sticks on its runners as I try to edge it out. I crouch down to see why. A thick book is wedged onto the tray below, blocking its descent on the rails. I reach in to try and extract it, teasing it outwards. With a rattle, the frame above it comes shooting out as well, clattering onto the floor along with the book. I swear under my breath.

'Are you all right, Miss Brown?' comes the voice from the bathroom, separated from me by only a thin wall.

'Yes, I'm fine, I just knocked over a tea tray.' I lift the tray up, hoping the butterflies have survived their fall. They are all still secure except one, which has come loose and sits at an angle. I give the tray a little shake, and the butterfly rights itself.

The book is still on the floor, and I pick it up. It's a photograph album, leather-bound and worn with age. Small flowers are embroidered over its surface, and a few of the sheaves of paper that protect the photos inside have come loose, whispering at the edges of the album like leaves about to fall from the tree. A strange clasp that looks like ivory holds it together. I open the album, and it settles at a page somewhere near the centre, the spine broken and no longer able to support the pages. The protective paper is embossed with spider webs, obscuring the picture beneath. Curious, I lift it.

This photo has been looked at many times. The paper around it is smooth, as if someone has brushed their thumb across it again and again, year after year. As the photograph catches the light, I can see its surface is peppered with fingerprints.

I have always found black-and-white photographs quite dull. They remind me of the tedium of history lessons at school, the warm, dark fug of a classroom full of bored teenagers watching scratchy reels of war footage. But this photograph is different.

A young woman looks out at me, her dark hair drawn back and hidden from view under a cloche hat. Behind her is the soft unfocused line of sea meeting sky. She isn't beautiful in the traditional sense of the word, but her face is unusual, her eyes bright and intelligent. She has sharp, delicate features that align pleasingly so that I find I can't tear my eyes from her.

Something about the picture makes it feel like a still from a film, paused for a brief moment. I can imagine the way she moves, light and precise, the soft clarity of her voice. The wind is pulling at her skirt, and she has a hand to her hat, laughing, and I find I'm smiling, as if I, too, am on the beach with her. Beneath the photograph is just one word and a date: *Nan, 1927.*

Would Miss Stourbridge have been alive then? I examine the girl in the photo. She's younger than I first thought, about fifteen or sixteen. I'm sure I read somewhere that Nan is an old-fashioned nickname for Anne. And Anne itself can be short for Marianne. Are they one and the same? Is this a photograph of the young Miss Stourbridge?

Quickly, I do the sum in my head. If this photo is of my employer, it would mean she's 106. It's possible: I'm sure I've read about someone living to 113, and Miss Stourbridge is a strange mixture of visceral energy and decrepit ailing flesh. I could almost imagine her going on forever. The sound of bathwater splashes nearby. I close the album quickly with a soft thud, creasing the thin protective paper inside in the process, and cram it back into the Chinese cabinet guiltily.

The sun has all but disappeared now, and the room glows with soft pools of gaslight. I lift the little lamp that Miss Stourbridge has given me, and make my way down the grand sweep of the staircase, creeping through the dark servants' quarters to my bedroom.

The bedsprings creak painfully as I collapse onto them, and suddenly I am wilting, everything I have seen today running and re-running across my eyes, and I wonder, just before sleep finds me, how long I will last on this strange and complicated isle.

Chapter Four

Tartelin

Summer 2018

The brightness in the room startles me awake. For a moment all I can see are the white walls and the grey, cracked ceiling through the barbs of my eyelashes, and I feel swaddled in this small, comforting space. This is what it must be like to live in a nunnery. Religious words flood through my head like a poem: silence, fasting, chapel, compline. I turn under the thin sheet, rustling like a bee in a waxen cell, and I hold my breath and listen. My bedroom is at the front of the house, facing west, and the light here is different to that of the panelled room. It is warmer, richer, yellowing the flaking paint. It is a light that comes from the mainland, a light of people and towns and living, not the clear, uncompromising light of the sea. It is the light of home, and I cherish it for a moment. A gull cries outside, and far off something howls. Beneath it all is a gentle repetitive rolling: Miss Stourbridge's wheels on the wooden floor above. She is up, then. Which means I must get up, too.

In the panelled room, Miss Stourbridge is already seated at her desk. It appears my duties do not include getting her breakfast. I hurry over to the mantel clock, and begin winding the key, counting in my head so that I don't damage it further. The hands are still stuck at eight o'clock.

'Sleep well?' Miss Stourbridge asks, not waiting for an answer. 'This morning I will be showing you how to deal with a caught butterfly.' She beckons me over as she talks. 'Then you'll be out on the island finding them for yourself, so watch well. I'm only going to show you this once.'

There is a large glass jar on the desk. Inside, a cocoon is suspended from a twig, a slice of it hanging open like a door left ajar. A peacock butterfly sits on the mulch at the bottom as if it has already explored every surface and knows there is no escape. I perch on the stool next to Miss Stourbridge's wheelchair.

'Pass me that jar. The small one with the laurel leaves in it.'

I pick the jar from a cluster at the edge of her desk, and hand it to her. She points to it with the sharp end of her scalpel.

'Killing jar,' she says. Then she points to the large glass box that holds the cocoons next to the desk, 'Puparium.' Finally, she lifts the lid of the jar and points to the green shreds at the bottom, '*Prunus laurocerasus*, or common laurel,' she says, shaking it slightly. The leaves shiver at the movement, and I smell almonds. Deftly, she unscrews the butterfly's jar and tips the insect into the laurel one, jamming the lid on with expert precision. Immediately, it tries to fly, then changes its mind and lands drowsily on the laurel leaves, its wings wilting. The smell of almonds lingers in the air, and I roll it round my mouth like the sugared almonds of my childhood, the memory clunking against my teeth.

'Laurel takes a while to kill, but it's a free and plentiful resource round here, and despite having a military base on the island, I've never yet found any cyanide to use instead.' She snorts quietly at her joke.

The butterfly lifts a front leg, and holds it in the air. Butterflies taste through their feet, I recall. I wonder if it can taste almonds, if its last memory will be the dense-sweet flavour of the nut. A pang of regret hits me, a wretchedness at the shortness of its life. Its antennae have drooped now, too. We wait.

'Is it dead?'

'God no! They're marvellously sturdy, these things. They come back from the brink as soon as look at you. I once had one try to fly away *after* I'd pinned it, little devil.' She glances at me slyly. 'Are you all right, Miss Brown? Not feeling queasy, are you?'

She is watching me, her eyes narrowed, and I sense this is a test to see if I'm up to the task. But watching something die is not new to me.

Miss Stourbridge leans forward in a quick, sharp movement and pats my knee.

'You need to toughen up, my dear. Life and death are a cycle that you can't get away from. Now,' she takes her hand away and straightens up, brisk once again, 'the good thing about laurel is that it keeps the subject soft. Perfect for setting. Other poisons have the effect of making the insect brittle. You really don't want to snap a leg or antennae off if you can help it.'

'Will we be pinning this one today?'

'The term is "setting", Tartelin. May I call you Tartelin?'

I nod, waiting for the comments to start, for the word 'unusual' to fall from her lips, a word I hear so often in relation to my name that it has become ubiquitous. But it doesn't begin. I don't dare ask her if I can call her by her first name.

'Open the drawer, child, and pass me a jar.'

I crouch down and pull open the deep drawer at the bottom of the desk. Inside is a blanket, folded roughly.

'Sorry,' I say, apologising for getting my first task wrong, and going to shut the drawer. But Miss Stourbridge's foot comes out of nowhere, wedging itself in the way, stopping me from closing it.

She is looking at the open drawer with a strange expression on her face, her features twisted and softened at the same time. I stand up slowly and step back from the desk, waiting.

'You can close it,' she says quietly, without explanation, removing her foot, and I push it closed.

Miss Stourbridge pulls open a small drawer near the top of the desk instead, and takes out an identical corked jar to the one on the desktop. She hands it to me silently, then pushes away from the desk and wheels herself out onto the galleried landing that sits above the staircase. I follow, the taste of almonds at the back of my throat, my mind still on the drawer with the blanket.

Hanging along the wall is a selection of nets of varying sizes. She points to one and I obligingly take it down.

'See how the net is deep and the material pliable. It means once you catch a butterfly, you can twist the hoop to keep the insect enclosed, like so.' She takes the net from me and demonstrates with a flick of her wrist. She seems fully recovered from her shock at whatever was in the drawer.

'Once caught, you pop it in the killing jar.' She points to the corked jar in my hand. 'Just one butterfly today, please. There's no need to be greedy.'

I notice a shiny black top hat hanging on a hook along with the nets. 'Who does that belong to?'

'It was my father's, then mine after a time.' She leans forward and uses the net to flick the hat off its hook. I catch it as it falls and peer inside. The hat is deep, and an unknown chemical smell rises up from within. Set inside the top is a layer of cork, punctuated with little holes.

'He used to pin his catches in there to keep them safe. Mama was forever combing butterfly dust out of his hair. I doubt you'll want to wear it, but it might prove useful one day, if your hands are full.'

But she is wrong: I do want to wear it. The hat is peppered with shimmering fingerprints of butterfly dust, and the silk slips against my fingers, recalling for a moment the touch of a moth, years ago: the shine of silver dust on my fingertips as I handled the poor, creeping creature, and I am back there, crouched on the playground.

I was only young. I didn't understand what I'd done. As I stroked it, a girl I barely knew stopped, looking down at what I was doing. My hands were brown-grey as if I had dipped them in graphite, and she gasped.

'What are you doing?'

'I just ... wanted to feel its wings,' I said as I released the moth. We watched it crawl away across the playground.

'It won't ever fly now,' the girl said, looking at me strangely. 'What were you thinking?'

She called across the playground, luring a group of children with her words like a magic spell. 'Tartelin's a moth killer!' The sound of it was like a taunt. A ring of children soon surrounded us, watching the poor moth's slow progress across the tarmac.

'No one play with her,' the girl hissed. 'She's a witch.' I could feel them all looking at me: looking at the birthmark on my cheek.

The weird magic of the moth's dust lingered on my skin for hours afterwards, made more potent by the knowledge that I had set it on a course to die. I can feel silver dust on my fingertips now. I rub them together. Out, damned spot.

As I step outside, a wall of heat hits me. The heatwave began in late spring, and now, in July, it's showing no signs of abating. Back on the mainland, the temperature was often unbearable, but here on Dohhalund there is a breeze, a wind that swoops and pulses in off the sea, and even though I can still feel the scorch of the sun on my shoulders, I'm thankful for it. Everything around me is parched, flecked with a salty coating that makes my throat sting.

I look longingly back through the door to Dogger Bank, where the rooms inside are cool and dark, but I have a job to do. *You cannot begin to help me until you have submerged yourself here*, she told me yesterday, and so submerge myself I must.

The house towers over me, its red-brick façade giving the impression of a great rusting ship dredged up from the seabed. It is satisfyingly square, with turrets and arches sprouting all over it, as if the architect plucked it straight from a gothic fairy tale. I can't imagine how many rooms must be inside: most of the doors as I made my way through were closed. I try to locate the windows of the upstairs sitting room, remembering the tall, thin pane of glass that looked out towards the military base. I find it eventually, spattered with salty sea spray, high up on the building's edge, closest to the sea. I think I can make out Miss Stourbridge's desk through it, and I turn away quickly in case she's watching me.

The bicycle is leaning against the side of the house where I left it. I look warily around for yesterday's dog and her puppies, but they're nowhere to be seen. I wonder how the dogs are faring in this strange heatwave, where they go to get out of the heat. Perhaps they've made their home in one of the houses that sits on the cliff next to Dogger Bank. There are three houses here, including Miss Stourbridge's. They're set in a staggered line next to the cliff. Dogger Bank is the furthest house from the edge, and the only one that hasn't yet begun to crumble into the sea. The other two are little more than husks, and it's plain that no one lives in them. The house nearest the cliff is now just a façade, its bulk crumbled away into the water a long time ago. Its front door is missing, and through it I can see blue sky and a wheeling gull. There are no rooms left – it is like the set of a play. The middle house has its front door, but half the roof tiles are missing. From somewhere inside I think I hear a yelping, and I get on my bike quickly.

As I leave Dogger Bank, the net tucked into my rucksack for safe keeping, it occurs to me that I didn't ask what type of butterfly Miss Stourbridge wanted, or where to start looking for one.

The road leads down a gentle hill. As the wind catches my hair, whipping it from my face, I forget all about my employer and her strange, dark-panelled room. Dohhalund stretches out before me, a vast, wild flatland punctuated by smooth, strangely geometric grey areas, and my stomach flips with nervous excitement. I pull up my bike and stop for a brief moment, mesmerised by the peculiar effect on the land, like a Mondrian painting, but in greys and browns instead of reds and blues.

At art school, I spent a term painting only landscapes. I sought out unusual scenes like this, and tried to imagine as I painted what might have been going on just before I arrived. What I had missed. Looking out at this scene, I have a sense that nothing has changed here for years, the only movement the slow creep of time.

I haven't done any painting for months. The bit of me that lit up with ideas and excitement when I saw new things has grown weary. But looking at this view, for the first time in a long time, my thoughts go to my pencils and sketchpads, back at home, carefully stored in Mum's studio. Deep inside me, I feel that light again, that spark of excitement, and I wish that I'd brought them with me. But it's too late now. I dismiss the thought, snuffing it out like a candle, and I get back on my bike.

It is a glorious day, the sun moving swiftly over the land in front of me as if the clouds are chasing it playfully. As I pedal over the cracked tarmac, I pass a single streetlight, bent and rusting. In the distance to my right, a huge patchwork of rectangles in varying shades of white and blue-grey glint in the sun, and I turn the rickety bike and head towards them, veering off the road and onto a track overcome with cables of bramble and curls of bracken.

To the north, I can see what looks like two people with rucksacks on their backs, but they are far away and indistinct. They could just as easily be the silhouettes of straggly bushes rooted to the barren landscape. After all, I'm sure Miss Stourbridge told me we were alone here. Crossing a bridge, I glimpse a dog lying in the shade. It lifts its head and watches me as I go past, and I set a wide path around it.

As I approach the rectangles, I see they are the size of small swimming pools, and they're low, set into the ground in rigid formation. Some of them are filled with water. In the distance there is a gnarled old tree. It looks a little like a plump figure, bent over the furthest one as if it's staring into the water.

I get awkwardly off the bike and lay it down, looking out over the strange pattern the rectangles make in the landscape. The water-filled ones have a steely surface, restless in the sea wind. Many contain only dry earth, their low stone walls crumbling so that they are hardly separate. The closest few are empty but for a thin crust of white, glinting in the sun. A gull walks across one, and I hear the soft crunch under its feet. I peer closer. The whiteness sparkles.

This island is indeed unusual. I can see evidence of lives lived across its strange, flat surface. I know from my correspondence with Miss Stourbridge that the island has a history of herring fishing. I imagine the boats out at sea, trawling through the water, pulling clouds of silver fish towards land.

'You're new.'

I jump at the voice, my heart drumming a tattoo in my chest, and turn towards the sound, my eyes still dazzled by the rectangle I have been staring at, filled with sparkling whiteness.

'You must be Miss Stourbridge's latest girl.' A figure shimmers into the shape of a small, dumpy woman with short grey hair. She grins up at me, her eyes encased in wrinkles so deep that they hold droplets of water, as if she often cries with laughter.

'I am.' My heart is still hammering, but I hold out my hand. 'I'm sorry, you made me jump: I didn't know there was anyone else on the island. My name's Tartelin.'

The woman takes my hand in hers and smiles, a gummy, toothless smile. She is dressed in a simple woollen tunic that is the colour of the muted heather dotted in shrivelling clumps along the path. Her feet are encased in sturdy sandals, but earthen-brown skin swells between the straps like softest leather, as if she spends much of her time walking barefoot.

'Oh, there are quite a few people here now,' she says. 'But I was the first. Arrived here two months ago, as soon as I heard the requisition had been lifted.'

'Requisition?'

'Yes. The army took control of the island, back in World War Two.'

She points to the north. In the distance, I see the buildings on the military base that I saw yesterday from the window of the panelled room, less hazy from here. They look odd, like wide, flat temples.

'They sent everyone away, even the Stourbridges later on, in the Fifties. It's only recently been handed back.'

I scan the island, seeing the barbed wire and strange geometric lines slicing across it in a new light. 'Why?'

'Oh, lots of reasons, I'm sure, but none that they would ever admit to. Islands are good for secrecy, after all.'

She is right. This place is tangled up with secrets. Not just the island itself: I sense Miss Stourbridge holds secrets here, too.

'Once the requisition was lifted,' the woman continues, 'word spread, it seems. People want to explore, and who can blame them?' She's still holding my hand, rocking it gently in hers, and I can feel the roughness of her skin. 'You're her third assistant, you know. The other two didn't last a month.'

I think I can detect the bones of a Suffolk accent somewhere within the base notes of the words she speaks. 'Perhaps the other two weren't as well suited,' I say.

The old woman cracks another smile, this one splitting her doughy face in two, and I am unable to stop grinning back.

'I saw her arrive,' she says, leaning towards me. Her voice is soft, as if from disuse, and a whiff of shellfish touches my nose. 'Not long after I got here. Crates and crates of cargo, and amidst it all a little old lady carried like a babe in arms up to the big house.' She juts her chin in the direction of Dogger Bank. 'Tell me, is she well, Marianne Stourbridge?'

'You know her?'

'I knew her a little, many years ago. It's been so long, I couldn't tell if it was her when they carried her off the boat. Is she well?' she asks again.

I think about Miss Stourbridge, shrunken and frail in her wheelchair. But despite her outward appearance, she seems quite robust, stoic even, as if she could live on for many years yet, enduring life. 'I think she is,' I say.

The woman nods, and her lips close together, as if my answer has helped stitch something tightly in her mind. She leaves my side and walks over to the white rectangle, rocking on the balls of her feet.

'You want to try my salt?' she says, nodding towards it, and I realise suddenly that that is what it is.

'It's yours?'

She nods. 'I used to tend it, a long time ago. It's good to see it thriving. It belongs to you, too, now that you live here. Come.'

She leads me to the edge of the salt pans. Many of them in the distance are defunct, broken and never mended, but the closest one sparkles with huge crystals of salt. The gull is still there, eyeing me intently. The woman reaches down and pinches a fingerful. She drops it in my palm and mimes me eating it.

'It's good. *Umami*. Go on.'

She nods at me and I lift a single crystal and hold it to the light. It is square-shaped, coming to a point at the centre like an inverted pyramid, its wide, flat sides thin as tissue paper. I touch it to my tongue. She's right, it is good. It's not the salt of fish and chips or crispy bacon, it has its own unique flavour and I dip my damp finger back into my palm for more. But her hand jumps out and covers mine.

'I wouldn't. Too much too soon can make you go mad. Sparingly, or you get the raging thirst.'

'But you're not mad.'

The woman shrugs. 'Oh, I don't know. Everyone here is a little bit cuckoo.'

'Even Miss Stourbridge?'

The woman chuckles. 'What do you think?'

'I only arrived yesterday,' I say with a glint in my eye.

She laughs again, a deep, throaty tremor that speaks of troubled lungs. She takes a pinch of salt herself and places it on her tongue, closing her eyes in rapturous delight as it melts. Then she leans in conspiratorially and whispers, 'Marianne Stourbridge takes her drink-water brackish.'

'She drinks salt water?'

'Not salt: brack. Half-and-half: fresh-and-sea from her own tap. All the pipes are crumbling on this island, they have been for years. The sea water sometimes leaks in,' the woman shrugs, 'and if she doesn't leave the house, she has no choice but to drink it.'

'Then where do you get proper fresh water from?' My mouth is suddenly painfully dry, the echo of the salt stinging the skin of my throat. I rub the crystals from my palm, worried it might enter me there by osmosis. I think longingly of the bottle of water I brought with me from England, sitting on my bedside table, an inch or so of fresh, clear liquid left at the bottom.

'It's here.' She waves her arms at the pans further along the salt field. They are filled with the ruffle of cool, fresh water, and my mouth fills with saliva at the sight of them.

'May I?' I nod at their deep surfaces, veined like chill marble, and she takes me by the hand and shuffles past the salt-filled pan to the next one. There is a fresh breeze coming off the surface of the water. It feels almost as good as I imagine a glass of water would taste. The woman produces an oyster shell from her tunic and mimes a scooping motion. I take it and dip it in, sipping at it greedily. The water is tart and cool. I have the feeling I am uncurling, stretching from the inside, relaxing for the first time since I began the journey from Lincolnshire.

'It's good, isn't it?' she says, winking at me, and she pulls her own oyster shell from somewhere near her bosom and ladles the water up, draining it in quick, sharp sucks, and then she sighs, the wind ruffling the short wisps of hair on her head.

'Where are you from?' I ask her.

'Not far, just across the water.' The woman nods in the direction of England. 'I haven't been here since I was a teenager.'

'Has much changed?'

'In some ways. In others it is exactly the same.'

I hold the oyster shell up. 'You get oysters here. Are there ever any pearls?'

Something flashes over her eyes, dulling their spark, and I wonder if I have offended her. She stops drinking, turning the wet shell over in her hands.

'I thought they had all gone years ago,' she says, reaching into the pocket at the front of her dress, 'but I was wrong. It looks like time has restored them.'

She pulls out a luminous pearl the size of a marble, and leans toward me, the light back in her creased black eyes. 'I've never seen anything like it before,' she says, 'never this big, never this perfect.'

But before I can get a proper look, she tucks the pearl and the shell away, and I am left blinking the imprint of it onto my retina, wanting to study it more.

'As I said, some things here are exactly the same. Others are very different.'

I go to hand her my oyster shell, but she brushes me away with angry hands.

'No, no, Tartelin, it's for you.'

I like the way she sings my name like a ladder, rising higher with each syllable.

'Thank you.' I pocket the shell and mount my bike. The sun bounces off the water behind me, reflecting on the salt pans.

'I think you'll stay longer than the last two,' the woman says confidingly as I get back on my bike. 'I think you're a good match. Marianne Stourbridge needs someone strong, someone who'll answer back. Don't forget that.'

I kick off and pedal back the way I came, waving behind me, knowing the woman is standing, watching me, and I wonder, with a sense of trepidation, if I'm as strong as she thinks I am.

Chapter Five

Tartelin

Summer 2018

Miss Stourbridge smacks her lips together and wipes her mouth with her napkin. She looks meaningfully at my own bowl. I still haven't taken a sip yet. I study the clear broth, the pungent steam so pervasive I wonder if I've inhaled half the bowl already.

'It is a delicacy of the island,' Miss Stourbridge says, nodding at me to try it, 'I have arranged to have it delivered to the house fortnightly, when the fisherman brings his catch. Get used to it, we live off it here, especially come winter.'

I wonder if she thinks I'll last that long. I came back from my expedition empty-handed, and Miss Stourbridge tutted at the sight of the killing jar, as if I had already failed her. Today's meeting with the grey-haired woman has unnerved me, too. It was naïve of me to assume that there was no one else but Miss Stourbridge and me here. The island feels suddenly sullied. I came here for solitude, for space to think, and now I feel as if I must be on my guard every moment I'm outside.

I debate whether to bring the subject up with my employer. I'm not angry, as such, just uneasy. I look at my spoon. There are unknown objects suspended in the liquid. As I sip, I feel the hardened jelly of what might be a mussel slide across my tongue, the thin, wet leather of seaweed following it down my throat. It feels like I am swallowing butterfly wings. She is right, I will have to get used to it.

'Miss Stourbridge?' I say, and she looks at me, her eyebrows cocked. 'You said we were alone.'

'What?'

'On the island. You said we were alone here.'

'Are we not?'

'No, I met someone today. A woman. And she said there are others here, too. She said word spreads quickly. That people want to explore now that the requisition has been lifted.'

Miss Stourbridge's brow folds down, as if she is trying to capture something long dismissed from her mind. She places her spoon delicately in her bowl, the metal clinking against the porcelain.

'Do excuse me for a moment,' she says, wheeling herself through the open door to the panelled room.

I try to ladle another spoonful of the clear broth into my mouth, but my stomach contracts at the thought, and I get up from the table instead and follow her through.

She is next to her desk, looking through the telescope.

'What are you looking at?' I ask, peering out of the window to see if anything's out there, but all I can see is the sea.

'Oh, just seeing if I can spy anyone on my island who shouldn't be here.'

I look longingly at the chaise, my legs painfully tired from the exertion of today's cycling, but I'm unsure if I'm allowed to sit down. This room feels inherently personal to Miss Stourbridge; to sit on the chaise the equivalent of sitting on the edge of her bed.

I go over to look at the framed butterflies on the wall instead, arranged around the Chinese cabinet, giving the impression they are bursting out of it, flying away across the wall in a spray of colour.

The clock on the mantel chimes suddenly, making me jump. I count to eight, and look at my watch. It's ten to nine. My eyes shift to the desk drawer that I opened by mistake this morning. It's firmly closed.

'It's beautiful, isn't it?' Miss Stourbridge says, nodding at the Chinese cabinet as she puts the lens cap back on the telescope.

'It is.'

'My father brought it back from one of his trade forays. Come, have a look.'

She joins me, pulling open the double doors to reveal the drawers of butterflies inside.

'Pull out the top drawer, would you? It sometimes gets stuck, and you're stronger than I am.'

A strange fizzing alights at the base of my skull. Does she know I've already looked in here? I think of the photograph album, crammed in between the shelves. Did I put it back in the exact place I found it? Is this a test? I shoot a quick glance at her as I crouch down, but her face is neutral.

I pull the top drawer out, and the regimented lines of butterflies are there, just as before.

'Brimstones,' she says. 'The larger yellow ones are male. The females are smaller, more delicate.'

'Why so many?' I ask.

'They're a record, I suppose. A timeline of a strange summer.'

I look down at the butterflies, frowning. How can butterflies be a timeline? She has a habit of talking like this, I notice, as if everything is a scientific puzzle that she expects me to crack.

She leans forward and pushes the drawer back in, and her hand hovers there for a moment. I can sense her deliberating whether to pull out the other trays. Will she notice the photograph album is not exactly where she left it?

'Miss Stourbridge,' I blurt out in panic, 'what was in that drawer I opened by mistake this morning? In the desk?'

She is silent for a moment, as if considering what to tell me, and then with a flick of her hand she bats the door of the Chinese cabinet closed. It swings sharply on its hinges, barely missing my fingers.

'That will be all for today, Tartelin,' she says. 'You may go now.'

She wheels herself quickly away, as if what I said has upset her, but I can't see how.

'I will see you early tomorrow. The forecast is calm and bright; I shall expect a butterfly from you by the end of the day.'

In the safety of my room, I climb into bed. Far above me, I hear the first soft notes of a piece of music. I think of the piano up there, Miss Stourbridge pulled up to it in her wheelchair, those claw-like hands clattering over the keys.

I turn off the gas lamp and pull the covers tight around me, and in the trickle of moonlight from the window, the oyster shell the old woman gave me shines a rainbow hue across the bedside table's surface. I pick it up and run my fingers over it, feeling only now what my eyes had not picked up before: there is something carved into the smooth, pearlescent dish.

Scratched into it is a drawing. A swirling, whirling animal, a porpoise perhaps, or a seal, curving round the luminous surface. Little air bubbles rise around it, its mouth stretched and teeth bared, and as I look at it, I am unsure whether it is smiling at me, or getting ready to kill.

Chapter Six

Marianne

October 1927

The creak of the floating bridge's chains lingered in Marianne's ears as she stood next to her father on the quay. It was a miserable, blustery day and she had wanted to stay at home with her mother and finish the embroidery she was working on. She had had an idea to incorporate a little girl into the already complicated composition: a miniature figure dressed as a maid, waving a feather duster at a cloud of fluttering silk moths. Mama had thought it a lovely idea, but Papa wanted her here by his side.

Behind them, she heard a click and whir as the photographer operated his camera. Papa had commissioned him to record the many changes to the island. It was the second time he had visited. The first had been excruciatingly embarrassing, with Marianne having to stand on the beach with her parents and the staff and try to look happy. At least today she was not being asked to pose.

Marianne frowned, screwing up her eyes to study the little cluster of people aboard the ferry, trying to search out anyone who looked as if they might not belong. She had overheard Cook that morning, talking about the arrival of Mr Stourbridge's 'snail-snapping frog'. Did

French people really bear a resemblance to frogs? She pictured a squat, leathery-skinned girl, her tongue long and supple from prising out snails deep in their shells.

From this distance, she could make out a large pile of boxes on the boat. Probably flour and pepper, and some tea and sugar if they were lucky. Or perhaps it was the silkworms. There was plenty of room left on the ferry; a pony could fit easily onto its smooth, flat surface. Even a hulking great carthorse, had her father desired it. She shot him a look under the brow of her hat.

As the floating bridge neared, she could make out a group of joskins, their shirt sleeves rolled up, revealing gleaming muscles earned from months of physical labour in the fields. Marianne sneered at their golden tanned skin, a by-product of their outdoor lives. They would be coming in to find work on Papa's Dogger boats now the harvest was over. They were in luck: Papa had said only that morning that it was to be another bountiful herring season.

Perched on the boxes at the front of the ferry was a girl. From here, she didn't look much older than ten or eleven. She was green about the gills, but other than that, she didn't look at all frog-like. One hand was on her hat to prevent the wind pulling it away, the other gripping the flimsy material of her skirt.

The silk-girl. Her title was so exotic, Marianne had imagined her to be made entirely of shantung or sateen, a life-sized doll with obsidian eyes and skin of the smoothest silk. She stood on tiptoe to get a good look at the girl. Her hair was black as Whitby jet, and her eyes appeared to match it in their shining darkness, but apart from that, she looked more or less the same as every girl Marianne had ever set eyes upon.

The quay was busy with herring packers, waiting to load their barrels and boxes to take to the mainland. You couldn't get away from the smell here. At least at Dogger Bank, high on the cliff, you were far

46

away from the stench of it. Some of the men and women around her had the trademark yellow hands characteristic of the herring curing and dyeing process. She wondered if they could smell themselves, as she watched them heave the loads towards the incoming ferry.

'Are you excited to meet her?' her father asked. There was an energy about him that made his whole body twitch, like the nervy thoroughbreds they had seen last year at Sandown Park.

'I suppose.'

The ferry came to a rocking halt, and the joskins spilled off onto the land before it had settled, their animated chatter infectious, lighting up the wind-worn faces of the herring girls who were mending the nets on the quay. The women didn't seem to mind the bronzed skin of the men: they giggled and whispered behind their hands to one another, their eyes following the newcomers as they wound around the lobster pots and the bright orbs of the glass floats. But then, she surmised, the herring girls' faces were deeply wind-tanned too, a perfect match.

She looked back at the ferry. The silk-girl remained perched on the boxes. Eventually she stood and picked up a small leather case. The girl's face was very pale, with a blue-green tinge. As she attempted to walk to dry land she teetered as if drunk, and Marianne felt a pang of empathy. She knew that feeling. The few times she had taken the trip to the mainland on a windy day she had lost her breakfast over the side within minutes of setting off. The floating bridge was the longest chain ferry in the world, bunny-hopping across the sea by way of a series of sunken pillars. The few miles could take hours, depending on the weather, the tide and the men pulling the chains.

The girl stepped off the ferry, clutching her suitcase like a lifebuoy. Close up, she was only a little younger than Marianne, perhaps thirteen or fourteen; that awkward, coltish age before the descent into adulthood widened the hips and attacked the skin.

Marianne's father stepped forward and removed his hat, bowing low. 'Welcome to Dohhalund.'

The girl dropped her eyes to the ground. Marianne saw that her clothes resembled the *à la mode* style of the London fashion houses. She had only ever glimpsed them in magazines, thanks to Mama's insistence that she wear the warm, unfashionable clothes that were suited to island life. Dohhalund was so far behind England's fashions, it was an embarrassment.

She took a sharp sniff in through her nose, searching for a whiff of onions about the girl, but detected only a blast of salty wind coming in off the sea. As they regarded each other, she thought she saw the girl's nose wrinkle slightly, and wondered if perhaps, under all their outdated finery, she and her father smelled the same to this new girl as the workers scurrying around them on the busy quay.

Three burly men heaved the boxes into their arms and followed her father as he set a course back to Dogger Bank. The six of them made a comical caterpillar, bunching and weaving their way along the path, Marianne and the new girl bringing up the rear.

'Do you speak English?' Marianne asked, speaking slowly and deliberately, her voice loud above the mounting gale.

'I *am* English.' Her voice was small, hesitant, but the words were clear and without accent.

'Pardon me?'

The silk-girl lifted her head and looked at Marianne for the first time. 'My father is English. I was educated in an English-speaking boarding school in France and, lately, in a finishing school in Hampshire. I am English.'

'But you weren't born in England, it isn't your home.'

'Nor is it yours.'

The comment stung, but the girl was right, Dohhalund wasn't England.

Marianne strode ahead, side-stepping the men and catching up with her father.

'Ah, here's my Empress of the Silkworms.' He lifted a hand as if to pat her on the head, but she ducked out of the way, hissing, 'I'm not a little girl, Papa.'

'Indeed you're not. I forget sometimes quite how much you have grown up in the past year. Are you ready to start our new venture?' He looked expectantly at her. When she didn't reply he rushed on, 'I've been thinking of a name. "The Dohhalund Silk Company" sounds rather grand, doesn't it? Or perhaps "Stourbridge Silk"?'

'Would it not be better to wait until we have produced some silk before we begin to think up names?'

Papa's walk slowed a little while he considered this. 'Soon there won't be any time to think,' he said. 'We'll be coaxing mulberry leaves into their little mouths like there's no tomorrow. Apparently, they're voracious eaters.' He clasped his hands together. 'Come on, come on!' he called over his shoulder, 'Let's get these little beasts into the warm. I must speak with the silk-girl,' he added, and turned abruptly, leaving Marianne to lead the way up the hill to the house.

As they approached Dogger Bank, the house rose toward them, quiet and imposing like a guard dog greeting its master. It was built in the gothic revival style, its red-brick walls standing majestically against the bleached white sky. The roof was composed of sharply peaked arches, and at the top of each one, a porthole-shaped window sat, so that it gave the impression of a many-eyed spider, crouching at the top of the hill, waiting for them to approach. Marianne thought she could sense her mother at the bedroom window, standing just out of sight behind the lace curtains.

They trooped into the annexe, a small anteroom off the kitchen that housed the coal-fired boiler and was therefore warm. It was also slightly humid from the washing strung across the ceiling. The men set the boxes on the ground and vacated the room, leaving Marianne and her father in the cramped space, with the new girl hovering in the doorway.

A soft step on the flagstone in the kitchen announced Marianne's mother. She entered the boiler room, brushing past the silk-girl and coming to stand next to Papa.

Marianne was surprised to see her downstairs. Papa treated Mama like a hothouse flower, attending to her every need, keeping the upstairs rooms tropically heated for her and decorating them with rich tapestries and sumptuous imported hand-painted wallpaper. Down here, in this small, dark room, she looked incongruous. She was one of those rare beauties, built for splendour in a way that Marianne and her father were not. Upstairs, she sat like a queen on her plump, tasselled throne, or else paced like a caged tiger, looking out of the huge windows. But down here, in the cold and dark, she appeared to wilt.

For a moment, Marianne wanted to rush to her, to squeeze her hand and look into her eyes and tell her everything would be all right. She didn't understand why she felt so melancholy – earlier in the day they had sat together in the upstairs sitting room, wondering what the silk-girl would look like, poring over a book of French oil paintings. They had stopped at one picture depicting a buxom young maid in rustic dress milking a butter-coloured cow.

Marianne glanced slyly at the girl now, wondering if she had spent her childhood pulling on the udders of a cow, sipping warm milk as it gushed straight from the teat. Was she really suited to living in a house as grand as Dogger Bank? And yet a second glance contradicted the peasant-charm: she was dressed in fine clothes, their cut and fabric far superior to Marianne's own. Maybe the girl might yet surprise and delight them all with her knowledge of French couture. Marianne could see Papa was delighted already, but compared to her imagination, the silk-girl was a sore disappointment. Perhaps this was why Mama looked so sad, too.

Outside, the peacocks started up their calling. Her father was crouched over the boxes, levering off the lids. He had not heard Mama come in, so intent was he on seeing the contents. Mama waited patiently next to him, her opaline face like a young moon in the dark room.

'Are we to stay in here for long?' Marianne asked in a bored voice. 'They're delivered now, can't we continue with our day?' Out of the corner of her eye she saw the girl stir at her words, perhaps hoping that Marianne might speak to her again, but she looked away, disinterested.

'The worms must be settled correctly,' Papa said, gazing into an open box, his eyes lit up as though he were staring at a boxful of gold. 'I wonder ...' He looked up and saw Marianne's mother hovering over him like a will o' the wisp. 'Kitty,' he said, 'you made me jump.'

He smiled, taking Mama's hand, and Marianne was reminded of the besotted way her father's collie dog had looked up at his master, even on the day when he had grown old and useless and Papa had shot him.

'Surely it's time for tea?' Marianne said, trying to break the soppy look between her parents. 'It was an awfully long walk down to the quay and back. I'm thirsty.'

'Tea,' Mama said, her beringed hand still in Papa's, diamonds glittering in the half-light, and not for the first time Marianne wondered how her father had secured such a catch. Mama was tall, taller than Papa (which wasn't difficult), her head ducking to avoid the washing strung between the beams. Marianne wished she had inherited some of her flawless dignity. Instead she was the image of her father, awkward and mousy, with a tendency to plumpness around the middle if she ate too much of Cook's suet pudding.

But it was more than just height that defined Mama's beauty; it was an otherworldliness, the way she held herself, floating, almost; the way she bestowed her smile on everyone, from the scullery maid who lit the fires to the visiting merchants and sea captains. But today she was not smiling.

Papa was back in his silkworm boxes. He had dropped Mama's hand and taken up a handful of silkworms instead. He was stirring them with his finger, nudging their fat bodies and crooning to them quietly.

Mama looked around the room, taking in the shelves that had been cleared ready for the worms' arrival, the hastily swept floor. Eventually, she said, 'All is arrived safe then?'

'Indeed it is, my dear.' Papa scrambled to his feet. 'Forgive me, here is the silk-girl. She has learned the skill of worm-rearing at her family's *magnanerie* in France, but has also had a good education. I believe she went to an exceptional boarding school in the South of France, and has for the past two years boarded at St Catherine's on the mainland – you know, where Georg Visser sends his girls. She will fit into this life perfectly.'

Mama's eyes found the silk-girl, and a few moments later, so did her smile.

'Welcome,' she said. 'Do you have a name? We can't keep calling you "the silk-girl".'

'It's Nan, ma'am,' the girl said quietly.

Mama took a step forward in the small space and laid a hand on her shoulder. 'Nan. I shall arrange for tea, you must be thirsty.' She surveyed the room once more, her eyes resting on the boxes, where a faint stirring was coming from within, before turning and leaving the annexe.

'Splendid,' Papa said, standing in the middle of the crates and lids, one hand on his moustache, staring at the empty space Mama had just left.

Chapter Seven

Tartelin

Summer 2018

The next morning, before I leave with the net and killing jar, I make sure to eat breakfast. On the scrubbed table in the kitchen is a strange assortment of hard-boiled eggs arranged on a porcelain plate, and I wonder who has put them there. Miss Stourbridge has no other help, as far as I can tell, apart from the fisherman who brought me here, and who also delivers our quota of fish. In the corner of the large kitchen is a stack of pallets, brought over from the mainland yesterday by the same man. He looked at me with suspicious, slitted eyes when I asked if I could help, and declined my offer of tea with a grunt before stomping back to his boat.

The pallets are heavy with powdered milk and tinned toma-toes. A huge sack of flour sits on the edge, threatening to tip the whole precarious load. Does she also expect me to bake her some bread, amid all her other demands, I think as I turn back to the eggs.

A tiny pile of salt crystals sits tantalisingly on the edge of the plate, and I surmise the whole thing is far too delicately arranged for the fisherman to have done it. The eggs are almost too pretty to eat, speckled and smooth-shelled and so small I can fit a handful in my palm, but I am famished, and I crack and peel and dip my way through them, trying not to think what bird they may be from.

Upstairs, I see Miss Stourbridge working at her desk, and I go over to the clock, glancing at the desk drawer I opened by mistake as I do. Is it my imagination or does she move closer to it, as if she's guarding it?

I begin to wind the clock, working as quickly as I can. She pays me no attention, but I'm not sure if it's because she's a little deaf, or just deliberately ignoring me. I tiptoe out onto the landing and look at the nets on the wall, wondering which was Miss Stourbridge's when she was a girl. I take one down. It is smaller than yesterday's, more delicate, with a brass handle, and I tuck the netted end into my rucksack to jostle with the remainder of eggs and some flat, dry bread I found in the larder. I have decided I will take the initiative today.

As I bike down the hill, ahead of me, at the bridge where I saw the dog, I can see the outline of two people sitting, their legs dangling over the edge. As I get closer, I see they have binoculars to their eyes. They are so focused on whatever it is they're watching that they don't notice me. Instead of crossing the bridge, I carry on, my bike juddering along a rutted tarmac road that leads eventually to the spit at the end of the island. I can see the military base in the distance, shimmering in the heat, and before that there appears to be a meadow. A perfect place to catch butterflies.

As I approach it, disappointment stings me. There is not a single blade of grass here. Instead, the ground is a deep, rich mud, densely covered by low-lying plants. Pools of brackish water are dotted across it. It smells like the salt pans, but with a tinge of meatiness, reminding me of last night's soup. I lean my bike up against a gate and ease my rucksack off my back, taking out the net and jar. Even though it's early, it is already so warm that sweat trickles down my spine. Each time I breathe in I can taste something like fish scales and decayed plants simmering just beneath the ground like a great stew. Here and there, dots of colour burst from the plants in yellows and purples. In the distance, a broad swathe of lilac covers the ground.

I lift my eyes to the sky in search of butterflies, but there is nothing there. Miss Stourbridge said rare species were sometimes blown off course and came down to rest. My mind begins to wander, to dream of catching a rare specimen, but then I feel the coldness of the killing jar, tangible in my hand, and I hear the sinister rustle of leaves inside.

Beginning to feel desperate now, I search the meadow for signs of insects, wondering what she will say if I fail to bring her a butterfly yet again. She only wants me to catch one, I think in exasperation. There must be a single butterfly, crouched low, wings folded, sheltering deep within a plant.

I step tentatively forward, and the soft ground gives beneath my feet just a fraction, the plants holding me up as if I'm walking on a cushion of air. I place the net and jar on the ground and crouch by the nearest pool. The water is clear, suspended on a soft layer of mud. Footprints of a wading bird wind along the pool bed. I dip my finger into the water and it swirls into a miniature hurricane at my touch. I put it to my lips. It tastes, not salty, but flavourful. What did the old woman say? *Umami*, and I wonder if the taste comes from the sea water, or if it is the mud that's the lifeblood of everything here, flowing beneath the pebbles like a rich lava.

I spot movement out of the corner of my eye, the dancing flight of a cornflower blue butterfly, and I stand up, but there is nothing there, just a crumbling stone wall.

My stomach rumbles, the eggs I had for breakfast seeming like a long time ago. The cycle ride here has tired me, and I realise I'm properly hungry for the first time in weeks. Is it this place, returning my appetite after so long, pulling my thoughts away from everything that happened on the mainland?

A flash of blue again, just to my right. I whip my head around, but it's gone. I think I hear the beginning of a dog's bark, quickly muffled. I stand on tiptoes to get a better look, but there is nothing but swathes of purple and the deep glow of nutrient-rich mud beneath. Then something white flits in front of me, and without thinking I grab the net and run.

It is the joyous run of childhood, the suck and pull of trainers in mud. I jump over clumps of leaves, my shoelaces catching in the wet and spraying a trail of brown water over my legs. I am gaining on the butterfly as it dances ahead of me, oblivious. It drops low to the ground, flitting round a patch of little white flowers until I can hardly see what is insect and what is flora. And then it stops, landing carefully on an open petal. Its tongue is already uncurling, preparing to feed. With a jubilant swish, I arc the net over, covering both the butterfly and the plant. Beneath the criss-cross of netting, I see the wings begin to beat, and I lift the net a fraction, the polished brass of the handle feeling again like a part of me, and I think, I was born to do this. The pulsing wings propel the butterfly higher, and quickly I twist the hoop, just as Miss Stourbridge showed me, trapping the butterfly within. I pick my way back, the net held carefully in front of me, bearing its prize.

At the pool I stop. The glass jar is there, corked and ready, a thin layer of chopped leaves lining the bottom. The butterfly taps at the netting, impatient, and I sink down, still holding the net, and take the jar in my hands. Trying not to think on what I am about to do, I lift off the cork and tip the insect inside, stoppering the jar immediately. And then I turn away, unable to look.

I can hear the tiny noises the butterfly is making behind me as it flaps against the glass. I look down at the net in my hands. There is a soft pearl shimmer on the woven fabric, and I touch a fingertip to it and rub it against my thumb, then to my cheek.

The tap of wing against glass is repetitive, like the faint touch of the high notes of a piano, the kind of soft strokes I used to make on the keys of the organ at St Andrew's Church. My mother's income as an artist was sporadic. She supplemented it by cleaning the church near our house and, when I was young, I went with her, waiting while she polished and swept, pressing the organ's keys as quietly as possible, trying not to be too loud in the vast, echoing space.

There was a butterfly trapped in the church once, I remember. Caught in a cobweb near the organ's pipes, the smell of furniture polish lingering in the air. Outside, drops of spring rain landed on the lead roof. Inside I watched as the spider began to wrap silken strands of web around the butterfly's wings, pulling it tighter and tighter. I remember the hush of the church as it tried to beat its wings to escape, the way the building tried to silence it. Churches do death very well.

The tapping has stopped. I turn around.

The butterfly is lying on its side, one wing resting on the laurel leaves. I crouch down to inspect it. Its tongue is out again, coiled and twitching. I lift the jar and hold it so close that my breath mists the glass.

'Please,' I whisper. But the butterfly won't die. It shivers, and a smear of its wing is left on the glass like a fingerprint.

'Just die.' I give the jar a little shake, angry at its hold on life. I feel like the spider from my childhood, spooling the silk tighter and tighter, slowly suffocating my prey.

'Just bloody die.' I rattle the jar again, watching the leaves swirl as if in a snow globe, and suddenly everything that's happened to me in the last few days overwhelms me: the lack of electricity, the loss of my phone, the thought of being stuck on this lonely, wild island for goodness knows how long, they all collide, and the tears that come are so sudden that the butterfly becomes a blur.

'You don't have to do that.'

I jump and almost drop the jar. There is a man standing a few metres away by the wall. He has his arm stretched out tentatively towards me. I wipe my eyes. Through my tears, he is just streaks of brown and blue.

'Here.' He walks towards me, his hand still outstretched, and, without knowing why, I hand him the jar, stepping back quickly.

I blink the tears away, and he comes into focus. He is only a few years older than me, perhaps in his mid-twenties, with a smattering of stubble and badly cut, scruffy hair. What is he doing here? I want to turn and walk away, but something holds me in place.

He holds the jar to the light, and the sun shines through the glass and pierces the insect's veined wings. 'It's not dead yet,' he says. 'You can still release it.'

He's wearing a threadbare brown knitted jumper with flecks of deep auburn that match the conker of his eyes. Round his neck is a thin scrap of cornflower material, tied as a neckerchief. It lifts in the breeze and I realise ...

'How long were you watching me?'

'Watching you?'

'Your scarf — I thought it was a butterfly. And there was a dog, I heard a dog.' I look around, suddenly alert. What if there is a pack of dogs nearby? Miss Stourbridge said they're only dangerous if they're hungry. What if they're famished? I feel all of a sudden slow and vulnerable in this muddy field, my bike far away across the marsh. Maybe they're stalking me right now, half hidden in the greenery.

'It's just Gabbro,' he says.

'Gabbro?'

He turns his head a fraction and makes a curious chirruping sound, and a speckled lump, invisible a moment ago, rises from near the meadow wall and begins to trot towards us.

I take another step back, grasping the net tightly, brandishing it in front of me.

'It's OK, she won't hurt you.'

The dog reaches us and sits patiently next to the man, leaning into his leg, and the man drops his hand without looking and fondles an ear. Gabbro's right eye is a deep muddy brown like her master's, but her left is a bright, clear blue.

With a sudden movement, the man steps forward, raising his free hand, and touches his thumb to my cheek, smoothing under my eye. I jump back, reacting as I normally do when people reach toward me like this, realising too late that he is touching the other side of my face, the smooth, unblemished side. I glare at him furiously.

'You had mud on you. And butterfly scales.' He lifts his thumb and shows me, and a brief flutter of surprised laughter escapes my mouth.

I sniff back the last of the tears, wiping my nose on my sleeve, and, with a sudden burst of courage, reach for the jar in his hand. 'My butterfly,' I say, my hand shaking.

The man releases it at my touch, watching me as he hands it back. At first I think he is staring at my cheek, but he is looking slightly to the left of my face, and I wonder if he just doesn't like making eye contact.

'What's your name?' he asks suddenly.

'Tartelin,' I say, before I can decide whether I want him to know or not.

'That's unusual.'

'I know.'

He drops his gaze. 'The mermaid said you'd arrived.'

'What mermaid?' I am aware again of how vulnerable I am here in this field with this strange man who talks nonsense and his obedient, sharp-toothed dog.

'An old woman I met on the south beach, where the herring girls used to work. I don't know her name, but she said she used to be a herring girl. They were known as the mermaids.'

'Did she have a tail?' I ask, thinking of the woman I met yesterday.

The man smiles. At his side, the dog yips softly as if she is in on the joke, her soft muzzle catching on a pointed tooth.

'What's your name?' I say.

'Jacob. Jacob Hall.' He lifts his right hand and I hesitate before taking it. It is the same hand that touched my cheek moments ago, I can see the silver mark on his thumb. His fist is strong and still around mine, the first proper touch from a human in weeks, and with it I feel a whole spectrum of emotions: disgust and anger and relief, and a light-headed, woozy feeling that hits me in the pit of my stomach, turning it over and over. The butterfly rolls over in the jar, clinking softly, and I drop his hand.

'I have to go.'

Jacob nods. 'You need to take your catch back home.'

'I don't live here.' I feel it is important to clarify this. This island is not my island. I am a mere visitor.

'Me neither. I'm just here for the summer.'

'Where are you staying?' I need to be on my guard, to know where he is so that I can keep an eye out, in case he starts spying on me again.

'All over. I have a tent. Gabbro and I are quite self-sufficient.' He pats the dog, and it lifts its head to him again, its eyes closed sleepily.

I nod, and set off over the uneven ground, looking back occasionally to check the dog hasn't moved, grasping the jar in my hand so hard I fear the glass may break.

Chapter Eight

Tartelin

Summer 2018

I set a course for the salt pans, not wanting to go back to the darkness of Dogger Bank just yet. The countryside around me feels less safe now, as if every shadow, every dark rooted bush contains someone who might step into my path, making me swerve on my bike and fall. I can feel the hard surface of the glass jar pressing against my back through the thin material of the rucksack, each rut in the path shaking the butterfly closer to death.

As I pedal along the wide, flat path, I'm hopeful I might see the woman who gave me the oyster shell again. I'm not sure why, but I have a desperate need to see a smile. It's not that I'm homesick, exactly, but I miss the feeling that a smile can give you. Back on the mainland, I was used to smiles. Genuine smiles that faltered when I turned and the person saw my cheek, but still, a smile. It appears that Miss Stourbridge rarely smiles. The man on the marsh just now didn't smile, and when I've looked in the mirror recently, all I see is a grimace.

At the bridge, the two men with binoculars are no longer there. Instead, there are four dogs, all lying flat out on the warm pebbles. One of them is flecked black and white, a little like the marsh man's dog, but when it turns its face lazily to follow the path of my bike, both its eyes are brown and nondescript.

As I continue to follow the path to the sea, to my left I see a straggle of people a few hundred metres away. Many of them have huge, dark green telescopes, and each one is pointed in the same direction, towards the dense rise of pebbles that heralds the beach. Sitting on top, silhouetted against the sky, is a large bird. The people are stock still, but whatever breed it is, I can't make it out from here. Is that why people are coming to the island? For a bird? A part of me wants to get closer, but I know that I might startle it, sending it off into the sky, to the fury of the people watching it, and besides, I have a job to do.

I pass the salt pans to my right and the path comes to a halt amid the cascade of pebbles that rise up ahead of me into the shingle bank. Over them, I can hear the sea. I lay my bike down and make my way across the stones. Here and there, swathes of white-flowered plants are lodged amongst the pebbles, growing almost all the way to the sea's edge. I spy a caramel-coloured butterfly flitting low to the ground, and I reach for the net, but something stops me. One death is enough today.

The sea rattles nearby, sucking and roaring at the ground like an angry toddler, and I think of my mother's stories, and wonder if this was the beach where she washed up, all those years ago. I look to the south, to the top of the cliff where Dogger Bank sits. The sea below the house behaves differently, a shimmer instead of a roar, and I strain my eyes for the circles I saw in the water on my first evening here. The beach beneath Miss Stourbridge's house is pale yellow in contrast to the piebald stones that I'm standing on. At the centre of the sand in the distance, a peculiar tower is perched. I crunch along the beach, shading my eyes to get a better look at it.

The bank of shingle to my right rises higher as I walk, compacting until it begins to form the start of the cliff that Dogger Bank is built on. Soon it's towering high above me, a vast compressed wall, the pebbles beneath me giving way to sand.

A wink of silver in the sun, and I see by my feet a small silver-grey fish. It's alive, convulsing on the sand, its mouth gaping. The movement is so sad, so desperate, that instinctively I reach down, wanting to help it. But as my fingers get close, I baulk at the thought of touching the shimmering scales. I am reminded of the butterfly in my rucksack, and I will the end to come quickly. The tears that started on the marsh film over my eyes again. Through them, I notice an indent in the sand next to the fish, a soft line marking its journey here from the sea, and then I see that the fish is moving, creeping infinitesimally slowly back towards the water, its small, sharp fins pushing against the sand. I watch in amazement as it makes its way to the sea until, with a silvery streak, it disappears into the cloudy water.

I blink the tears away, not sure what I've witnessed. I know there are fish in the world that can move across land. But here? I start to walk again, looking at the island with fresh eyes. Dohhalund is a part of England, but there is something so foreign about it, something I can't put my finger on, as if the meaning is hidden too far beneath the scarred surface for me to find.

Above me, Dogger Bank rears up, high on top of the cliff. The two houses next to it look so sad, half crumbled away into the sea, and I skirt around the sand as I walk beneath them, wary of falling bricks and debris. There is a half-submerged toilet cistern here, part buried in the sand. I hope the owner wasn't sitting on the toilet when it fell.

The strange tower on the beach is close now. It's a rectangular structure, almost like a chimney, made of flint and old, worn stone. Here and there, shells are embedded into the bricks. At its top a wooden frame holds a bell in place, and I realise that it's the remains of a small church. The tower is set at such an angle that I fear it might topple over, except that it's sunk into the sand. I wonder how far down it goes; or if, in fact, there is a whole building below it, anchoring it in place. Is it empty, beneath the sand, the pews still in place? Or is it full of the same grains that I'm walking on, trickling into every crevice, pushing out the air?

Scattered around are strange structures pointing up out of the ground. They look like anchors, but they appear to be made of stone. I scrape the sand away from one that leans precariously on its side. Words are engraved along its curved arms.

In Loving Memory of Edward Cantlay
Captain of Zilver
1875–1928
'The sea is made up of unspeakable sadness'

They are gravestones, or else memorial stones. I wonder if this man died at sea, or if he was buried in the churchyard, his body falling over the cliff at the same time as the stone anchor.

Further along the beach, there is what appears to be another gravestone, but this one is different from the rest. It's crudely fashioned, with no words other than an X and the year *1928*. It is mottled from the constant assault of sea spray so that it appears to be composed of little craters, as if the stone it's made from is so soft that mere salt air is strong enough to lick it away.

I walk back to the church tower, dusting sand from my hands. There is a crumbling opening near the tower's base here, a broken crag of pale bricks, big enough that I can crouch down and duck my head inside. It is dark within, and it smells of dried wood and polish, reminding me for an instant of the hours spent with my mother while she cleaned

St Andrew's Church. The wind rushes up the tower, and a faint knelling keens from the bell above me.

I sit down with my back against the knapped flints and stare over the sea to the horizon, my thoughts drifting to my mother.

She always loved the water. 'We're people of the sea, you and I, Tartelin,' she said to me often on the last days, shrouded by morphine. I try not to think of the black-crazed stones of her eyes, unseeing and omniscient, raking around the room as she said it. Instead, I pull my phone from my jeans pocket and, before I can change my mind, I press the button to turn it on.

It blinks into life quickly, as if it has been waiting for me. I glance at the battery – 10 per cent – before touching the photos app.

I can see it, now I know what to look for. There is a transparency to her skin, as if it is thinning before my eyes, the colour of the bone beginning to show through. She is laughing, holding her hand up as if to grab the phone from me. Her eyes and forehead are wrinkled up with laughter, and she is beautiful, in the way that all dead people are beautiful because an image is all you have left. I remember she took the phone from me and told me to delete it, told me her teeth looked yellow and her fingers looked horrid. I had always thought up until then that she was proud of the webs strung delicately between the digits.

I hold my phone up, searching for a signal, but there is none.

We're people of the sea. I look at the shifting, mercurial water, and I'm certain that *she* was. But me? I don't yet know. I'm trying it on for size, putting on my own metaphorical webbed gloves to see if they fit. I look down at my phone. Eight per cent. Hurriedly I switch it off, hoping there will be enough energy to boost it into life one more time, trying not to think about how I might feel if there isn't.

✻

Tonight's meal is a concoction of tinned goods I found in the kitchen. Everything on my plate is familiar, trusted, everyday ingredients that I have eaten before. It is a relief. The slightly soft and rubbery potatoes that I found at the back of a cupboard that morning have been baking slowly all day in the Aga, and the little sprouting tubers that dotted their skin this morning have shrivelled and all but disappeared (they are known as eyes, Miss Stourbridge tells me, and in future should be cut off before cooking). The potatoes are crisp with sweet, tumbling insides. I wish there was a little butter left in the ice box to melt into them, and I sprinkle more salt instead. I lift a spoonful of mushy peas to my mouth, and notice that Miss Stourbridge is not eating.

'You're not hungry?'

She hasn't even lifted her knife and fork. Perhaps because her hands have been shaking more than usual. I drop my eyes, hoping she doesn't ask me to help her. I remember spoon-feeding my mother, the pathetic little sips of soup, wiping her lips and chin. Miss Stourbridge has made it clear that I am not here to be her carer. If she doesn't want to eat, it's up to her.

'I'm sorry I only caught one butterfly,' I say when she doesn't answer. 'I know you need more.'

My caught butterfly lies just out of view in the panelled room, pinned and laid out in the top left-hand corner of a new frame, the first catch of what she has dubbed my 'nouveau arrivé'.

'You did well today,' Miss Stourbridge says.

We're sitting apart at each end of the table, and her words are almost lost, catching and sticking somewhere in the middle of the polished oak surface.

'The girls before you baulked at the idea of catching lepidoptera at all,' she adds, by way of explanation. 'Now you've caught one, it will become easier, I'm sure.'

I think back to the meadow, to the way the world blurred behind my tears. 'It's definitely not as easy as it sounds,' I admit, thinking of its wings clinking softly against the glass, and the odd man with his dog: the way he looked, not *at* me, exactly, but around me, as if he was taking in something about me that I couldn't see.

'I saw more people today,' I tell her. I can still feel Jacob's thumb pressed against my cheek, his hand around mine as he shook it.

'Really? Where? How many?' She is alert all of a sudden, her eyes narrowed, but I find I don't want to talk about my meeting with the marsh man. It feels too private, too confusing.

'There were a couple of men with binoculars on the bridge, and a few people with telescopes near the beach. Birdwatchers.'

'Did you see what they were looking at?'

'The bird on the beach was quite big, but I didn't get close enough to see what it was.'

Miss Stourbridge's brow creases again, in a way I'm becoming familiar with. 'I'm sure you'll find out for me sooner or later. You're my eyes and ears, after all, don't forget that.'

The responsibility of my position presses down on me again, and I search around for something else to talk about, something lighter.

'Why do you wind the mantel clock if it doesn't work?'

Miss Stourbridge blinks, her eyelids fluttering. 'Tradition,' she says at last, her mouth set in a thin line that tells me not to pry.

I take another mouthful of potato, chewing thoughtfully. The dining room we're sitting in is small, unlike the panelled room next door. It has fitted glass-fronted cabinets covering every wall. Inside, instead of butterflies, strange dark shapes peer out at me from all sides.

'This is a beautiful room. It reminds me of a museum I used to go to with my mum.'

We would troop through the syrupy-dark rooms on our way to the brightly lit galleries, where Mum would stand me in front of a piece of smoothly polished alabaster, looking both ways to check no one was watching before putting a hand onto the cold stone and saying, 'Isn't it wonderful, Tartelin? Feel.' But I always preferred the dark corridors lined with cabinets, the dimly lit exhibits, the thrill of the musty cards that whispered of secrets in inky handwriting.

'How did your mother feel about you coming to the island?'

I'm not braced for the pure cut of pain that sears through me at the mention of her.

'She's dead,' I say, more sharply than I mean to.

'Ah. I see. Still, one less tie to the mainland,' she says. 'Easier, I should think.'

I'm not sure I've heard her correctly. Surely even severe Miss Stourbridge couldn't be so lacking in empathy? I get up from the table, my eyes sparking with tears, not trusting myself to reply, and approach the nearest curio cabinet. Inside are a collection of crudely made figures. I wipe the tears away, and they come into focus. Some are a dull yellow-white, others the colour of the wooden banister on the stairs where hands have touched it for hundreds of years.

'Are they ivory?'

'They're the ivory of the sea,' Miss Stourbridge says. 'Walrus bone mostly. And baleen.'

'Baleen?'

'The bony bit of a whale's mouth. They used to make corsets out of it. It's set into the doors too.' She indicates slivers of yellow-grey, inlaid into the wood around the edge of each door.

I move on to the next cabinet. In here are tusks, or horns, polished smooth. I lean closer. They have patterns scratched into them, fish and flowers, hearts and ships.

'Where did you get them?' I ask, thinking of the oyster shell, the strange, eerie animal carved onto it.

'They're my father's collection. The mermaids used to find them washed up and carve their own designs onto them. Sometimes he paid them a penny for their work.'

I look up at the familiar word. 'Mermaids?'

'It's what we called the herring girls.'

I nod, remembering, and turn back to the cabinets. 'Are they all sea ivory?'

'Mostly. We think that one,' she leans over and points to the next cabinet, where a huge tusk sits, supported on its own stand, 'is a mammoth. Sometimes we get mammoth leg bones washed up, too. Papa used to use them as doorstops. The area round Dohhalund was land thousands of years ago. My great-grandfather once found a lion's skull, or so the legend goes.'

I sit back down and begin to eat again, thinking of wild animals prowling round the island. High up in the top cabinets are lines of blown eggs in stippled shades of pastel blue and pale pink. They range from ones so small and fragile that I wonder if they are goldcrest eggs, to dimpled orbs so large I can only think of ostriches or emus. On the wall behind Miss Stourbridge is a frame of the inevitable butterflies.

'What will you do with the butterflies I catch?'

'I dissect them. Sometimes I set them: you've seen me. They'll form a collection of sorts, I suppose. My father used to say there was such a thing as a "collecting gene", that he and I both had it; that insatiable need to amass more and more.'

She waves at the butterfly frames on the wall, smiling as she reminisces, but this comment strikes me as nothing more than greed.

'But are you looking for something in particular?' I say, thinking of the scores of butterflies in the Chinese cabinet, lying in rows, all so similar.

She sighs and reaches out to touch the tines of her fork with the back of a fingernail. The tiny sound it makes is sharp, reaching my ears across the table in a way that her words have struggled to.

'It's not just the butterflies. It's the island as a whole,' she says. 'I suppose you could say my work is about change.'

'Do you mean mutation?'

'Yes and no. I try to think like a scientist, but this island is unusual. Science says that if A happens, then B will follow. But I am still in the process of proving that A happened at all.'

'And what is A?'

'A is immutable, in here, at least.' She presses the tip of her finger to her forehead, tapping gently. 'But out there,' she points in the vague direction of the island, 'it is fancy: just the ramblings of an old woman. Until I can *prove* it happened, I will remain here in this house, on this isle, searching for evidence. And you will help me.'

It's as if she's speaking in a scientific code that makes no sense unless you already know her language. Perhaps she's writing a paper on mutation, or trying to prove that something exists; some slightly different butterfly with a marginally lighter pair of wings. Perhaps she will be able to name it the *Mariannus ancientus*. I stifle a giggle, disguising it with a cough, and bend over my plate, licking the last of the peas from my fork.

'Did you explore well today?' she asks. 'I thought I spied you down on the beach earlier.'

I swallow the peas uncomfortably. It unnerves me that I am being watched. But then, what else has she got to fill her days, stuck within these four walls?

'There's a tower down there,' I say. 'And some gravestones.'

'Ah yes. My family's chapel. My great-grandfather had it built in 1840.'

'What happened to it?'

'It went over in the Fifties. We get a lot of erosion here, as I'm sure you've seen. The houses next to Dogger Bank are nearly gone now, too. They were still standing when I left the island.' She touches the shrivelled eye on her potato. 'It's so odd how some things on Dohhalund have changed so much in my time away, and yet, others feel just as if it happened yesterday.'

A tingle of exhilaration touches me. 'As if *what* happened?'

What is she referring to? Her words are bittersweet, as if tangled up with regret. And they feel familiar, like a trickle of déjà vu. And then I remember the mermaid at the salt pans. *Some things here are exactly the same. Others are very different.*

Miss Stourbridge's eyes take on that faraway look, the one that scares me a little, as if she's caught many years ago, trying to pull her way back to the present.

'Lots of things happened,' she says at last, and I let out a sigh.

It is frustrating, this evasiveness, but perhaps it's just old age. Perhaps when you reach a certain age, your whole life feels like that, so far away, and yet gone in the blink of an eye.

'Was it something in particular?' I push, but she just raises a hand and waves it. 'Oh, I don't know. I'm old, Tartelin, I get muddled.'

'What's *Zilver*?' I ask her, trying another tack.

That faraway look is back. Or perhaps it never went away. 'It was one of Papa's herring boats,' she says. 'It was lost at sea in a storm in 1928. The whole crew was killed.'

'That's awful. Were you alive then?'

'I was fifteen. I slept through the whole storm, but in the morning –' her face is as pale as cobweb as she remembers – 'the sea was silver with dead herring.'

'Dead? Why did they die?'

71

'I don't know. Lightning, was the most plausible answer. But who knows why anything happens, what its rhyme or reason is? The sea is made up of unspeakable sadness.'

Those words again. They were on the gravestone too. An island saying, perhaps, a way of dealing with the inevitable tragedy that comes with living in such close proximity to the sea. I can picture fifteen-year-old Marianne Stourbridge, standing on the beach, surveying the silver scales floating on the water.

After we finish our supper, I tidy away the plates and stack them in the dumb waiter. Before I go downstairs to the kitchen, I stop at the mahogany desk by the window and look at my butterfly frame. The white butterfly looks odd all on its own in a corner of the blank frame, and I'm not yet sure how I feel about it being there at all. I can still hear the sound of its wings, tapping against the glass. The lowering sun is creeping across the desk, stroking the frame, turning the veined-white wings of my butterfly to orange, and then to a deep, violent red that makes my skin shiver.

Chapter Nine

Marianne

October 1927

Mama was drawing her morning bath. Marianne watched her from the panelled room as she sprinkled a handful of salt into it. The steam made her look even more unreal than usual, as if she were half mist.

'Mama?' she said, not bothering to knock before entering the bathroom. 'Why must the new girl sleep in that bedroom? Why not the maids' quarters downstairs?'

'Your father has his reasons.'

'What reasons? He never explains them to me. Or to you,' she said, trying to keep the whine in her voice to a minimum.

The bath, a huge, copper affair sunk into the floor, always smelt slightly of herring. It had been built with a dual purpose – to bathe in, but also to store the excess live fish during profitable seasons. As well as the usual set of bath taps, it boasted a larger tap which drew water directly from the sea to keep the fish alive. Marianne had seen herring in here too often to be comfortable bathing in it. She preferred to use the smaller tub in her bedroom, set close to the fire, even if it meant keeping her knees drawn up to her chin.

'Nan isn't your servant, Marianne,' Mama twisted the taps off. 'She has been brought here to do a job, yes, but she is also the daughter of a friend of Papa's, however else she came to be. We will treat her like a guest.'

'She's not one of us, Mama.'

'We all see things differently,' Mama said. She was looking out of the window. Marianne went to stand with her. The sea today was white with waves, mesmerising.

'Her job isn't even that important. Even Miss Stanley sleeps downstairs.'

Miss Stanley was Marianne's latest governess. She had had many governesses over the years. She had vague memories of the first few, keen and young and pretty. They had never lasted long. She remembered one – a Miss Pemberley – a smiley, freckled young woman, not much older than Marianne was now, with white-blonde hair wrapped artfully in a plait around her head. She had left very suddenly, boarding the last floating bridge of the day, clutching a handkerchief, her pretty eyes red-rimmed. Marianne had been very sad to let Miss P go: she had been jolly good at croquet.

Since then, all her governesses had been old spinsters. The current one, Miss Stanley, was a meek, untidy woman with teeth like a squirrel. She certainly hadn't complained at her living quarters. Whenever Marianne walked past her bedroom on the way to Papa's study, she glimpsed the bedcovers, wrinkled and twisted like a dormouse's nest. She could imagine Nan tucked up in a nest like that, sitting primly like a delicate little bird: a blue tit, perhaps, or a wren.

Mama turned back to her bath, standing over the steam. Through the window, Marianne glimpsed Papa down in the garden, taking Nan to see the mulberry trees. They had stopped on the grass outside the house, and he was pointing something out to her on the horizon. The wind was fierce out there, and Marianne smiled as Nan tried to hold her skirt in place. Papa bent to help re-tie the silk scarf that had started to unravel from round her neck, and Marianne frowned, trying to remember the last time he had done anything so thoughtful for her.

Nan had spent her first night on the island in the bedroom next to Marianne's, a room they usually reserved for important guests. It was dominated by a huge oak bed. Papa had bought it from Liberty's when Marianne was a baby, and had it shipped across the sea to Dohhalund at great expense. She had always coveted the huge headboard, the pretty little upside-down heart that was cut out at its centre. When you lay in it, the heart looked the right way up, as if it had been carved that way just for you.

Last night she had lain in her own bed, knowing she and Nan were inches apart, merely a thin wall separating them. Next to her, perched on her bedside table, was a little rosewood mouse with a leather tail. It had been her favourite toy when she was a child, and when she had thrown all her other toys out in a fit of maturity a few months ago, the mouse had stayed.

She'd picked it up, its round little body worn smooth from all the times she had held it.

'It's not fair,' she whispered to it, her eyes drilling into the wall between her bedroom and Nan's as she spoke. She thought nastily how Nan's face was a little bit mouse-like, a little bit too sharp and pointed to be called pretty.

As a child, when she had talked to the mouse, she could have sworn it squeaked back at her in reply, but this time, it remained silent.

'Did you know that your bedroom used to be mine when I was a child?' Mama said, interrupting Marianne's thoughts. 'When I was your age, sometimes I had friends to stay on the island, and they would always sleep in the room that Nan is in. When I was about twelve, I knocked a picture off the wall by accident, and the nail that had held it there fell away. It left a small hole – you know how paper-thin these interior walls are – and with a bit of effort I made it large enough to whisper through. I don't think my mother, your grandmama, ever knew. I used to lift up the edge of the paper and put my mouth to the hole, whispering secrets to my friends. I spent many happy evenings chattering away like that.'

'But Nan isn't my friend, Mama,' Marianne said. She couldn't think of anything worse than having to gossip away to the help every evening. Not for the first time, she wished her father had allowed her to go to boarding school. Perhaps it was not too late. She would ask him over breakfast. Papa was always at his most receptive with a grilled bloater in his stomach.

As their maid, Peggy, doled out seconds of fish and bread and butter, Marianne shot a glance at Nan, sitting by herself at the far end of the table, spooning a small amount of herring into her neat little mouth.

'Papa,' Marianne said, turning her attention to her father, hidden behind the morning papers, 'I really think it's time you let me go to boarding school. It's simply not fair to leave me here on the island with no one to talk to. How am I to be expected to know how to conduct myself in society if I've never learnt the proper way to behave?'

Her father lowered the paper and wiped bloater grease from his moustache, his voice muffled behind the napkin. 'Who on earth will run The Dohhalund Silk Company if you're away, *mijn lief*?' he said, 'Poor Mama can't be expected to do it, she has a house to run, and Nan has only just got here.'

'Can't *you* help, Papa?'

'It's the start of herring season, Marianne. You know what that means. And besides, I have another plan to get under way.'

Mama came in, late from her bath. Her luminous skin was tinged with pink. She smiled at the table as she sat down.

'Kitty darling,' Papa said, closing the paper. He laid a hand on hers, and she turned her smile in his direction.

Papa cleared his throat. 'I have been looking for something to invest in since the herring have been so remunerative, my dear.'

'I thought the silkworms were your investment?' Mama's voice was quietly curious, and Marianne wished, not for the first time, that she had half the backbone of the fish that lay, dissected and clean, on the plate in front of her.

'Well, yes, of course, but they will take time to get going. Nan, how are the *Bombyx* after their journey?'

Nan lifted her gaze from her lap. 'As you feared, Mr Stourbridge, the live silkworms you took delivery of did not fare well, but the eggs appear to have done much better, and have started hatching already.'

'Excellent. When should we expect our first harvest?'

'The first brood should start to spin their cocoons in a few days. I suggest we leave those to hatch and mate so that we can rear a larger brood next time. If all goes well, the first sample batch of cocoons for silk harvesting will be ready towards the end of the year.'

It was the first time Marianne had heard her speak more than a few words, and she tried to search for the dregs of a French accent within the delicately enunciated words.

'Excellent, excellent,' Papa said. Turning to Mama, he carried on, 'This year is pivotal, my dear, I can feel it. The Stourbridge name moves on to ever greater things. The silver darlings were so plentiful last year, and the captain of the *Schoonheid* says he thinks we're heading toward another bountiful year. One must spend money to make money.'

As her father continued to discuss with great excitement his plans for the herring and the island, Marianne leaned towards Nan.

'Is it true they eat snails where you come from?' she hissed under her breath. 'Snail snappers, they call your kind, if I'm not mistaken.'

Nan placed her knife and fork together on her plate. 'You eat winkles,' she whispered sweetly back, her eyes flashing. 'They're the snails of the sea, so I hear. Surely that makes you a snail snapper too?'

Marianne sat back as if she had been slapped. Nan wiped her mouth delicately, a small smile half hidden behind her napkin.

Papa had not heard their hurried discussion. He had picked up his pipe and was packing it as he spoke, eagerly pushing the tobacco into the barrel with his thumb. 'You know the old building over by the oyster beds?' he said, the excitement palpable in his voice.

'Great-grandfather's pavilion?' Marianne interrupted, turning away from Nan.

Papa nodded, biting down on the end of his pipe, his eyes crossing as he lit it. 'Don't you think it would make a wonderful summerhouse?'

Marianne clapped her hands together in delight. 'Oh Papa! I've always wanted a summerhouse. Think of the parties!'

Her mother spoke sometimes of the parties that went on in the pavilion back in the 1890s: butlers with trays of martinis stacked ten high, live flamingo brought in from Africa, strutting through the rooms, people covered head to toe in gold paint. Of course, Mama had been too young to attend, but she had witnessed the preparation, seen the guests arrive on the floating bridge. Great-grandfather knew how to put on a party.

'No, my dear, you misunderstand,' Papa said, 'it's not for us: I want to bring people to the island, have them holiday here.'

Marianne felt the heat rising in her cheeks. 'Not for us?' she repeated.

But Papa was so taken by his idea that he didn't hear her. 'I want Dohhalund to become a great holiday destination. All decent folk want to holiday by the sea, do they not? The fresh air, so good for the constitution, not to mention the health benefits of salt water. And we are surrounded by the stuff! I was thinking of building a narrow-gauge

78

railway. I'm still trying to work out the finer details – I'm not sure the floating bridge could support a steam engine, but I know of a barge that might carry one. Where there's a will, there's a way.'

He had forgotten the origin of the conversation. He sat back in his chair, puffing on his pipe contentedly, gazing at the breakfast table as if the picture he had painted were laid out in front of them all like a map of war.

'But Papa,' Marianne said, 'surely you don't need me? Perhaps I could go to a finishing school for a little while? I would be back in the summer. Think what I could learn, how I could help with your business—'

'Marianne, you will learn so much more here. No, I need you three girls to work together, to keep the silkworms weaving.'

You three girls. Marianne shot Nan a look, irritated to see her head low over her plate, trying not to listen.

'Mama says you're to learn from the mermaids,' Marianne said as she latched closed the little gate at the end of the garden. 'It'll soon be herring season. Everyone helps. Even I know how to gut a fish.'

This was not strictly true, and she pulled her hat down to hide the lie, and began to climb down the little curved staircase that was etched into the cliff. Nan followed cautiously, lifting the edge of her skirt to keep from tripping. Marianne had managed to convince Miss Stanley that her studies could wait; she had the important job of showing the new help around.

She reached the little beach below the cliff first, and turned to see if Nan would slip on the stones, but her tiny feet in their lambskin slippers curved over the large pebbles, balancing like a ballerina.

Nan came to a stop by the sea's edge, and stared out at the great expanse of water in front of them. Marianne thought she could see the blue-green tinge beginning on her cheeks again. She set a swift course around the peninsula, not looking back to see if the girl was keeping up.

'I don't normally come this way,' she shouted against the wind over her shoulder, 'it's the herring girls' area, but needs must.'

High up beyond the tideline, what looked like patched, grey sails billowed out over the stones. As they got closer, the sails became the skirts of a group of women sitting on the beach. The women turned their heads a fraction as the girls approached, but continued to chatter. Some were tanned and walnut-wrinkled, others smooth as the pearlescent inner shell of a mussel. A few of the older ones she remembered from her childhood. Others, like the two younger girls sitting slightly apart with mud-coloured curls and shawls around their shoulders, must be newcomers, fresh for the autumn herring season.

Marianne had never been to this spot before. It wasn't the done thing, just as the mermaids never approached the house. This stretch of beach was their territory while they were on the island, and it was as alien to Marianne as if she had stepped into a different country.

The chattering stopped as Marianne and Nan reached the little group.

Marianne cleared her throat. 'I want to introduce you to Nan. She's going to be helping with the herring when she's not up at the house. I thought you could show her the ropes.'

One of the older women pushed herself up from the pebbles, her joints audibly creaking. She wiped her hands on her apron and picked up a basket, nodding at Marianne.

'Turns out we were just off to gather winkles. Maybe your friend would like to join us?' She looked at Nan doubtfully, her eyes hovering over her pale pink dress and flimsy slippers.

'She's my servant,' Marianne said in a flash of annoyance, but she felt a rush of jubilation at the thought of Nan's beautiful clothes getting ripped and dirty. A wisp of shame clung on as an afterthought, but she brushed it away.

Nan seemed to gather herself in a moment, breathing in the sea air through her nostrils and pulling herself taller. The other women had begun unlacing their boots and pulling them off, and a few had got to their feet, hoicking their skirts up, twisting them over at their waists or tucking them into their knickers. Marianne averted her eyes.

Nan copied them, lifting the pretty layers of cotton around her legs and tying a loose knot in her skirt so that it hung high out of the way of the water. She slipped off her shoes, and began to follow the first of the mermaids who were already striding across the stones, as sure-footed as if they were wearing leather boots.

Marianne followed Nan's progress with her eyes, wincing to herself as she watched her tentatively place her small feet on the sharp stones. For the first time she allowed herself to feel a little sorry for the girl.

They had crossed the beach now, and were climbing onto the barna-cled rocks that had begun to appear from beneath the receding water. Marianne's toes curled in her shoes: she knew how sharp the barnacles could be, especially on soft feet that had always been encased in leather.

'They'll be back before you know it,' a small voice fluttered up from the stones next to Marianne. 'Come keep me company 'til then.'

She looked down at the shrunken woman who remained, cupped in a nest of pebbles, a blanket wrapped around her legs. She thought perhaps that she had spoken to her before: this woman was one of many who must have watched her grow up on the island, watched her play in the big house on the cliff while they worked down here, gutting herring on the beach.

Marianne had spent time in the mermaids' company over the years. Once, when she was younger, she had escaped her governess and gone exploring without Mama's permission. She had got stuck trying to cross the creek, the mud holding her fast, the rising tide creeping closer and closer.

A mermaid had come to her rescue, laying wooden boards across the mud and sliding out along it with a rope to pull her out. The sucking sound the mud made as it released its grip still woke her at unexpected times, gasping and cold.

In later years she had envied the herring girls just starting out: how new and exciting the island must be to them. Unlike Marianne, they were allowed to go where they pleased without an adult to keep them from harm. But over the years she had come to realise that their life was not to be envied. Home comforts were far more important than freedom.

She wrinkled her nose. The smell on this part of the beach was cloying, the stink of the sea lingering on these women even after they had washed. She wondered if Nan would come back smelling the same.

'How long will they be?' she said, nodding at the women in the distance. They were far out now, bending and picking at something on the rocks. She could hear laughter slide across the open space. What have they got to be happy about? she thought.

'Sit with me,' the woman said, and Marianne, who knew her manners, folded down onto the stones next to her. The woman's legs were swaddled in blankets, and they juddered under the heavy cloth.

'What's ...?' Marianne stopped.

'What's wrong with my legs? Come, child, you can speak freely. My time is running out, I appreciate a girl who gets to the point.' She laid a hand on her jiggling legs, and they stopped moving just for a second. She sighed. 'Ah, it's such a beautiful feeling, being still.' Her legs began almost immediately to shake again and the woman frowned. 'It's the peas,' she said. 'The sea peas that grow all around here.' She gestured to a small plant growing out of the stones by Marianne's shoe, little fingers of brown pea pods hanging from it. 'It's fine in small amounts, but come the winter there's little else to eat. And when you have a choice between shaking and starving ... well.'

'What about herring?'

'Herring?' the woman opened her mouth in a silent crack of laughter. 'The silver darlings? The herring belong to your father, Miss Stourbridge. We are paid by the weight to gut them and pack them. It does us no good to eat them. It is like eating money that does not belong to us: neither tasty, nor legal.'

'But if you're hungry?'

The woman looked at Marianne with pity and she slowly shook her head, turning her attention to her legs again. 'It's a slow poisoning. Tremors, muscle wastage. We all have it to a degree.'

Marianne had a sudden urge to put her hand on the woman's leg.

'She's a pretty young thing,' the woman said, nodding out to sea, where Nan was silhouetted with the rest of the women, bending and straightening. 'Is she to sleep in our quarters, too?' She indicated a small brick building further up the beach, a smile on her lips.

Marianne felt the shame creep up on her again. 'Mama says she's my father's pet.'

'Oh?'

Marianne sighed, stirring the stones with her finger. 'Papa has always had pets. They hold his interest for a while and then he drops them. Doubtless Nan will be the same.'

The woman was staring out at the silhouettes of the girls on the rocks. Marianne took the opportunity to study her face. Something about the crack of her lips, the clam-like eyelids, was familiar, and she wondered again if this was the woman who had rescued her. She debated whether to ask.

'Is that what you should do with pets?' the woman said lightly, 'Lead them astray until they are lost, never to return?'

Marianne shot the woman an angry look.

'Perhaps you're one of his pets too. Is that it? Have you been dropped in favour of something more exciting? More interesting?' the woman reached out and picked a pea pod from the plant between them, snapping it crisply in two.

Marianne could see the beginnings of a tremor in her hands. 'You should speak to Father,' she said. 'I'm sure he will allow you a few herring if you're hungry.' She thought of the remains of the cod she had left on her plate at luncheon, the fat slices of potato rich with butter and dill. She imagined this woman, approaching for scraps like a stray dog.

'Pardon me, miss, but you don't know your father in the same way I do. He is a businessman. And besides, have you not heard the rumours coming down from Scotland? The tides are turning on the herring industry. Less and less every year. They're swimming elsewhere, so they say.'

'That's not what Papa says. The captain of the *Schoonheid* assures us it will be a bountiful year,' She was aware she was parroting her father. She picked up a stone and studied it in embarrassment.

'Think as you will, miss. I'm only repeating what I hear.'

They looked out to sea, watching the women on the rocks who had stopped bending over now, and were making their way back to the beach. Marianne followed Nan's progress over the sharp barnacles, surprised by her finesse.

'Besides,' the old woman continued, 'we mermaids don't need herring yet: we have winkles aplenty at this time of year, and there is no law to stop us eating those.'

Chapter Ten

Tartelin

Summer 2018

Over the next fortnight, I do as I'm asked, collecting butterflies and bringing them back to be observed, killed and set. Each day I find it easier to catch them, both the act of sweeping the net over them, and the torment that comes with tipping them into the jar. Sometimes, this scares me. Am I becoming like her?

After our supper each night, we retire to the panelled room and sip tea in silence, watching the sky turn, as the gas lamps hiss into life around us. My legs ache pleasantly from my exertions in the day, and the resonant, irregular chimes of the broken clock make us both jump and laugh at ourselves.

Sometimes, when I feel her austere façade softening, I try to push her on what she is really looking for: what the A of her example of the other night is. But she never gives anything away. After these conversations, the atmosphere always chills noticeably between us. I never stay long after that. I understand that she craves her own space, as do I.

Down in my bedroom, exhausted from my day on the island, I lie in the narrow bed and listen as she begins to play the piano above me. It's the same song every night, a beautiful melancholy piece that builds to a crescendo, becoming joyful where once it was sad, and I wonder when she learnt it, which part of her life it comes from. Perhaps as a teenager she had piano lessons. She might even have been playing this piece on the eve of the storm that shipwrecked the Dogger boat and killed all the herring.

I would love to hear more of Miss Stourbridge's stories, to find out about what it was like here all those years ago. I tell myself it's because I want to learn about the island that's now my home, but there's another reason too. Of all the things I miss about Mum, it is her stories that I ache for. Listening to Miss Stourbridge talking about the island's past is a comforting substitute. Her voice is full of an ancient wisdom, cracked and honeyed, as if what she is telling me is not fact, but folklore and myth. I have tried on a few occasions to bring up her past again, but she is defensively prickly, as if she thinks I'm probing, when all I want to do is get to know her better.

In the last few days of Mum's life, when I sat by her bed in the hospice, she told the story of webbed hands and fishes and the sea so often that it became a mantra. On a too-bright day, when the sunlight poured across her weakening body, highlighting the jutting bones and thinning, grey skin, she turned to me, raking my face with her barely conscious eyes.

'The sea,' she said, her voice scratchy, reaching out her birdlike hands and clawing at mine. 'I ... the sea ...'

'I know, Mum, it's OK.' I looked desperately out to the corridor, wondering whether to press the button to call the nurse but, just as quickly, she closed her eyes again and drifted back into an uneasy sleep.

As I sat by her bed, watching her eyes flutter beneath her lilac eyelids, it occurred to me that perhaps her tale of fish and webs and water was more than just a story. There had been an urgency to her words, her poor sinewed muscles taut and fragile as she tried to lift her arms, to make her point from the drugged depths of her hospital bed. As I gazed at her, sleeping peacefully now, it struck me that she might have been trying to tell me, in her own, creative way, something about herself.

Mum didn't have many friends; she was quite at peace being on her own. As far as I could tell, no one else visited her in the hospice. I had never arrived to find fresh flowers in a vase on the bedside, never looked through the door to see a gnarled old hand holding onto my mum's.

I knew she hadn't had a good relationship with her parents. I had never met my grandparents; I didn't even know if they were still alive. But surely if your daughter is dying, you would lay your differences aside? Was there something about her past, about where she came from, hidden in the words I knew so well? A lone egg, drifting in the tide. Was that her?

The longer I'm on this island, the more I realise I know nothing about my mother's past before she adopted me, and I curse myself for not asking her before she died. Now that I can't ask her, I want to know everything. I want to know what she ate for breakfast as a child, what her first kiss was like, what her last thoughts were each night. *We're people of the sea*, she said to me often in those last days, but what did she mean? What did she mean?

Perhaps this is why Miss Stourbridge's early life fascinates me so much. If I can find out about her past, I can begin to understand her in a way that I never managed to with my mum. I can assuage the guilt, and pave my way to forming new relationships, to begin to care for people again.

On a dull, muggy morning, I get up earlier than usual, ensuring I rise before my employer. This isn't hard: I've been here for two weeks now and for the last week I've noticed that Miss Stourbridge has been getting up later and later. It's as if she's beginning to tire after many years of vim and vigour, reminding me how old she must be. Sometimes she gets up so late that I don't see her until I come in from my day out on the island, bringing with me my haul of butterflies.

Today, instead of going straight outside, I quietly climb the stairs, pausing after each step to listen for movement. I have never been in her bedroom, but I know it's off the galleried landing, the door just along from her collection of nets hanging on the wall. It's closed, and I tiptoe into the panelled room.

The early morning light is like a translucent pool, lapping over the floor, and I'm distracted by the sea and the garden outside the window. They're the same colour, merging as if joined, as if there is no cliff there to divide them.

I can see a pair of people walking through the shallows, far below the cliff. They look as if they've come from a handful of tents which are just visible, pitched in the dips of the dunes. I'm no swimmer, but I have felt the pull of the water on my ankles down there, and I silently hope that they know how strong the current is. I feel a sense of pride in my knowledge: I am getting to know the island's secrets; the fissures and cracks that only an islander would be aware of.

I stand at the window and watch the two people paddling in the sea, sure that they have no idea anyone is looking down on them from high up on the cliff. It makes me feel like a god, and I wonder if this is how Miss Stourbridge feels, watching the world, day after day. As they stride out of sight, I turn to the Chinese cabinet. Its lacquer has taken on the colour of the sea, a petrol blue that looks wet to the touch.

I've come up here to look at the photograph album. I have an urge to see the face of the laughing girl again; the girl who I suspected for a while was Marianne, but the more time I spend in Miss Stourbridge's company, the less likely it seems that the girl in the photo is my stern employer. The girl's laughing face has become a fixture in my dreams of late, replacing my mum's wasted one, and for that I'm grateful.

I pause and listen for any sign she is getting up, but the house is silent beneath the ticking of the clock. Quickly, I open the doors of the Chinese cabinet and crouch down to look between the trays. But the album is no longer there.

I pull out the butterfly frames hastily, one by one, in case I've missed it right at the back, but they slide out easily with nothing trapped between them. Frustrated, I turn and look around the room, wondering where Miss Stourbridge might have put it, and my eyes settle on the large drawer at the base of the desk. I think of the soft blanket within, how she thrust her foot into the gap so that she could stare at it for a moment. Perhaps whatever is wrapped inside it might give me a clue about what she's doing here on this island. The clock behind me seems to quicken, the tick of it matching the beat of my heart.

With mounting excitement, I hurry over to the desk. I can hear the scratching of the cocooned butterflies in the puparium. One or two are twitching, as if preparing to emerge. I wonder if Miss Stourbridge will want to pull each of them from their chrysalis before they have a chance to hatch naturally.

I check over my shoulder, and quickly pull the drawer open.

The blanket is gone, the drawer empty. Disappointment sweeps through me. I close it carefully and then open each of the other drawers, but there is nothing but lepidoptery equipment in these, glass jars and sharp, pointed instruments.

I have left the door to the Chinese cabinet open, the trays of butterflies half pulled out, and I flit across the room, my ears straining for sounds of my employer. As I go to close them, my gaze settles on the top tray. The larger males are a striking yellow, the petite females a pale green that almost appears white. Since learning their name, I've spotted them on the island too, flitting far out of reach, a bright, yellow-green flash in the sky, like leaves caught in the wind.

I pull each tray out in turn. There must be twenty in each frame, and five trays in the cabinet. A hundred brimstones, dead and pinned. What did Miss Stourbridge call them? A timeline of a strange summer?

On the fourth tray down, I notice something unusual. The change is so slow, so delicate, that it has crept up on me. I look hard at the butterflies, at their dead, dried-out bodies and wings. The insects in this tray are marginally smaller. The orange-brown dot that should sit so perfectly at the centre of each wing has strayed, as if a painter has grown weary while marking hundreds upon hundreds of them. One or two of the butterflies have tiny slits to the edges of their wings.

I pull out the fifth and final tray. These insects are markedly different from those that came before them. To look at them, you wouldn't think they were the same species, and yet in all of them, the same bright yellow-green shines through. One butterfly has so many dark dots on its wings that it looks as though it has freckles. Another has such small, stunted wings that it must never have been able to fly. Yet another has one overlarge hind wing and one extremely small. There is a butterfly near the bottom that has what looks like a second tongue, half unrolled and sticking to the bottom of the drawer. I peer closely at it. Its eyes are flat instead of round, as if they have collapsed in on themselves. I begin to feel sick.

Beneath each butterfly is a tiny rectangle of paper with a date on. The top tray begins on 8 July 1955, and as my eyes flit over the dead insects, I see that they were killed and set consecutively over a number of days, the last one labelled a few days after the first. A crackle of excitement trickles over my skull. What happened to these poor creatures? Could they be mutations, like Miss Stourbridge said? The thought makes me nervous, the tingle in my scalp flooding my ears with white noise. Beyond it, I think I hear the rolling of Miss Stourbridge's wheelchair, and I quickly slide the tray back into the cabinet and close the doors, suddenly not wanting to be near its contents at all.

I manage to creep back downstairs and leave the house without being seen. I'm not sure what I would say to my employer if I saw her. In my haste to get out of the house I have forgotten the net and the killing jars, but after seeing so many butterflies, dead and pinned, I cannot contemplate catching more today.

As I step outside, I can't shake off the image of the trays of butterflies, the date, 1955, scratched onto a label below each one. I look out over Dohhalund. From here I can just make out the military base on the spit of land that Miss Stourbridge warned me about. *Things happened there*, she told me on my first day.

The island was requisitioned in the war, I remember, the Stourbridges told to leave later on in the Fifties. The butterflies were caught in 1955. Slowly, something slots into place.

Science says that if A happens, then B will follow, Miss Stourbridge told me, *but I am still in the process of proving that A happened at all.*

A shiver runs down my back. What if something *did* happen here, something massive, something disastrous?

I kick off and start down the hill on my bike, aiming for the northern spit and the peculiar buildings that sit on it. If she won't tell me what happened, I need to find proof of my own. A trayful of dead butterflies isn't enough.

There is a fresh breeze today, skimming off the sea from the west. It ripples at the canvas of three small green tents that are pitched at the edge of the road, their inhabitants zipped away inside, probably still fast asleep, and I think of the breeze touching England before it came here. Did it pass through Lincolnshire, swooping over my old house? I think of it licking at the chimney, dropping down for an instant into Mum's studio, stirring the flakes of gold leaf, the strands of peacock feathers that may still be there, abandoned on the workbench. The house is for sale now. It had been too much to deal with, in the weeks after Mum's death, so before I left for the island, I gave instructions to the solicitor to deal with it all. Perhaps even now it's being cleared, ready for a new family to move in, and the realisation comes to me that I have no home now, other than on this island. It's an unsettling feeling, the last tether to the mainland – to my mum – gone.

I take a deep lungful of the air coming in off the sea. It doesn't smell of England, this breeze, it's entirely Dohhalund, a taste more than a smell – salt and something acidic that promises to strip away memories. It sloughs away the feelings of anxiety, and I revel in the newness of it all. As I pedal down the hill, I realise it's a smell I'm gradually beginning to love, and I embrace its chill in the morning, sucking it deep into my chest. I can feel the air catch on the small patch of ruffled skin on my cheek, and today it doesn't feel cumbersome to be different. It feels beautiful. In a flash, the hill is behind me, and I pedal confidently round the dogs that lie, curled up on the sides of the road, as if I have been doing it for years, not days.

I freewheel over the tarmac, zigzagging to avoid the cracks and clumps of plants, swerving round odd strings of barbed wire left to rust on the ground. A small tan-coloured dog trots past me, and I find myself calling out a friendly hello that's lost to the wind as soon as I shout it.

I pass the marsh to my left, keeping a wary eye out for Jacob and his bright-eyed dog. I cycle on, the marsh giving way to a low field punctuated by clumps of sedge.

Ahead, I see a man in his fifties, dressed head to toe in khaki. He waves me down as I approach, and I slow to a stop. He has one of those waistcoats that seems to be made of pockets, and each one is stuffed full. I can see a pair of sunglasses, a penknife, and a compass peeping out. An expensive pair of binoculars hang from his neck, the strap nestled in his slightly too long sandy-coloured hair.

'I'm looking for the mulberry trees,' he says. His voice is gruff, as if he hasn't spoken in a while. 'It's where it was last seen.' His orange eyebrows twitch at me like poisonous caterpillars.

'Where *what* was last seen?'

'The bird. The *Morus* hybrid?' He speaks the name slowly, as if he thinks I'm dim.

'Oh. I don't know, sorry.'

'You might know it as the old silkworm plantation? Apparently, you can't miss it, it's a, umm ...' He pulls out a piece of paper, and unfolds it, squinting to read what's printed on it. 'It's a field of trees planted in lines.'

'Sorry, I don't know. I'm not here for a bird.'

'Then what *are* you here for?' He looks about at the island, then up at the clouds, as if the answer will come soaring down from the sky.

I shrug, and the man tuts in frustration and starts walking away, the many objects in his pockets clanking.

Why *am* I here, I ask myself as I watch him go? I push off on my bike, the question rolling around my mind.

If I'd asked myself two weeks ago, my answer would have been something to do with escape. Escape from my grief, escape from the memory of my mum's death. Coming here was an attempt to leave my sadness behind. But of course, you cannot escape grief, it clings to you in ways you can't just brush away.

So why did I not leave as soon as I realised? Why am I still here now?

I look around me, and the answer comes in the pleasant ache I feel in my legs as I pedal: I'm here because I relish the feeling of strength in my muscles as I bike further and walk longer each day. I'm here because I'm having to make decisions for myself, and I like the feeling of power it gives me. I'm here because there's something about this place: it has done something to me, changed me intrinsically, and it fills me with hope that one day I will love the person I'm becoming. My grief has followed me here, yes, but there is so much more space for it on this wild, windy isle.

The island is longer and thinner than I realise, and as it stretches out in front of me, the sea is suddenly presented to me on both sides, like a book opening, and I feel as if I'm not on land, but on the back of some great, hulking blue whale that has risen for a moment to take in air, before dropping back down, fathoms below. Instinctively I breathe in too and hold in the air as long as I can. I used to play this game with Mum when I was younger, as we drove into tunnels. We would both hold our breath as we went down. She always lasted longer than me.

Far ahead of me on the spit, a building is shimmering into view. It looks a little like a Japanese pagoda. As I get closer, I see there are two, one behind the other. But the furthest one is different. Where the roof of its sister rises majestically into the air, the further building is lower, the roof flat and crumbling, as if the pillars it rested on have dissolved.

I reach the edge of the spit and raise my hand to shield my eyes from the sun. So, this is the military base.

The two buildings are little more than blocks of concrete, windowless apart from the gaps between the struts that hold up the temple-like roof of the nearest one. The furthest one is surrounded by a circle of rubble, and I see why: the struts have collapsed, the roof slammed tight onto its walls like the lid of a huge sarcophagus. My heart patters in my chest. Has it crumbled over time, or is this the result of something more sinister?

A weedy path winds through the shingle towards the buildings. I dismount from my bike and pause, heeding Miss Stourbridge's warnings about the spit ahead. The heat of the morning is beginning to lift from the stones and shimmer into the air, the last clouds clearing. In the distance, past the buildings, I think I see someone walking at the very end of the island, but the skyline is a molten shimmer of blues and yellows and I can't be sure. I try to make the shape into Jacob, searching for his dog running with him, but from this distance I cannot tell. I wait, looking around, as if I'm sure someone will call out and stop me should I step any closer, but there is no one here to tell me what to do.

I start forward, wheeling my bike beside me.

The path is longer than it looked at the start of the track, the buildings not seeming to get any closer as I push my bike over the compacted stones. Every now and then I look warily at the great swathes of pebbles on either side of me, and each time I look back, the buildings are closer, as if they have crept up on me while I was looking the other way.

As I approach the closest one, the day cools suddenly. It's as if a cloud has passed over the sun, but when I look up, the sky is bright and clear. There is a single door set into the nearest wall. It's painted green, but the paint has peeled, revealing dark, pitted metal beneath. Above me, the breeze sings through the gaps between the struts. It reminds me of the intonation of prayers in the church Mum cleaned, and I listen, distracted. It sounds as if someone is in there, humming as they work. I sway towards the building, and I know with a certainty that I cannot put into words that my mother is inside, her yellow Marigolds on, floral apron tied at the waist, and I can smell polish, fresh flowers.

The last time I went to St Andrew's Church was a year ago. I was nineteen, just back from my first year at art school. I'd been so happy to come home. At art school, the other students were all so full of a confidence that I couldn't see in myself, and I had struggled to navigate their complex nuances. One boy asked to photograph me, only to bring the lens so close to my cheek I could feel it brushing the ruffle of skin there. After that, whenever I sketched myself, staring at my face in the mirror, I always rubbed my birthmark away.

I was so happy to be home, to see my mum, to get in the studio and begin to apply all that I'd learnt while I was away. I dropped my suitcase in the hall, calling for my mother. I looked in the studio, but there was nothing there but stillness and peace, and a note, telling me where she was.

'Tartelin.' Her voice is far away. I stare at the door, not sure what is real and what is not. I take a step closer. My mother is in there, I am sure of it.

I went straight to the church, brimming full of excitement and stories and a yearning to see her. A year away at art school had shown me just how special a person she was. The church was beautiful. Cool and smelling of flowers left over from a wedding the day before.

We sat in a pew, my mother and I, and she took my hands in hers, overjoyed to see me again, and I took a breath, ready to tell her everything that had happened in my first year away, how happy I was to be home, with her.

But her hand came to my face, a soft finger touching my lips, quietening me.

And she told me she had cancer.

The finger against my lips shook, and I saw the thinness of her arms as she reached out to hug me, the sockets of her skull as she looked at me.

And we stayed there, in each other's arms, not wanting to leave, as if by staying in the church we would never have to move on from that moment.

The light around me changes, softening. It is the clear, harmonious light of a church. I look at the building in front of me. My mother is in there, I know it. I drop my bike, hardly aware of what I am doing, and step towards the door.

'Tartelin.' The voice again. I stare at the door, listening. Waiting for her.

'Tartelin, what are you doing?' The voice is closer now. It's behind me. I blink and look around.

Jacob is running down the path towards me. As he nears me, he stops and bends over, panting, his hands raised. His dog is at his side as if they are one creature.

His breath coming in sharp rasps, he says, 'You can't come here. Don't you know what these are?'

The word 'church' is on my lips, but when I look at the buildings again, I see they are nothing like a church. They are ugly and broken and enclosed like a tightened fist; like a mausoleum.

'They're bomb-testing facilities,' he says. 'And this,' he waves his arm over the sea of stones surrounding us, 'is where half the bombs they tested are buried. Any that didn't make it as far as the sea landed here; they might be still live.' He pulls himself to standing and points to a crater thirty feet away. Stones lie in ripples surrounding a shallow pit. 'That's where one exploded. See the bones on the edge?'

I squint at the pebbles, and eventually focus on a horseshoe of bones that looks like a ribcage.

'A deer, probably,' he says, 'I can't get close enough to check, but the dogs don't dare cross the stones, as if they instinctively know it's dangerous.'

I feel so stupid. And angry too. Angry at Miss Stourbridge for not making it clear how dangerous it is out here. I wish, not for the first time, that she wasn't so mysterious with her warnings and her stories. I could have been killed.

The dog whines at Jacob's side and lies down quickly, her nose between her paws. I see the blue flash of her eye before she closes her soft eyelids and sighs.

'Are we allowed inside?' I nod at the closest building. The other one is too dark, too damaged to think about entering. It's not just the rubble and the collapsed roof: there's something about it that's the opposite of what a church should be, and I find I don't want to see inside.

'We're allowed where we want. It's whether it's safe or not.'

There is a glint in his eye now, a twinkle, as if he is just a boy, really, young and innocent, full of the joy of exploring.

'Is it safe?' I ask.

He cocks his head, examining the building over my shoulder. I am reminded of a robin, watching from between the branches of a tree. 'It's safe enough,' he says. 'I want to get in there, actually.'

'For your work?'

'Partly for my work. Partly out of curiosity. How about you? Is it work, or curiosity?'

'It depends if there are butterflies in there.'

'There might be. And I'm hoping there'll be spiders.'

I start forward, towards the green door. 'Come on, then,' I say over my shoulder.

At the door, we stop. It doesn't seem to have a handle, just a keyhole. Jacob bends and looks through. 'Can't see a thing. Probably blocked with cobwebs.' He stands up, and I am conscious of the scratch of his wool jumper against my bare arm. It feels both comforting and disturbing. I take a step back.

'Is that it, then? We can't go in.'

I can hear the relief in my voice, but Jacob isn't listening. He is scouring the floor. He picks up a thin shard of flint at his feet, and, jamming it into the crack between the door and the wall, he pushes against it, and the door creaks slightly. A puff of air escapes, something avian in its smell, and I shiver.

'It's not locked,' he says, 'whoever was here last didn't want to stick around to lock it up.'

I think of Miss Stourbridge's words. *Things happened there. Things I don't like to dwell upon.* I look at the other building, the roof flush against the top, the rubble around the base.

Jacob is heaving at the door, and slowly it eases open. He turns to tell Gabbro to stay, and then slips inside.

Before I follow him, I take one last look at the building further away, its sarcophagus-like lid firmly closed. The sound that is like humming is still there, but it's just the wind, I realise now. My mother was never here. It suddenly feels more dangerous outside on my own than inside with Jacob. I swallow down my fear and step inside.

The first thing that strikes me is the light. I expected it to be dark, but the spaces between the struts above us let in so much sunlight that it is a lattice of brightness and shadow divided into geometric chunks. Here and there, rusted grids of metal strike sharp, cross-hatched silhouettes across the ground. Everything about the place is linear, mathematical, and I can envisage how modern and functional it must have been in its heyday.

But flora and fauna have taken up residence now. Ferns grow in every crack. Small rectangular holes in the walls are filled with twigs and dried grass. A rustle comes from one, and then something pale launches itself out and swoops at us. I stumble back, but at the last moment it rises sharply, soaring up to the gaps near the struts where it lands for a moment, silhouetted against the blue sky. Then, with a shriek that chills my bones, it drops away outside.

'Barn owl,' Jacob says, going immediately to the nest it came from. 'Sadly no chicks. They've probably already fledged.' He drops his backpack onto the ground and goes to examine a far corner of the building.

I notice the walls have strange metal plaques along them. They look like elongated crosses, making me think again of the church and my mother. The eerie singing is still here if I listen for it, the wind's vibration catching on the concrete and emitting a deep hum that seems to collect low on the ground by my feet and swell outwards, as if trying to escape.

Above me are old, rusted lights, pendants strung from the ceiling, but they, too have been taken over by nature. Great chalky stalactites hang down from their metal shades. I hear the slow drip, drip that signifies they are still in the process of evolving.

'It's the sea salt from the concrete.'

'Sorry?' I pull my eyes from the weird structures. Jacob has come back from the other end of the building. He's looking up at the lights too.

'When they built these facilities before World War Two, they used stones from the beach to make the concrete. Ever since, the salt's been seeping out.'

'How do you know all this?'

Jacob shrugs. 'Knowledge is important,' he says. There is a glint of excitement in his eyes, as if he wants to tell me more, but is unsure whether I will want to hear it. I find I'd like to know, and I open my mouth to ask, but at that moment he takes hold of my elbow, and I jump at his touch.

'Come and see this,' he says, beckoning me over to the corner he's been exploring.

This wall has more of those rectangular holes in it. Jacob leads me to one right in the corner. Apart from a layer of dust at the bottom, it looks empty.

'There's nothing there,' I say, peering into the dark space, wary of birds flying out without warning.

'You're looking too far into it. Adjust your eyes.'

'How can I adjust my eyes?'

'Like those magic eye pictures. Do you remember them? Change your focus and the picture appears out of nowhere.'

I have no idea what he's talking about, but I try all the same, attempting to relax my gaze.

'Just there,' he says, turning back to the hole and lifting a finger to show me, 'strung across the entrance.'

I wait for my eyes to filter out the dark hole behind, and then I see it: a spider's web. But it is not like any web I've seen before. I take a step closer. This is the web of a master weaver. Its outline is the same shape as any normal web, the fine silk shining like slivers of silver wire, but within the jagged circle, something miraculous hangs.

I try not to blink, keeping my eyes as still as possible so as not to lose focus on the translucent silk. The web resembles the veins of a leaf more than anything else I can think of, and yet I am aware of how wholly inadequate that description is. It's like a story laid out before me, a book that you can read without words, and within this story are tiny whorls, leading your eye into smaller and more complicated patterns. Ferns and fractals appear as my eyes rake over its beauty, so that it becomes a galaxy of stars, and suddenly I'm aware of how unimportant I am in this vast, bewildering universe.

'Try not to breathe too hard,' Jacob whispers, close to me, and I real-ise that my breath is becoming laboured, as if I have forgotten how to do it properly. The web is vibrating, pulsing against the air from my lungs.

'How is it real?' I whisper.

'Look in the top right corner,' he says, hardly moving, and I follow his eyes to a compressed part of the web, as if the silk has been wound around itself to make something solid. It is so dense that it glows, so white that it makes everything around it look dark, as if it has collected the light and is drawing it in slowly, carefully, until this whole building will be dark as pitch, this white dot the only light in the world.

'Isn't she beautiful?' Jacob breathes, and for a moment I don't under-stand, but then the clot of silk moves ever so slightly, and I realise: this is the spider.

She is small, her body no larger than a pearl, her legs delicately tucked beneath her.

'Is it a rare species?' I say, my eyes distracted by the web again, marvelling at the intricacies of the spun silk. I can almost see faces in it, landscapes, seascapes, forests and trees.

'I've never seen one like it. She resembles an orb weaver, see the markings on her back? But I've never seen a white one.'

I look closely, and I can just make out a pale grey pattern on the bulbous body. I think of Miss Stourbridge and her mutations, the man in the waistcoat and his hybrid bird.

'Could it be a new species?'

'It could, but it's more likely a species that has been breeding on this island for so long that it's gone off on its own genetic route.'

'You mean evolution?'

'Yes.'

'Or mutation?'

Jacob frowns. 'I'm not sure you could call it that, although mutation and evolution go hand in hand. This isn't the first unusual spider I've found here. The island is littered with them. Mutation almost never happens on this scale. You'd need an event. Something catastrophic.'

My scalp prickles. 'Like what?'

Jacob shrugs. 'An ice age? A huge change in temperature? Who knows?'

He turns back to the spider, inching closer to it. 'Leucistic spiders are rare,' he whispers. 'The only time I've seen any before were in caves so deep they never see the light of day.'

Leucistic. Miss Stourbridge used that word. I think of the swallows above her window, the pure white mother and baby. 'There's a leucistic swallow nesting at the house where I'm staying,' I say.

Jacob looks up. 'There is?'

Outside, Gabbro barks softly.

'Come on,' he says,' I don't think we're going to find any butterflies in here.'

I'm relieved to be out in the sunlight, where there are no black shadows slicing into the brightness.

'Why are you so fascinated with nature?' I ask him, collecting my bike.

'You say it like it's a bad thing,' he says.

'No, I . . .' I have offended him. I stop, trying to find the right words. 'It's nice. Watching you.' It reminds me of being out on a walk with my mother, her eyes darting from bird to bird, the way she got home and immediately wanted to recreate them.

'It's my job,' he says, shrugging.

But it's more than that, I think. There's something raptly passionate about the interest he has in the world around him, something that goes far deeper than just a job. I like the way that sometimes he hardly sees me at all. I am not his focus; I am just there in the background. His passion reminds me of some of the students on my art course, but without their overinflated self-importance.

'What is it you do? For a job, I mean?'

'I'm a university lecturer. I specialise in arachnids.'

'You're Spiderman?'

Jacob snorts softly. 'Not quite. I *know* a lot about spiders, I'm not one myself.'

I glance at him to see if he's deliberately missed the joke, but his expression is passive, giving nothing away. 'And this is part of your job?' I gesture at the island, the sun pouring down on us, the scant bushes twisting out of the stones.

'No, this is something I'm just interested in. But I'm hoping I can write a paper on the spiders I find here.'

Gabbro wags her tail as we approach, her whole body wriggling in greeting. Jacob rests a hand on her head, and she stops moving, relishing his touch, trembling submissively. I almost want to put my own hand on her head and feel her soft fur, but she turns her eyes on me, and I think, maybe next time.

As we walk back along the path, Jacob says, almost to himself, 'I have Autism Spectrum Disorder. I get interested in things. It's always been nature of some kind or another. When I was little, I spent whole weekends living out in the garden, searching for bugs. My parents didn't really get it.' Out of the corner of my eye I see him risk a quick glance in my direction. 'I thought you should know,' he says, 'because sometimes I focus on something, and it feels like everything else is blotted out because of it, and it's not that I'm ignoring you, it's just … I'm just … looking through a different set of eyes.' He says it as if recalling a phrase learnt by rote, as if he doesn't know quite how else to describe it.

We walk along the path, our shoulders touching so we don't stray into the swathes of pebbles on either side. Gabbro trots obediently behind Jacob, occasionally dipping her head and pretending to nip at his ankle.

We continue to walk in companionable silence. I think how wonderful and difficult it must be to love something so much. It reminds me of the way Miss Stourbridge is consumed by her butterflies. Everyone I've met on this island seems to have a passion for something, except me. Is there something inherently wrong with me? Why don't I feel emotion about things in the same way that Jacob does? And then I remember my first butterfly, the sound of it in the jar as it died. Perhaps I'm not made of stone after all.

Ahead of us, a group of people with camouflage backpacks emerge over the bank of shingle.

'I didn't know there'd be anyone else on Dohhalund when I got here,' I say. 'You gave me a fright on the marsh the other day. I'm sorry if I was rude.'

'No, it was my fault: I shouldn't have approached you. You just looked sad.'

I take a breath, thinking again of the white butterfly, the tears that were for both the insect and my mother. 'I think I'd just begun to realise what I'd taken on by coming here. Why do you think so many people have started turning up?'

'Word spreads,' he says. 'The requisition was lifted in the spring, and an island nobody's set foot on for sixty years does sound appealing, you've got to admit. It certainly did for me, anyway.' He shoots a glance at me. 'The summer holidays were coming up, and after a year of standing in fuggy lecture halls, it was like paradise coming somewhere so ... freeing.'

'Overwhelming though,' I say, thinking of my first few days, the doubt I'd felt that I'd done the right thing by coming here.

'What made you decide to do it?'

'My mum.'

'She encouraged you?'

I pause. 'Sort of. It was something she used to tell me. A story, about how she loved the sea. I've never spent much time by the water, and I suppose I wanted to experience it for myself. Anyway, I'm not the only one,' I say, uncomfortable under the beam of his focus. I've never been good at talking about myself. 'I spoke to a man earlier who was looking for a rare bird. Some kind of hybrid?'

'Oh yes. There was a whole boatload of day trippers last Saturday. They're all after a sighting.'

'What is it? The bird?'

'I don't think anyone can agree. Nobody's been able to get close enough to confirm. I suspect they're hoping it's a new species.'

'Do you think it could be?'

'There's always a chance, I suppose, like I said with the spider. But I haven't seen it, and I'm not a bird specialist. I tend to look down, not up.' He indicates the ground, a shy grin touching his mouth. 'How did you find out about the white swallow you told me about?' he adds.

'My boss showed me. She's lived here on and off her whole life, in the big house up on the hill. Dogger Bank.'

'You mean Marianne Stourbridge?'

I look up at him. 'How did you know?'

'I had to apply to her to come to the island. I did some research before I wrote to her. Did you know, her family have owned Dohhalund down the mother's line for over two hundred years? Silk makers.'

'Of course,' I say, remembering what the birdwatcher had said about the mulberry plantation. 'I wonder if that's why she's so interested in butterflies and moths: she must have spent time with silk moths when she was younger.'

'What does she do with the butterflies you bring her?'

'She dissects some, and she pins ... sorry, *sets* others. She's looking for something, studying change on the island, though I'm not sure what.'

Jacob nods. 'You'd learn a lot about nature, growing up somewhere like this. Her family were herring fishers before the silk business, until the fish moved into different waters. I think they also cultivated pearls at one point. I suppose living on an island means you need to make use of the raw materials it provides, especially such rich pickings as this island seems to throw up.'

I think of my oyster shell with its strange, scratched drawing on it, and the fat pearl the woman at the salt pans showed me.

'They used to eat all kinds of birds' eggs here,' he adds. 'Some of the birds are ground-nesting, and it was customary to go egg collecting in the spring. Imagine trying to do that now, you'd have the police on to you.'

'Oh?' The little speckled eggs come back to me, how delicious they tasted, how delicate their shells were. What bird had they been from, I think guiltily. Who left them for me?

'I get the feeling she's a bit of a hermit,' Jacob says. 'Miss Stourbridge, I mean. I haven't seen her since I've been here.'

'You're right. She doesn't leave the house.'

'At all? Why?'

'Well, she's in a wheelchair for one thing, and she lives upstairs.'

Jacob looks appalled at the idea.

'But I don't think she wants to go outside,' I rush in. 'She's certainly never asked.'

'Trapped animals don't ask to get out,' he says. 'How did she get up there?'

'I have no idea.' It feels as if she's always been there, a permanent fixture of Dogger Bank, prowling its rooms. I forget that she only arrived on the island a few months before me. 'I think the fisherman who brought her to the island carried her upstairs,' I say, remembering my conversation with the woman at the salt pans.

I can imagine Miss Stourbridge, directing him from her wheelchair as he heaved up cases and foodstuffs, wheeling herself around the panelled room, wiping dust from the desk. It hadn't occurred to me that she might want to go outside.

'Could you introduce me? Show me this leucistic swallow? I'd love to see it.'

I pause. The thought of Jacob in that house fills me with an unknown dread, as if surrounding him with the decaying husks of insects, and the heavy, wood-panelled walls might have the power to dampen his bright, sunny mood. I cannot put the feeling into words, and I stay silent, trying to untangle it in my mind.

He's looking down at his dog. 'I'm sorry,' he says, 'I didn't mean to presume.'

'You didn't presume. It's just, you said it yourself – she's a hermit. I don't feel I know her well enough yet to start inviting people into her house.

Talking to Miss Stourbridge isn't as easy as talking to you. I don't feel I know her very well at all, yet.'

Jacob nods, clicking his fingers for Gabbro, who is trotting behind a little way, a piece of bone in her mouth like a clay pipe.

'Island folk are renowned for building a wall around themselves. I hear she can be quite ferocious. You know, the Stourbridge family left Dohhalund in 1955, when it was still very much a working military base?' he says. 'They were told they had to leave with hardly any time to prepare. Can you imagine? It must be very strange for her to come back and see it like this, taken over by nature.'

We have reached the end of the shingle path now, back onto safe land, and we stand, looking out over the island. I try to imagine what it must have been like here the year they had to leave. With a start I realise it was also the year the brimstones were caught and pinned. I look back the way we've come, at the furthest bomb-testing building that stands, half crumbled to rubble.

We walk on in silence, Jacob bending down here and there to examine the soft tendril of a plant, the sea-washed curve of a shell. I'm so close, I can see the curl of his hair over his collar, and I have a sudden urge to touch it, in the same way that he is touching the land with his fingers, exploring with his senses.

Jacob stands up, a pebble in his hand. He rolls it in his palm, looking at it.

'What you said earlier,' he says, 'about me giving you a fright … I … I won't hurt you. There's no need to be scared of me.' He's still looking at the pebble.

I grip the bicycle's handlebars, dipping my head to hide my red face behind my hair. Jacob pockets the pebble and bends down again, his fingers peeling the grass apart, burrowing into the stones.

'Look here,' he says, and I go closer, thankful for the distraction.

It's another spider web. This one is the opposite of the web we saw in the pagoda. It's hardly complete, the few strings that bind the edges together jagged and asymmetrical.

'I've found lots like this.' He sits down on the shingle and watches the web, drifting into a fascinated stillness that reminds me of the way children become absorbed by the tiny worlds around them, and I think, I was wrong, he's not like the students at art school: his passion is inherently different to theirs. This thought spreads pleasantly through me, and I feel as if I have gulped down a cold glass of water on a hot, hot day.

Something nudges my thigh, and I look down with a jump to see Gabbro standing next to me, her soft muzzle pressing against the denim of my shorts. Tentatively I reach down and rest my hand on her head, just as I've seen Jacob do. My fingers tremble as they touch her, and I am surprised by how warm she feels; how full of life. I realise that this is the first living thing I have wanted to touch since Mum died, and I bury my fingers into her warm fur.

Mum was so cold in those last few weeks. I bought her the softest lambswool socks to keep her chilled feet warm, and I wrapped her up in shawls and blankets. But it is impossible to keep warm when there is so little flesh left under your skin.

Gabbro leans her warm head heavily against me, so that I can feel the soft vibration of life within her. She lifts her eyes to look at me. They are sleepy and long lashed, and there is something very human about that dazzling blue eye. And suddenly it is too much. I take my hand off her and step away quickly, feeling the ghost of her heavy head against my leg still.

Jacob hasn't noticed. He stands up and blinks, as if he is coming out of a trance. 'Everything leaves a trace,' he says, 'like a map to the past.' He points up to the sky. 'Even the birds tell us things. Look at those geese. They normally form a V, but they're scattered, as if none of them want to take the lead over the island. There's something about this place that I can't quite get a grip on. It's as if it's trying to tell me something, but I don't know the language.'

He turns his serious face to me, studying my features as if I am part of the answer. 'I'll be on the west of the island for the next few days,' he says, 'if you need me.'

We watch the geese as they fly away. When they reach the sea, they pull together, forming a sleek pincer, and I think, everything leaves a trace. Not just animals, but other things too: I think of the oyster shell with its scratched drawing; the long-dead brimstones in the Chinese cabinet, the fingerprints littering the photograph in the album. I look over at the bomb-testing facility, its roof destroyed, and like the strands of the spider webs that Jacob admires so much, I try to link them all, criss-crossing them in my mind, searching for patterns.

Chapter Eleven

Tartelin

Summer 2018

I am late back to the house, and, as I climb the stairs to Miss Stourbridge's rooms, I sense something is different. Outside, dusk brushes against the windows, and inside, the walls are drenched in a shade of violet that makes everything shimmer, as if ghosts are hiding around every corner. It's my job to light the gas lamps on the walls, and I wonder if Miss Stourbridge will be angry with me for my lateness and lack of caught butterflies; if she has at least had the sense to light the Tilley lamp on her desk.

As I turn the corner on the stairs, I stop. The door to the panelled room is closed. I've never seen it shut before. I continue climbing nervously. The closer I get, the more unsure I am of what I will find on the other side. Miss Stourbridge is old and weak. What if the door has blown shut and jammed, and she has been unable to open it? What if she has shut it on purpose, the better to lay down on the chaise, and close her eyes for the final time? I turn the knob and push against it tentatively. A high-pitched hum whirs in my ears, and something soft brushes my face.

'Close it! Quickly, girl, quickly!'

I do as she says, and turn to face the room. My immediate impression is that everything has lost its gravity. A microclimate has opened up in the space, and a hurricane of leaves and soft, grey snow is whirling toward me. A rhythmical tapping, soft and hesitant, fills the room.

There are perhaps seventy or eighty butterflies and moths spiralling in the dim light. The room is awash with daubs of colour. Little puffs of air tickle my face as they flit past. Through them, I can just make out Miss Stourbridge across the room, lit by the single gas lamp on the desk.

'If you walk slowly, you can make your way through without causing too much damage,' she says, an energy in her voice I haven't heard before. 'I think I've crushed a couple under my wheels, so do be careful.'

I make my way over to the desk, treading carefully, focusing on the rush of wings in front of me. I feel one against my cheek, and then it's gone. A butterfly lands in my hair. It is surprisingly heavy and I can sense its wings slowly opening and closing before it takes off again, lost amid the clouds.

To my left, the puparium lid is standing open. Rows and rows of empty cocoons hang inside like discarded clothing. Miss Stourbridge is sitting at her desk, pincers in hand, as if nothing out of the ordinary is happening. I sidestep a bowl of cut-up pears, peacock butterflies lapping at the soft flesh.

As I reach my employer, she turns and looks up at me, smiling. It is so startlingly unlike her that for a moment I don't trust that it's actually her at all.

'It's magical, isn't it?' she says, looking around the room. Her voice is light, and I forget for a moment how old she is. It's as if I'm talking to a much younger Marianne.

A red admiral alights on her outstretched hand and she draws it close, examining it with her intelligent eyes. 'It's so rare that I see them like this,' she says wistfully, 'I forget when they're under my scalpel how beautifully they move, like they're in a world of their own and we are merely structures to land on, like trees or rocks.'

The butterfly takes off again, the crimson bands on its wings flashing in and out of view, and we turn to watch it until it is lost in amongst the fluttering.

When did she stop caring about living butterflies, I wonder? At what point did she take up a scalpel and start treating them as objects, things to be experimented on, with little or no thought for the life that she was snuffing out?

'They all decided to hatch at the same time, little devils.' She indicates the open puparium. 'Not much else I could do – they'd have died all piled up on top of each other in there.'

'What will we do with them now?' I have visions of attempting to catch them all before having to watch her slice into them with her scalpel.

'Oh, I don't think we need do anything. I'll open a window soon. It is rather marvellous, though, don't you think?' That nostalgic look in her eye is back. 'It reminds me of when Nan and I left the silkworm cocoons too long before boiling them and they all hatched at the same time in the annexe.'

Nan. A flash of excitement runs through me. 'Nan? That's … that's not you, then?' It's only after the question comes out that I realise how strange it sounds.

'Of course not.' Miss Stourbridge's eyebrows draw together, and I flush, hoping it's too dark to notice.

'Who was she?'

But her eyes snap away from me and land on a peacock butterfly that's dancing towards her. Her expression changes to one I haven't seen before, something unreadable.

'Miss Stourbridge?'

But she still doesn't answer. She's staring at the butterfly. The clock ticks its irregular beat, and I find my nervous breathing matches it as I wait. I can feel I'm on the verge of discovering something. The butterfly lands with a soft pulse of its wings on Miss Stourbridge's lap. She stares down at it, hardly breathing, but it takes off again, and she lets the breath out like a sigh.

'Nan lived here for a while,' she says. 'In the Twenties. She … she taught me a lot.'

'Like a teacher? A … a governess?'

'No, not like a governess.'

The clock begins to chime, making me jump.

'Be a dear and light the other lamps, would you?' she says. 'It's getting too late for this type of work.' She takes the glasses from her face and wipes them on a fold of her apron. Her face looks different without them. Not pretty, exactly, but handsome, austere.

'Can I get you anything to eat?'

Miss Stourbridge shakes her head. 'No thank you, Tartelin, I'm fine. I find I am less hungry on this island. It's strange, it used to give me such a voracious appetite. But that was when I was gallivanting around it like you are now.' She looks at me for the first time, and I shrink away from the severity of her gaze. 'You are eating enough, aren't you?' There is a tenderness in her voice. She lifts a hand and touches my wrist, her fingers encircling it easily. I'm surprised by her affection.

'I'm OK.' I take a step back and begin to light the lamps. 'Was Nan someone you worked with?' I ask lightly. 'I mean, if she taught you things?'

There is silence behind me, and I turn to look at Miss Stourbridge. She is so still she appears frozen. As I watch, a single tear falls from her eye, and rolls unchecked down her papery cheek. She turns her chair so I can no longer see her face.

'Goodnight, Tartelin,' she says.

Chapter Twelve

Marianne

December 1927

As November ended and the cold north-westerly gales sucked up the island air and batted it around like a cat playing with a mouse, Marianne rarely saw her father. He was often at the pavilion, overseeing its repair and conversion into a summerhouse, or else shut in his study, in talks with the captains of his herring fleet.

Yesterday, the photographer who had plagued them back in the autumn arrived again, setting up his camera in Papa's study, the bright flash of the camera's bulb visible from underneath the closed door. From out in the corridor, Marianne could hear Papa and Nan laughing in surprise at the sudden burst of light, and she remembered how it had made her blink in shock the last time he came. This time, apparently, the photographer was not there to document her.

Papa was always asking for Nan's help with new things now, frequently leaving Marianne alone to deal with the silkworms. She wasn't jealous of the time they spent together exactly, but she missed her father, and wondered why he didn't think to ask her instead. After all, one day all of his businesses would be her husband's, and by association, hers: she needed to learn their ways.

One evening at the beginning of December, Papa came late to the dinner table, his moustache twitching. Marianne sat impatiently, waiting for him to settle, her stomach rumbling. She could smell the *erwtensoep* in the tureen on the side, and her stomach gave a cruel growl as her father sat down and opened his napkin painstakingly slowly.

Nan was already seated. She looked less meek and mild these days, compared to her first few weeks on the island. No longer were her eyes lowered, her hands in her lap. It must be the fortifying island air that Papa was always going on about, Marianne decided. Perhaps she was starting to become one of them at last.

She thought back to when Nan had first arrived, and she'd taken her down to the south beach to pick winkles with the mermaids. She remembered the steely glint in the girl's eye, the way she had hoisted up her skirt without a word and followed the herring girls out onto the rocks. That day had pricked at Marianne's conscience like a thorn in the pad of her thumb. I really ought to give the girl a chance, she thought, and she opened her mouth to engage her in conversation, but Papa beat her to it.

'Nan made a wonderful discovery today,' he said, taking a gulp of *schelp wijn*. 'I don't know how much she's told you about herself, but her family comes from the Gironde Estuary, a place renowned for its remarkable pearl yield. I showed her our old oyster beds, and I am pleased to tell you that she has an uncanny ability to find oysters that still – incredibly – contain pearls.' He leant back to allow Peggy to ladle the thick pea soup into his bowl. 'Leaving the beds to fallow all these years must have given them the nutrients they need to make beautiful Dohhalund pearls again. There won't be many, but their rarity will make them extremely valuable.' He lifted his glass and inclined his head to Nan.

Marianne lifted her own glass, which contained the small amount of *wijn* she was allowed. 'Papa, this is such good news! At last I will be allowed my own Dohhalund pearl necklace.'

'Let's not be hasty, Marianne, we don't know how many pearls we will be able to harvest. They are a commodity, after all: they must first and foremost be offered for sale.' His tone was sharp, and Marianne took a sip of wine, stung. She looked over to Nan, who had not touched her glass.

'May I see them?' Mama's voice drifted over the table, mingling with the steam from the soup bowls.

'Soon, Kitty my love, soon. I have sent them to a contact to grade them properly. It is so long since we had pearls on the island that I fear I may be a little rusty. Although Nan assures me they are of Gironde quality, if not even better. Imagine!'

Marianne took a sip of the soup, watching over her spoon as her father proceeded to bolt his own bowl down before abruptly pushing his chair back and giving his excuses. That evening, he was to host a soirée at Dogger Bank. The soirées were a quarterly event, a selection of invited dignitaries and old friends: men Papa knew from the herring trade; old university chums; even pearl merchants sometimes, if they were in the area.

The soirées were always filled with the rich smell of cigar smoke and the clink of brandy glasses as the men moved from the dining room to the library, and on into Papa's study. The staff downstairs knew to lock their bedroom doors on these nights. Men often got lost in the maze of passages down near Papa's study, finding themselves opening the door of a bedroom and making the maids squeal.

Papa had also invited a silk weaver from Norwich to this particular meeting, a man he had been courting for months. Marianne remembered meeting him at a party they had attended in Norfolk last year: a pompous, monocled man swathed in a shining purple waistcoat, his bulbous belly straining at the seams. It had been the first party she had been allowed to attend on the mainland, having finally been considered grown up enough. Usually, she was left behind on Dohhalund with her governess while her parents took seasonal sojourns across England and Europe. If there were enough pearls in the Dohhalund beds, she hoped that next year she might accompany Papa to France to witness their transformation into jewellery. Nan might even come in useful then as an interpreter. Marianne had never quite managed to grasp foreign languages, other than a smattering of Dutch, which had peppered their island speech for hundreds of years, due to the proximity of the country.

The women finished their *erwtensoep* and stood as one, retiring upstairs to Mama's sitting room, where they were to remain for the rest of the evening. The soirées had been a part of Dohhalund's heritage for years. Marianne knew the women's job was to remain out of sight, to allow the menfolk to make their deals and ensure the island would continue to prosper.

They sat in silence, listening to the revelry as it began downstairs. Outside, the moon was bright, and they gazed, mesmerised by it, until Peggy came in to stoke the fire, and pulled the curtains closed, blocking out the world.

'Congratulations on finding the pearls, Nan,' Marianne said, turning to her. 'You seem to know so much about Dohhalund's businesses. First silkworms, now pearls. Perhaps you'd like to run them all.'

Mama looked up from the book she was reading. 'Marianne,' she said warningly.

'If you took more of an interest in your father's projects your-self, I wouldn't need to,' Nan said, her dark eyes glittering in the firelight.

Marianne stared, winded, and then she burst out laughing. Mama went back to her book, but Marianne continued to flick glances at Nan, her brow furrowed. She wasn't used to people talking back to her.

As a rule, people were always nice to Marianne, probably because they were paid to be, she conceded. Perhaps because Nan was not receiving payment, she didn't consider herself to be among them. Nan was not from this island; she didn't understand the way things were done. It was quite refreshing.

The party continued below, getting louder as more brandy was consumed. Late in the evening there was a noise in the entrance hall, muffled laughter quickly quietened as heavy feet mounted the stairs. Then the sitting-room door was thrown open, and Papa stood there, his wiry body weaving on the threshold.

'Nan,' he said, his eyes crossing, a cigar in his hand, 'Nan, my fellow gentlemen would like to practise their French on you. You can tell them all about the pearls you found.'

'I really don't think that would be appropriate.' It was rare for Mama to speak up, and Marianne shot her a look. Since when did Mama care what Papa did with the help?

'Nonsense, Kitty darling. With great respect, you don't understand how these things are done. Come, Nan.' He swayed, holding the door open for her. From downstairs came a great whoop of drunken laughter.

Nan got up slowly and pressed her hands against her dress to smooth it. She darted her eyes at Marianne as she walked past.

She was gone so long that Marianne and Mama went to bed. Marianne hid her ears under the pillow to drown out the sound of the revelry downstairs, but it was uncomfortable, and she lay, eyes open, staring up at the ceiling, thinking of Nan.

What were they doing, down there with her? She imagined her in the dimly lit library, the men leering drunkenly as Papa paraded her in front of them like a prize-winning colt. Now and again a great bellow of laughter bubbled up, and, unable to bear it any longer, Marianne got out of bed, curiosity getting the better of her.

She tiptoed to the door, listening. She could hear the faint hum of voices, far off in the bowels of the house. She pulled on her robe and opened the door, making her way quietly along the landing.

At the top of the stairs, she stopped, leaning over the balustrade to see if the entrance hall was clear. It was forbidden to go downstairs on soirée nights, and yet some compulsion drove her onwards. As she began to descend the stairs, she clutched the banister, ready to run back if anyone were to spy her.

The voices were still distant. They were coming from the direction of the long channels of corridors off the kitchen – the staff's rooms. Papa's study was also down there, and Marianne walked carefully, her bare feet cold on the flagstones.

At her father's study, she stopped. The heavy oak door was closed. The hinges, made from silver and shaped like giant oyster shells, winked in the gaslight. From inside, she could hear the low chatter of many voices. Cigar smoke seeped from under the door, and she stood in the hazy light, wondering if Nan was in there with them. And then the handle began to turn, and Marianne bolted, past the study, further down the corridor, coming at last to the utility room at the back of the house. She slipped inside and pushed the door to, holding her breath to listen. She heard the study burst open, and a handful of men poured out in a great cloud of cigar smoke, chattering enthusiastically and making their way back to the main part of the house.

As her heart slowed, a voice behind her said, 'Marianne?'

Marianne turned in the darkness, her heart spiking again in panic.

Nan was standing in the middle of the room. Her shawl had slipped and a tendril of dark hair had escaped her bun.

'What on earth are you doing here?' Marianne said. 'I thought you were teaching them French?'

'I don't think they were very interested in learning a language.'

Marianne looked about her for the first time. 'But why are you in *here?*' she said, wrinkling her nose. It was a large storeroom, packed full of quarter crans and nets. Above her, the base of the great copper bath hung down from the ceiling. The place stank of herring.

'I just wanted to be alone for a while.'

'Well, don't let me stop you.' Marianne began to pull open the door, but Nan's hand reached out, touching her arm.

'Stay with me? Just for a little while?'

Marianne heaved a sigh, shaking her head in resignation. 'All right.' She turned over a basket and sat on it, taking care not to let the wicker catch the delicate fibres of her robe.

The party had moved out to the garden now. She could hear the men somewhere outside, whooping and caterwauling. The faint smell of cigar smoke drifted under the door into the room.

'What was it like, in there?' She nodded in the direction of the study.

'The silk man from Norwich tried to engage me in French conversation, but it was so slurred I couldn't understand him.'

A thought struck Marianne. 'You don't think Papa is looking for a husband for you, do you?' she said.

Nan considered this. 'He did kiss my hand.'

'What was that like?' Marianne pictured the man's great walrusy moustache prickling at Nan's pale skin, and a brief flash of jealousy coursed through her. Surely *she* should be the one receiving kisses from suitors: she was older than Nan, after all.

'His nose was long, and a bit wet,' Nan said, looking down at her hand, rubbing at the skin as if to banish the memory.

Nan was too young to be married, Marianne decided. And yet she wouldn't put it past her father to try, if it meant strengthening relationships with the right people. The idea unsettled her somehow, but then, Papa had married Mama for the same reasons all those years ago, and that arrangement had worked out perfectly well.

'Do you think that's why Papa brought you to Dohhalund, to find you a husband?'

'I don't know,' Nan said, gazing out of the window. 'I'm not really sure why I'm here at all.'

'The silkworms, Nan,' Marianne said with an exasperated sigh. 'You're an expert, remember? And don't forget the pearls.'

'The silkworms don't need expert care, Marianne. You're more than capable. You haven't needed my help for a while.'

Marianne brushed away the compliment, getting up and looking out of the window. It was a calm, clear night. 'I wonder if Papa will ever invite *me* to one of his soirées,' she said.

'So your father can find you a husband?'

'God no!' She began pacing through the room, winding between the herring baskets and nets. 'I'm not ready for marriage yet. I just ... I'd like to know what they do in there, that's all.'

She had hardly given marriage a thought before. Mama had mentioned it, of course, but it had always seemed years off, something a different, much more grown-up Marianne might contemplate. But of course, she was her parents' only child, and in order for the island to flourish, she would at some point need to continue the family line. Papa had come here from the mainland to marry Mama and take over the family duties. Had Grandfather organised their union? Would Papa in turn organise hers?

She was distracted by a rustle coming from the window. Nan looked up at the sound too, and reaching up, extracted something from a large cobweb. Marianne peered through the gloom, trying to make out what it was.

'It's a butterfly,' Nan said, opening her hands.

The insect lay there, coiled in spider silk. One of its hind wings was torn, and it was fluttering helplessly against the spider web that held it. Carefully, Nan pulled the silk skeins from it and held her palm open to release it, but the butterfly would not fly.

'Poor thing,' she whispered.

'It would be best to kill it,' Marianne said, looking around for something heavy with which to end its life.

'No,' Nan said, shielding the little thing. 'We should try to save it. It deserves a chance.'

She tipped the butterfly into Marianne's hand, and went to the shelves, rummaging through the bric-a-brac. She came back with a scrap of tissue paper and a pot of animal glue.

'Hold it still,' she said, tearing the paper into small pieces.

'How?' asked Marianne. She had never had to keep a butterfly alive before. Normally she just tipped them straight into the killing jar.

Nan showed her how to gently secure the butterfly's legs to stop it escaping. Marianne watched the concentration on her face, the tip of her tongue poking out between her teeth as she coated the tissue with glue. Carefully, Nan pressed the paper onto the torn wing.

'Come closer,' she said, tearing another piece of tissue, 'I need to mend the other wing.'

Marianne stepped closer, aware of the insect's fragility in her hands.

'Hold still,' Nan said, repeating the gluing process with the insect's other wing. She pressed the paper onto the butterfly, trying not to rub away the silken dust.

'Have you done this before?' Marianne asked.

'Not exactly. But every living thing deserves a chance, doesn't it?'

'Well yes, but—'

'Where I grew up in France, we were poor. If something was broken, we tried to fix it. We never gave up on anything; never threw anything away or used it only once. We couldn't afford to.'

'But then your father came along and claimed you as his own,' Marianne said in a bored voice, 'and suddenly money was no object ...'

'No.' The tone in Nan's voice made her look up. 'It's more than that, Marianne. We have a duty, don't we, to make things better? If *I* was broken, you'd try to fix me, wouldn't you? I would fix *you*, if you were.'

Marianne didn't have an answer for this. They stood in silence, waiting for the glue to dry, watching as the butterfly gave a little shake, its feelers dipping.

Nan went to the window and unlatched it, and Marianne lifted her hands, feeling the sea air brush across her fingers. The butterfly perched on her palm for a moment, as if contemplating the night sky, then it took off, weighted but repaired. The girls gasped, watching it spiral up and out of the room towards the moon and the clouds that scudded across the dark sky.

The next day was a Sunday. Papa appeared rather later than usual, his red face sweating off the excesses of the night before. As they got ready for chapel, Marianne watched him help Nan with her coat, and she remembered what she'd told the mermaid on the beach: that Nan was his latest pet, and she felt a pang of wretchedness for her, because Nan had no idea that his pets were often dropped as quickly as they were picked up.

After chapel and a hot lunch of battered *kibbeling*, Marianne went to the annexe to check on the silkworms. They had begun weaving the silk thread around their fat white bodies two weeks before, cocooning themselves inside. It fascinated Marianne to think of the insects deep in the soft silken balls, changing silently into winged creatures.

Nan had harvested a sample batch of silk a week or so ago. These remaining cocoons would be left to hatch into moths, and then the cycle would begin again. The next brood would be the first attempt at producing Dohhalund silk thread. The few cocoons that Nan had tested had showed a good yield of silk, and both Nan and Papa were pleased that the project was running along smoothly.

As Marianne ran her eyes over the shelves, looking for the signs of movement that would indicate the moths were starting to emerge, the smell of Papa's pipe drifted down the corridor from his study. She followed the wisps of smoke, coming to a stop at the study door. Beneath the familiar smell, she could still detect the acrid remnants of last night's cigars, and she gritted her teeth at the memory of all those men leering over Nan.

'Papa!' she said quietly, knocking lightly.

The door opened swiftly, and her father stood there impatiently, his eyebrows raised.

'Are you working on the pearls?' she said hopefully. 'May I help, Papa?'

'No need, my dear Marianne. Why don't you go and practise your Dutch with Miss Stanley? Or else read up on sericulture. Nan can help me if I need an extra pair of hands.' He reached forward and patted her cheek. 'After all, I need my Empress of the Silkworms to be fully educated on her chosen subject.' He stepped inside and closed the door, the silver hinges glinting at Marianne as it settled into its frame.

But I never chose the silkworms, she wanted to shout. Instead, she pressed her lips firmly together, seething inwardly, and crept back along the corridor, thinking of that elusive necklace of pearls she had been promised years ago.

Chapter Thirteen

Tartelin

Summer 2018

I leave the roomful of escaped butterflies and make my way downstairs, the little gas lamp lighting each step ahead of me.

If somebody had asked me, before I came to this island, if I could live without electricity, I would have baulked at the idea. But over the weeks I've found there's something comforting about the glow of my lamp, the way it lights only a small pool around me. The darkness that stretches away from me is not threatening. It buffers me from the rest of the world. There exists on this island only the gentle tug and pull of my needs, of Miss Stourbridge's needs. The rest of the world is kept at bay, as if lost to fog. I've never had the luxury to focus so fully on myself before, away from the intrusion of everyday life – phones, social media, news, all of them gone.

My world now is the size of this island, and at night, when darkness descends, I live only in the pool of light that I hold in my hand, the moonlight on the sand outside, the flicker of gaslights illuminating the butterfly wings in the sitting room. Is this how Miss Stourbridge felt as a young woman? Was she comforted by it, or did she yearn for more?

My mind reaches back up the stairs to my employer. I can't stop thinking about her; about the single tear I saw on her cheek at the mention of Nan. It feels as if we've taken tentative steps towards friendship tonight. A loose butterfly has slipped through the door with me, and it spirals up into the great cavern of the grand stairwell. It is soon lost to the darkness.

In the kitchen, I gather a small plate of dried bread and olives and sit at the table to eat. Next to the sink, I spot the basket of dirty laundry that I haven't yet begun to wash, and I groan with tiredness at the thought of starting now. It has been a strange day, the oddest one yet in a string of peculiar days. As I eat, I examine a jar of cauliflower chutney sitting on the pallet next to the table. Its contents remind me of something preserved in a specimen jar, and I leave it unopened. Miss Stourbridge is right, I'm not eating enough, especially since I'm covering so much distance each day, and I'm surprised again by her concern for me. With the surprise comes a softening towards her.

I push the food around my plate, making an effort to take small bites. My first days here were punctuated by hunger, but the longer I live here, the less of an appetite I seem to have. I estimate I walked ten miles today, and I didn't eat breakfast or lunch. And yet I'm still not hungry.

In the days that followed my mother's death, I ate voraciously. I had always thought that grief was meant to make you lose your appetite, but it's only now that I have the distance to reflect on her death, that my body has decided it doesn't need nutrients any more.

After Mum was diagnosed, I didn't return to art school. No one was able to tell us exactly how long she had left, only that she was dying. How could I leave her, not knowing if she would be there when I returned?

It struck me that our time together in those last weeks mirrored the first few months after she adopted me, when she bestowed care and love on me in abundance. It felt as if these two moments were our beginning and our end, like bookends to our time together. But now our roles were reversed, and I was the one caring for her.

I brought paints to her bed, and we worked on the same sheet of paper, looping and swirling our brushstrokes together, laughing when the colours mingled and turned muddy. I still have those pictures somewhere, hidden away until I'm brave enough to look at them again.

On those first days, when the illness was just beginning to course through her body, I found myself going to her studio, locking the door and letting out a sob of frustration in the quiet space. It had always been a place of comfort for me, her studio, but now it seemed to take on an even greater significance, as if the collections of materials that lined the shelves contained the key to understanding this new version of my mother.

I ran my fingers through the bowls that sat haphazardly on every available surface: tiny pine cones smaller than bees, sea-glass fragments that, when I buried my nose in them, still clung to the briny tang of the sea. I scooped pieces of bark and empty acorn cups, pulled wisps of sheep's wool and picked out thin bones from long-dead birds, and I began to create.

I wove these materials together in my own way, making from my mother's ingredients something that was inherently mine. I glued and stitched, painted and stapled, until the creations in front of me resembled something akin to the birds she used to make, but different, too: strange, winged creatures, neither good nor evil. I strung them from the studio's ceiling.

Over the weeks, I made bird after bird, slathering my hands with slip, and moulding clay into tiny brittle skulls, bony, frail bodies. These I covered with skins of fabric. I added wings made of feathers, wings made of silk, wings made of bone and mud and glass. And at the heart of each bird I sewed a small scrap of paper, a word scribbled onto each one, words that described the feelings I couldn't say out loud: *pain* and *scream*, *sour* and *death*.

As my mother grew sicker, it seemed inappropriate to talk of happy things, better things, and so I added these words to my birds, too: *love* and *beauty*, *touch* and *softness*. I held them deep inside myself, scribbled on twisted scraps of paper sewn near to my own heart.

It is impossible to watch someone you love die. I spent my time in the studio instead of by her side, the smell of paint thinner and white spirit in my nostrils, obliterating the sickly sweet smell of the cancer as it spread its cells through our house. Whenever I checked on my mum, she appeared to have grown smaller and weaker, until by the end, in the hospice, she could hardly speak at all, her language rendered down to the liquid babble of infants.

The funeral was short and to the point. I read a poem she had liked, but halfway through, the words snagged in my throat like something solid. I stopped, gaping at the people watching me, unable to carry on. The celebrant took over, smoothing the tear-stained piece of paper. But the words sounded all wrong in her voice, evaporating away over people's heads like smoke from a crematorium chimney.

My mum came home in a cardboard urn decorated with hearts, and I put her in her favourite place: her studio. I arranged little bowls of all her favourite materials around her on the workbench. From above, she looked like the sun casting light over a glittering orrery.

At the kitchen table, I align my plate with the olive jar, pulling the bowl of salt close, remembering, and I cannot eat any more. As I get up, I look again at the crumple of clothes in the basket, but I am too tired tonight. I will do it tomorrow.

I go to my room and sit on the creaking bed. I take my phone from the drawer, desperate to see my mother's face again, craving the look she had only for me: full of love and emotion. I press the button to turn my phone on. Nothing happens. I press it again. Nothing. It is dead.

I stare at the blank screen, trying to conjure her face in its blackness, but there is only my own dark reflection staring back at me, and then, memories of her last days begin to flood towards me like a high tide, spilling over until I am submerged: her bloodless arms, her poor, bony fingers, gripping onto mine.

Somewhere above me, the piano starts up again, and slowly, like an anaesthetic balm, my mother's face fades. I lie down on the bed, still in my clothes, and allow myself to drift towards sleep.

I dream that I am cycling across the island. I pass the long-dead remains of a lone tree, its twisted trunk stunted and grey. A flash of purple catches my eye, and I twist round as I go past, spotting the mermaid I met at the salt pans. I screech to a stop, my bike hauling up a cloud of dust, and pedal back to her at a slower pace. She is hanging something silver on the branches of the tree. They glitter as they catch the light.

'Tartelin,' she says as I approach, her smile stretching across her face. 'How are you finding Dohhalund?'

Behind her, the silver things dangle from the branches, and I see they are small fish, their milky eyes staring.

'It's a strange place,' I answer, 'beautiful.'

'Yes,' she says, the word coming out in a sigh. 'It is rather beautiful, isn't it? It was never this wild when I lived here before. But the wildness suits it, I think. The island was always going to win, in the end.' She pats the tree, and the movement sets the fish spinning.

I look down, and the oyster shell she gave me is in my hand. I lift it up so that it catches the light, the animal on it appearing as if by magic.

'Where did you find this?' I ask her.

The woman sees the picture on it, and her eyes grow round with interest 'Ah,' she says, nodding wisely. 'The mermaids used to find them washed up and carve their own designs onto them. The sea has always given us gifts, wouldn't you say? Given and taken away.' She looks suddenly very old. Her soft skin has the fuzzed sheen of a peach, and her earlobes hang, round and flat down by her neck.

I tuck the shell away. 'I ought to go,' I say, though where I am heading, I don't know.

The woman reaches out a pudgy hand and squeezes mine. 'Go well, Tartelin,' she says, and she turns back to the fish as they spin lazily in the air, reaching up, as if to caress them.

The next morning, I take two bowls of porridge upstairs. I know Miss Stourbridge doesn't eat breakfast, but I want to do something for her, to show her that I care.

As I approach the top of the stairs, I see her through the doorway in the panelled room. She is sitting in front of the mantel clock. The wheelchair is turned away from me, and I can't see her face, but she's so still, it's as if she's hypnotised by the strange, irregular ticking. I stay where I am, not wanting to interrupt, the steam from the porridge rising towards the ceiling. Eventually, I clear my throat and enter the room, but she doesn't turn as I tiptoe past.

I sit on my own in the dining room, picking at the bowl of watery porridge. It tastes slightly briny, and I wonder if seawater has leaked into the pipes again. The little creatures in the cabinets eye me curiously as I stir the liquid oats, and a mouse – or something more unsavoury – patters, unseen, behind the walls. I can hear Miss Stourbridge now, her wheelchair running smoothly over the floorboards, the sound getting closer until she pushes the door wide open and wheels herself inside. She is accompanied by a few of the remaining butterflies from yesterday's hatching. Many escaped through the open window and have no doubt been blown out to sea, but some remain, flitting around our heads, crawling into the creases of the curtains, their colours already beginning to fade.

'Where do you think you'll go today?' Miss Stourbridge asks, customarily plunging into the conversation without the need for a greeting. There is no reference to the strange scene I found her in. I watch in surprise as she picks up her spoon and begins to eat the porridge I brought her.

'I wondered about going to the west side of the island,' I tell her.

'Ah, then you'll see my great-grandfather's pavilion. You can't miss it, it's out past the oyster beds.'

'What was it used for?'

'Oh, parties, mostly.'

'Did you go to any?' I imagine jazz and flowing drinks, the sound of the sea beneath the chatter of guests, beautiful dresses spinning across the dance floor.

'No, no. It had changed by the time I was old enough to attend. Fell into disrepair. I always held a desire to go dancing there when I was a child, but it wasn't to be.'

'That's a shame.' I find it hard to imagine a version of Miss Stourbridge, bright and young, wanting to go dancing. Surely she's always been old and stiff and serious.

'Take a good look at it, would you?' she says suddenly. 'I'd love to hear how it is.' She pauses. 'I haven't been to visit it in years, not since I was a girl.'

'Why?'

But she doesn't hear me. 'I'm sure it'll be in a terrible state,' she says. 'It was taken over by the military during the war. I'm afraid the soldiers got their hands on it. Covered it in graffiti, I heard. I didn't dare go and look. Would you look for me? Report back?'

'Of course.' Jacob said he'd be on that part of the island today. I quash down a stirring feeling of excitement.

'Oh, and if you get to the oyster beds at low tide, you might be lucky and catch a good haul. They love the salt.'

It takes me a moment to realise she's talking about butterflies. I see her watching me, waiting for my still sleepy brain to catch up.

'Don't forget why you're here, Miss Brown,' she says, fixing me with her steely glare.

Do I imagine it, or is there a twinkle of humour behind the usual fierce gaze? I wonder if she's been watching me, if she's seen me with Jacob. I feel heat rising up my neck and into my cheeks.

She reaches out suddenly, taking my hand.

'It's good to see you happy,' she says, squeezing my fingers carefully in her own, and I smile back at her.

I push my chair away and take my porridge bowl to the dumb waiter. Through the door to the panelled room, the eyepiece of the telescope catches the pale light of the morning, winking in the sun.

'What do you look at through that?' I ask, nodding towards it.

Her head whips round to follow my gaze. The telescope is pointed to the sea, its lens cap hanging.

'The water, of course,' she says.

Perhaps she lost a lover to the sea years before, and she's pining for his return. His handsome, rugged face might be in the photograph album. I make a mental note to search for it again next time I'm alone in the panelled room.

'It looks like an expensive one,' I say. 'You must be able to see for miles.'

'It does the job,' she says, her eyes narrowed, as if she doesn't appreciate my probing.

She has always been so secretive about the amount of time she spends looking through it. Sometimes I come into the room and the binoculars are in her lap. Occasionally I hear her chair move quickly away from the window as I'm coming upstairs, as if she doesn't want me to know what she's been doing. She always looks guilty, as if I've caught her in the act of doing something subversive. Once, I put my eye to it, hoping to discover what it was she was so intent on looking at, but it was just flat, grey water.

Miss Stourbridge has finished her porridge, the bowl scraped clean, and I collect it up, pausing at the cabinets on my right. I haven't looked in these ones before, but now the morning light is just at the right level to filter inside. I crouch down. Dust motes tap lazily against the glass. On a shelf near the bottom are two objects. I hear Miss Stourbridge come to a stop next to me, the cane-work creaking as she leans in.

'Ah,' she says, 'baleen, if I'm not mistaken. Looks like a corset stay.' She pulls the door open so we can see the object more clearly. It is a long, thin strip of what looks like yellow bone, coiled like the tongue of a butterfly. On it someone has scratched crude flowers and hearts interspersed with fish. For a moment I wonder who would have given a piece of their corset to the Stourbridges: it seems a very personal item, but I'm distracted by the object beside it.

It's an oyster shell, balanced on a wire stand so that its concave iridescence is clearly visible. Carefully, I lift the shell out and turn it in my hands, admiring it. The image etched into it has faded with age, but I can just make out two women walking arm in arm under a tree. The design is nothing like the one on the oyster shell the mermaid gave me, yet I haven't seen any others in Miss Stourbridge's collection.

'Who made this?'

I'm unsure if I sense a slight pause before Miss Stourbridge answers.

'I don't remember,' she says, looking away, 'one of the herring girls, probably.' She wheels her chair away, making her way back to the panelled room.

'I thought the herring girls usually scratched pictures onto baleen, not oyster shells.'

'They decorated whatever the sea spat up. There must have been hundreds of discarded oyster shells drifting around these waters. We harvested pearls for years, after all.'

I look at the picture again, running my finger over the image of the two women. At the bottom, so small and faint that I almost miss it, there is a small circle, a tiny moth set within it, and it strikes me that it looks like a signature.

'It's an unusual scene for a herring girl to draw, though, isn't it?' I call after her. 'It's not like the others I've seen: no fish, no hearts, no ships.'

Her chair pauses far across the panelled room. 'It's a strange island,' she seems to say, her voice drifting back to me from the room beyond.

Chapter Fourteen

Tartelin

Summer 2018

Dohhalund feels different on foot. On my bike, it has felt like a fluid thing, shingle blurring as I speed past. But today it's slow and still as if it's basking in the sun. It is another hot day, tempered by a breeze coming off the sea.

The west side of the island is a low land consisting of succulent plants and pebbles so small you might mistake them for sand. A lazy creek stirs through the middle of it, and it's here that the oyster beds are laid. The tide is creeping out, revealing the mud-encrusted oysters like strange, grey plants, a thousand sharp-edged leaves cresting up from the ground. I make a mental note to stop on my way back, to watch for butterflies dipping down to suck at the salt.

I wonder if Jacob is nearby, if he can see me from whatever crouched position he occupies, and I stride across the flat land, keeping an eye out for his tent, for the scrap of blue tied around his neck.

My walking pace has picked up while I've been here, and today the ground flies beneath my feet. I pass a young couple with rucksacks on their backs, camping mats coiled beneath them. They nod and smile. The girl has pink hair, and I notice how they link their fingers loosely as they walk.

I turn back to continue on my way, my feet crunching over something on the ground. A small heap of cockle shells, discarded by whatever bird or beast has feasted on them. Without thinking I crouch down and begin to sort through them, removing the broken pieces from the intact shells, and laying them out neatly. At first the pattern is a circle, but as I spy more and more shells nearby, it becomes a tight spiral, growing outwards until it's almost a metre wide. I stand back and admire my work. There are butterflies here, too, flying too high at the moment for me to reach. I see more shells, scattered over the path a little further away, and I collect them up, dislodging them from the stones and sandy soil.

As the spiral gets bigger, twisting further outwards like a strange vortex, I think of the birds I made in Mum's studio while she was ill; how I became so lost in making them that I was taken away from my own thoughts.

After she died, I continued to make birds, but they began to evolve. The first few began as wire structures, like the skeletons I remembered from Mum's beautiful bird book. I intended to cover them, but when the wire bodies were finished, I realised that I liked their starkness. I liked the way I could see inside them, see through them, that in their vulnerable fragility they had nothing to hide: they could not scare me.

My mind has drifted away from the island as I work on the shells. It is a simple pleasure, losing myself in the swirl of them, in the need to make the pattern bigger, longer, wider. There are so many shells here that I wonder just how huge I could make it: whether I could cover the whole island.

I stand up and stretch, taking in the wide vista that's laid out before me. When I first arrived on Dohhalund, I was disappointed that it wasn't the beautiful island I had hoped for, but now I can see its strange beauty everywhere I look. It is a wild beauty, a secret beauty that twists and burrows inside me until sometimes I can't separate myself from it. I've never felt like this about a place before. It's an exhilarating feeling.

A mottled blur is moving fast towards me in the distance, and I put my hand to my eyes to shade them. It's Gabbro, her salt-and-pepper coat rustling as she gallops my way, and even though I feel scared, I stand my ground and wait. As she approaches, she slows to a walk, as if she senses I'm nervous. She sits at my feet, that startling blue eye trained on me, her tail thumping up dust from the ground.

Jacob isn't far behind, and as he reaches me, Gabbro turns her watchful face to him. He reaches down and strokes her muzzle, looking with fascination at the spiral of shells that stretches across the floor. Suddenly I'm embarrassed. It seems childish, somehow, what I have been doing here, alone.

'Can I help?' he asks, and before I have time to answer, he dips down, scooping up some shells and placing them on the ground, continuing the spiral. Gabbro finds a half-eaten cockle and takes it between her paws, licking at it like an ice cream.

I lose track of time as we work on the shells, and soon they're coiling further and further out, as wide as the salt pans in the distance, and all I can see when I blink is the imprint of white going on and on, seemingly for ever. The sun tracks across the sky, and eventually we stand back and admire our work.

'It looks a bit like a spider web,' I say, squinting at it, seeing patterns and shapes. I think of the silk strands that hold webs onto bushes and trees, and I stand and shade my eyes again, looking for things to secure our cobweb to.

The house rears up in the distance, and I begin to lay a line of shells in its direction. Jacob understands without me needing to tell him, and he starts a strand towards the testing buildings in the north.

We lay four or five lines out from the spiral. Eventually we can find no more shells, and we smile at each other, suddenly shy.

'Well,' he says, 'I ought to get on.'

'Me too.' I dig my toe into the shingle, uprooting one last cockle shell and placing it at the end of the spiral.

We go in different directions, and as I walk away, I force myself not to turn, not to look at him, in case he is turning back too.

I head west past the oyster beds, and the pavilion appears ahead of me. It's a low wooden building, so at ease with its surroundings that you wouldn't notice it unless you were looking. Up close, it has a large veranda at the front, peacock blue paint peeling away to reveal the grey, salt-washed wood beneath. It feels like the sort of building a colonial English family might have owned in India, and I imagine men in well-cut cream suits stepping out onto the veranda, whiskies in hand, the evening sun painting their linen jackets to pale peach.

As I climb the wide steps to the door, it doesn't feel quite so imposing. The wooden balustrade that lines the veranda is like a rotten grin with half its teeth missing. The glass in the windows is cracked, and here and there a pane is missing. It feels undignified, as if someone has stripped it of all that's important.

The door stands partly open. Inside I hear something like leaves skittering across the floorboards. From here, the building protects me from the roar of the island's incessant wind, and for a moment everything is still. The skittering sound is there again. A tap-tapping inside, like nails on glass, and I peer cautiously in through a window, but it's fuzzed with age. I push the door open a little more, and it squeaks against the floor, bloated with sea water.

Something hurtles towards me, hissing and rattling. At first, I think it's a swan, its wings raised in anger at my entrance, and I raise my arms in defence. But then it comes to a standstill in the middle of the room, and I see that what I thought were wings are in fact tail feathers, held high over its head. It is a peacock. A white peacock. It twists its neck, eyeing me beadily, and I drop my arms and watch it. It is trying to raise its feathers in an arc over its head in a display of aggression, but they're knotted and ungainly, hanging in a matted heap over its back. I step forward, pity taking the place of fright as I look at its yellowing, flea-bitten body. Where the tail feathers should take the shape of eyes, they look as if someone has taken a pair of shears to them and savagely cut them away. The peacock fixes me with its stare, but this time it is resigned. It gives itself a shake, and struts away.

A feather disentangles and falls to the floor, and I pick it up. It's like a thin twig, with pale, knotted, bud-like structures sprouting from it. Sharp filaments hang from these like single white hairs. There is something otherworldly about it, something wrong, and I recoil at its touch, dropping it quickly, watching the bird warily as it makes its way out of the room, dragging its monstrous tail.

It's only now that I see how large the room is. It is a vast space, with floor-length windows on three sides. Beneath the dust and dried-out leaves, polished black-and-white tiles sweep across the floor. I walk over to a window, my footsteps echoing through the room, and run my finger over a swathe of burgundy velvet hanging at the dirty glass. The pile is so rotten it dissolves at my touch.

On the main wall at the back of the room is a mural. Several feet wide, it depicts three life-sized soldiers in uniform. They're sitting on the ground, playing cards. One of the men is holding a black-and-white photograph. It's a portrait of a young woman. Her hair is set in waves, and her lips are dark and sultry. It's so real that I think it must be an actual photograph, and it's only when I run my fingers over it, feeling the tiny brushstrokes, that I realise it's painted. My hand automatically goes to my pocket in search of my phone to take a photo of it for Miss

Stourbridge, but of course, it isn't there. I wonder if there's a way of bringing her down here. This place obviously means something to her, although I sensed that her memories of it aren't entirely happy. It's probably best that I just try and describe it to her, as she asked.

I turn from the mural and look around the deserted room. Along each wall are a number of concave insets, framed with plaster vines and flowers. One of them holds a marble statue, what looks like a Greek god. Another statue is on the floor, lying on its back, staring up at the ceiling, as if it never quite made it to its frame.

On the floor beneath the mural, I see more evidence of the army's occupation: rusting buckets that must once have contained water for washing, an old kettle lying on its side, the ashy remains of a fire staining the black-and-white porcelain beneath. In a corner, two modern sleeping bags have been rolled up next to a small camping stove. Whoever is sleeping here, they are braver than me. I can't imagine spending a night in this place, the soldiers staring down at me from the wall, the white peacock roaming the halls. I'm suddenly thankful for my little bedroom in Miss Stourbridge's house, safe and hidden away.

I can sense so many stories in this building, ebbing and flowing, lapping over each other, and I cannot make out Miss Stourbridge's story within them all. Why has she not visited this place since she was a girl? I stand in the middle of the room and slowly turn around, taking in all of the sadness and the decay.

I find a spot on the floor clear of dead leaves, and I sit down and open my rucksack, rummaging inside it for my bottle of water. I take a long draught of the cool liquid, thankful that I remembered to fill it up from the salt pans the day before, and try to untangle all that I've learnt so far about this island.

There is evidence here more than anywhere of the army's occupation, and I wonder how Miss Stourbridge felt when the war ended. Most of the military must have left then, leaving her and her family almost alone. Did it feel as if she had reclaimed her island? Or were the testing facilities on the other side of Dohhalund a constant reminder that nothing could ever go back to how it was?

The wind rustles noisily around me, and as I look up into the cavernous space, an odd feeling comes over me. Right at the centre of the hall, amid the ornamental ceiling roses, a dusty chandelier hangs, swinging gently in the breeze. It is a beautiful relic from a time long before I came here, maybe even before Miss Stourbridge's time too. What has it witnessed? What will it watch over in the years to come?

Somewhere behind me I think I hear the scratching sound of the peacock's claws again, and I scramble up and collect my bag, and go quickly to the door.

I walk back to Dogger Bank along the creek. In the distance, a dense fog is beginning to accumulate over the sea between Dohhalund and England. I pause to watch it. It creeps slowly, as if it's alive and stalking prey.

On the boat trip over here, we went through a similar patch of fog. It was so thick I could swipe it aside with my hands, leaving my fingers cold and dew-drenched. When we came out on the other side, the fisherman pointed over the edge of the boat.

'Nearly at Silver Pit,' he grunted, nodding at the water. I clasped the side of the boat and looked down. We were speeding through a shallow patch, the last wisps of fog melting away on its surface. As I watched, the sandy shelf beneath us dropped away, and with a plummeting feeling I was aware of a yawning, black depth below, a place so dark that only sightless creatures could survive.

I think of Jacob and his blind cave spiders. I think of all the untouched places in the world. Will Dohhalund become one of them soon? When the excitement of exploring a new place dies away, who will come to this island, once we have all gone? Who will care? Nature has taken back this land once, and will do so again, just as every part of the world goes through cycles, be it seasons, or years, or timescales so large that I can't even hold them in my mind. Perhaps, whenever I leave here, it would be better to think of Dohhalund as a place reclaimed by nature, the island I knew lying dormant below the surface, clutching its secrets to it like buried bombs, not yet exploded.

I continue to walk until I come to the edge of the oyster beds, and I sink down onto the shingle, waiting for butterflies, watching the fog as it curls slowly towards the island. There are prints in the mud here, curling around the oysters, perhaps seagulls or egrets, the impressions of their feet revealing the webs between their toes. I lean forward and push my hand into the mud. It oozes between my fingers, and I recall doing the same with my mother, not with mud, but with clay.

It was perhaps the third or fourth day of our life together. We were sitting at the kitchen table, a great slab of clay in front of us, and together we pushed our hands into it, feeling its warmth grip our fingers.

'What's it for?' I asked.

'It's a memory,' she said, pressing her hand against the clay.

'But a memory is something before,' I said, my small eyebrows drawing together, confused. 'Like my foster home. That's a memory now, isn't it?'

'It is, my darling. And one day this piece of clay will remind us, years from now, of the story of when you were small and came to live with me: of how you came to be my daughter, and how I came to be your mum.'

'I like that story,' I said, pulling my hand from the clay, enjoying the way it tried to keep hold of me.

I climbed into her lap, fingers smearing clay on her shirt, watching as she peeled her own hand away and frowned at the imprint left behind. The fingers in the clay were linked by the faintest trace of webs.

'Let me tell you another story,' she said, her eyes drifting off, a look I would come to know as the one reserved for storytelling.

'Long ago,' she began, 'I was a tiny jellied spawn no bigger than a pearl ...'

It was the first time that she told me the story of the sea and the fish and the pearls.

When I was growing up and beginning to think about where I came from, I often wondered what my life would have been like if she hadn't adopted me.

If I had been born three hundred years earlier, I might have been drowned at birth, the strange shape on my cheek marking me out as cursed, dangerous. My birth mother might have dropped me into the same river that the chamber pots were emptied into, with hardly a backward glance.

Society has changed, but even now there are some people who will give a baby up simply for its imperfections. We tainted children are not drowned any more, instead we're passed on to someone else, adopted by people who never had a chance to have their own child, perfect or not.

When she adopted me, my mother believed it was important that I should know where I came from. And so, she named me for my birth surname, Tarttelin.

I have always loved and hated my name in equal measure. At school, the same bullies who laughed at my birthmark abbreviated my name to *tart*, shouting it at me in the playground until my eyes stung from the shame.

But at home, I was always Tartelin. I am bound to the people who gave me up by the very existence of my name, and yet my mother chose it to anchor me, so that I might know my beginnings. I wonder again if her story of the sea was something more than just a fairy tale. If it was her way of telling me that we weren't that different from one another:

both alone, both drifting, until we found each other. I wish again that I could ask her, but it is too late now.

Mum chose me *because* of my differences, not in spite of them. She knew what it was like to be different. *We're people of the sea, you and I, Tartelin.* Webs and scales. Disfigurement and deceit. Lone eggs floating on the tide, waiting for the current to land us who knows where.

I stare at the fog, mesmerised by the way it roils and clings to the sea, becoming a land of its own, a place even more mysterious than this strange, wild island.

The oysters are in front of me, tantalisingly within reach. I lean forward and take hold of one. It's like gripping onto a piece of concrete, and it comes out with a wrench of my wrist. It's an ugly thing, bulbous and slick with mud. I put it in my rucksack, hoping I can find something to open it with back at the house.

As I click my rucksack closed, the hairs on the back of my neck rise, and I become aware in a tingling moment that I'm being watched. A shiver runs through me, sending goose bumps down my arms. Slowly, I turn my head to the left, taking in the bunches of sea lavender that pepper the stones. A few metres away, a pair of grey eyes blink at me. I almost laugh with relief. It is a little dog, far too small to be dangerous, its coat the same rusted tan as many of the pebbles. It's breathing quickly, panting in the sun. Through its fur I can see the shape of its ribs on every in-breath. It's nibbling at a plant by its paws, a thick-leafed, rubbery-looking thing, and I realise it's trying to quench its thirst.

I pull my rucksack to me and take out my water bottle. The dog eyes me warily. Pulling off the lid, I inch closer and pour a little water on the stones. The dog pauses for a moment, then shuffles forward, rolling its tongue out and lapping at the wet patch, its eyes never leaving my face.

'Would you like some more?' I say quietly. In response, its ears lift, but it carries on lapping, licking at the stones, drawing whatever it can into its mouth. I cup my hand and pour a little water into my palm. Cautiously, I move my hand forward, daring myself. The dog's ears flatten against its head, and my hand shakes, but its muzzle is inching towards me and before I know it, soft, whiskery breath is tickling my fingers, and a warm tongue is folding and bunching, sucking the water held by my fingers into its mouth.

I let out a quiet exhalation of pleasure. The dog licks my hand clean and withdraws, eyeing me again.

'You're not so scary,' I whisper, pouring more water into my palm and offering it, and again it drinks, creeping closer in order to lap at it more quickly. As it moves, a line of fat nipples are revealed, pressed against the stones. Where are her puppies? I look around, but all I can see are hummocks of pebbles and clumps of grass. The dog is still drinking. I want to run my free hand across her back, to feel the knobbled bumps of her spine that I can make out with my eyes, stroke away the fine powder of dandruff clinging to her fur. When was the last time anyone went near this little dog, showed her some kindness, if ever? I move my hand to the sharp blades of her shoulders, and, very gently, lay it on her back.

Immediately she stiffens. In panic, I whip my hand away, but the dog remains still. She has stopped drinking. I look at her face, but she's not watching me, her gaze has shifted to something over my shoulder. Ever so slowly, I turn my head.

There is a deer on the other side of the creek, about twenty metres away. It is quite small, with little tusks sticking out of its mouth. The water is low, and it's picking its way through the mud, leaving a trail of hoof prints.

I can feel the rough whiskers of the dog's muzzle on my hand. She is so still as she eyes the deer that I think I can feel her heartbeat pulsing through her body. I daren't take my hand away, the movement might make me vulnerable to her razor-sharp teeth.

The deer has reached the river. It leaps over the water and begins to make its way towards the oyster bed. It hasn't seen us yet. I want to make a noise, move, anything to warn it, but I am frightened of the dog, her keen muzzle resting on my hand.

She moves without warning. She is so quick that all I see is a blur of rust. She reaches the creek in seconds, and it is then that I realise she's not alone. At least three other dogs are behind her, closing in on all sides. Too late, the deer sees the dogs. Before I have a chance to wonder where the pack has come from, they are on the deer. I stare, paralysed, as they take hold of its neck and a hind leg, snapping at its flank. With a sickening smack, they bring it down onto the oyster shells, and I stumble to my feet and run, not looking back, my water bottle spilled and abandoned on the stones.

Chapter Fifteen

Tartelin
Summer 2018

It's barely midday when I reach Dogger Bank, breathless and sweating from the panicked run here. For the first time, the house feels like a place of comfort: a home. I am approaching the back door when I realise I haven't got my rucksack. I look down at my hands. The net is also gone. Cursing myself, I turn back and retrace my steps.

When I reach the oyster beds, there isn't much left to tell the story of what happened. The deer's footprints are slowly being erased by the rising tide, and where it fell, a few paw prints are dotted between the oysters. There is an indent in the mud where the dogs must have dragged the carcass away, and the ground is a little darker there, but I can't tell if it's blood or just dredged-up mud.

There are no dogs in sight, but I have learnt that this doesn't mean they're not there. I look around warily as I reach for my rucksack. The net is lying a little way off, as if I managed to carry it some of the way, before abandoning it in panic. The sun is blazing in the sky, not yet obliterated by the sea fog, and I pick up my water bottle and knock back the last dregs of liquid. I swipe the hair from my face, tucking the sweaty strands behind my ears.

A butterfly comes flying towards me as if from nowhere. I watch its jittery dance, the net flexing in my hand. It zigzags over my head and swoops down low over the oysters. I wait for it to settle, following it with my eyes. It is large; larger than any other butterfly I have seen, and there's something else unusual about it, something not quite right. A feeling of hope tinged with sadness begins to trickle into my chest, a sensation I haven't felt since I caught the moth all those years ago and rubbed off its dust.

The butterfly hovers over the oysters, then loops back towards me instead. For a moment I think it's going to land on the net in my hand, but then, with one last pulse of its wings, it settles on my bare arm. It spreads its wings lazily, and I can feel it tickling the hairs on my skin. I watch, fascinated, as it lifts one leg, then another. Then a tongue unrolls daintily and it begins to suck at the beads of sweat on my skin.

The light around me changes, and I look up to see the fog, dense and dark, moving closer, curling around the sun. The island is suddenly swathed in a hazy glow, and in this strange, new, ethereal light, the butterfly appears to glow, too. It has large, pale wings the colour of thin cream. It has finished feeding now, and it closes its wings slowly, as if the unclarified sun is too warm for it. As they come together above its body, something deep in my stomach flips, like the first kick of a baby.

Where normally there would be dull, plain underwings, a striking blue eye stares straight at me. It has a small black pupil and a huge, blue iris flecked with hazel. There is a depth and emotion that I have only ever seen in human eyes, and, like the eyes of people in portraits, it seems to stare at me accusingly, daring me to look away.

I lift the net quietly, trying to keep my arm still, and lower it slowly over the butterfly, trapping it. Unlike the last butterfly I caught, it stays still, balancing on my arm, its wings firmly closed. I can feel the eye on me, gazing at me intently through the net's fine mesh. It is like looking into the eyes of an animal imprisoned in a zoo; the stare of a cow in a slaughterhouse, and I let out a silent moan.

The eye isn't real, I tell myself, it's just a pattern on a wing. I shake my head and look again. The blue iris gazes at me mournfully. Is it just the strange translucent light, or are there tears collecting in it, trembling, ready to spill?

With a cry of exasperation, I lift the net and drop it at my feet. The butterfly stays on my skin. Slowly, it lowers its wings, and the feeling lifts. The blue sky rushes back all around me, the fog dissipating as quickly as it had arrived.

I'm angry, but whether with the butterfly or myself, I don't know. I give my arm a flick, trying to dislodge the insect from where it clings to my skin, and it takes off. I watch it as it flits away, the eyes on the underside of its wings flashing in and out of sight, as it follows the creek southwards, disappearing into the distance.

I take a deep, shuddering breath, and look up at the sun, high over my head, its warmth nourishing me.

Already, I'm questioning what I saw: the butterfly can't have been crying. I must just still be reeling from what happened with the dogs and the deer. I shake my head, dispelling the fuzziness that's descending. I look at my watch. It's still only lunchtime. I have hours until I need to be back, but I'm hot and tired and I've had enough of exploring for one day.

Back at Dogger Bank, I tramp up the stairs, exhausted and muddy. Miss Stourbridge takes one look at me and says, 'Bath.'

I'm grateful to her, and as I lie in the huge copper tub, fragments of mud spiralling up through the water, I look out of the window at the sea beyond, searching fruitlessly for the circles I saw on my first night, and it comes to me, is this what Miss Stourbridge is searching for each time her eyes strain at the telescope lens?

The sea today is calm and clear. The bathwater cools around me, and I stand up and reach for my towel.

In my bedroom, trying to take my mind off all that's happened, I heft my mum's book from the bedside table and open it on the bed, comforted by the familiar pages.

I come to a drawing of a large seabird, something about it making me pause, and then I see it: *Morus bassanus*.

The Morus hybrid, the birdwatcher said when he stopped me the other day.

It's the Latin name for a gannet. I study the illustration, remembering a photograph of a gannet in Mum's bird magazine once. This picture does not do the bird justice. It cannot convey the startling blue eyes, or the incandescence of its white feathers.

I turn to look out of the window. Is it a gannet they're looking for out there? And if so, why is it so special?

We eat a late lunch in the dining room, and I tell Miss Stourbridge about the deer. When I finally get to the butterfly with the blue eye, I try to convey how unusual it was, my words stumbling over one another as I fail to describe the effect it had on me. The memory of it still haunts me, but of course it couldn't have been crying. It was just a feeling, that's all, brought on by the shock of the deer attack.

'Sounds like a hawk moth,' Miss Stourbridge says. 'Some sort of hybrid perhaps.'

Hybrid. The word jolts in my memory. 'There's a hybrid bird out there somewhere. The bird I told you about, the one all those people were after? Some sort of gannet, I think.'

'Hmm,' Miss Stourbridge isn't listening. She's still focused on the puzzle of the butterfly. 'Are you sure the eye was on the *underside* of the wing?'

'I'm sure. I got a good look at it; it landed on my arm,' I say without thinking.

Her voice is suddenly cool. 'And you didn't manage to catch it?'

Guilt streams through me. It occurs to me only now that if it was an unusual species, it would have been a valuable specimen to have. 'I'm so sorry. I … I made a mistake. My mind was still on the dog attack. It's just been such a weird day.'

I can feel tears at the corners of my eyes, ready to spill. What if I let the butterfly go on purpose because somewhere, deep inside, I knew how important it might be? If it was exactly what Miss Stourbridge was looking for, would bringing it back to the house have meant the end of my job here? Is that why I let it go?

Perhaps my job is *already* at an end, I think, seeing Miss Stourbridge wheel herself towards me, the look on her face severe, as if she's about to boil over with anger. But as she reaches me, the fury swiftly dissipates.

'I think you ought to spend the rest of the day here,' she says, patting my shoulder stiffly, but her voice is kind. 'It sounds as if you've had a bit of a shock.' She reaches up and wipes a tear that has fallen on my cheek. 'It is extraordinarily hot out there. I've never known a summer like it. Some time in the cool will no doubt settle your nerves.'

'Thank you,' I say, feeling pathetically grateful. Her hand is still on my face, cupping my cheek, and I lean into it, inordinately comforted by it. I'm reminded of the way Gabbro pressed against me that day down on the military base.

'We all make mistakes. Now, some tea, I think, child.'

Downstairs, I make a pot of tea, bringing it up on a tray. I offer to pour, but she bats my hand away, and I watch as she hefts the teapot awkwardly and pours, her wrists twisting from the task. A spatter of tea dribbles across the table, the teapot landing hard on the tray. My tea ripples with rings from the drops, and I'm reminded of what I was thinking about earlier.

'What are those circles, out at sea?'

'Circles?' She frowns.

'When I first came here, I saw three or four large circles in the water on the east side of the island.'

'Are you quite sure the sun hasn't got to you? Perhaps you ought to go and lie down.' She seems genuinely baffled by the question.

'It doesn't matter,' I say. 'I must have imagined them.' My eyes settle on the cabinet behind her. 'Did the mermaids always sign their work?' I ask, pointing. I can just make out the oyster shell in there, glimmering.

'Your mind is more erratic than a butterfly today, Tartelin. Have some tea. It cures all ills.' She refills my cup, though I've barely taken a sip. 'The mermaids rarely signed anything. I shouldn't have thought it would have occurred to them. Why do you want to know?'

'I thought there was a signature on the oyster shell you showed me, that's all. A moth or something, in a little circle.'

She takes a bite of the dried seaweed that she likes to finish each meal with in lieu of dessert. She chews for a long time, as if she's chewing on my words, too, and I wait for her to give her usual dismissive reply.

'That piece was made by Nan,' she says at last.

The name has taken on such a strange significance to me that my stomach flutters at the sound of it.

'Nan?' I study her, trying to work out what's going on in that dusty old brain. Her hand trembles as she brings her cup to her lips. I wait impatiently for her to swallow, so that she can elaborate, but instead she says, 'Now, tell me about the pavilion.'

I clench my cup a little too hard, and grit my teeth. But I'm not going to give up. Not yet. 'Who are the two girls, on the shell?'

She puts her cup down heavily, and tea slops onto the table. 'Tartelin, I really am not in the mood to indulge these questions today. Now, please will you tell me what you saw at the pavilion?'

I debate whether to question her further. My heart is beating hard, partly with frustration, partly adrenalin: I don't think I've ever pushed her this far before. But as I try to find another way to ask, I see for the first time the look on her face. She doesn't look angry; instead, her expression is open, her eyebrows raised, and I realise she is desperate to know.

I glance once more at the shell, and then put it from my mind. I can ask again another time. Instead I dig through everything that's happened today, trying to recall my visit there. It feels so long ago, and yet it was only a couple of hours.

'You were right,' I say, 'it's not in a good way. But it's still beautiful. I can see how opulent it must have been, once upon a time.'

Miss Stourbridge's cup stops at her lips. 'Tell me more,' she urges, without taking a sip. 'How did it feel?'

How did it feel? What an odd question, and yet I sort of understand: in the short space of time I was there, the place touched me. I think of the people using it to sleep in while they stay on the island. Perhaps they don't see ghosts in the same way I do.

'It was a bit spooky,' I admit. 'A bit sad.'

Miss Stourbridge nods knowingly. 'Yes,' she says, 'yes, I expect it would be.'

'There was a peacock in there.'

She raises her eyebrows in surprise.

'It was white, and its tail was all ... knotted.' I'm struggling to convey how strange it was, how it made me feel.

'We kept peacocks for years,' she says. 'Papa brought them with him when he married Mama. I did wonder what had happened to them after we left the island. They must have carried on breeding.'

'Where did you go, when you had to leave Dohhalund?'

'We moved to Lowestoft. I nursed my mother there until she died. With a good telescope, you can see Dohhalund on a clear day from the tip of Claremont Pier.'

'Did you go to work?'

'Not at first. I took care of Mama. She wasn't used to mainland living. I think it broke her, leaving her beloved island. Sometimes I think she left a part of herself here.' She breaks off and looks about the room, as if her mother might come in at any moment. 'In her last years, she used to go missing from the cottage, and I would find her, barefoot and in her nightdress, standing on the shore, always facing Dohhalund. It does something to you, this place.' Miss Stourbridge clears her throat, taking a sip of tea.

'After Mama passed, I became a secretary in the office of one of the local fisheries. The herring had dwindled by then, but boats were going much further afield. I always managed to bring back a fat bit of cod for my supper.'

'Oh.' I had assumed that Miss Stourbridge's life had been a full and rewarding one, decades of scientific research, perhaps. Working as a secretary in a fishing town didn't seem all that interesting. 'I thought you might have been a scientist,' I say.

Miss Stourbridge lifts her cup, draining the dregs of her tea. 'Life doesn't always take you in the direction you want to go, Tartelin,' she says. 'I liken it to the pull of the tide: you can fight against it if you wish, but often it's easier just to let it take you.'

Was it the pull of the tide that brought her back here? Is the tide pulling all of us, even now?

'I do class myself as a scientist, though,' she continues. 'When I was fifteen, we began the Dohhalund Silk Company, and I spent all my free time with the silkworms, learning. I've never stopped learning, even now. Your specialism doesn't have to be your job, you know. Remember that.'

'Do you miss it, making silk?'

'Sometimes. I miss the feel of the finished silk beneath my fingers. I miss the warmth of the annexe where the caterpillars lived. I miss the way this house was alive with people.' She lifts the tea things and stacks them on the tray. 'I miss my mother,' she says, and there is a heft of emotion in her voice. 'I miss the mother she was. She shone in the years we made silk. My father kept her like a valuable pet for years. She was a beauty, you see, Tartelin, truly a queen of Dohhalund. I think he was in awe of how she looked. No wonder he gave up his whole life to move to the island and marry her.' She sighs, looking over at the wall of framed butterflies.

'But when she was at last allowed to work, once the silk company was up and running in the late Twenties, she bloomed like the rarest of orchids.' She pauses, her eyes on the butterflies still. 'They did an experiment – in the 1980s, I think it was – to test the strength of the swallowtail butterfly. You know what a swallowtail looks like? There's one, there.'

She points to a frame with just one butterfly at its centre. It's quite large, and spectacularly pretty, its yellow wings dotted with black rectangles. Circles of cerulean and ruby line the base of its hind wings, and at the bottom, two little black prongs fork out below.

'Our most elegant and beautiful butterfly,' Miss Stourbridge says. 'In the experiment, they tied silk string to each tail tip, and added weights to it. And do you know how much the butterfly was able to carry, how many ounces it actually managed to lift into the air?

'No.'

'Have a guess.'

'Five ounces?'

'Not close.'

'Ten?'

'Nope. The swallowtails were able to carry precisely nothing,

Tartelin. They tried and tried, straining against the weight, until, with a great weft of their wings, each and every butterfly ripped off the little tails and flew haphazardly away.'

I put my hand to my mouth, trying to turn my mind away from the image.

'My mother was a swallowtail,' Miss Stourbridge continues. 'She was beautiful and delicate, her strength not very obvious to an obstinate, spoiled teenager like me. But there are different kinds of strength. My mother's was there, quietly building up, until the time came when she was able at last to demonstrate it.' She sighs. 'But like a swallowtail, her time in the sun was short ...'

'What do you mean?'

But Miss Stourbridge has placed the tea tray on her lap, and is halfway across the room with it. I'm beginning to see a pattern to these conversations: it feels sometimes as if she wants to talk, but it becomes too painful, and she slams shut again.

I get up, stretching, and go through to the panelled room, stopping at the piano.

'Do you play?' she calls through, the tray clinking as she pushes it into the dumb waiter.

'No. I never learnt.' I lift the lid. The keys are unusual: I think I recognise ridges of baleen divided by fingers of deep purple mussel shell. I press one gently, and the note rises into the room, its echo remaining even after I release it.

'What's that piece of music I hear you playing sometimes, Miss Stourbridge?'

She doesn't answer, and for a brief moment the hairs on the back of my neck rise. What if it isn't her playing it at all? But then I hear the wheelchair rolling across the floorboards. 'Sit,' she instructs as she approaches. 'I'll teach it to you.'

I do as she says, and she draws her chair up next to me. She begins the song I've heard so often through the floorboards. The music is so much louder in here, swelling around us, filling up the room. As it progresses, building to a crescendo, I can feel the floorboards humming with the sound of it, the glass of the butterfly frames around us vibrating. After so long without music of any form, it's hard to put into words how it affects me. It feels as if it's inside me, painting a picture so faintly, so delicately, that I can't quite see what it's meant to be, but I know that it is as fundamental, as necessary, as breathing.

When the music stops, I take a deep breath, as if I have been under-water for a long time and am only now able to gasp for air.

Miss Stourbridge shows me how to play the first few notes, taking my fingers and placing them in the correct position, smiling when I get it right. After a little while, I'm able to do it from memory, playing the higher part while she focuses on the more complex chords. We play for a while, enjoying the way our fingers appear to move as if connected, a strange and complex dance across the keys.

As the music comes to an end, I ask, 'What is it?'

Her fingers rest lightly on the keys. 'I never learnt the name. It was Nan's.'

I wait, hoping for more, but she is silent.

'Who was she, Miss Stourbridge? Who was Nan?'

She shakes her head. Not in a dismissive way, more like an act of desperation.

'You change when you talk about her,' I persist. 'She was important to you, wasn't she?'

She leans back in her chair and lets out a flutter of breath. 'Sometimes,' she says, 'I forget what she looked like. But when I play this song, I can feel her sitting next to me on the piano stool. I haven't played the piano in sixty years – we didn't have one on the mainland, there wasn't room in our little cottage. But when I came back here, it was as if the music was waiting for me, lying dormant in my fingertips.'

'Was she your friend?'

Miss Stourbridge looks up at me. I almost expect there to be tears in her eyes, but they are as dry and devoid of emotion as could be.

'I don't know who she was,' she says, and she takes the lid and closes it softly and, just like that, my piano lesson is over.

That night I dream of pearls and mussel shells, of the moon in the water and my mother as an egg, floating on the ebb tide, further and further away from me, until she disappears altogether. But instead of sadness at her departure, I feel a kind of release.

In the morning, when I wake, it's the first time I haven't reached for my phone to look for my mother's face. I wait for the rush of guilt to start trickling over me, but though I can sense it's there, it is thin and delicate, like silk. It is easy to bear.

I think instead of Nan, wondering why Miss Stourbridge finds it so difficult to talk about her. It feels as if she is the key to all of this. My mind drifts to the photo album. If I can find out more about her, I might be able to find a way to talk about her with Miss Stourbridge, and once we can do that, maybe we will both be able to lay some ghosts to rest.

I climb the stairs, my feet barely gracing each step, my nightie trailing out behind me. The panelled room is empty, and I stand in the doorway, trying to think where Miss Stourbridge might have hidden the album. Last night's dream is still fresh in my mind, Mum's story so visceral that it feels as if it is caught inside me, floating through my veins.

I scour the room, trying to put myself in my employer's shoes, to think like she thinks. I pull open the desk drawers at random. Glass bottles clink and metal instruments rattle, to no avail. And then I see the drawer; the one that she stared at with such soft sweetness when I accidentally opened it. I pull it open.

The blanket is still missing, but with a flash of exhilaration I see the album is in there. Quickly, I scoop it up and settle cross-legged on the floor, opening it eagerly to the first photograph.

It is a picture of Dogger Bank, standing on beautifully manicured lawns. It appears to have been taken from a point in the garden that no longer exists. I knew the cliff had eroded, but it's hard to imagine the house with such extensive grounds. A peacock is strutting across the grass. Tightly clipped yew hedges frame the wide, flat lawns. It is beautiful and imposing, and so very different to the weathered, battered house I'm sitting in now.

I turn the page. This photo is of a group of people. They are standing in a neat line with their feet pushed into the sand, the unmistakable wall of the cliff below Dogger Bank towering behind them.

I search the faces for the laughing Nan, but she's not there. Beneath the picture, in Miss Stourbridge's scratchy scrawl, it says, *September 1927*.

This looks like a family portrait. A small, wiry man stands on the left of the group. He has a perfectly waxed moustache and his eyes are small and sharp like the eye of a needle. To the right is a woman so tall she appears to hover over everyone else. She is beautiful, and her skin, even in the black and white of the photograph, is luminous. Her face shines out of the picture so brightly that it has the effect of obliterating everything else. My eyes are drawn to her again and again.

Standing between this otherworldly beauty and the wiry little man is a stocky, mousy girl of about fifteen. I feel a flip of sadness as I recognise my employer, for even though so many years have passed, that unmistakable sour expression thunders out from beneath her scowling brow.

Here is Marianne Stourbridge, standing between her parents. Imagine spending every waking moment with a mother like that, only to look in the mirror and see such an ordinary face looking back at you. The young Miss Stourbridge is about the same height as her father, and she has inherited an unbecoming blend of her parents' features, so that her hair is lighter than her father's, but less tame than her mother's. She is slouching, as if she has failed to inherit her mother's grace, or perhaps it's just the insolence of adolescence, the distaste for having her photograph taken.

There are other people in the photograph too, lined up at the back. They look like staff: a cook, perhaps, and a maid, even a governess, and I run my eyes over them to double-check that none of them is Nan.

Outside the panelled room, I think I hear a door creak, and I hastily flick through the photographs, searching for a clue. There's a picture of a ferry boat, Marianne and her father standing in front of it. In the background, herring girls are crouched, sorting through fishing nets on the ground.

I come to the picture of Nan, laughing on the beach, and I stop for a moment, taking a strange kind of comfort from it.

There's something in the background that I hadn't noticed last time. Right down near the water's edge stands a figure, and she is laughing too, carefree, her hand on her hat to stop it sailing away in the wind. And even though she's far away and her face is blurred, I can see that it is Marianne, her face transformed in a fit of giggles, her expression in complete contrast to that of the family portrait.

Another creak, and I close the album quickly and place it in the drawer, pushing it closed as quietly as I can. On the landing, Miss Stourbridge is just appearing, and we nod to one another as I walk sedately down the stairs.

I set out towards the herring girls' beach on the south of the island, keeping to the west path, tracing yesterday's walk along the edge of the oyster beds. The dogs gave me a fright yesterday, but I've learned that avoiding something does not make it easier. The creek is clear of dogs and deer today, any evidence long since washed away by the tide.

I pass the spiral of shells, stopping to marvel at the sheer size of it. I wonder if Jacob is on this part of the island today, and my stomach tilts at the thought. As my eyes range over the shells, I realise that one of the lines – the one heading back towards Dogger Bank – is significantly longer. I wonder if it was Jacob who added to it, or someone else.

I continue south, making my way towards the curved piece of land in the distance that forms the rounded southern end – the head of the leaping fish. There is a patch of gorse ahead, the flowers a waxy yellow, trembling in the wind. On one side the flowers are denser, a huge patch of gold, as if the gorse has been overcome with a desire to bloom. I walk closer, wondering if this is some form of mutation, but as I approach, the thick patch of yellow separates itself from the bushes, and I see it's not flowers, but a tent. I have seen tents on the island before, but usually they're pitched in groups of two or three. This one is on its own, and there's something different about it. It is very small and low to the ground, and scattered all over it is a pattern of spider webs, and I think, *Jacob.*

I approach quietly, looking around in case he's nearby. The tent is zipped closed.

'Jacob?' I say tentatively. There is no answer. Carefully, I pull the zip upwards and look inside.

A sleeping bag is laid out neatly on a thin roll of foam. There is a metal water bottle, and a blanket covered in black-and-white dog hairs. I glance behind me and, before I have time to question what I'm doing, I quickly slip inside.

It's suffocatingly warm beneath the fabric, and I breathe in the nostalgic smell of hot canvas, remembered from childhood. As I zip the tent closed around me, the sound, metallic and crisp, instils in me a feeling of safety. When I was small, Mum and I used to go camping every summer. Last summer, after her diagnosis, we began again: little trips, just her and me. For some reason that defies logic, I have always felt perfectly safe with just canvas between me and the rest of the world.

I lie back on the sleeping bag. Above me, the pattern of spider webs criss-cross over the fabric in random lines. I trace my finger over them, and it dawns on me that Jacob has drawn these himself: I recognise the fragmented, scattered skeins of the web that he was looking at when Gabbro put her soft head against me, and the miraculous web he showed me in the testing facility. He has tried to convey its beauty, its sense of depth, but no picture could capture the feeling it gave me, the way I lost all sense of time and place while I looked at it.

The sleeping bag beneath my head smells of him, a dark, woody smell that reminds me of the curls of his hair, the brown filaments of his woollen jumper. It makes my stomach flip pleasantly, and I breathe it in. I trace the webs above me like constellations in the sky. It feels as if I'm looking deep into Jacob's mind, seeing the intricacies of his inner thoughts, and I know suddenly that I've stepped too far, carried away with the idea of seeing a part of Jacob that he hasn't yet allowed me to see.

I leave the tent as quietly as I can, zipping it up and making my way toward the south beach, a place I haven't set foot on before.

I pass a mass of gnarled bushes, their scant leaves withered. There's something orderly about them, despite their ragged appearance. They're squat and stunted, growing in regimental rows. I take a leaf in my hand and pull. It comes away easily, speckled and dry, and I put it to my nose. Its smell is potent, evoking the earthy, vegetative scent of dense woodland. Except for the old oak in Miss Stourbridge's garden, these bushes are by far the largest plants I have seen here.

I look at the cross-hatched rows, the wayward branches reaching out and twisting together as if they are clutching at each other for dear life, and I rub the shrivelled leaf between my fingers. This must be the mulberry plantation, where the rare bird was spotted. There is no one around now, and I wonder where the bird has flown to; if the gaggle of birdwatchers I saw the other day are following it across the island as it swoops and dives.

I carry on towards the beach, and as I step onto the shingle, the wind hits me. The cliff rises to my left, and high up at its top I can just make out the tips of Dogger Bank's chimneys.

The remains of a little brick building stand halfway to the water. Part of the roof has long since gone, and some of the bricks have fallen away and lie scattered amid the stones, their corners softened by the sea. Beyond it, the tide is just beginning to cover a swathe of flat rocks grizzled with barnacles.

I peer inside the building. It's small and functional, and smells faintly of salted fish. There are four bunk beds, their grey paint rusting onto the floor. Behind them, fishing nets hang on a far wall. One of the lower bunks has a pile of blankets on it, and nearby, there is a small kettle on a single gas burner on the floor. An old oilskin coat hangs from the corner of the bunk bed, and a damp roll of toilet paper sits nearby. Feeling for the second time as if I'm trespassing, I duck back out of the building.

Far along the beach, I see a figure stepping sure-footedly across the pebbles. She – I think it's a she – is coming towards me, walking confidently on the shifting stones as if she has done it all her life. I blink away the blur in my vision from the relentless wind, and the shape condenses into the round, stooped body of the old mermaid.

'An unusual mist,' she calls as she approaches, pointing out to sea where the fog that had coated the island yesterday is still coiled, its wispy fingers trailing in the water. 'I thought I saw animals in it earlier, like you do in the clouds. Fish and butterflies.' She sits on the pebbles, patting the space next to her. 'It's Tartelin, isn't it? Come, have a pew.'

I sit down on the stones and we look out to sea together.

'Is this where you used to work?' I say. 'It's the mermaids' beach, isn't it?'

'It is. It still smells the same, even after all these years.' She takes a deep breath and smacks her lips. 'There's nothing like it.'

'Did you leave when the island was requisitioned?'

'Oh no, long before that. They stopped fishing for herring here many years earlier.' She reaches up and touches a necklace strung round her neck, a mussel shell, deep purple like the keys of Miss Stourbridge's piano, shining metallically in the low light. 'I've missed it, this island, this beach,' she says. 'It has always had a hold on me.'

'Is that why you came back? Because it pulled you back?'

'I suppose so. I've never had to put it into words before, but, yes. The pull of it. Magnetic. As if it wants me to search out its secrets.'

I nod in agreement. There's something intoxicating about Dohhalund that feels indescribable. Both the mermaid and Miss Stourbridge have been pulled back here. The birdwatchers must feel its pull, too, in a different way, and Jacob as well. Will I, too, be drawn back here? Will I be able to leave?

The woman is quiet, watching the fog dissipate. 'There are many secrets here, I think,' she says at last, her hand on her necklace still. Then she pushes her thick, bulbous knuckles into the stones, and heaves herself up. 'I'm sure you'll find the answers you're looking for, you're a clever girl.' She winks at me, and then starts to walk back along the beach, her bare feet dipping into the salt water. I watch her go, and it's only when she's a distant speck on the shore that her words penetrate me. How does she know I'm looking for answers?

I get to my feet and begin to jog to catch up with her. Far in the distance, she stops walking, and in one swift motion, slips off her dress and deposits it on the pebbles. I stop still. It feels for a moment as if she turns to me, considering me, then she steps into the water, completely naked, and dives fluidly under a wave. I watch, waiting for her to reappear, but the water is calm and nothing breaks the surface. With mounting concern, I scan the sea, willing her to come up, and in panic I reach into my back pocket, but then I remember my phone is back at Dogger Bank, the battery flat, and besides, there is no signal out here.

I start running towards the place she disappeared, my feet sliding over the stones. I debate whether to pull my shoes off and wade in, but then, far away, her head pops up, like a seal. I breathe a sigh of relief, and my toe nudges against something on the sand.

Her dress is lying crumpled in a heap, the mussel-shell necklace on top of it, and I bend down and pick it up by its string. It has been prised open and laid flat so that the two shells are still attached to one another, resembling a moth's drooping wings. Scratched onto the bottom of each wing is an eye. I run my thumb over the shell, remembering with a shiver the butterfly with the blue eyes that landed on my arm. But as I look closer, I see that the scratches on this shell aren't eyes, after all. Each one is a moth set within a circle.

And just like that, I know who this woman is.

She is the same woman who Jacob called the mermaid; the woman who gave me an etched oyster shell. But she also gave Marianne her own shell too, many years ago, a delicate etching of them walking, arm in arm, beneath a blossom-filled tree.

Nan.

Chapter Sixteen

Marianne

Winter 1927–8

December washed over the island in a fine mist that drenched you before you'd taken two steps out of the house. Marianne relished the weather, enjoying the way it swallowed her up as soon as she went outside. Out there, she could pretend she was far away from the mysteries that were locked up inside the house. But by mid-December, the winds had intensified, keening through Dogger Bank like the cries of a hundred bereft children, and Marianne conceded that it was too wild outside even for her.

She and Nan sat by the fire in the sitting room, working on a jigsaw composed of hundreds of butterflies' wings. At this time of year it always took a long time to thaw out after the Sunday service, the chapel so cold that their breath plumed above them into the air like a sea mist. From downstairs, deliciously delicate wafts of *gebakken* sole drifted up from the kitchen, and Marianne found her stomach rumbling in anticipation of the thin slivers of fish.

Nan went over to the piano, putting her hand covetously on the burnished lid that covered the keys. 'Do you play?' she said. 'I don't think I've heard it since I've been here.'

'No,' Marianne said, getting up and following her over. 'It belonged to Great-Grandmama. She always slapped my hand away when I asked to have a go. She said my fingers were far too fat to play well.'

Nan took Marianne's hand in her own, examining her fingers. Nan's own hands were slight and pale and perfect.

'They look fine to me,' she said, squeezing her hand briefly. She touched the gleaming piano lid, stroking it as if it were made of gold. 'May I?' she asked.

'Of course. I didn't know you played.'

'I don't. Not very well, at least. My mother taught me a few songs when I was little.' She sat at the stool and lifted the lid, taking in the long stretch of keys before her. They were an unusual shade of brown, with thin, rigid lines running down each one. The smaller keys were dark blue and shiny. Nan looked up, puzzled.

'Oh, it was commissioned for my great-great-grandmother,' Marianne explained. 'The keys are baleen and mussel shell.'

Nan nodded, and placed her fingers on them lightly. With a quick inhalation of breath, she began to play.

The piano had not been touched in a long time, and it was in need of a tune, but the soft, sad notes rose into the room. The sound was silvery, like sea water might sound, and Marianne watched, mesmerised.

When she stopped playing, Marianne said, 'It's beautiful.'

'Shall I teach you?'

'What, with my fat fingers?'

Nan laughed, and shifted along the seat so that Marianne could sit down.

They spent the afternoon absorbed, the notes flowing from the piano, laughing at their mistakes. At one point, Mama came into the room to listen, stopping at the door so as not to disturb them.

When they had finally had enough, Nan closed the piano's lid, and

Marianne wriggled her stiff fingers, finding a sort of satisfied pleasure in the ache that thrummed through them.

She looked at Nan. She was still touching the piano, stroking it as if it were human.

'Are you all right?'

Nan gave her head a little shake as if coming out of a reverie. 'It … it just reminded me of playing with my mother.'

With a flush of guilt, Marianne remembered that Nan's mother was no longer alive. Awkwardly, she put her arm around her and squeezed her tightly.

On a bright, crisp Saturday in early January, Papa came into the dining room dressed in khaki slacks and a matching shirt. Balanced jauntily on his head was a black top hat – a relic of his bachelor days, and only worn now when he went butterfly catching. He rested his palm on the handle of a net, the hooped end pressed to the floor as if it were a cane.

'Are you off dancing, dear?' Mama said, looking at his outfit over the rim of her teacup and trying not to smile.

Papa spun on the spot, lifting the net in his hand and swooping it through the air. 'Not today, my dear. Today, Marianne and I are going hunting for butterflies.'

'But Papa, it's the middle of winter!'

Her father came over to where she sat at the table, and crouched down next to her. 'Marianne, I don't think we've spent enough time together these past few months. There have been so many new things: silkworms, pavilions, pearls. We have always had the most fun when we go out hunting butterflies together, regardless of whether we catch any or not, so I wondered if you would do me the honour of accompanying me across Dohhalund, nets and all?' A loose corkscrew of wiry hair had escaped his hat. He extended his free hand, eyebrows cocked, and Marianne took it, laughing.

'Papa, you're very silly,' she said.

'Nonsense. Now hurry and finish that breakfast, Marianne, we have butterflies to catch!' He raised his hat to her, inclining his head, his dark hair strewn with the glittering dust of long-dead butterflies.

Marianne couldn't remember the last time she had gone for a walk with her father, he had been so busy for so long. It was a still day, mild for the time of year. She was wrapped in a new silver fox-fur cape, the matching muffler encasing her hands. It had been delivered the previous week, and she hadn't had the opportunity to wear it yet. It was deeply soft, and far too warm for today's weather. Wisps of fur stuck sweatily to her neck, making her skin itch, but she was too proud and too self-conscious to take it off.

At the quay, they passed two joskins hauling the herring barrels, and she thought she saw them whisper something and stifle their laughter. She looked at her father, marching ahead, oblivious to the men, his top hat foppishly askew and his net resting over his shoulder. She looked down at the silver fur of her cape, far too resplendent for a walk across Dohhalund, and her cheeks flamed red. How dare they make fun of their employers? Ignoring their laughter, she lifted her skirt over a foul-smelling puddle, and trotted to catch up with her father.

When she was a child, she and Papa had spent every free moment in summer striding over Dohhalund in search of butterflies. She had cherished the time spent alone with him. Sometimes, when she was little, she secretly pretended she was a boy, stamping across the shingle, learning the ways of the island that would one day be her responsibility to run.

As they neared the salt marsh, Papa came to an abrupt halt, throwing a hand out to stop Marianne.

'What is it?' she asked, peering round him.

But Papa was in his element, far too distracted to listen to her. Rocking on the balls of his feet, he raised the net high in the air and arced it down, bringing it to a close over a scraggy patch of sea spurrey. 'Got it!' he exclaimed, crouching down.

Marianne tried to see what he had caught, but his body was hunched over the grass, and she stood and waited, tapping her foot impatiently. When he straightened up, he was cupping something between his palms.

'Shouldn't you pin it in your hat, Papa?' she began, but then he opened his hands.

Sitting on the creases of his palm was a butterfly. For an anguished moment, she thought it might be the one she and Nan had rescued on the night of the soirée, but as she leaned in, her heart began to flutter.

It was small and delicate, its crimson wings catching the light. And it was made of rubies.

Marianne gasped, taking in the intricate detail, the fine gold antennae. At the centre of each hindwing was a pearl, positioned just like the eyes on a peacock butterfly's wings.

'For *mijn parelmoer*,' her father said, lifting the butterfly and pinning it to the lapel of her cape.

'Papa, it's beautiful,' she said, her eyes lighting up as the rubies caught the cold winter sun and sparkled.

'Nothing is too fine for my daughter,' he said, touching the butterfly brooch lightly, his fingers reaching up to stroke her cheek, and she leaned into him, caught up in the full beam of his focus.

'Are they Dohhalund pearls?' she said. His fingers on her cheek stopped their stroking.

'Of course. I promised you some, after all,' he said, rather shortly, turning his attention to the net that he'd dropped on the ground, and

Marianne felt the light that had surrounded her dim. She drew away from him, confused.

But Papa didn't appear to notice. He was balancing the net on his shoulder now, and righting his hat, which had slipped to the side. Without looking back, he set about carrying on with their walk, calling over his shoulder, 'Come, Marianne, let's go and spy on the seals.'

That night, she dreamed of the island as she had envisaged it as a child: the feeling that beyond Dohhalund's beaches, the sea stretched for all eternity, and Mama and Papa were the only people in the world. When she awoke, she felt a yearning need for that innocence again. She turned to look at the butterfly brooch next to her bed. Even in the dark, the rubies glowed, like the last embers of a fire, and she wondered just what Papa thought he had bought by giving it to her.

By mid-January, Dohhalund began to take on a stillness, a feeling of calm, as if the island were resting, collecting itself, deep beneath its crust, in readiness for the great flush of the spring.

Marianne had taken to caring for the silkworms almost completely on her own now, since Papa was borrowing Nan so often to help with his many projects.

She had been surprised by how much she enjoyed working with the caterpillars, their gaping mouths reminding her of the young swallows that sometimes nested outside the sitting-room window. As she had observed them over the weeks, they'd grown fat from the lush mulberry leaves, moulting their skins in succession until they began to slow down, their plump, round bodies too heavy for them to move far.

Eventually they stopped eating altogether, and over the last few days she had plucked them up one by one, trying not to feel squeamish at the touch of their soft, maggoty bodies, and placed them safely out of harm's way on the shelves so that they could start to spin their cocoons.

Now, she saw how the last few had begun to weave threads of the fine filament around themselves, their barely visible bodies pulsing beneath the silk. Before long, it was impossible to tell that anything at all lay within the little white orbs, and she thought longingly of the reams of silk they would make.

It was quiet in the annexe, the soft puffs of silk sitting on every available space like strange fruit dotted around the room.

From out in the kitchen, Marianne heard Nan's voice.

'Mr Stourbridge, I must talk to you about the pearls.'

Papa's reply was muffled, and Marianne tiptoed to the edge of the door and peeped round.

Nan was standing in the middle of the kitchen, the weak winter sunlight shining on her hair, turning it to mahogany. 'It's not right,' she was saying, 'what you're doing with them.'

Papa stepped closer to her, his voice barely a whisper, but still Marianne detected the anger in it. 'Hush, Nan, not here.'

At that moment, Cook shuffled wheezily into the kitchen, a large saucepan in her hands, and Papa stepped back and said, rather too loudly, 'Come, Nan, let us see to those pearls.' Marianne watched as he stalked off towards his study, patting his hair down as he went.

Nan took a moment to collect herself, tucking her hair behind her ears before following. Cook was still standing in the kitchen, her meaty arms holding the saucepan. Through the crack in the door, Marianne watched as the old woman shook her head, hitching the pan to her bosom. 'Folks are queer round here,' she muttered, slopping stew onto the tiles.

Marianne stayed in the annexe, too stunned to move. What was Papa doing with the pearls? She unpinned the little butterfly brooch on her lapel, examining it. The two pearls that studded the wings glowed like mist-covered moons. Her gaze travelled round the room, trying to make sense of what she had just heard, but however she tried to twist Nan's words, they simply didn't add up.

Later that afternoon, she sat at her dressing table on the pretence of reading up on sericulture, gazing out of the window. England seemed very far away today, hidden beneath a haze of cold cloud.

A soft tap on the door made her jump.

'Come in,' she said, hastily looking down at the book.

Nan slipped through the door. She had a thick shawl around her shoulders, and her normally sleek hair looked windswept. The rims of her eyes were red.

Marianne looked up from the book. 'You've been crying,' she said, frowning. Perhaps Papa had torn a strip off her for being so insolent.

'I've just come from the mermaids,' Nan said.

'The *mermaids* made you cry?' Marianne said with surprise.

The herring girls had taken to Nan in a way they never had with Marianne, welcoming her onto their part of the island as if she was one of them. She sometimes spent her free time down on the south beach, helping mend the quarter crans and listening to their stories, or else tending to the salt pans on the west of the island.

'No. I ... I wanted to ask them about your father's herring business,' Nan said. 'They say there are fewer herring this year.'

'They're herring girls,' Marianne scoffed, 'how on earth would they know the ins and outs of Papa's businesses?'

'They know more than you give them credit for, Marianne. They told me some of the girls were dismissed last week; there wasn't enough work for them.'

Marianne got up and went to the window, remembering what the old mermaid had told her about the herring stock, and a quiet buzzing started up somewhere at the base of her skull. She gazed across the sea, trying to make out the long thin line of the English coast, imagining people out there, getting on with their own lives, oblivious to the conversation that was happening in a room in a house on an island far away.

'But once the pearls you found are sold,' Marianne said, 'things will go back to normal.' She turned to Nan, trying to gauge the emotion in her face. 'This sort of thing happens all the time, Nan, honestly.' Her voice belied the trickle of worry that had begun to collect in the pit of her stomach.

'I just think you should be prepared,' Nan said, not meeting her eyes.

'Prepared? For what?' She bunched her fists in frustration. 'I'm built of strong stuff, Nan. If you have something important to say, please say it.'

'It's nothing, it's—'

'I heard you, this morning, talking with Papa in the kitchen,' Marianne said.

Nan looked up sharply.

'I was in the annexe,' Marianne added hastily. 'I wasn't spying or anything, I just … happened to be there.'

A tinge of pink crept across Nan's cheeks. She grasped the shawl closer to her body.

'What was it about?'

'It was nothing,' Nan said, shaking her head.

'It can't be nothing, for goodness' sake, you've been crying. Tell me,' she demanded.

Nan took a breath. 'Your father … Mr Stourbridge, he has taken on a lot—'

'Papa always takes on a lot,' Marianne said dismissively. 'And soon we will have the money from the pearls, and then he can move on to the next part of all his projects.'

She turned back to the window, straining to see through the low-lying cloud. Papa had hired an engineer somewhere over on the mainland to design a narrow-gauge railway for the island. She imagined the man now, far away across the stretch of water, drawing designs to Papa's specifications. Behind her, Nan was silent.

Marianne turned back. 'It will all be fine, I promise you, Nan,' she said, a note of finality in her tone. 'You just ... don't understand the way we island people do things.'

Nan remained silent. She reached into her pocket. 'I brought you this,' she said, pulling out something small and grey, and Marianne took a step forward to see.

'The mermaids scratch pictures onto the pieces of whalebone that wash up on the beach,' Nan said. 'I wanted to make one for you. It's on an oyster shell because, well, it seemed more appropriate, coming from me.' She pushed the shell forward, tipping it into Marianne's hands.

She had scratched a drawing of two girls into the curved pearlescent sheen of the shell. They were walking arm in arm under a tree in blossom.

'It's us,' Nan said.

Marianne ran her eyes over the picture. Other than the gorse bushes that grew in straggly patches over the island, she had never seen a tree with flowers on before. Dohhalund's sandy soil was not made for large trees, and the only one was the oak in their garden, regularly watered and fertilised by the gardener.

She stroked the little blossoms, looking at the two girls – herself and Nan – beneath the tree. The picture was incredibly intricate, and she marvelled at the neat cross-hatching, the tiny leaves and blossoms trembling on the branches.

At the bottom of the shell was a tiny scratched silk moth, set within a perfect circle.

'I signed it like that so you will always remember it's from the silk-girl,' Nan said, the start of a smile curling at the edges of her mouth, trying to reach up to her red eyes.

Marianne ran her finger over the fine lines in the mother-of-pearl.

'It's beautiful,' she said.

That evening, as she lay in bed, thinking of Nan's gift, she turned to the wall and traced the patterns of seaweed that wound across the wallpaper, wondering what Nan was thinking on the other side of the wall. She stopped, frowning, her finger pressing into a dent beneath a feathery tendril in the pattern. Finding a corner of wallpaper, she hooked her nail under it, and it came cleanly away.

Underneath, in the bare plaster, was a small hole. She touched it tentatively with her finger, and then she leant close and whispered, 'Nan, can you hear me?'

There was a rustle on the other side of the wall, and Nan's voice whispered back, 'Marianne?'

Marianne scrambled up on her knees and put her eye to it. She saw Nan's dark eye looking back at her.

'I'm sorry,' she whispered. It was somehow easier to talk with a wall between them. It masked the shame she felt on speaking the words, for they were not words that she was used to saying.

'What for?' came the reply.

'For not accepting you. For making your life here difficult.'

A soft pattering of plaster dust, and then Nan's finger appeared, small and vulnerable. Marianne reached out and hooked it in her own. She lay back on her pillow, the small touch between them soft as velvet.

Chapter Seventeen

Tartelin

Summer 2018

I walk back from the herring girls' beach in a daze, my mind filled with the image of the old woman, diving into the sea.

Nan.

The woman in the photograph, here, all these years later. And yet, Miss Stourbridge doesn't appear to know she's even on the island. What happened between them? When did they last see each other?

I reach Dogger Bank without noticing which way I've come, and go in by the back door. A delivery has arrived from the mainland: a fresh pallet stands in the kitchen, and I'm momentarily distracted by the promise of normal food. It's heaving with slabs of meat and cold cheeses, packed in the rapidly melting ice that's also keeping our order of fish fresh. There are tins of baked beans and sweetcorn, too, and even a wooden box containing a rainbow of earthy vegetables. I rejoice at the thought of not having to eat seaweed again for a week or two.

I open my rucksack, searching for the stale sandwich I made this morning so that I can throw it out ceremoniously, and my hand brushes against something hard and rough. It's the muddy oyster that I collected yesterday. I go to the sink and rinse it under the tap, thinking of the pearl Nan showed me on one of my first days on the island.

Thin slivers of shell flake off, sticking to the porcelain, pearlescent and pale. I try to prise the shell apart, but the two halves are jammed tightly together. I take a knife to it, sliding it deftly between the lips, careful in case it slips, and twist sharply. The oyster eases open, and I blench at the jellied body inside. It is grotesquely bulbous at one end, and I push my finger into it, feeling slightly nauseous. A fat white pearl slides out, bigger even than the one Nan showed me. It's the size of a cherry, and perfectly round, and it appears to shimmer in front of my eyes, as if its surface is moving, a tiny planet swirling with gases.

Lost in thought, I become aware of a dark shape approaching the kitchen door. It pauses briefly, blocking out the light of the frosted glass, and I look up, the pearl slipping from my fingers in my surprise. Something is pushed roughly through the letterbox, and just as quickly, the dark shape is gone and light floods the kitchen again.

The fallen pearl rolls across the tiles, coming to a stop near the door. On the doormat is a piece of paper, coarsely torn and folded. I reach down and pick it and the pearl up.

The writing is round, and hard to read, as if the person who wrote it isn't used to holding a pen.

Tartelin, it says,

Meet me at ten o'clock tonight on the beach, near the ruined chapel. I have something to show you.

Jacob.

I run my eyes over the piece of paper, trying to read meaning between the hastily scratched words.

It has been such a strange couple of days. My mind drifts towards Jacob. The smell of him comes to me again, as if I am back in his tent.

It's a comforting smell, familiar. I tuck the pearl away in my rucksack and shoulder it to take back to my bedroom.

That afternoon, I spend the time in my room, leafing through Mum's ornithological book, my mind on the south beach and Nan, wondering why she hasn't come to the house to visit her old friend.

As the sun lowers towards the distant mainland in the west, the oyster shell on my bedside table catches the afternoon rays. I pick it up, turning it over and over, searching fruitlessly for a signature.

The sun catches my glass of water, sending rays dancing across the bedside cabinet, and with sudden inspiration, I dip the shell into the glass, bringing it out, burnished and dripping. I turn it over again. It's on the third turn that I notice it, half hidden beneath the calloused wave of the outer shell: a tiny moth scratched inside a circle, and I smile. I touch my fingertip to it, thinking.

Far away in the kitchen a bell tinkles, but I am too lost in my thoughts to make sense of it. A minute later an angry call comes from upstairs, and I realise it's Miss Stourbridge.

I pocket the oyster shell, and leave the room to return to my duties.

That evening, as I deliberate over whether or not to meet Jacob at the beach, I rustle up a plain supper of soft white bread and thick yellow butter. I cut slabs of strong cheddar and arrange an array of colourful, crisp peppers along one side. At the last minute I scatter a little pile of Dohhalund salt onto each plate. As the sun gets lower in the sky, my stomach dips and churns at the thought of the darkness that will descend soon over the sand outside.

There is a strange atmosphere at dinner. Miss Stourbridge, usually eager to hear about my day, is silent. I'm pleased to see her appetite has returned, watching her as she bites with satisfaction into the bread, chewing with her eyes closed.

I take this opportunity to study her face, searching her features for the young Marianne I saw in the photographs. There is something about the sharpness of the cheekbones, the straight slope of the nose. She opens her eyes, catching me looking, and they narrow as if in anger. I look down at my plate, my cheeks flushing.

'No butterflies,' she says. 'Yet again.' There is a sharpness in her voice that I haven't heard before.

'I'm sorry. I was a bit distracted today.' After my discovery of Nan on the beach, the thought of butterflies had gone completely from my mind. I glance guiltily over my shoulder at her desk in the sitting room, noticeably devoid of fresh specimens.

Miss Stourbridge lays her breadcrust on the edge of her plate. 'Don't let it become a problem, this distraction, Miss Brown.' The anger is still in her voice.

'I'm sorry, I—'

'Do remember, I *need* you to catch them for me. It's not as if I can pop outside, brandishing a net, and bring in a jarful myself, is it?'

Where has this rage come from? 'I *am* sorry, honestly. I'll do better tomorrow.'

'I hope so.' She taps her fingers on the table, as if she's weighing something up in her mind. 'I'd also appreciate it if you didn't go rooting through my possessions.'

'I'm sorry?' A cold rush of salt water seeps through me, and as if in slow motion I watch as she pulls open a drawer in the dining table, and suddenly the photo album is there.

'If I want to show you something,' Miss Stourbridge says, placing the album on the table, and the anger in her voice chills me, 'I will do just that. Drawers and cupboards are closed for a reason, Tartelin. I would appreciate it if you'd remember that.'

I look down at my plate. I want to tell her that I was only trying to fit her story together, so that I could understand her better. I want to spell out just what is going on out there on her island, how her past and her present are overlapping.

'It's just—' I begin.

'That's enough, Tartelin! I have had enough! You're here to do a job, that is all.'

That's all? What about the moments we've shared in the last few days, the friendship I thought we were both edging towards? 'But I—'

'You will catch me a butterfly tomorrow,' she says, cutting me off, her voice sharp with venom. 'That's an order.'

A flash of frustration tears through me, its edges rippled with anger. 'Do you really need more, Miss Stourbridge?'

I hadn't known my anger was so close to the surface, but now that it is there, I revel in it. 'It seems a bit bloodthirsty. Surely you have enough already?'

She looks up sharply, her eyes narrowing at me again. 'Tell me, Tartelin, why do you think you are here?'

I pause before answering. Is this a trick question? 'To help you study the island,' I tell her. 'To bring things back for you to examine.' I want to add, 'To indulge an old woman,' but stop myself just in time.

'And why do you think I want to study this place? Why would an old, disabled woman come back to an island she left more than sixty years ago, and imprison herself on the first floor of a crumbling old house to eat poorly cooked meals and await the return each day of a girl she barely knows and, frankly, right now, hardly likes?'

She is leaning towards me now across the table.

'Why?' she says again, and with a flush of guilt I see clearly the picture she's painted.

'I don't know,' I say quietly.

'Pardon?'

'I don't know, Miss Stourbridge,' I say, the words coming out louder than I intended.

'I see. So, you're curious enough about my life to go riffling through my private things, but you don't pause to think about what your rummaging might do to me, how it might make me *feel*?' she says, her eyebrows raised.

My stomach swoops with guilt. She's right. I was so set on finding out about everything that she's so secretive about, that I hadn't stopped to wonder how she'd feel if she caught me at it.

'You're curious about my past, but do you not find it strange that I am here, now, in the present,' she continues, 'without family, shedding modern comforts? You mock my peculiar, obsessive ways, I'm sure, but you have no idea what has gone on in this part of the world, my dear, no idea at all.'

'I would, if only you'd tell me.' My voice is barely more than a whisper, the shame of what she has implied almost silencing me, but I need to get this through to her, I need to fight my corner.

'I'm sorry?' her voice is quiet, deathly.

A fizzing feeling begins at the very top of my skull. What did Nan say on the first day I met her? *She needs someone who'll answer back.* I clear my throat. 'As soon as you knew I was capable of finding and killing animals for you, you didn't bother finding out anything else.'

'*Insects*, Miss Brown. Lepidoptera are insects.' She bangs her hand on the table and the photograph album jumps and lands on the floor with a thump. She leans over the arm of her wheelchair and tries to reach it, the cane-work groaning as she stretches.

I jump up and pick it up, placing it next to her plate. The interruption seems to have defused her anger, and she sighs, leaning back in her chair.

'Some things are private for a reason, Tartelin. Not just because I'm a stubborn old woman who enjoys keeping things from you. You have to understand that I am not a story to be unravelled. I may be old and crotchety, but I have feelings and emotions too, just like you. I know that the death of your mother is still raw, but trust me, things that happened decades ago can feel like they were only yesterday, too, especially when you're plunged back into the very house where they happened.'

She darts a gnarled hand towards me, then withdraws it, as if she is trying to grab at a memory flitting between us. 'I don't know what sort of story you're searching for in me, but I can assure you that – whatever you find – it will not have a happy ending.'

'I know that, Miss Stourbridge. It's just that I think you're sad about something, something that happened a long time ago, and I hoped that if I knew why, I could – I don't know – help you somehow.'

From the panelled room, the clock strikes eight, its chime drilling into my skull. I check my watch automatically, knowing before I do that it will be wrong.

'Shall I adjust the clock?' I say, needing suddenly to move, to breathe.

'Do what you want,' she says. 'The bugger always thinks it's eight, every damn hour. Has done ever since the blast.'

A tingle reaches for my wrists and my chin, pulling my gaze to her like a puppeteer. 'The blast?'

Miss Stourbridge lets out a sigh that seems to come from deep within her. 'Sit down,' she says, resignation in her voice, pointing to a chair.

I pull it out and sit down obediently. I haven't sat this close to her before. I can smell a muskiness, a strange vitality that only runs through ancient things.

'The blast,' she says, and the two words feel familiar, though I'm sure I've never heard them before. 'You want to know about me?' she says with a sigh that ruffles the water in her wine glass. 'Then we shall start with the blast.'

I wait, not sure I believe she's going to tell me anything of worth.

She takes a sip of water. Her hand is shaking so much that it quakes as it reaches her lips.

'The island was requisitioned by the military at the start of World War Two. Most people were told to leave then, but my family were allowed to stay because it was our island, and besides, we had been making parachute silk for the military. They needed us. But in July 1955, nearly ten years after the war, they told us we must go, too. No explanation. Everyone must go.'

She lifts her trembling hand and touches my cheek. I want to pull away, my nostrils flaring at the reek of her, but I close my eyes and force myself to listen.

'I stayed,' she says, 'and I saw what they did.'

My heart jumps at her words. I open my eyes. 'You stayed?'

Her finger has come to a stop on my cheek, high up on the cheekbone near my eye.

'I stayed,' she whispers. 'And I *felt* what they did.'

I can feel her breath on my skin like a solid thing, thick and curded. 'You mean …?'

She nods, and turns to look past me, through the door to the panelled room, and far out to sea. 'The blast,' she says again.

'A … an explosion?'

She pulls her eyes reluctantly from the window. 'On the military site,' she says, 'they were testing bombs. Nuclear bombs.'

'But they can't—'

'There's no proof they were nuclear, I know. Except that there is.'

'The island,' I say, realisation dawning.

'Mutation,' she adds, nodding, pleased I've made the connection. 'These changes we're seeing, Tartelin, they're not down to chance or evolution. They're man-made aberrations.'

'And you … you actually felt it?' I try to keep the doubt out of my voice.

She nods again. 'There are … no words to describe it. But afterwards I became ill. Very ill. Feverish and hallucinatory. If I'm being truthful, I thought I might die.'

'And you're back here now, studying the island so that you can — what — alert the authorities? Write some kind of report?'

Miss Stourbridge shakes her head slowly. 'No. I'm not powerful enough to do anything about what happened. I wasn't meant to be here. It is better that no one other than us knows.'

'Then why?'

'This is a personal crusade. I need to understand what happened here.'

We sit, as the light fades all around us.

'What will it take,' I ask, 'for you to form a conclusion?'

'I'm not sure. I'm really not sure. I don't know if I ever will, to be honest, but I have to try. You see that, don't you?' She is looking at me almost pleadingly.

'I do,' I say honestly.

I think about what she's told me, and I try to put myself in her place. I don't know if I really believe she was here, or that, if she was, that whatever she witnessed was as terrible as she says, and I'm not certain even now that she has told me everything, but at last I'm beginning to understand the reasons behind what she's doing here.

'Did you know,' she says, 'butterflies' wings are made of scales?' She looks closely at my cheekbone. 'Flattened hairs, overlapping just like this. Like the scales of a fish.'

'My mother used to say we came from the sea.'

'We all come from somewhere. But she was wrong. With these butterfly scales you are more likely to have fallen from the sky. Descended from archaeopteryx instead of apes.'

'You don't agree with Darwin?'

'Oh, I agree all right, but we'll never stop evolving. Who knows where we will go next?'

She traces the shape of the mark on my cheek, stroking the skin so that it brushes the wrong way, like a wave of sequins. I've always had this, strangers touching my face without asking. I think of the gold pincers lying on her desk, the sharp scalpel glinting in the last of the day's sun, and I have a feeling she wants to dissect me, to pull me apart and see what I am made of.

I stand abruptly, unable to take the tension between us, and I go into the panelled room. I can hear her following me, the chair creaking over the floorboards, and for one angry moment I want to tell her to leave me alone, to give me the space to breathe. I stand at the window, staring out at the dark night.

'Why are you so interested in the photograph album?' she says behind me.

I stay looking out of the window. It's so dark now that all I can see is a glimmer of my reflection. And then I remember the oyster shell in my pocket, and, before I have time to think, I pull it out.

Miss Stourbridge is by the chaise. I go over to her and sit down, placing the shell in her hands, my eyes catching a glimmer of the fierce-looking animal as her long-fingered hands cover it.

'What's this? Light the rest of the lamps, child.'

I go round the room, and the lamps hiss into brightness. One or two of the last escaped butterflies take off in fright, dancing near the ceiling.

'An oyster shell? Where did you find it?' she says, pushing her glasses up her nose and bending to inspect it. 'Not here, in the house?'

'No, not in the house.'

As the image flashes in the gas light, her face drains of all colour, and the shell clatters to the floor.

My stomach lurches. What have I done?

'Are you all right, Miss Stourbridge?' I sink down by her chair and rub her back. She is bent over, wizened and pale. 'Miss Stourbridge?'

But she is lost in some other world, her hand to her mouth. This is an odd reaction. I had thought she might realise that Nan had made it, but I certainly never meant to upset her. I keep rubbing her back in smooth circles, waiting for her to come out of her reverie.

'Where?' she stutters out, 'where?' And then she appears to compose herself. She reaches out her pale, ghostly fingers. 'May I have another look?' she says. 'I'll be careful this time.'

I pick it up from the floor and tip it into her waiting palms, watching as she bends and studies it again. Tears prick at the wrinkles beneath her eyes, flowing over the soft folds of skin and down onto her cheeks. I look away, embarrassed.

'Where did you get it?' she asks abruptly, the childlike voice gone.

'She gave it to me when I first arrived,' I say.

Her head snaps up. '*She?*'

'Nan.' Even before I say her name, Miss Stourbridge appears to crumple in her chair, as if all the breath has been knocked out of her.

'Good God,' she says. 'She came back.' To me she says, 'Was she well? Was she happy?'

It's the same question Nan asked me of Miss Stourbridge when I first met her. I smile at their symmetry. 'I think so, yes.'

Something seems to pull together inside Miss Stourbridge, and a smile flits across her face, before it is gone. She straightens her back and studies the shell again, a look of wonder on her face. 'Tell me,' she says, 'have you seen her again since?'

'I saw her this morning. I think she's living in the old building on the herring girls' beach.'

'Well, if you see her again, tell her ... no, *ask* her, if she would pay me a visit.' She looks at the shell in her hand. 'May I keep it, for a while?' she says, raising it, her wet eyes transfixed by the creature on its surface.

'Of course.'

She tucks it away in the pocket of the sailor's smock she is wearing, signalling that the conversation, for now, is over.

I clear my throat. 'I'm going out this evening,' I say, the words coming out before I can change my mind.

This catches Miss Stourbridge's attention. 'Out? Where?'

'To the sea. If … if that's OK?'

Her eyes bore into me, the way they had bored into the oyster shell, and I catch a trickle of the emotion that she had reserved for the shell, seeping into me.

'Will you be all right without me? I'll run your bath first, of course.'

'I'll be fine, but yes, a bath would be nice. Don't forget that tomorrow is Sunday: there is no hurry to go out early. We all need a morning off now and again.' She smiles at me, as if she knows more about what I will get up to tonight than I do.

'Take me to the window,' she orders, and I push her chair around the desk. She leans towards her telescope, removing the lens cap with a shaking hand. As her face aligns with the eyepiece, she goes still.

I go into the bathroom, and turn on the taps, and then I return to the dining room to clear away the remains of our meal. As I pass the piano, I see that the lid is open. I run my fingers over the keys, and then, with a quick glance at my employer, I slip onto the piano stool.

I begin to play quietly, conjuring the music Miss Stourbridge taught me, surprised by how easy it is to recall each note. I play it through once and, as I come to the end, I let my hands rest there, listening to the last silvery sounds as they evaporate away into the walls.

'Don't stop.' Miss Stourbridge has turned from her telescope. 'Please?'

I lift my hands and play the piece again, getting used to the rhythm, the different pressure needed for different notes. This time, when I reach the end, Miss Stourbridge's eyes are shining.

I close the lid and push the stool back into place, going into the bathroom to wait for the bath to fill. As I stand at the window, my eyes take in the royal blue of the darkling sky. The music I played is still in my head, and I hum it quietly, trying to make out the sea beyond the cliff, wondering what Miss Stourbridge is looking for out there. To my left, out of sight at the north of the island, the military base stands. Could she be right? Was there a nuclear explosion here? It's a fanciful idea, but then I think of all the unusual things on the island: the animals and birds, the giant, swollen pearls and gnarled, stunted trees. All of these are just as fanciful, yet they are real.

I look down to the beach far below, the pale sand lit by the moon-light. What does Jacob want with me down there, alone at night? And can I give it to him? Am I ready?

Chapter Eighteen

Marianne

February 1928

Whilst the silkworm cocoons incubated in the warmth of the annexe, outside, the mild weather they had encountered gave way to the crackling ice of a stark island winter. The sea grew so cold that it froze Marianne's joints when she dipped her hands into its flurrying waters. She liked the way the pain of the cold water took away the thoughts in her head. So many things were clouding her mind now: all the unfinished projects on the island, the dwindling herring stocks, and the confusion over the pearls. She had never seen the island in such muddied disarray, and it disturbed her.

Entering the women's sitting room after breakfast on a glitteringly cold morning, Papa looked out of the window, rocking on his heels, his hands in his waistcoat pockets, and said, 'Doesn't the sea look pearlescent today, ladies?'

Marianne glanced out of the window. The sea did indeed have a strange, luminous quality to it. When she looked back, Papa had already gone, and Nan was halfway across the room, hurrying along in his wake.

Marianne slumped down on the chaise, watching as her mother

picked up her latest piece of embroidery and settled into the wicker chair by the fire.

'Have you noticed, Mama, how Papa is always making Nan work?' Marianne said, searching her face for a reaction. 'She came here to help with the silkworms, but he has her helping with other projects at every opportunity: he never gives her a moment's peace. She's my friend, yet I never get to see her,' Marianne complained. 'It's just not fair.'

Mama looked up from her embroidery just as the cruel east wind howled down the chimney, damping the flames and making her skirt rustle.

'Nan was brought here to work first and foremost, Marianne, you know that. Why, only a few weeks ago, you were referring to her as "the help". You can't have it both ways.'

'Oh, why do you always side with him?' Angrily, Marianne got up from the chaise, and was about to sweep indignantly from the room, when Mama's hand sprung towards her, grabbing at her arm.

'He is my husband,' she said, and her face was full of a beautiful anguish. 'That is how our lives here work, Marianne. Whatever your father is doing to my beloved island, I am bound by marriage to support him, just as one day you will be bound to your husband.' Her eyes were glittering with a furious sadness, and then suddenly they cleared, opening wide in surprise. 'Wherever did you get that?' she said, pointing at Marianne's lapel, where the ruby butterfly was pinned as if it had just settled moments before.

'Papa gave it to me in lieu of a real one when we went out butterfly hunting,' she said.

Her mother reached out a pale finger, tracing the pearls on the butterfly's wings, her brow creased. 'However could he afford …?' she said, the sentence drifting away before she finished.

'Do you think they are Dohhalund pearls, Mama? Papa says they are but I have yet to see …'

But her mother wasn't listening. She was fumbling with the pin, and then the butterfly brooch was sliding away from Marianne's lapel.

'Mama!'

'I need to borrow it, but you will have it back, I promise.'

In frustration, Marianne mouthed at her mother for a moment, and then, unable to think of something suitably scathing, she stamped her foot in anger and strode from the room.

In her bedroom, she slammed her door and swore under her breath like a common herring girl. Everyone was behaving so oddly in this house.

She threw herself on the bed, feeling the sting of tears pinch at her eyes. The little wooden mouse on her bedside table caught her eye, and she went to it, picking it up and cupping it in her palm as she used to when she was a child. It felt awkward, as if the mouse knew she was only pretending to play.

'What should I do, Mouse?' she said, but it remained silent, and she threw it with frustration onto the bed and went to the window instead, hoping the sea would calm her.

When she was little, at times like this she would go to her father, and he would welcome her on his lap, stroking her hair from her forehead and soothing her with kind words. But Papa had not shown that sort of interest in her for years. As she had grown older, he had withdrawn from her, leaving her bewildered. What had she done to make him so distant?

But now she understood. It was simple: she had grown up, that was all. He had wanted a sweet little girl, not a stubborn young woman who would need to be married off or else become yet another drain on the family finances.

Marriage. Was that what all this was about? And what had her mother meant, when she said that she was bound by marriage to support her father? Did she not love him? Did she not support his plans for their island? Marianne pressed her lips together, hardly seeing the sea in front of her. She wished that she could teach her parents a lesson; something that might remind them both that she was still here, still in need of them. Papa especially needed to be shown that the whole world didn't revolve around him. She racked her brain, trying to think of something that would disrupt his perfectly oiled working life; something that would make him forget about his hundred-and-one business ideas, turning his gaze inward instead, to the family he was supposed to love.

The next morning, with Papa safely overseeing the preparation of a new mulberry plantation near the pavilion, Marianne found Nan out in the garden, where she was harvesting leaves from the older mulberry trees.

In whispered breaths, she imparted the plan she had come up with.

'But Marianne,' Nan glanced at the trees, 'I have so many things I still need to do today. Your father wants me to write some letters, and then—'

'Oh! Are you his secretary now, on top of all your other duties?'

Nan took a mulberry leaf in her hands. Her fingers looked so white against the dark green leaves. 'But isn't it a bit ... childish?' she said.

'We *are* children, Nan. I'm fifteen, and you're even younger. Come along, I've seen the way Papa treats you. Don't you want some respite? Some time to spend at leisure?'

Nan's eyes glittered at the thought, and her bright smile appeared at the corners of her mouth. 'Well, all right, but we'd better be quick: he's due back in an hour for another meeting.'

They stole into Papa's study, carrying between them a heavy herring barrel, handkerchiefs wrapped over their noses to dampen the smell. Together, they scraped out the bottom of the tub, trying to quieten their nervous giggles, their fingers slipping against the tiny jellied bodies of discarded shrimps. Marianne cut a hole along the hem of the curtain, and they pushed the shrimps in, wiping the stray eggs onto their handkerchiefs.

As they worked, a sort of manic energy began to overtake them. To Marianne, it suddenly didn't seem so funny any more: it wasn't just a practical joke. Behind the trick, there was real intention to do harm. Neither girl spoke as she scraped the last of the shrimps from the barrel, stuffing them neatly into the curtain's hem, neither wanting to vocalise their reasons for doing it.

When they were done, Marianne stood and looked around her. She was rarely allowed in Papa's study, not since she had been a little girl and Papa had welcomed her in here, sitting her on his lap and introducing her to the mysteries of his working life. It was a grand room, full of leather-bound books and strange beach finds displayed artfully on the shelves. Taking in the sumptuous luxury of a room that had been denied her for so many years, she felt unexpectedly melancholy. She wished suddenly to be that little girl again, young and innocent, a girl whose father cared for her, and loved her above all else.

She took a needle and thread from her pocket and passed it to Nan, watching while she closed the cuts up with an expert hand.

The study began to smell. It was a fishy odour, and at first Papa just opened a window and left his boots at the back door in case he had stepped in something. But after another day, the rank stench of ammonia began to spread down the hall. Even Mama, who never went in his study, commented on the smell, sending Peggy in to give the room a thorough clean and airing. Papa began turning out the curios on the shelves in case a piece of leathery sealskin had begun to go off. He peered into the cracks between the furniture, and even levered up the floorboards to check for a dead mouse. Nan and Marianne kept poker faces, watching from afar.

It gave Marianne immense satisfaction to see how much damage they had caused, however childish it was, and the reprieve meant Nan was finally free to spend time in other pursuits.

Marianne stood in the doorway of the annexe, watching as Nan examined the soft balls of silk. It was the first time she had had time to visit the silkworms for weeks.

'How long since they began weaving their cocoons?' she asked Marianne, holding a particularly large cocoon up to the light.

'Oh, not long.' Marianne's voice was muffled as she tried to tie a tea towel over her nose. The smell from Papa's study was strong down here, permeating the air. Nan seemed oblivious to it.

'Do you think they'll yield enough silk?' Marianne asked her.

'Everything so far points to it being extremely good. But we need to make sure we harvest them as soon as they've completed spinning their cocoons, and then we can move onto the next stage.'

The smell from the decaying shrimps continued to intensify, until it was so strong that it began to invade the whole house. Marianne found it hard to sleep, the acrid odour permeating her pillow as she tossed and turned in bed. The staff were suspended from their usual duties, and instructed to give the house a thorough spring clean instead. Marianne shrank closer to the fire as windows were opened wide to air the rooms, but still the smell persisted.

The next time Papa was out all day at meetings, she and Nan tiptoed into his study again and cut away the hem of the curtains. Marianne tried not to gag, but Nan was made of stronger stuff, calmly sewing them up as quickly as she could, before standing back to assess her work.

The next day, the smell was almost gone. At breakfast, Papa placed his knife and fork together.

'Nan,' he said, 'we have lost much-needed working time. Meet me in the study after breakfast. I need your excellent writing skills.'

Marianne's heart sank. She wanted to shout at him, What about my writing skills? But her voice deserted her. Nausea roiled in her stomach as she watched Papa's tongue searching out the remains of a winkle caught in his teeth, reminding her of a mollusc withdrawing into its shell. It had all been for nothing. Papa hadn't learnt a thing, and now he was taking Nan away from her again.

'Please may I be excused?' she said, getting up abruptly without waiting for an answer and dropping her napkin on the table. 'I need to check on the cocoons.'

Her father called after her, 'Of course, of course, *mijn lief*. It's good to see you being so attentive.'

Once out of the dining room, Marianne went, not to the annexe, but to her bedroom. She flung herself down on the bed and screamed into her pillow. If Papa was intent on stealing Nan away from her, then the silkworms could wait. She swept the little wooden mouse from her bedside table and clutched it tightly until her fingers hurt.

What kind of pointless, childish plan had it been? A prank that had hardly stopped Papa in his tracks at all. She rolled over and lay, looking at the loose flap of wallpaper, the hole just visible underneath. It occurred to her that perhaps the problem might not be her father's study after all, but Nan herself. If Nan weren't here, then perhaps Papa might turn to Marianne for help instead.

She rubbed at her face, willing the tears to come, but her eyes were as dry as a dead fish's, and she curled up in a ball instead and stared at the seaweed patterns on the walls.

The next evening, a great storm blew up over the mainland. Marianne was sitting at her dressing table, watching it crackle over East Anglia, creeping ever closer to Dohhalund. There was a tap on the door, and she padded barefoot across her bedroom, unlatching it. Nan was on the other side, her arms wrapped tightly around herself, her dark hair hanging loose down her back. Marianne opened the door wide, stepping back to let her in, and Nan tiptoed past her, her teeth chattering. She was wearing a thin cotton nightdress, and there were goose pimples on her bare arms. Lightning careered across the sky, splintering around the moon and illuminating the clouds for a dizzying moment. The crash of thunder that followed made Nan jump.

'It's quite normal,' Marianne said, getting into bed and drawing her knees up. 'I do hope the Dogger boats got home safely. Storms around here work up so quickly. Come.' She lifted the edge of the quilt, and Nan crept in next to her.

Papa had kept Nan busy since they had removed the shrimps from his study, and Marianne hadn't seen her for more than a passing greeting in the corridor, or a rushed dinner. She looked exhausted, Marianne thought, her small face pinched and pale.

'I'm sorry our practical joke didn't work quite as well as we'd hoped,' Marianne whispered.

Another boom of thunder crashed around them, and she felt Nan stiffen next to her.

'We'll be all right in here, won't we?' Nan said, shooting a look out of the window.

'Of course. This house is as strong as an ox.' She lay back on her pillow, feeling Nan uncurl next to her. She was still shivering. Marianne rubbed her arm. 'Try to get some sleep,' she said kindly.

In the morning, Marianne woke to a bright, cold light pouring in through the window. She had left the curtains open so that they could see the storm, and she squinted in the brightness that flooded in. Nan was already up, sitting at the window, looking out over the island.

They dressed quickly. In the sitting room, Mama was standing at the picture window. She turned as they came in. Her hand was at her necklace, her fingers tangled in the pearls.

'Two of the Doggers didn't come in last night,' she said. 'Papa has organised a search.'

'Do you think they've gone down?' Marianne said, her mind full of the drifting hulls of shipwrecks. Nan sank down on the chaise, her hand to her mouth in horror.

'We're not privy to the sea's thoughts,' Mama said distractedly, turning back to the window.

'But surely Papa could—'

'Your father cannot fix everything, Marianne.' Mama's voice was sharp, stinging at her as if she had flung a handful of shingle. 'The sea is made up of unspeakable sadness,' she added quietly. The words were an island tradition, recited in times of great need.

Marianne joined her mother at the window, her eyes scanning the water. 'Where can they be?' she said.

'The sea will give up its secrets when it wishes.' Mama placed a hand on Marianne's shoulder.

The girls forwent breakfast, going straight down to the beach instead. There was no wind, the storm had blown itself out. The light was strong and mushroom-coloured. Over to the east, they could just hear the hush of the sea. Everything was so still.

'Isn't it peculiar?' Marianne said to Nan as they walked through the garden. The mulberry trees were silent, their usually rustling leaves motionless.

The steps that had been carved into the cliff for as long as Marianne could remember had been hit by the storm and begun to crumble away, so they took the longer route via the salt pans instead.

As they reached the east beach, they saw the mermaids had congregated down by the sea. They were huddled in a group, a patchwork of linen and wool, their white caps bobbing as they talked among themselves. Nan went to them immediately, and was soon lost amongst the knot.

Marianne stood at the top of the dunes, straining her eyes to look for the missing vessels. It was not common to lose a boat, but it did happen. In '21 one of the Doggers had been caught in a storm, and the whole crew washed up along the southern stretch of the beach.

She walked down the dunes towards the water, watching the crowd of mermaids on the shore, pointing at the sea, gossiping together. It was strange to see them away from their own patch of beach, but as Marianne neared the tideline, she understood why they were there. The water was a mass of metallic flashes, sifting gently as the waves lapped at the shore.

One of the mermaids waded into the sea, her skirts darkening in the water. She pulled up a fistful of fish. They lay in her wool-gloved palm, completely still, their flat eyes staring.

'They're saying it was the storm,' Nan said when she returned. 'The lightning hit the sea.'

Marianne put a hand to her mouth in shock. Out of the corner of her eye she saw her father appear over the brow of the dunes. He came to a stop, staring out across the water, his eyes fixed on the herring that floated on its surface like a thick scum.

'Poor Papa,' Marianne whispered.

As the tide came in and receded, depositing the herring on the shore, everyone abandoned their usual jobs to help clear the beach of the fish that would soon rot.

'At least the mermaids will be able to store plenty of salted herring for themselves this year,' Marianne said as she hefted a pile of dead fish into the quarter crans lined up on the beach. She thought of the herring woman she had sat with that day on the beach, her legs quivering under the blanket. She was glad she wouldn't go hungry again this winter.

'They won't touch it,' Nan said, casting a glance at the women working further along the beach. 'When something like this happens, they believe it's a curse or a blight; that it's happened for a reason. The fish are tainted.'

Marianne wondered how Nan, who had only been here a matter of months, could know all this, and yet she, who had lived here all her life, did not. 'What a strange superstition. What will happen to all of it, then?'

'They'll burn it,' Nan said simply.

They watched the women hefting the large baskets full of fish across the beach. Unlike Nan and Marianne, who were wrapped up in thick knitted sweaters, hats and scarves, cosseted against the winter weather, the herring girls had on their usual cotton dresses and shawls. Marianne's eyes watered from the cold as she continued to gather up the slippery haul.

Later in the morning, there was a wave of relief as the *Schoonheid* returned to port, damaged, but with a full crew. Papa's other boat was still missing.

At the end of a long day, they walked back to Dogger Bank, weary from their efforts, as spirals of fish-scented smoke began to rise up from countless bonfires across the island.

They closed the kitchen door against the smell, the sting of the sea's spray still ruddying their cheeks. Marianne sighed with pleasure at the welcoming warmth of the Aga.

'I don't think I've ever worked so hard in all my life,' she said.

As they were pulling off gumboots, a bloodcurdling scream came from the annexe, and Peggy burst through the door towards them, a bundle of damp sheets trailing after her.

Nan ran to the annexe door and looked inside. Marianne followed cautiously, hopping behind, one boot half unlaced. They were met by a flurry of rustling wings on the annexe floor.

'We forgot to check on the cocoons,' Nan said, her face pale. Hundreds of silk moths seethed across the floor. She stepped down carefully, beckoning for Marianne to follow.

It was like entering a room full of recently fallen snow. And, just as with snow, a chill settled over Marianne as she stepped down into it. A moth crawled over her bare foot, making her start. Behind them in the kitchen, Peggy was slumped in a chair, white-faced and ashen, while Cook gave her a shot of jenever for her nerves.

Nan picked up one of the silk moths. It circled her palm, its wings vibrating. 'The storm ... the herring, I completely forgot to check on them. And it's so warm in here,' she said. 'They've incubated too quickly.'

'It doesn't matter,' Marianne said, surveying the carpet of moths and the discarded cocoons. 'No one need know; we have the silk now.'

'You don't understand.' Nan's anxious face looked almost blue in the shadowed light of the annexe. Marianne put a hand on her arm to steady her, fearing she might faint. 'When they hatch, they break the thread,' Nan said. 'The silk is ruined, look.' She lifted one of the empty cocoons from a shelf, and Marianne saw that there was a hole at one end. Nan began unspooling the cocoon, but the silk came off in fragmented skeins, floating down onto the seething mass of moths below.

'Mr Stourbridge will hang me,' she said, sinking down amid the moths.

Marianne knelt down next to her, trying to ignore the flutter of moths as they crawled over her knees. 'Nan, it's all right, really. Papa won't be angry. It's no one's fault, after all.'

Nan looked up at her, her eyes wide and staring. 'But he has nothing now, Marianne. Nothing. The herring had already started to dwindle, but with the stocks gone completely, the silk was all he had.'

A soft finger of fear trickled down Marianne's spine. 'But ... but the silk is just a hobby,' she said. 'It was a present for my birthday. Papa won't mind if we get it wrong.' A moth climbed over her toes, its wings vibrating, making her shudder. 'Why aren't they flying?' she said suddenly, looking around at the myriad moths crawling near their feet.

'They can't fly,' Nan said distractedly, getting to her feet and stepping carefully across the room. 'We've bred them over thousands of years to weave silk, not to survive. They will mate, lay their eggs and then they'll die. They don't even have a proper mouth to eat with.'

Marianne picked up a moth and inspected it in her hand. Its grey-white wings were flecked with fine lines of gold, like the marble around the sitting-room fireplace. She looked at the insects on the ground, feeling a pang of regret that their life was so near its end. The moths were moving as one, like flotsam washed up on the seashore. Some were already connected, performing the mating ritual that they had been bred to do.

Nan was whispering to herself, standing in the middle of the sea of white, her eyes flitting from the moths to the cocoons. 'What have I done?' she said. 'What have I done?'

Marianne went to her, taking hold of her arms and looking into her eyes. 'Really, Nan, it's not our place to worry about these things. Papa will have got it all under control. When I get upset or worried, I try and think of something nice to take my mind off it.' She wracked her brain to find something that would cheer Nan up. 'The pearls,' she said at last, smiling. 'Turn your mind to those instead. After all, Papa says the Dohhalund pearls are unrivalled.'

Nan jumped away from her, pushing awkwardly through the moths. 'We must collect the eggs,' she said distractedly. 'At least we can salvage the next generation. Help me, Marianne.' She picked up an abandoned cotton sheet and nestled it in a wicker basket, then she began to gather up all the mating pairs, placing them gently on the cotton. 'They will begin to lay as soon as the mating is done. Please, Marianne, help me.'

Squeamishly Marianne picked up a pair of moths attached to each other by their back ends. She tried not to look at the way they were connected: tried not to think of how people somehow connected in the same way.

As they placed the mating moths together, Nan looked up at her warily. 'They're not what you think,' she whispered, shooting a glance at the door. 'The pearls, I mean.'

The finger of fear on Marianne's spine grew nails, scraping icily down her back. 'What do you mean?'

Nan looked down at the floor. A lone moth crawled over her toe. 'We never found ... I mean to say, we ...'

Marianne stared at her; the enormity of what she was saying rushed over her like a cold, salted wave. 'Nan, are you saying there were never any pearls?' she said.

Nan nodded once, her eyes downcast.

'But ...' Without the pearls, they had no businesses to fall back on, no money. Marianne thought of the half-finished pavilion, the plans for a railway and a pier, the wages for joskins and fishermen, herring girls and maids, and she began to feel sick. 'But that's impossible,' she said.

'He ... he will be in a lot of trouble if anyone finds out what he's done,' Nan said. She was pacing now, her feet wading through the moths.

'Finds out about what? What has he done?'

'It's all my fault. I gave him the idea when I told him about the pearls at Gironde.'

'The idea for what? Nan, talk to me!'

But Nan's lips were trembling. Shaking her head, she ran out of the room, and Marianne was left with the sea of moths crawling all around her, the vibration of their wings so loud that it blocked out all thoughts but one: if Papa really was bankrupt, what would become of them all?

Chapter Nineteen

Tartelin

Summer 2018

I have never stood on a beach in the dark before. The sand feels different beneath my feet, cold and crisp. The world around me is violet, the sky a melange of cloud and clear, the sea a hushed lullaby of little waves, lapping at the shore.

Jacob is nowhere to be seen, and I shiver, even though I'm warm. The tide is out, further out than I've ever seen it, and I pad down to the water, my feet sinking into the wet sand. I put my hand in my pocket and bring out the pearl that I found in the oyster beds. I hold it high so that it covers the moon, and for a moment I am transfixed with the idea of throwing it into the water, returning it to where it came from.

I feel my mother standing next to me, her feet planted in the wet sand too. I want to turn to her, to show her this pearl, and say, look, I have found you, but I daren't because she isn't really there. We stand next to each other and stare out to sea, lost in our thoughts.

Something breaks the surface, far away: the smooth, black head of a seal. For an instant, the sea around it cascades with pinpricks of light, and then both the seal and the light are gone. I turn to my mother, to share in the small miracle, but she too is gone, and I am alone.

There is the crunch of sand on pebbles in the distance, and Jacob is beside me, so suddenly it is as if he has emerged from the night like a spirit. He looks different in the moonlight, his brown hair bleached to pale, his eyes so faded they are an echo of the violet world around us.

'My mum would have loved this place,' I say, looking out to sea.

'Is she ...?'

'She died, two months ago.'

'I'm so sorry.'

I shrug. 'It's not your fault. It's no one's fault, really. She had cancer. It was good, in the end, that she died. She stopped suffering.' I put my hand in my back pocket and pull my phone out. 'I have a photo of her on here, but my phone's run out of battery, and as you know, there's no electricity on the island. Sometimes I miss seeing her face so much it hurts.' I run my thumb over the screen, as if I can caress the photo within, even if I can't see it.

'I've got a charger,' Jacob says. 'It's solar powered. I can charge the phone if you'd like?' He's standing a little way away from me, tentative, unsure.

'Yes,' I say, 'I'd like that very much.' I give the phone to him, holding on for a second too long.

He places the phone on the pebbles along with his jumper, and straightens up. 'I wanted to show you something,' he says. I notice his voice is softer at night.

'Show me what?' I whisper.

In answer, he opens his mouth to speak, but for the first time, words fail him. Instead, he takes my hand and pulls me towards the sea. The water swells at our ankles, and he bends down, rolling up his jeans.

'I can't,' I say, pulling my hand away when I realise what he means for us to do.

'It's not dangerous,' he whispers back.

'It's not that.' But I can't explain what it is. It is the touch of his hand in the middle of all this open space, the feel of the water as it closes over my ankles. It is my clothes: the tightness of denim on my legs, the heavy wool of my jumper. I imagine wading in, my clothes sucking and pulling at the sea, weighing me down. I have been heavy with sadness for so long, I want to feel light now. I want this to happen on my terms.

'Wait a moment,' I say, turning back to the shore. Where the pebbles begin, I stand for a second, mustering the courage, and then I unzip my jeans and pull them off, feeling them peel away from my skin where they're soaked at the bottom.

Jacob is still standing in the shallows, looking down at the ground, a blue blush spreading up his neck. I can feel a blush starting on my own neck too, but I carry on, resolute.

'Come on,' I say, peeling away my jumper and T-shirt and indicating that he should do the same.

He deliberates for a moment, glimpsing my bra and quickly turning away, and then he seems to make up his mind, stepping out of the water and unbuttoning and pulling at his clothes in a flurry until we stand facing each other on the stones, blushing in our underwear, our clothes heaped in a pile on the shore like skin that has been sloughed.

The breeze coming off the sea is warm, and it licks pleasantly at my skin. *On my terms*, I think, savouring the feeling. I offer Jacob my hand, and together we walk into the sea.

We move slowly, lifting our hands clear of the water, watching the dark liquid move viscously around our thighs, then our hips, then our waists. As we wade forward, sound changes, the sea steadily creeping up our bodies. I am aware of the warmth of Jacob's hand in mine, the cold spreading over my skin. I look up and stop. Ahead of us there is a large ring rippling in the water. It's like the circles I saw from the bathroom, but this one is lit with a silvered scattering of light, like a nocturnal halo. I scan the sea. Further out I can make out more rings, each one lit with a bluish-white light.

'Can you see them?' I whisper.

'Of course, that's where we're going, come on.'

He tugs at my hand again and we begin to move faster, and the water around us starts to change. It is like wading through electrical sparks, like water made of diamonds, as if a shoal of crystal fish are swarming round us, fleeing away at our touch.

'What is it?' I ask, swirling my hand through the water, mesmerised.

'Phosphorescence.'

The word is alien to me, but it reminds me of another word. Luminescence. Lumen essence. Essence of light. I wonder for a moment if the bright dots in the water are a reflection of the light from the moon, but no, they are too strong for that. They are flickering on and off, appearing and disappearing under the water, and I think, *phosphorous*.

'It's beautiful,' I say, turning to Jacob, and he is looking at me. He's not looking at my cheek like other people, but instead, it's as if he can see deep inside me. The sea water licks against my stomach, making it twitch, and I remember the words he spoke at the military base:

When I focus on something, it feels like everything else is blotted out.

'I ... I can't swim,' I stutter, feeling foolish. I've always lived in land-locked counties with a mother who loved the sea but feared swimming pools for the chlorine and clientele.

'Don't worry,' he says. 'Here, do what I do.'

Slowly, he sinks down until the water lulls over his shoulders. He puts his hands on my shoulders, his thumbs touching the base of my neck, and pushes gently down. I feel myself dipping into the water, my chin touching salt. The phosphorescence has gone now, and the black sea surrounds my body, encasing me completely as if I am disappearing within myself.

'Do you trust me?' Jacob whispers. He's looking at me in that same, penetrating way, looking into my eyes for the first time, as if he sees something inside me that even I'm not aware of.

I nod.

Gently, he places his hand on the back of my head. 'Lean back,' he says.

The shock of the cold water on the back of my skull almost tips me over, but I relax against his hand, trusting him, and slowly my feet begin to leave the sea floor.

My whole world becomes the basin of sky above me. The inky clouds have moved on and the stars stretch away into the future, the past. My ears fill with sea water and all I can hear is the singing rush of water over shells, and a high, cold call from somewhere deep. I think of the Silver Pit, the great underwater chasm I went over to reach this mysterious isle, and I wonder if this song comes from there.

Water pools in my clavicles, encircling my neck, eating me up. A drop leaks into my mouth, and suddenly I am struggling to plant my feet on the shifting ground. I twist and stand up, clawing at the sea, beads of salt water diffracting off me in torrents as I gasp for air.

'It's OK,' Jacob says. His voice is calm, and I realise he still has his hand on the back of my neck.

I take a breath and stand, dripping, my feet firmly on the ground. The water is shallow here, it laps at my thighs where moments before it had reached my waist.

'I'm sorry, I …'

'It's OK. The sea can be frightening.'

'Everything new is frightening,' I say. His hand is still on my neck. I find I don't want him to let go, as if he's the one thing anchoring me here in this soft, black world.

'The tide is still going out?' I say.

'Yes, it's nearly turning. Are you warm enough?'

I realise I'm trembling. 'I'm fine,' I say. I am not cold at all.

He takes a tendril of my hair between his fingers. It is dark with water next to his white hand, like the antithesis to light. My face must look moon-pale against it. We are close now, barely millimetres from each other.

'Touch my cheek,' I whisper.

Jacob's eyebrows draw together. I take his hand and guide it to the place on my skin. Ever so gently, he trails the tip of his finger over the soft scales, and I hold my breath. This touch feels different to the others. I feel my pupils grow large, the blood rushing through my skin, my body prickling with desire, and I see it in his eyes, too.

A rush of phosphorescence swirls past us, and we both look down. When we look up again, the moment is gone.

'Now, we wait,' Jacob says, turning to the horizon.

'Wait for what?' I ask, but he is quiet.

Here and there the water lights up as shoals of fish flash by. Eventually, I see what he is looking at. The rings in the distance are becoming solid. They are no longer ruffles of disturbed water, but actual circles rearing from the sea.

'It's rare that the tide's low enough to see them completely,' he whispers.

'What are they?' I ask. They're appearing quickly now, forming before my eyes, their roughly hewn sides revealed in flashes as the waves sidle against them. I can make out bricks and chunks of curved flint glinting in the moonlight, circular walls like some sort of round tower. It is as if a lost city is pushing up from the water. I imagine a million towers far out to sea, stretching towards the sky, a million Rapunzels locked inside. I think of the chapel on the beach.

'Are they … church towers?'

'No, think of something that goes down, not up.'

'But they *are* going up.'

'That depends on your perspective,' Jacob says.

I am annoyed now, tired of his riddles. 'What *are* they, Jacob?'

'They're wells.'

'Wells?'

He nods. 'The island used to stretch out much further here.' He indicates the sea in front of us. 'As the land eroded, the structures of the wells remained. There's a freshwater spring beneath each of them. Sometimes, the sea here is hardly salty at all.'

I stare at the strange, magical pillars. It's still too deep to wade out to them. I can feel the pull of the current on my legs as the tide begins to turn. We will not get closer tonight.

I turn to Jacob, trying to put into words how the magic of this place has touched me.

But there is salt water beading on his dark eyelashes, and his eyes have taken on the purple sheen of mussel shell, and his hand is twined again in my hair, and he is pulling me closer until our skin touches and I feel him, slick with salt water, against me.

His lips taste of salt, and I close my eyes, and it is dark beneath my eyelids and sparks of luminescence stir there, too, like fireflies or moths, drifting towards something warm, something safe.

There is a splash, a roar of sea nearby. I open my eyes, and pull away from Jacob. The sea has begun to close over the nearest tower, and inside the ring of brick and stone, I can make out the head of the seal again, watching us, its eyes just above the water, dark and wet like oil. I hear Jacob's intake of breath. The seal twists over and dives down, but not before the moonlight catches it, and something gleams at its neck. But it can't be. I turn to Jacob, and the expression on his face mirrors my own.

'Were those gills?' I say and, even as the words leave my mouth, I know it can't be true.

But Jacob nods. 'And I thought I saw ...' He shakes his head disbelievingly.

'What?'

'It had ... hands,' he says. He lifts his own hands up and examines them, as if he's never seen them before. 'It clasped the side of the well before it pushed off.' He rubs his face. 'What happened here?'

For a moment, I consider telling him everything that I have learnt, but I know that if I try and put it into words, it will sound inconceivable.

Instead, I look up at the sky, and for the briefest flicker of time, I think I see a spider web of silver strung between the stars, as if the creature of Nan's oyster shell has judged that I am finally wise enough to see, and has scratched an image into the universe, revealing itself to me in all its glory.

Chapter Twenty

Tartelin

Summer 2018

When I wake in the morning, I can sense it's later than usual. The light in the room is whole and full, yet not as bright as I am used to.

I didn't get to sleep for a long time after I said goodbye to Jacob at the door. I think of him now, and a swooping sensation tumbles in the pit of my stomach.

My memories of the strange night on the beach are blurred. Every time I blink, the creature on the oyster shell is etched behind my eyelids, fuzzy and out of focus like an after-image, as if it is lacking detail.

Was it only a seal we saw last night? What can you really see in moonlight, after all? There is a reason people generally see ghosts at night and not in the day. Their emotions are heightened, the world they know is strange, distorted. The improbability of the evening on the beach replays itself in my mind: the phosphorescence, the towering wells, the kiss in the midst of it all. Perhaps none of it happened. Perhaps I never left the house; I fell asleep early and dreamt every moment of it.

As I sit up, my hair peels away from the pillow, and I see I've left an imprint of salt on the cotton, a white ghost of myself indented there.

My hair feels crisp to the touch, hanging in shaggy ringlets where the seawater has dried into it, tangible proof of last night's starlit expedition.

Somewhere far away, I hear a noise: a thin, mewling cry. I get up and put my head round the door, listening. The corridor is long and thin, the lamps along it unlit. The only light here is the sunlight from my bedroom window. It filters out, reaching fingers of hazy light down the hallway.

There – I hear it again. Far down the corridor. It sounds like a new-born baby. Quickly, I tiptoe out of my room and begin walking the long stretch of corridor. I've never been this way before. There are lots of doors, all of them shut. It gets darker as I make my way along, the light from my bedroom left far behind.

I reach the end and strain my ears for the sound. I'm standing at the entrance to a dark room. The door is ajar and a faint smell of fish drifts through. Suspended from the doorway is a piece of old fishing twine, and knotted into it are several stones with holes at their centre. My mother had a stone like this. She called it a hag-stone. She used to hang it over my bed when I was small to stop my nightmares. I remember falling asleep to its gentle rhythmic sway. For a fleeting moment I wonder where it went, and then the cry comes again, and I step inside the room.

I'm momentarily confused by the ceiling above me, where a huge, oval, copper structure is suspended. Then I realise: this is the bathtub upstairs.

The room is only a little lighter than the corridor outside. There is a small, square window at one end, and as my eyes adjust, I can make out metal pipework covering much of the walls. On one side, shelves and shelves of bolts of material are stacked, in varying jewel colours and hues. Damson and sloe, chartreuse and vermilion.

Silk, I think, wanting to lift one down and unroll it, to feel the slippery sleekness of the fabric beneath my fingers. I start towards them, but as I do I brush against a tower of old wicker baskets piled up, and the musty smell of salted fish drifts up from them as if I've disturbed it after years of settlement. I stop and look around me, taking in the years of history in this room. It is some kind of storeroom. Stacked beneath the copper tub are some crates and, in the gloom, something white flickers, caught on the edge of one of them. I hasten forward and pluck it from the rough wood.

It's the body of a long-dead moth, its white wings so flea-bitten that they look like lace. I can just about make out faint golden lines crazing the wings, tiny horns rearing from a noble little face. I wonder if this was a silkworm that got away, if it found a quiet corner to weave its cocoon, only to hatch, forgotten in this dark, claustrophobic space.

I'm about to go when I hear the crying sound again, closer now. I freeze, feeling the hairs on my arms rise. It's a soft whispering sound, at times sharper and full of pain, and I fight the urge to turn and run back to the safety of my bedroom. The sound is coming from the far end of the room, and I peer through the gloom towards the small square window, clutching the moth in my hand, and let out a breath of relief: the window is open a crack, the wind catching in the gap, keening in sadness.

I can feel my pulse slowing. I turn to go.

As I make my way back towards my bedroom, my eyes used to the dark now, I notice a rather grand door halfway along the corridor, very different to all the others nearby. It feels out of place, with its solid oak panels and great silver hinges in the shape of oyster shells, as though it's been hidden down here. I reach out and twist the doorknob, half expecting it to be locked.

It opens on well-oiled hinges and I step inside.

It is a study. The light from a single window shines hazily through a gold silk blind, letting in a pale imitation of the morning sun. I run my hand over the leather-bound books on the shelves, my fingers bumping over their rigid spines. The opulence of the silver hinges on the door does not reflect the room within. There is no luxury here, although traces of it remain. No pictures, no sumptuous rugs or other signs of comfort. This space speaks of a clinical way of living; work and home combined, sparse and utilitarian. Across the room is a large chest with labelled drawers, and a metal filing cabinet stands in one corner with a rotary dial telephone perched on top. It's the first phone I've seen here, and I rush over to it and lift it, a joyous fizz of excitement coursing through me as I press it to my ear. But of course, there is no dial tone. As I replace the handset, I realise I don't have anyone to call anyway.

In one corner, a small gas stove and kettle sit on a planter, and on the far wall there is a calendar with an illustration of a stag beetle on it, the image sliced in two so that you can see its insides, the parts labelled. The calendar is open to July 1955.

I stop by the desk. It feels far older and more luxurious than anything else in the room. It's made of a deep mahogany, similar to Miss Stourbridge's desk upstairs, but larger and much more cluttered. There is a set of scales here, an old brass contraption, the metal dull from disuse. On one side is a flat brass plate for the weights to sit on, and on the other, a large brass bowl. Nestled in the bowl is a blanket, the same soft woollen weave as the one I saw upstairs in the desk drawer weeks ago, and I wonder what fragile things Miss Stourbridge might have been weighing. Eggs? Swallows caught from their nest?

Next to the scales is a scrap of paper, and on it, in Miss Stourbridge's familiar scrawl, are row after row of numbers, measurements weaving drunkenly across the page. Dates and times, and sometimes words too. *Pale today*, it reads under 18 July and, below it on the next day, *breathing quickly*. Under 22 July she has written, *Hardly slept, won't drink. Head seems larger, or is body smaller?* I notice now that the weight is slowly decreasing over time, ounce by ounce.

Far away, I hear the soft mewling of the wind at the little window again, and my eyes settle on the dull brass of the scales, the blanket carefully tucked into the bowl, the soft indent in its midst.

I sit down in the chair, thinking, looking around the room. This is a room of mysteries. It belonged to Miss Stourbridge, of that I am certain; I can feel her in here, the practical, no-frills way she goes about things.

My eyes fall on the blanket again, and I remember the way she stared at the open drawer upstairs, and a thought crystallises, as if the room has been waiting for me to make the connection.

I can feel the stag beetle on the calendar eyeing me with its gleaming, pin-black eye, and I get up and go to examine it. The days have been crossed off up until late July, but there is one day in the midst of all these crosses that is different. Instead of a cross, there is a little drawing of a fish. I trace the lines of it with my finger, my head ringing with discoveries. I look down and see that in my distracted excitement I have crumpled the dead silk moth in my hand. I dust its flaking powder from my fingers, and suddenly I need to be far away from the stagnant air of this closed-off room, away from Dogger Bank completely, breathing in the salt-spray sting of the island air.

In the time it's taken to explore the bowels of the house, the sky has waned from sunshine to a scud of grey cloud. It is a surprise to see it after so many days of sun.

As I open the back door and step outside, I stop, my eyes catching something on the ground. At my feet is a line of cockle shells. It travels over the shingle, leading off into the distance, and I start forward. I walk next to it until at last I come to the shell spiral I made with Jacob. It's changed since last time I was here; it's bigger, each of the strands that hold it in place much longer, disappearing from view. I follow the direction each one goes in with my eyes: the testing buildings, the house, the pavilion. I look at the spiral of shells in front of me, and wonder what it looks like from above; if it draws all the important places on this island together like a strange brainstorming diagram.

I head for the south beach, and crunch over the stones, the grey clouds making the flat shingle beach feel oppressive. I try to pretend to myself that I came to this part of the island out of chance, but deep down I know I'm here for a reason. I just hope she turns up.

I leave my rucksack by the water, the net in my hand, and catch two butterflies very quickly, a small white one and my first brimstone, flitting near the sea peas that grow under the cliff. I leave them to their fates in the jar, and walk down to the water's edge. I take my shoes off and dip my toes in the sea, thinking of the dark rooms I explored in the depths of the house, and what I found there.

The shiver of stones beneath my feet pulls me back, and Nan is walking towards me as if she's been waiting for me, and perhaps she has. She lifts a hand when she sees I've noticed her, and I do the same in return.

All of a sudden, I don't know how to be around her. I watch as she makes her way over, her eyes focused on the stones she's crossing. Her body is bent over, the ankles beneath her dress swollen, the skin of her upper arms doughy. As she approaches, I can hear a wheeze deep within her lungs, a voice in its own right, like a swish of laughter.

She comes to a stop close to me and raises her hands high in the air. 'Tartelin!' she says, 'you've brought the clouds.' She chuckles to herself, looking up at the sky. Her breath continues to crackle long after she stops laughing, filling the silence.

She is grinning at me, and for a moment, the folds of her double chin stretch out, and I catch the profile of the laughing young woman in the photograph, hidden beneath the layers.

'You're Nan,' I say.

She lowers her arms, looking at me questioningly, her eyes going for a second to the top of the cliff.

She makes us tea on the little stove outside the herring girls' hut. With enamel mugs clasped in our hands, we talk.

'It is always easier to talk over tea,' she says wisely. 'It gives your hands something to do, gives you something to focus on when the conversation is a difficult one.'

'You said before, you hadn't been here since you were a girl,' I say, blowing the steam from my mug. 'When did you leave?'

'It was the spring of 1928, I think.' She says it lightly, vaguely, but I have a feeling the date is imprinted in her thoughts. It's so long ago that the intervening years spiral in my mind. She is so very old, this mysterious woman.

'Where did you go?'

'I went back to where I had grown up in France.'

'You're French?'

'Half French. But when I got there, I realised I had changed too much to ever be happy there. My mother had died years before, the silk farm I grew up in closed. Besides, I'd been pulled from that life and taught a very different way of living. In the end, I came back to live as close as I could to Dohhalund. I settled in Great Yarmouth and married a local man there.'

'Is he—'

'He passed away a few years ago, yes.'

'I'm sorry.'

'Don't be. We had many happy years together.'

'Nan, why did you leave Dohhalund?'

Nan takes a sip from her mug, licking her lips thoughtfully. 'I left because she asked me to,' she says finally, with a swift look towards the clifftop again. Above us, the first drops of rain land softly on our hair.

'Does everyone always do what Miss Stourbridge tells them to?'

'No,' Nan says, 'not always.' She lifts a hand and pats my knee. 'But occasionally, you know, she's right.'

I think about the blast. Is Miss Stourbridge right about that, too? I want to ask Nan her opinion, but I know that Miss Stourbridge has entrusted me with her secret, and it's time I started to take her trust seriously.

Nan's hand goes to the mussel necklace around her neck, rubbing her thumb against the little signature etched onto the shell.

'The oyster shell you gave me,' I say suddenly, 'you drew the animal on it, didn't you?'

'Yes,' she says, a hint of wariness in her expression.

'Is it a seal?' I ask, thinking of Miss Stourbridge's startled reaction when she saw it.

'I'm not sure,' Nan says, and I frown, not understanding.

'Sometimes,' she says, 'you can think you're drawing one thing, and it transforms before your eyes into something completely different.'

Comprehension floods through me. I remember the birds I made while Mum was ill, how I didn't realise they were an embodiment of my grief until long after they were finished, until long after she was gone.

Nan raises her head, looking out to sea. 'Sometimes you can't tell what it is you've drawn, even when it's finished and staring right back at you.' She turns to look at me. 'I have an idea what that animal is,' she says. 'Only an idea. I think perhaps Marianne knows more about it than I do.'

'Because she knows so much about animals?'

'Yes and no. I expect she has done research, of course, but that thing is not in any books.' She leans toward me. 'I've seen it, out there,' she gestures to the sea. 'And I think she's seen it too.'

'You've seen it?'

Nan lifts her eyebrows, nodding. 'It reveals itself,' she says, 'sometimes when you least expect it.'

I think back to the seal with gills that I saw last night. 'I think I've seen it, too,' I say.

Nan nods sagely, as if she had already guessed I had.

'What happened between you two?' I ask her. 'Why did you leave the island?'

She fixes me with her glinting eyes, a weary smile crossing her face. 'She was angry. And she was grieving, of course,' she adds with a barely discernible shrug of her shoulders.

'Grieving?'

Nan looks at me sharply. 'How much has she told you?'

'Barely anything. The storm that killed the herring, the silk moths hatching. The piece of music you taught her on the piano.'

Nan's mouth lifts, and she laughs softly, but there is sadness in it. Her eyes have clouded over until they're indistinguishable from the sky above.

'You weren't just a herring girl, were you, Nan? You seem to have spent a lot of time in the house. You were friends with Marianne, weren't you?'

'We *were* friends,' she says. 'Or so I thought. I was brought to the island to teach her how to look after the silkworms.'

'It must have been very difficult coming here, having to settle into such a different way of life.'

She chuckles. 'I think you're implying that *she* must have been very difficult.' Her eyes sparkle. 'I doubt she's changed, has she, in all these years? I bet she's a cantankerous old coot.'

It's my turn to smile.

'I thought as much,' she says. 'When I saw her being carried into the house all those months ago, her arms aloft, directing the fishermen to carry her belongings as if she were conducting an orchestra, I thought, that's the Marianne I remember.' She smiles at the memory. 'I'm glad she still has her spirit after all this time. I've thought about her often over the years, wondering what became of her. She was spoilt and rude, but she was honest. And deep down I believe she cared for the things that mattered.' She pauses, stirring the stones with her finger. 'You care for her, don't you?'

'I do.'

Nan is right, Miss Stourbridge is cantankerous and stern, but beneath all that is something else, something I've been searching for ever since I said goodbye to my mother.

'I've never met anyone like her,' I say. 'She's just so ... vital. So alive.' It's hard to put it into words, but Nan nods all the same, as if she understands.

'Why did you leave Dohhalund, Nan? What happened? Why was she so angry with you?'

'It's not my place to tell you. I don't mardle, not in other people's business.'

'But it's *your* business too, isn't it?' She starts to shake her head, but I interrupt. 'You gave me that oyster shell; you knew Miss Stourbridge might see it.'

I'm tired of having to deal with whatever has gone on between these two women. I finish my tea and stand, passing my mug back. 'She wants to see you,' I say. 'She knows you're here.' And then, because I'm beginning to realise I must take responsibility for my actions, 'I told her.'

Nan gets creakily to her feet too. She takes the mugs over to the edge of the sea and swills them out with sea water.

'I don't know, Tartelin. It's one thing coming back to Dohhalund, it's another seeing someone you last saw decades ago, particularly when we parted on such terrible terms. I had no idea that she would follow me here so soon after I arrived.' She comes back to me and regards me for a moment, then she reaches forward and squeezes my arm. 'It's been nice chatting,' she says with a sad smile, and turns to go.

'She has a photograph of you,' I call after her, and she comes to a stop. 'It's battered from being looked at so often. Every other photo in the album is in perfect condition, but the photo of you is cracked from being touched so much.'

Nan takes a deep breath, and it rumbles out in a sigh. 'I remember that photograph album,' she says, turning. 'I remember the man who came to take the photographs. It felt miraculous, back then.' She looks out to sea. 'How things change. How miracles change.'

Her eyes have cleared until they are reflecting the water. 'So many years,' she says, shaking her head, and when she looks at me, her features have settled into a look of acceptance.

'All right,' she says, 'I'll do it.'

A bloom of relief seeps through me. 'Thank you,' I say. 'When shall I tell her you'll come?'

'I think we should do it now,' she says. 'Once a decision has been made, it's best to get on with it, in my opinion.'

'Maybe I should prepare her first,' I say, looking nervously up at the cliff, thinking of Miss Stourbridge in there with no idea of what's coming.

'Nonsense. It's best to surprise Marianne. Less time for her to get angry about everything.' She chuckles, linking arms with me, and we begin to cross the shingle.

We enter Dogger Bank via the kitchen door. I'm expecting Nan to react to being back after so long, but she hardly gives the room a glance, and I realise she's been inside before.

'Was it you who left those eggs?' I ask her, remembering the plateful of freckled eggs on one of my first mornings, and she nods.

'Marianne and I used to gather them for breakfast sometimes,' she says. 'I thought they might hint to her that I was here.' She pauses. 'Perhaps I've wanted to see her more than I've admitted to myself.'

'I ate them,' I tell her, my hand to my mouth in horror. 'I'm so sorry. I was so hungry; I didn't even think to take them upstairs.'

'It doesn't matter. We got here eventually, didn't we?' she says, winking at me, her infectious smile lighting up her face.

At the bottom of the stairs, the smile fades. It's clear she hasn't dared go any further since she came back.

'Ready?' I ask her, and she nods, her mouth set in a determined line.

The stairs seem twice as long as normal. As we approach the panelled room, I listen out for the rolling of the wheelchair on the floorboards. The room is silent but for the ticking of the clock.

'Miss Stourbridge?' I call.

'Ah Tartelin,' comes her voice from over near the desk.

I take Nan's hand, and we cross into the room.

'Just in time,' Miss Stourbridge says, turning. 'I know it's Sunday, but I ...' She stops mid-sentence, and the pincers in her hand drop to the floor with a clatter.

'Hello, Marianne,' Nan says.

The two women hold each other's gaze, and for the first time I see something, something I should have seen all along. Their eyes, dark and compelling, and so very similar.

And then Nan is rushing forward, and Miss Stourbridge has clutched her wheels and is moving swiftly across the room, and then they are clasping each other, Miss Stourbridge's arthritic hands gripping onto Nan, their cheeks pressed against one another's, and, 'Welcome home,' Miss Stourbridge says, 'my dear, dear sister.'

Chapter Twenty-One

Marianne

February 1928

Marianne stood outside Mama's sitting-room door, collecting herself. She had spent the morning thinking about everything that she had found out, trying to make sense of it all: the storm, the pearls, the herring, the silkworms. But it was like trying to keep hold of a handful of slippery fish, and she wondered how her poor father managed to keep afloat with so many choices to make every day.

But of course, he didn't. *Papa*, she thought, trying to calm the terror that was threatening to spill over and consume her. She remembered Nan's words: *He has nothing now, Marianne, nothing.* She pushed open the door.

'Mama, I need to talk with you.'

Mama was in her customary place, by the picture window, looking out to sea. The *Zilver* had still not come home, but early that morning its nets had been spotted, alone and floating on the water near the quay. Four souls were still missing. Her mother's hand was at the string of pearls around her neck again, worrying at the beads. She continued to look out of the window as if she had not noticed Marianne enter.

Marianne went to stand by her, sharing in the view from the window.

Even now, each time she looked out to sea she hoped that the boat would be out there, a small dot on the horizon growing bigger all the time. But the sea was calm and still and empty.

Her eyes went to her mother's pearls again. Mama's necklace was reputed to have been harvested by her great-great-grandmother, the first of the pearl-mermaids. Before the herring girls inherited the term, the women in Marianne's family were known as the Dohhalund Mermaids, collecting the finest pearls to send to high-end jewellers around the world. It was said that only the gentlest of the women had hands nimble enough to remove the pearls without harming their delicate nacre.

When Marianne was younger, reaching up to stroke the orbs at her mother's neck, Mama had told her that the pearls had touched the skin of so many of their forebears that a little bit of each of them was impregnated into each one, and they shone all the brighter for it.

One day, Marianne had thought when she was little, they will be mine to wear, and I will watch over this island like my mother does, like *her* mother did before her.

But now, seeing her mother's hands rub distractedly over them, the notion of having the oils of her long-dead relatives against her skin made her feel sick. It all came back to the pearls, and she fixed her eyes on her mother, feeling anger and fright build inside her.

'Mama?' she said again, trying to keep her voice calm, feeling the worry and danger and nerves fighting in her throat to get out. 'Mama, something Nan said has been worrying me. Are Papa's businesses safe?'

Her mother's hand came to a stop, her fingertip touching a pearl at the base of her throat. Marianne marvelled at how still she could be, while the household continued to rattle around her like a storm over a Dogger boat.

'It's just,' she continued, 'first it was the awful luck with the herring, and now I think the silkworms might be ruined. And Nan says ...

Nan says the pearls that she and Papa found are not real. There are no Dohhalund pearls in the oyster beds.'

Her words sank into the deep silence of the room, so quiet that she could hear her mother's finger tapping against the pearl at her throat. She put her hand on Mama's arm, willing her to stop.

'Is she telling the truth, Mama?' she whispered. 'They must exist, because, if they don't, then what are we supposed to live on, with Papa building railways and piers and summerhouses?' She came to a stop with a gulp of air, her throat constricting from the force of it all. When Mama didn't respond, she slammed her hand on the Chinese cabinet.

'For goodness' sake, Mama!' she burst out, the words venting out of her like the cry of an angry child. 'Why won't you tell me anything? You let Papa do just as he wants, as if he is the king of Dohhalund, but it's *your* island, Mama, it's yours.'

Slowly, her mother turned from the sea and fixed Marianne with her large, silver eyes. Even at times like this, in the middle of an argument, Marianne was breathless at her beauty.

'One day,' Mama said, 'when it is your turn to marry, and care for this island, you will understand how the world works, Marianne. It is not *my* island, we do not own it; we are only keepers of this place, charged with its safety. Likewise, I cannot control what your father does. I am his wife, not his jailer.'

'But he's been doing it right under your nose,' Marianne said, stamping her foot. 'Bringing Nan here, concocting some mad and stupid plan with her to try and keep us afloat, while out there,' she threw her arm towards the window, 'all of his businesses are falling apart!'

Mama sighed. 'Of course I care, Marianne,' she said. 'But there is no point challenging your father on any of this. He knows that he's done wrong, and he's trying to put things right in his own way. Arguing with him will only make it worse.' She looked at Marianne searchingly for a moment. 'Promise me you'll leave things be,' she said, and for the first time Marianne felt an emotion in her mother stronger than a wisp of mist.

'Why do you care what I say to him?' she asked.

'Because there is no point in stirring up trouble. It has happened already: we cannot change the past.'

'But it's happening *now*. You can change the present, the future, surely!'

'What would you have me do, throw Nan out?' Mama's hand went to the pearls round her neck again.

Marianne was momentarily confused. 'Of course you mustn't throw her out,' she said, watching the way her mother's hand tangled with the pearls at her neck, the usually smooth skin there chapped and sore, and her own thoughts felt as jumbled as the pearls, ricocheting against each other, being chipped away. She wondered for the first time if Mama's outwardly calm appearance was just a façade, if inside she was just as confused and angry as Marianne.

'Why would you throw Nan out?' she said quietly.

Her mother stilled.

'It isn't her fault,' Marianne continued, and then, her voice quavering, trying to understand, 'it isn't her fault, is it, Mama?'

'Of course it's not her fault, Marianne. But she is involved, you can't deny that.'

'But we're all involved,' Marianne scoffed. 'Even the mermaids and the joskins are involved. Why single Nan out?'

Her mother turned to face her. There were lilac shadows under her eyes. 'You really don't know?' she said.

The room seemed to keel, and Marianne grabbed the edge of the cabinet to steady herself. 'Know what?'

'Nan is his daughter,' Mama said.

'She is ...' All sorts of possibilities whirled through Marianne's head, fitting together like the jigsaw Nan and she were working on in the corner of the sitting room. 'She is Papa's ...'

'Why do you think she was brought here?' Her mother was looking at her steadily, questioningly.

'But she is the daughter of a friend of Papa's,' Marianne said, clutching at the facts as they disappeared into the air like thin wisps of fog.

Mama was shaking her head. 'No,' she said, 'no, she isn't.'

Marianne threw herself into an armchair and stared out to sea, trying to make sense of what her mother was saying.

'Does she know?'

'I don't know. I don't think so.'

'But she must at least suspect.'

'Did *you*?'

Marianne shot her mother a look under her brow, a glittering anger coursing through her. She felt her cheeks flush with it. 'How long have you known?' she said, her eyes narrowing.

'Your father is as transparent as a jellyfish.'

'But you let it happen. You let him bring her to our island.'

'How could I not? She is your sister, Marianne, however she came to be.'

'She's Papa's bastard,' Marianne spat, standing abruptly. She regretted the words as soon as she had spoken them but, turning, she strode from the room, wrenching the door closed behind her and running down the stairs, her mother's call echoing after her.

At the bottom she stopped short, the words Mama had spoken catching up with her.

Nan was her sister, her own flesh and blood. But how could she be? They were so different in looks and in temperament, their first years on this earth separated by hundreds of miles and a thousand disparities. A small voice whispered, but you *are* alike, in so many infinitesimal ways. She saw the wicked glint in Nan's eye, the fiendish smile she bestowed on her that mirrored her own so exactly, and she let out a cry of shame.

Outside, the peacocks began to call, and Marianne unlatched the front door and set out across Dohhalund.

She strode across the island, winding through Papa's new mulberry plantation, crushing the saplings beneath her feet, not caring where she ended up. Eventually she found herself standing in front of the pavilion. From outside it appeared to be empty, the absence of sound snapping her out of her sorrow. She walked up the steps and turned the handle. The door creaked open into silence.

Inside, the floor was finished now, stretching ahead of her like the giant shining chessboard she had envisaged. A cluck behind her made her turn, and Ebisu strutted warily into the room, coming to a stop next to her. She looked down at his shining blue head and thought, with the desperation only a girl on the crumbling cusp of adulthood can have, *my only friend!* and she threw herself down on him, engulfed by emotion, and began to cry.

When she finally stopped, gulping loudly into the silent room, Ebisu stood and shook his feathers. He strutted away from her, feet clicking on the tiles, as if he couldn't bear to be smothered again.

Through a film of salt water, she looked about the room, her gaze resting on the tools that lay abandoned on the floor around her: saws and hammers, knives and axes. She was aware again of how eerily quiet it was, the only sound the tap, tap of Ebisu's great clawed feet on the porcelain. Where were the workers? How long since they had downed their tools? How long since Papa had last deigned to pay them? There had been clues, of course, and Nan had tried to warn her, but Marianne had refused to listen, so blindly adoring was she of her father.

It all came back to Nan: that's when everything had begun to go wrong, when Papa began to grow distant, when the island's businesses began to fail. Nan and Papa and their obsession with the Dohhalund pearls.

She sifted through everything she had been taught about pearls, trying to understand what her father and Nan had been up to. Most people thought that pearls formed from a grain of sand, lovingly coated with layers of luminosity until a round, fat pearl emerged. But Papa had taught her years ago that cultured pearls start with a parasite introduced by human hands; something irritating, gnawing away inside the shell. The oyster tries to protect itself by wrapping it up in the shiny nacre as a way of defence. However beautiful a pearl looks from the outside, there is always a parasite, ugly and dangerous, at its heart. Just like Nan.

Marianne's stomach flipped unpleasantly. Was that really how she felt about her? Nan hadn't chosen her parents, just as Marianne hadn't. And she certainly hadn't asked to come here: she might not even realise she was a Stourbridge at all.

Or perhaps Marianne was being naïve, and Nan had known all along. Anger simmered inside her, and along with it came an excruciating twist of embarrassment. Perhaps everyone had known except her: Mama and the maids, the joskins and the mermaids. Had they all been gossiping away behind her back? She blanched at the thought, imagining Papa and Nan shut away behind the study door, laughing heartily at her expense.

There was nothing for it: she needed to confront Papa. Perhaps if she explained how the situation made her feel, he might see fit to send Nan away to another finishing school, or better, she thought with a thrill of satisfaction, back to the French backwater she had come from.

Marianne got to her feet, brushing plaster dust from her skirt. Clicking her fingers for Ebisu to follow her, she went to the door, pausing for a moment for one last look around the pavilion's silent hall, and then she stepped down onto the veranda, and began the walk back towards the house.

Chapter Twenty-Two

Tartelin

Summer 2018

They are sisters.

I watch as they pull back from their embrace and look at one another, studying the other's features as if looking at a portrait, and I feel as if I'm intruding. I step quietly from the room and tiptoe back downstairs, leaving Nan and Marianne to their reunion.

Outside, the sun is slipping towards the west, inching away from the sea where it rose this morning, where it has risen every morning. Some things on this island will always be the same, I concede, but others have changed irrevocably.

Dohhalund is quiet today. I've been here for so many weeks now that I've lost track of the days, but it must be late August. It's still inexorably hot, the island parched after a record-breaking summer. Perhaps, at last, people have begun to drift away now, back to the demands of their jobs, of their families, their lives in the real world at last pulling them home.

There is nothing on the mainland to pull me back. My home is here now. This thought would have frightened me a few weeks ago, but now it brings comfort. It means I can go anywhere, do anything. I can stay on this island for ever if I wish, roaming the countryside as if it were my own. Will Miss Stourbridge and Nan live out their days here, too? Will they manage to get past whatever it was that tore them apart? Are they, even now, reconciling? I don't know if I'll ever find out what happened between them, but I'm beginning to understand that that's OK: it's not my story.

I look out over this island that I have grown to love. This is *my* time now, I think, *my* story, and I realise with a rush of exhilaration that I need to start living it.

I pass the bridge that leads to the salt pans, and keep on walking, my eyes on the strange marsh where I first met Jacob. When I reach it, I sit on the crumbling stone wall, letting the heat from the sun-warmed stones penetrate the backs of my legs.

There are fewer butterflies on the island now, the first flush of hatching long gone. I wonder if any have attempted to journey across the salt water; if any will survive?

The marsh is a haze of colour, late summer flowers blooming so that I can hardly see the pools of water, the rich mud beneath. Far up on the hill to my left I can see Dogger Bank next to the two derelict houses, and I think of the two sisters inside.

There is no breeze here, a perfect stillness as if the world has paused, and it's because of this absolute calm that I see it: a tiny flicker of movement. I scan the area again, practised in the art after so many days spent catching butterflies, and my eyes settle on something glimmering. Not a butterfly this time, but a bird.

It's about the size of a large gull, sitting so low and still that I wonder how I noticed it at all. It is white and well-muscled, but for a shimmer of iridescent green feathers at its neck. And it is this gleam at its throat that I can't take my eyes off, for although there's no hint of a breeze, the feathers there are moving, flickering open and closed. *Like gills*, I think.

Ever so slowly, I turn my head so I can see it properly, trying to make sense of what I'm looking at. I can feel the sting of my eyes as I try not to blink. Is this the *Morus* hybrid that the birdwatcher told me about? If so, he was wrong: this is no gannet, no mere hybrid. I watch as thin gaps appear at its throat, wisps of feather moving as if air is rushing through them.

As if it senses my stare, it takes off suddenly, powerful wings beating the air. A trail of water arcs from its feet as it climbs towards the sky. I watch it until it's lost from view, heading for open sea.

Later, as I climb Dogger Bank's sweeping staircase, I hear the piano start up above me. I pause on the stairs and listen, realising it's two people playing. It has a depth that stops me on the stairs, rooting me there, and suddenly I am full of a desperate joy, a mixture of emotions that is impossible to unravel. This island is like nowhere I've been before, its wild arms clutching at me, drawing me in, opening my eyes to its miracles, and I pull myself up the staircase as if making my way through a strong current, my hand clenched around the banister.

At the door to the panelled room, I pause, bewitched by the music. I can hear the low melody of the two women's voices as they play. I cannot interrupt them.

I turn back towards my bedroom instead. Mum's bird book is there, waiting for me, and I while away my time, searching for the bird I have just seen, though I know it will not be there.

Later, I lift my eyes from the page and realise the music has stopped. My hand rests on the book's mottled pages, the black outlines of a hundred drawings of birds swimming before my eyes.

The house is eerily quiet. I can no longer hear the two women talking. I get up from the bed and stretch.

The door to the panelled room is open. Miss Stourbridge is sitting in the middle of the room, looking at the photograph album in her lap. She looks up as I come in, and her face is different: there's a look of the young Marianne about her, as if something has lifted.

'She's gone,' I say.

'Yes, we were both quite tired from our meeting, as I'm sure you can imagine. She'll be back.'

'She's your sister.'

'Half-sister, yes. We shared a father. Her mother was French.' Her answer is short and sharp, as if she's simply ticking off the facts, and I see in her face how difficult she's finding it to say out loud.

'It's OK, you don't have to tell me.'

'I know I don't have to,' she says, blinking up at me. 'But I find for the first time that I want to, which is quite a strange feeling, for me. No one has ever got under my skin like you, Tartelin. Well, not since Nan, anyway. I find I want to tell you the truth.' She looks a little puzzled at the thought.

I don't know how to react to this. It is the fondest declaration she has yet made to me, and I'm aware how much of an effort it must have taken for her to admit it. I sit down on the chaise, not sure where to put myself.

'I've been sitting here since she left earlier, trying to understand why I thought it right to send her away,' Miss Stourbridge says. Her hand is on the photo album, her arthritic fingers stroking the picture of Nan. 'Has she spoken to you about what happened? About the reasons behind her leaving?'

'No. Only that she left in 1928.'

'Yes, that's right, in the spring. She was only here for six months or so, but they were pivotal, in so many ways. So much was going on at that time, it felt as if everything I knew was spiralling away from me.'

'Did you know you had a sister, before she came to the island?'

'I did not. In fact, I only found out who she was a few weeks before she left.'

'Was that the reason you sent her away?'

'In truth? It was part of it, but many perplexing things happened around that time. The island was on the cusp of change, and I failed to notice the signs until it was too late. Poor Nan got tangled up in it all. Of course, none of us was wholly innocent.' She heaves a trembling breath, her frail shoulders lifting and settling like a wave. 'Nan says I should explain it all to you properly,' she adds. '"She's not just the help, Marianne," she said, and she's right, of course: you're not.' She reaches out and takes my hand carefully in her painful fingers.

'Miss Stourbridge, I ... '

'You can call me Marianne,' she says, squeezing my hand in her own. 'Come, let us get this over with.'

Chapter Twenty-Three

Marianne

February 1928

Marianne put her ear to the keyhole of Papa's study and listened. Hearing nothing, she ducked her head, peeping through the hole to the room on the other side.

She knew that Nan was down in the annexe, checking on the young silkworm eggs. Nan rarely left that room now, preferring to take her meals with the staff in the kitchen so that she was nearby. Marianne wouldn't have been surprised if she slept down there, too.

There was no sign of Papa through the keyhole. Yesterday afternoon, two men had arrived on the floating bridge. They were shut in the study with her father for a long time. When they left, they took with them a painting of a Dogger boat that had taken pride of place on the wall behind his desk.

'Dealers in Fine Art,' Papa had said over dinner. 'Apparently the brushstrokes are very *Cotmanesque*. It's to go in an exhibition in London – alongside a Turner, apparently. What an honour, eh?' His smile was stiff and thin under his moustache. 'Don't worry, my dear,' he said, seeing Mama staring down at her plate. 'We'll have it back soon, I promise.' Mama flinched when he put his hand over hers.

At the time, it had struck Marianne as an odd conversation, but she conceded that more and more peculiar things were happening in the house at the moment. She wondered if the painting's removal had anything to do with the problems with Papa's businesses. Perhaps he had sold it to make some extra money to tide him over whilst he got the household's finances in order.

Earlier, when she'd come back from the pavilion, wiping her sore, red-rimmed eyes, she'd gone to the kitchen door to ask Cook if she'd seen Papa. Hearing a voice drifting out of the open window, along with the steam from a suet pudding, she'd stopped on the grass outside, listening. It was Peggy, her voice brimming with excitement.

'There's rumours he's given every one of them joskins their notice without paying them their wages,' she said, and Marianne could hear the thrill of gossip in her voice.

'Aye, and fights have broken out on the quay, so I heard.' Cook's voice now. 'What is that man doing, eh? I've lived and worked here long before he came along, and never have I seen this place in such disorder.'

Marianne had wondered if there was any truth in the rumours, and she thought to ask Nan next time she saw her, before reality crashed around her and she remembered afresh who Nan really was. In anger, she had burst into the kitchen, scowling at the staff and storming off down the corridor, and now here she was, standing outside Papa's study, her heart beating a tattoo in her chest.

She peeked through the keyhole one last time, her ears straining to detect any hint of breathing, but the air passing through the keyhole was calm and untainted. Looking to left and right to check that the coast was clear, she turned the handle and pushed the door open, stepping cautiously inside.

She had always loved this room. Her eyes ran over the walls lined with books, beautiful volumes nestled on the shelves, interspersed with fossils and pieces of baleen art. A single vertebra of a mammoth rested next to a collection of Darwin's textbooks, and a group of clay pipes with grotesque faces stood in a rack next to a beautifully bound copy of *Culpeper's Complete Herbal*. Everything had its place, ordered and tidy. Marianne wrinkled her nose at the faint trace of fishiness that still lingered from the episode with the shrimps. She tried to banish the bittersweet memory of Nan and her sewing them into the curtains, giggling at the sheer audacity of what they were doing.

She closed the door and turned to face the room, and then she saw that not everything was as it should be: Papa's usually tidy desk was a chaotic shamble of papers.

Marianne crossed the room, taking in the mess spread across the leather. Coffee rings and pipe dottle peppered the topmost papers, and there was an acrid smell in here, too. Not just the fishy remains of the shrimps, but another smell, sharp and close, as if her papa had been working so tirelessly, he had not had time to crack open a window for days. On the wall, a rectangle of wallpaper glowed brightly, marking the place where the oil painting had been.

She sifted through the papers, almost knocking over a half-empty coffee cup in her haste. A fat pile of bills were stacked beneath a heavy walrus tusk. Hurriedly she flicked through them: porcelain flooring, velvet curtains, the shipment of silkworms. Marianne's eyes grew round, her fingers slowing as she saw the numbers totalling on every page. How on earth had Papa intended to pay for all of this? Even if it had been a bountiful herring year, these costs were monstrous.

Beneath the bills were plans for the summerhouse: diagrams of the layout, and a map of the proposed railway route across the island. An architect's drawing of the grand pier caught her eye, and she was momentarily distracted, taking in the marble columns, the long board-walk that stretched far out to sea.

What had Papa got himself into? She slumped into her father's chair, surveying the mess.

When she was small, she remembered, long before she was old enough to have a governess, Papa used to sit her on his lap in this very room and tell her about his hold on the island. Back then, before the silkworms, before the pavilion and the railway and the pier, he had dealt only in herring and pearls. Marianne's favourite days were the ones spent sitting on his lap in the study, the smell of pipe smoke and leather books in her nostrils, listening to him talk about pearls. She sat with rapt attention as he talked of the mermaids who harvested them and the men who cleaned them and graded them, and sent them to London and Paris to be set in fabulous jewellery.

But those days were long gone. She stood up and turned her attention to the bookshelves, her eyes ranging over the leather volumes. She began pulling out books at random, searching through their pages. With great effort she hefted out a particularly large sealskin book, and stopped. In the deep, dark space behind it, something glittered. She reached in, and her fingers met the cold curves of countless glass bottles. With a shaking hand, she took hold of the closest one, and carefully lifted it out.

It was a small bottle, about the size of the blue medicine bottles that Cook kept for coughs and colds, but this one was clear, with a glass stopper. Marianne held it up to the light. It was half filled with what looked like murky water, but as the light hit it, she saw there was a layer of silvery-grey fish scales at the bottom, and on the water's surface, a scud of opalescence frothed like sea foam, and she knew immediately what it was.

She took it back to the desk with her, and sat once again in her father's chair, placing the bottle on the pile of papers.

'*Essence d'Orient*,' she said.

A memory came to her. She was sitting on Papa's lap in this very spot, the light streaming in through the window, slanting across the books on the shelves, making the dust dance in the air.

'Now, Marianne,' Papa had said very seriously. 'If you are to follow your forebears into the art of pearl cultivation, you must know about *essence d'Orient*.'

'What is it, Papa?'

'It is a luminous liquid that comes in delicate little glass bottles,' he said. 'Quite magical looking. Pearlescent, if you will.'

She remembered being struck by the prettiness of the name. It sounded like a perfume, and she imagined her mama dabbing it behind her pretty ears and on the insides of her slender wrists.

But Papa had laughed when she told him this.

'No, no, *mijn parelmoer*, it's not a perfume; it is paint made from the putrid remains of fish scales.'

The young Marianne screwed her nose up in disgust.

'Everyone in the pearl trade should know about it,' he went on. 'It's the stuff of paste jewellery-makers and con artists. As the daughter of a pearl trader, you must learn to tell the difference between a real pearl and a glass one painted with Orient essence.'

He leant around her and reached into a compartment hidden at the back of the desk. With a snap, a little drawer in the pigeonhole sprung open, and inside, beautiful, luminous pearls rolled about, clicking against one another. He picked one up and held it to the light.

'This,' he said, 'is a real pearl. Look at the way the light radiates from it. Feel it, go on.'

Marianne took the pearl. It was cool. It felt almost soft in its smoothness.

'Rub it on your teeth,' Papa said, 'it should feel gritty.'

She did, trying not to swallow it. 'It feels like sand,' she said.

'Exactly,' her father said, nodding approvingly, and she swelled with pride.

He dipped his fingers into a different segment of the drawer. 'Now,' he said, pulling out a small cream-coloured orb, 'this is a fake pearl. It is important to have a collection of these to show visiting merchants; it makes your own pearls look even more luminous, even more luscious. It proves that what we are selling is genuine and beyond compare.

'The fake pearl is covered in a layer of *essence d'Orient* – pearlescent paint. See if you can tell the difference.' And he dropped the two pearls into her outstretched hand.

Marianne tried to keep her eyes on the real pearl, but the two orbs rolled and slid together in the creases of her palm until she lost track of which was which.

'The trained eye can tell them apart immediately,' Papa said. 'The fake pearl is hard and brittle.' Here, he ran his finger over them both. 'The sheen peels off in your hands, look.' He scraped his nail over one of the pearls, and a curve of paint peeled away and flaked into her palm, revealing clear glass beneath.

'Have you got any, Papa? Any essence dor ... dor ...'

'*Essence d'Orient*. Gracious no, child. Why would I? We have the real thing.' He lifted the remaining pearl from her hand, holding it up between finger and thumb to catch the slanting sunbeams. 'Genuine pearls are cool, but become warm to the touch. They are soft and lustrous. Nothing man-made compares, and that is why we are one of the most eminent pearl traders in the world. Dohhalund pearls, Marianne. They are the best, and when you are a young lady, you shall have your very own set.'

The pearls he had promised her had never materialised. By the time she turned twelve and had begun to think covetously of the necklace she would soon receive, the pearls that Dohhalund had been so famous for had begun to degrade. Fewer and fewer oysters proved fruitful, until Papa took the decision to stop trading in pearls altogether.

Now, she lifted the bottle and shook it, watching the scales lift and settle, thinking.

Papa was perfectly within his rights to have these bottles. He had herring scales aplenty, why not make use of them to make a little more money? Fake pearls in themselves were not illegal. It was only if you pretended they were real that you could get into trouble.

A shiver ran down her back, and she glanced at the bottles hidden in the bookcase, dark and mysterious.

Papa wouldn't, would he?

And then she remembered. Sitting at the dinner table, supping on pea soup. Her father's words: *Nan made a wonderful discovery today.*

Was it Nan who had given him the idea? A white-hot thrill passed across Marianne's shoulder blades. What had her father said, all those years ago? *Orient essence is the stuff of con artists.*

She slammed the bottle down on the desk, a squirming mixture of anger and fear overcoming her. The herring, the silkworms, the pearls: everything had soured since Nan arrived, and she felt an effervescent rage run through her. She shook her head, trying to dislodge the thoughts so that they swirled away like the silver scales in the bottle in front of her.

She took a breath to calm herself and looked at the desk, summoning the memory of the pearls again. She reached carefully into the corner of the pigeonhole and felt around, her hand closing over a tiny lever. With a click that transcended through memory, a small drawer jerked open, the sound of its contents giving the pearls away before she could see inside.

She pulled the drawer towards her. Tiny orbs were ricocheting off each other like a set of billiard balls. But they weren't pearls. They were clear, smooth glass.

Mixed in with these glass balls were what at first glance appeared to be real pearls. Marianne picked one up and dug a fingernail into it. The essence came away from the glass bead in a clean crescent, like a piece of broken eggshell.

She lifted the bottle again, shaking it harder this time, and held it to the light, frowning. The scales swirled and settled to the bottom like a snow globe.

Were these the pearls that Papa and Nan had whispered about? How many fake pearls had they already sold?

Marianne looked down at the bewildering amount of paperwork on the desk, the huge number of bills, and her heart crashed through her chest.

'Oh Papa,' she said to herself, 'what have you done?'

The following evening, the family sat in silence, sipping mussel soup. Even Nan had managed to peel herself away from the silkworm eggs and grace them with her company.

As she looked around the table, Marianne could feel anger radiating out from her, creeping towards each member of her family like a thick, poisonous fog. She looked from face to face, trying to work out who knew what. The house felt as if it was made up of a long spool of lies and whispered truths, zigzagging out like a spider's web until nobody could tell what the other knew, and nobody dared speak of it at all.

Did Nan know that the man sitting opposite her was her father? Across the table, Papa was sipping his soup thoughtfully, his usual noisy slurping noticeable by its absence. Marianne thought of the pavilion, the tools abandoned on the floor. She remembered Ebisu's great, clacking feet echoing on the porcelain in that huge, empty space. She thought of the dead herring floating on the water, eyes staring helplessly upwards, and the fake pearls coated in *essence d'Orient* rolling around in Papa's desk, and she felt like throwing her bowl of soup across the table to get her father's attention, demanding answers right there and then. But then she remembered Mama's words: *promise me you'll leave things be.* She looked over at her mother and something squirmed in her stomach, an uncomfortable mixture of pity and love.

In the silence at the dinner table, the only sound came from the tapping of spoons against china bowls, the polite sips as the food that had been bought with tainted money flowed into each of their stomachs. Marianne felt sick.

Over the next week, Nan began to spend more and more time with the remaining mermaids down at the beach, leaving the silkworms once again to Marianne. She got back so late in the evening that Marianne was often already asleep, and she was gone before Marianne awoke. It was a blessing, really: Marianne didn't know what she would say to her if she saw her alone. She was angry at her, yes, but beneath the anger, there lay a shameful embarrassment that they had spent so much time together and yet Marianne had never guessed who she really was.

On a cold February day, when the wind blasted off the sea so strongly that the curtains in the sitting room lifted almost horizontally, the same two men who had taken the Dogger boat painting came to see Papa again.

Marianne was out walking near the quay when she saw them stepping off the floating bridge. They looked like businessmen, but even with her naïve islander's eye, she could see there was something improper about them. They didn't look like art dealers, certainly. One was small and shrewd, the other barrel-chested and well-muscled. Close up, their clothes were cut from cheap cloth, and a day or two's stubble smattered the small man's sharp cheekbones.

They shut themselves away with Papa for even longer than last time, and Marianne finally admitted to herself that they weren't there to buy more art. With an uneasy dread pulsing in her blood, she wondered if they were policemen. What if they had discovered the Orient essence too, and were even now shackling Papa to take him back to the mainland to await trial?

Mama remained in her sitting room, a half-finished embroidery of a painted lady butterfly in her hands, staring out at the sea. She hummed whilst Marianne paced the floorboards around her, but the needle remained plunged into its cushion, the embroidered butterfly's wing unchanged in her lap.

The men left as it began to get dark, thankfully leaving Papa, white-faced and perspiring, behind. It was too late for them to take the ferry back, but her father generously offered them the *Schoonheid* to take them to the mainland. Marianne watched them from her bedroom window. They carried with them boxes of files and a basketful of artefacts pulled from the shelves in Papa's study.

'Good riddance,' she whispered to them under her breath, watching as their lonely lamp wound its way down to the quay, growing smaller and smaller until it was no more than a pinprick in the dark.

When she was sure they were not coming back, she took her own lamp and tiptoed downstairs, through the kitchen and along the passages to Papa's study.

She rapped softly on the door. There was a muffled rustle inside.

'Come in,' said Papa, his voice so soft and sad that Marianne leant her forehead against the door for a moment, before pushing it open and going inside.

She stopped in the doorway. The shelves that lined the walls were empty of the artefacts that Papa had collected over the years. The piles of papers that had littered the desk had been cleared. The room felt like a shell, as if her father had wiped it clean of any trace of him.

'Papa,' she said, rushing to him, and he opened his arms to her. She clung to him awkwardly. She could feel the boniness of his arms, the clunk of his skull against hers as he held her tight.

'Is all our money gone?' she whispered, her voice muffled in his shirt. 'Are we to be thrown out of Dogger Bank?'

Papa's breath was ragged as he pulled away from her. 'The house is safe,' he said. He looked at her, his gaze tracking between each of her eyes, trying to pull something from her to sustain him, and she saw for the first time how glassy and frenzied his own eyes were, like a pair of black buttons sewn onto a toy.

'My sweet *parelmoer*,' he said, and she sank down onto his lap, feeling like a little girl again.

'Why did you choose her over me?' she said. 'Why couldn't *I* sit in your study with you and paint the pearls?'

Her father took a deep breath and pushed her gently from his lap. She stood, her hand on the arm of his chair, refusing to move. 'I'd do anything for you, Papa,' she said. 'Anything.'

At these words he appeared to crumple, his usually ebullient face collapsing in on itself, and Marianne didn't know where to look. She hadn't known that men could cry.

Papa pulled himself up from the chair and took her face in his hands, smoothing his thumb over her cheek, and cupping her chin. It felt to Marianne as if he was looking at her properly for the first time in years.

'It is because I love you that I couldn't ask it of you,' he said. 'You are my *lief* – my *darling*. You are my world, dear, dear Marianne.'

He sighed, taking his hands away and opening a drawer in his desk. For a moment, Marianne expected to see pearls, but he pulled from it instead a piece of notepaper.

'Forgive me,' he said, picking up a pen. 'I have work to do.' He sat and began to write, and Marianne took the lamp and tiptoed out of the study.

As she closed the door, she thought she heard him say again, 'Forgive me.'

That evening, Papa went missing.

Nobody saw him go. It got dark quickly at that time of year, the island falling under a cloak of black as if a spell had been cast. One moment the pale light was washing in from the west, the next they were all plunged into the bleak, starless black, and unknown to them all, Papa's study stood empty. Nobody saw him steal out of the house, or spied him creeping across Dohhalund in the deep dark of the night.

One by one, the women pulled away from the warmth of the fire and went to their beds. Marianne went to bed with a stirring feeling of unease, the faces of the two men in suits swimming before her eyes.

Marianne awoke to the peacocks' call, and her first, happy thought was of Ebisu, his royal blue neck shimmering as he strutted across the lawn. She got up, washed, and dressed herself. In the dining room, bread and pickled winkles were laid out, and she breakfasted alone.

After she had eaten, she called upstairs to Mama, but there was no answer. The house felt eerily quiet. She peeped her head around the kitchen door, whispering a tentative, 'Hello?' but the kitchen was empty too, the table scrubbed clean. At the back door, she pulled on a coat and gumboots, and went outside.

It was a glorious, crisp winter's day. Marianne spied Cook over near the mulberry trees, and she broke into a run, thankful to at last have found someone. But halfway across the garden she slowed to a stop. Cook was calling out Papa's name with a quivering, mournful mouth, her face the ashen grey of cold porridge.

And then, beyond the trees, Marianne heard it: Papa's name being called again and again. Across the garden she began to hear different voices, all calling: Mama, Nan, Peggy and the rest of the staff were all there, calling, calling, until his name seemed to become a melodic chant, round after round of it relaying across the grounds, and at last Marianne joined in too, her voice, high and clear, rising above everyone else's.

People go missing on islands, in sea communities, it has always been so. Islanders hang hag-stones up to keep themselves safe; they pray to nautical gods and name their families, their pets, after the spirits of the sea, in the hope of calming its raging temper. But still people die.

The sea is made up of unspeakable sadness, its tragedies always remembered. With every hour, Marianne grew more worried for her papa. He knew the island like the back of his hand, but he was not from this isle. He had the blood of a mainlander: he lacked the islanders' respect for the sea.

As she called his name, Marianne began to tremble, her teeth chattering, her hands shaking.

And then Peggy was coming across the grass, a piece of notepaper in her hand, a handkerchief to her mouth, and Marianne found herself on her knees, the wet grass searing through to her skin.

Behind her, Cook began to wail.

He had left a note.

Marianne sat at the kitchen table, looking at the piece of paper. It was soft from the tears of all the people who had clutched it, crushed from the emotion of the hands that had held it. She smoothed it out on the scrubbed pine.

Forgive me

She traced the two words with her finger again and again, trying to feel her father's touch within the familiar slanting scrawl.

Outside, someone raced past the window. She could still hear Papa's name being called, far away down on the beach.

As soon as Mama saw the note, she had rallied, hurrying away through the gardens and down to the beach. She had lived her whole life on this island, the sea in her coral bones, and she knew exactly what she must do. She organised the herring girls into groups, and had them sweep the beaches across the entire island. She ordered the *Schoonheid* to scour the sea.

But though she was born of nautical stock, she forgot that Papa was not. He was an immigrant; a land lover, and a businessman above all.

Marianne sat at the kitchen table, trying to focus on the simplest thoughts in her mind, but the words he had uttered the last time she saw him kept swimming before her eyes.

Forgive me, forgive me.

Somewhere outside, the peacocks started up their call, and she remembered the moment she had found out about Nan: the softness of Ebisu's feathers as she clung to him in her sadness, the whole world as she knew it crashing down around her. She remembered the flash of black-and-white tiles beneath her feet, the sharp tools abandoned on them, and suddenly, she knew where her papa was hiding.

She pulled open the kitchen door and stood for a moment, facing the mainland, before turning south, towards the oyster beds and the pull of the pavilion beyond.

She ran all the way, her skirt gathered in her hands. When she arrived at the old building, she sank down on the shingle for a moment, her lungs screaming. When she straightened up, the pavilion was ahead of her, sad and forlorn. The wind had picked up again, and she could make out the deep red curtains billowing through the half-finished window frames. It made the building look as if it was bleeding, the blood pulsing through its cracks.

She climbed the steps to the veranda. The double doors ahead of her were old and grand, their wooden panels speckled with salt. She put a hand on each, and pushed.

The wind entered the hall at the same time as she did, rushing around the room, caught between the walls with nowhere to go.

Papa was hanging from a length of fishing rope at the centre of the room, his face purple, the breeze playing with him as if he were a part of the landscape, and nothing more.

Chapter Twenty-Four

Tartelin

Summer 2018

Dogger Bank is so still, I can hear the wind rustling in the leaves of the oak tree outside.

'I'm so sorry,' I say eventually, looking down at the photograph album on Miss Stourbridge's lap. It is opened to a picture of her father, sitting proudly at his desk. He has a pipe clamped between his lips, his expression serious and business-like.

'Is that why you told Nan to leave?' I ask her.

'Yes.'

'But …' Miss Stourbridge shifts slightly in her seat, and I almost stop myself from saying it, but something inside me makes me carry on. 'But she wasn't responsible for your father's death, surely? It was his decision to end his life.'

At these words, Miss Stourbridge's face appears to collapse with grief, and I realise that it's still so raw for her. I remember her telling me how coming back here after so many years was difficult, and I can imagine how it must have awakened ghosts she thought she had buried long ago. Has she never talked about what happened, discussed it with another person?

'You have to understand, Tartelin,' she says, 'I was grieving. I needed someone to blame, and she was there.' As she speaks, it's as if she's dredging the words up from many years ago, as if she has gone over her decision again and again across the decades, trying to understand why she responded like she did.

'But couldn't you have blamed your father?'

She lifts the edge of the photograph album with her finger, letting it fall back down. 'In death, he couldn't answer for his actions. He was no longer there to take the blame, to put forward his side of the story, and so I turned to Nan.' Her voice is infused with a tremor of guilt.

'Did she put her side of the story to you? Did she try and fight you?'

'Of course she didn't. She had been involved in whatever Papa was doing to save his businesses. She hadn't known that what they were doing was illegal, of course, but she felt at least partly to blame. She had already told me she thought it was her fault: I just took her for her word. I used that against her. It was wrong, I know that now. I would have known it then if I hadn't been so wracked with grief.'

She pauses, her eyes settling on mine. The sharp wisdom I've seen every time I look in them has gone, to be replaced by a film of milky sadness. 'I don't tell you this because I want your sympathy, Tartelin,' she says. 'You're perfectly within your rights to be disgusted by my actions. I certainly am. It's the first time I've spoken about my father's death to anyone.'

I try to take in what she's saying. I have wanted to understand this strange, obstinate woman since the day I arrived, but now that she's laying her truths before me, I don't know what to say.

Miss Stourbridge speaks again, into my silence.

'When you first arrived, you told me about your mother's death, and I'm afraid I was rather rude. I want to apologise. As you may have gathered, my relationship with my own parents was ... strained. Death is an odd thing. I am surrounded by it here, and I may have become a bit too matter of fact about it. I apologise.'

I reach for her hand, and she jumps at the touch, then encloses her fingers around mine.

'What was she like,' she says, 'your mother? Tell me about her.'

I prod gingerly at the memories of my mum in my mind, finding that it doesn't hurt quite so much as I thought it would. I tell her about Mum's joyfulness at life, and the cancer that ripped it from her. It's a relief to say the words out loud, as if speaking them makes what happened real.

She sighs deeply. 'Tartelin, I——'

'I came here to get away after she died,' I interrupt her, not daring to look up, not wanting to see the sympathy in her eyes. 'She always loved the sea.'

When I look up, Miss Stourbridge is looking at me, but she's not smiling, and there are no tears in her eyes. I find I can meet her gaze. We have both lost people we loved, after all. Something passes between us, and I feel stronger.

'I can't imagine how awful it must have been, finding your dad like that.'

Miss Stourbridge looks down at the photograph of her father. It is the last photograph in the book, and she closes it slowly, the pages coming together with a dull thud.

'I've never been able to go back there,' she says, pushing the baleen clasp closed. There is something final about the click it makes as it secures the photos within. She places the album on the chaise, and turns to stare out of the window. With a sigh, she rouses, as if coming out of a trance.

'It's time we found you better accommodation,' she says. 'Come.' And the wheelchair jolts forward, as if it has a mind of its own.

We leave the panelled room and go out onto the landing. She leads me past the nets on the wall to what I assume is her bedroom door. Pushing it open, she goes through, and I follow behind, wiping my tears away, momentarily surprised that what I'd thought would be Miss Stourbridge's bedroom is actually a long corridor.

'I remember those little rooms downstairs,' she says over her shoulder. 'My governesses used to sleep in the one you're in. Awfully tiny space. Cramped. Nan says you deserve better. Come this way.'

Before I can object – I have grown to like my little cell – she leads me swiftly down the long hall.

'That is my room,' she says, nodding at a door on our right, 'and this is yours.' She stops before a second door, and inclines her head. I turn the handle.

The room is much bigger than the room I occupy downstairs but, judging by the view from the window, it sits directly above it. It is a beautiful room, with pale honeyed floorboards and an immaculate tapestry rug. My eyes are drawn to the headboard of the bed, where a little upside-down heart is cut out.

Miss Stourbridge follows me inside, stopping in the middle of the room. 'This was Nan's room,' she says.

I swing round. 'Then surely Nan should be staying in it?' I say, thinking of her current accommodation in the old herring hut down on the beach.

Miss Stourbridge raises her hands. 'I have asked her, Tartelin, but she says she is perfectly comfortable where she is. Perhaps one day she'll move in here, but we are only at the beginning of our reconciliation, remember. We have a long road ahead of us, Nan and I.' She looks around the room. 'She said she thought you might like it, and it is her room to give away.'

I turn and look at my new room, marvelling at the space around me, the motes of dust dancing in the golden light.

'I haven't been in here for years,' Miss Stourbridge says. There is a strange huskiness to her voice, what my mother would have referred to as a church voice. She clears her throat and adopts her usual brisk manner, 'I'm afraid it will need a good dust.'

She goes over to the wardrobe, pulling it open with some difficulty. A cloud of dust erupts, followed by a few tiny moths. I peer round her to take a look inside. The wardrobe is filled with dresses, jostling colourfully for space. Before I came to this island, I lived in dresses and skirts, but I have worn shorts for so many days now that I can hardly remember what it is to feel the swish of material around me.

'Were these yours?' I ask, eagerly stepping forward. I run my hand over them, fingering the silks and satins, the thick linen and brocaded bodices that compete in the small space. I am no historian, but these are many years old. Here and there I can see small holes where the moths have chewed at them.

'Some of them,' she says, trailing her hand over a dress of cream linen striped with navy. She casts her eye over me, standing next to her, the look on her face critical, assessing. 'I might have something that fits you,' she says, looking me up and down, 'you're a petite little thing.' She riffles through the dresses, her practised fingers searching until they land on a swathe of silk the colour of the sea.

'This was one of the first pieces made from our own silk, the year after Papa passed.' She reaches up to try and unhook it, and I help, lifting the dress down. It peels away from its neighbours, the long skirt flowing out like a peacock's tail in its wake.

'It's beautiful,' I say. Its colour shifts and changes in the light from blue-green to grey, as if clouds are scudding over the sun. 'Was it yours?' It's hard to tell how tall Miss Stourbridge is in her chair, but her legs under the blanket jut out quite far, and she sits proudly, her shoulders straight and tall: she is certainly taller than me. I hold the dress against me, and it rests on my ankles, as if it has been made for me.

'I had it made for Nan, but she never wore it.'

'Why not?'

'It was made months after she left,' she says.

I wonder why you would make a dress for someone you know you might never see again? Was there hope stitched into this dress? Hope that Nan would one day return?

Her eyes linger on the silk. 'Try it on, Tartelin,' she says at last. 'A dress is only a dress when it is worn, after all.'

Her eyes linger on me, and they are brighter than normal, as if she has shed a great weight in the last few hours. She gives me a sad smile, reaching out and touching my hand briefly. And then, abruptly, she turns and makes her way back to the door.

'I'll leave you to your room.'

When she's gone, I lay Nan's dress on the bed and go over to the window. I push the sash up with an effort, and dust spirals up from the dressing table as fresh air enters the room for what must be the first time in years.

I lean out and look to the west, searching the distant scrubland for the pavilion. It's just visible, rising above the gorse, and I take a long, shuddering breath, as if I've been holding it without realising. Marianne and Nan's father, gone, just like that. I think of Miss Stourbridge's severe demeanour; the wall that she has constructed, layer by layer, to hide herself away. What she has told me today goes some way to explaining it all. The image of her father swings like a pendulum before my eyes, and I force my mind to think of something else.

Over by the bed, a triangle of shadow catches my eye, flickering on the wall. I go over and run my hands across the wallpaper, admiring the curls and swathes of what looks like seaweed in its pattern. A corner of wallpaper has lifted away, flapping in the breeze, and I sit on the bed and hook my finger under it, lifting it up. Beneath is a hole, just big enough for a small finger to reach through. Marianne's bedroom is on the other side of this wall, and I think of Nan, lying here, Marianne barely inches away.

I go down to my old bedroom and pack up my meagre possessions. I lift the delicate bird that Mum made from the windowsill, and take the Quality Street tin from the bedside cabinet. I collect my belongings together, taking them all upstairs, unpacking slowly in my new room. I lay shells and dried seaweed that I've collected in spirals across the dressing table, a flecked pebble that reminds me of Gabbro at their centre.

I stand, looking about the room with Mum's little bird on my palm, wondering where to put him. The window in this room is too far from the bed, and besides, he might be blown outside by a puff of air. I decide instead to sit him on the bedside cabinet so that I can gaze at his round little body as I curl up each night.

I look at the silk dress on the end of the bed. The fabric has settled into the colour of a still rock-pool, and I lie down next to it. This bed is much comfier than the lumpy mattress downstairs. As my head nestles against the pillow, I see the little cut-out heart just above my brow, the right way up now. I think again of Marianne, sleeping just the other side of this wall, and I touch the loose wallpaper next to the bed, lifting it up and tracing the hole beneath. I put my mouth to it and whisper, half hoping the teenage Marianne is on the other side, listening.

I get up and remove my clothes slowly until I'm standing, naked, in the room. The silk dress shivers over my skin, smoothing my sharp hip bones and glancing off my thighs. The cowl neck cascades like a waterfall between my breasts, and I open the wardrobe door and look in the mirror.

The glass is old, the silvering speckled with rust, and I hardly recognise myself in its flattering light. I pull my hair into a soft bun and secure it with a tortoiseshell clasp that is sitting on the dressing table, as if waiting for me. The blue-green of the silk and the deep black of my hair makes my milky skin look almost metallic white, and I think how Miss Stourbridge knew Nan would never wear it, and yet she had it made anyway.

When I turn back to the room, I see the Quality Street tin where I left it on the bed. I lift it carefully in my arms, cradling it to me, and I know that now is the right time.

As I start towards the door, somewhere downstairs a bell rings, and I wonder why Miss Stourbridge is ringing for me when she has only just left. I go out onto the landing, the tin still in my arms. The sound is louder out here, more insistent, and I realise it isn't the tinkling bell that summons me to my employer, but a different bell, brasher and more forceful. It's coming from the front door.

As I begin the descent downstairs, I'm aware for the first time of the great curve of the grand staircase before me, the feel of the silk dress on my skin, and I think, this is what it must have felt like in Dohhalund's heyday, sweeping down the staircase, the warm summer's night pouring in at the windows, bringing with it the promise of dancing and music and the heady excitement of the balmy evening ahead.

Through the blue glass of the grand front door, a silhouette stands, and as I reach the bottom of the stairs, I sense who it is, even though they're just a blur. I know intimately the tall, broad shoulders, the way their posture is relaxed, yet aware. A feeling of happiness surges through me, pushing through the grief that lingers in this house, and I unlatch the door and open it wide, and it's like inviting the sun into an overcast day.

Jacob is holding a bunch of wild flowers. He stands in the doorway, staring at me, and I look down at the dress, embarrassed by its splendour. He opens his mouth, but no words come out, and he pushes the flowers towards me instead. I recognise sea lavender and thrift, and little dots of veined white flowers that I don't know the name of. A small strand of sea-pea pokes up like tiny amethyst bells, and I dip my nose to it and smell its delicate perfume.

'It's a beautiful evening,' Jacob says, standing on the threshold. 'You look ... incredible.'

He's wearing a different jumper, this one without the holes and plucks I've grown accustomed to. It is a deep, flecked purple, like the flowers, and it reminds me a little of Nan's tunic she left discarded on the beach. He's still watching me, as if the shimmer of the silk has bewitched him and he can't take his eyes off it. Behind him, I can just make out the line of shells, travelling off into the distance. He manages to pull his eyes away from me at last and follows my gaze, giving his head a little shake as if he's coming out of a trance.

'I saw some people adding to it the other day,' he says. 'I think you've started something.' He reaches into his pocket. 'I came to give you this. I promised you I'd charge it.' He pulls out my phone, and I take it, a rush of excitement flooding through me.

'It works?' I look at him, and he nods.

'Fully charged.'

The phone feels alien in my hand: heavy and unnatural. I press the button, and it lights up almost immediately. It is an inexplicable joy, holding its weight in my hand, knowing my mother is moments from my eyes. My finger hovers over the screen. It's been so long without a phone, and I'm momentarily unsure what to do, and then, remembering, I tap the photos app, and she is there, waiting for me, the expression on her face saying, *as if I could be anywhere else.*

'Thank you,' I whisper.

'Tartelin?' Miss Stourbridge's scratchy voice echoes down from upstairs, 'Tartelin, who is it?'

I can hear the wheels of her chair squeaking across the wooden floor above. In a moment she will come close enough to see Jacob. I hover on the doorstep, wondering if we have time to slip out of the house. Upstairs, I hear the first chimes of the mantel clock beginning again, and the wheels of her chair come to a halt.

'Can I come in?' Jacob says, 'I'd like to meet her ... if that's OK?'

I waver for a moment, but he has every right to meet her. And besides, he has the ability to brighten even the saddest of places, and Dogger Bank feels so desperately sad today.

'Of course,' I say, stepping back to let him in.

I lead him up the stairs, conscious of the way the silk dress flows behind me, the way it settles at the base of my spine, revealing the bare skin of my back. He's so close I can feel his breath on my skin, and I ache for the warm touch of his hand there as well.

At the panelled room, I knock, but there's no reply. The door is ajar, and I push it open.

Miss Stourbridge is sitting, not in her usual place at the desk, but in front of the mantel clock, facing away from us. She doesn't turn straight away, her head lowered, as if in prayer. I pause on the threshold. It feels as if we've interrupted something private.

'Miss Stourbridge?' I venture.

She turns sharply, as if she has forgotten anyone was downstairs, and her eyes fix on Jacob. 'Oh!' she says.

Jacob smiles an easy smile. I see that he's not intimidated by people in the same way that I am, and pride swells within me. He reaches out to her and they shake hands. Something intangible passes between them, a beam of mutual intelligence that I'm not party to, and then it's gone.

'This is Jacob Hall,' I say. 'He likes spiders.'

Jacob laughs, the sound flowing easily around the room. He looks so at home, so relaxed, that part of me is envious: it has taken me weeks to begin to feel like that around Miss Stourbridge.

'Very nice to meet you, Mr Hall. Tell me, do you like butterflies?'

She takes him over to her desk, showing him her latest dissected specimen. They begin comparing notes on their finds, and I stand on my own, clutching the Quality Street tin, feeling like a spare part. I'm reminded of my first day at Dogger Bank, when I stood as I do now, waiting, looking at this old woman about whom I knew nothing.

I think of what I know about her now: of her life as a young woman, of her grief and sadness. I think of the notion of the blast. Of the brass scales in the study, the measurements written in a wavering hand. I look over at the Chinese cabinet, the strange butterflies inside it, and then I remember the pagoda with its roof slammed shut, and suddenly I'm desperate to take Jacob's hand and lead him back downstairs, outside to the beach and the water and the air, to tell him everything I've learnt, and see if he thinks it's plausible.

It's a strange feeling, wanting to confide in another, caring enough about them that I care about their views, too. I've been so self-contained for so long that it feels as though I am a flower, opening up. Miss Stourbridge would no doubt say I was a butterfly, emerging from my chrysalis.

I look over at the clock on the mantelpiece. It's still stuck at eight o'clock, ticking intermittently as if time means something else on Dohhalund, something that isn't constricted to moving in straight lines.

'Tartelin, be a dear and bring us some tea, and then we can have a good long chat,' Miss Stourbridge says, settling back in her chair and extending her arm towards the chaise, looking pointedly at Jacob.

He pauses, his mouth slightly open, as if he wants to say something

264

but cannot find the correct words. 'I … I actually came to see if Tartelin would like to go for a walk with me. I would love to talk with you properly later, Miss Stourbridge, but I wanted to look at your garden while the light is still good, if you'll permit me.'

If she is affronted, she doesn't show it. She smiles at him beatifically.

'Of course, what's left of it, anyway. Please go ahead, but be careful near the edge.'

I shoot a glance out of the window. I haven't been in the garden for a few days. From up here, the house feels very close to the cliff. I estimate there are perhaps five or six metres of grass, if that. The proximity to the sea feels momentarily unsettling.

'Actually,' I say, and my voice is unexpectedly strong. Jacob turns his attention to me, and I feel, again, the laser assurance of his eyes deep inside me. 'I was just going down to the beach. I need to do something, and I'd like you to come, Jacob, if you wouldn't mind. But then, yes, a walk in the garden would be nice.'

Jacob smiles and nods to Miss Stourbridge, who dips her head in return.

'Come on, then,' he says to me, taking my hand and pulling gently.

I leave the flowers on the chaise to take to my room later.

As we reach the doorway on the way out, Miss Stourbridge calls out to me, 'It suits you, Tartelin, the dress. I am so glad it's been worn.' And she smiles.

Something passes between us, a look that cements a bond we have been working on for days, and I smile back, and follow Jacob out of the room.

'What on earth can be in that tin that you need to bring it all the way down here?' Jacob says as we step onto the sand beneath Dogger Bank.

I look down at the tin I'm hugging to me, tracing the letters with my finger. 'They were my mum's favourite chocolates,' I say, remembering how she would always steal the toffee pennies before I got a look-in. 'It was the only thing she would eat, in the last days.'

Her hospice bed was littered with the wrappers. She used to peel the see-through cellophane away from the foil and look at the room through the different colours. The blue ones were her favourite. She said they made her feel like she was underwater.

'After she died, when I collected her ashes, she was in a cardboard urn. It was cheap and tacky, and she would have hated it. So I gave her a new urn, one she would have found both funny and joyful, and I brought her with me.' I hug the tin close. 'She always said we were people of the sea. I wanted to return her to where she came from.'

Jacob nods, his small smile understanding, and we walk down to the edge of the shore. It feels like the right time. My feet are bare, the tendrils of the dress caressing my ankles. I lever off the lid, and step into the sea, and the ashes that were my mother stir in the breeze. I crouch in the water and submerge the tin, and she is released, rolling away in the waves, becoming a part of the sea.

I straighten up and stand there for some time, letting the magic of the place settle over me.

The last birds I made before I came to the island were small and light, designed to gather in flocks, to flit and shimmer in the slightest breeze. I am reminded of them in this moment as I imagine the molecules of my mother, moving through the water away from me and out into the world, and it occurs to me that we're not designed to stay in one place, rather to always reach for the unreachable, to stretch out our arms and touch the myriad possibilities laid out before us. I turn and walk from the water.

Jacob is sitting a little further back on the sand, and I sit down next to him.

'Your mother was very special to you,' he says, looking out over the water. It isn't a question.

'I needed to bring her with me. All she talked about in her last few days was the sea.'

I take my phone from my pocket and, switching it on, show Jacob the picture of her, laughing at the camera.

'She looks like a good mum,' he says.

'She would have loved you,' I say, knowing it's true, and the corners of his mouth lift.

We sit for a long time, watching the sky change as the sun goes down behind us.

Eventually, I say, 'What about that walk then?'

Dogger Bank's garden feels smaller than the last time I walked here, and I wonder if a little more of it has crumbled over the cliff in recent nights. As we walk, I picture the fallen chapel, back in its rightful place, superimposing it onto a garden that stretches far into the sea. There is only an oak tree here now between the cliff edge and the house, its roots stretching out into the air above the sea like Adam reaching out to God.

Jacob's hand touches mine, and our fingers interlace as we walk. I feel the silk of the dress sweep over my skin as I step barefoot through the lush grass, and I am, for a brief moment, living in a different time, a time of silkworms and pearls and the silver swash of herring scales.

Jacob stops at the oak tree and his hands reach up to stroke the trunk as he peers into its crevices, peeling away the leaves, examining the bark beneath. I leave him to pore over his new find, and continue walking through the garden, knowing he will be lost there for a while yet.

I come to a stop at the edge of the cliff. The sky all around me is tinged with yellow. On evenings like this, there is a moment, just before the dark descends, where the sky turns from yellow to green.

It only lasts a minute, but sometimes, as I watch it, it's as if the world has tipped upside down and the sea is above me, and I am hanging, clinging to clouds, while below me phosphorescent stars begin to light up in little pinpricks. It's moments as unreal as this that I can start to believe my mother's stories of eggs floating on the tide, and I can begin to hope that love and happiness — the things she wanted for me — are real, tangible things.

Far below me, at the bottom of the cliff, leftover sea water pools around the bricks of the chapel. The tide is receding again, the sheen of ebb-water like a skin on the sand. In the distance, the wells are visible, and I think, with a prickle to my skin, the tide will be even lower tonight.

The prickle intensifies, trickling down my neck to my back. Someone is watching me. I turn and look for Jacob, but he's still deep in his oak tree. I scan the garden, but there's no one there.

It's as I begin to turn back to the sea that I see Miss Stourbridge. She is sitting in the picture window upstairs, half hidden in shadow. She withdraws as soon as I see her, but not before I register the expression on her face. There is a nostalgic look in her eyes, and something else, a touch of melancholy, and I put my hand up and touch my hair, feeling the tortoiseshell clasp. Did I look like Nan to her, standing there, with the sea and sky as my backdrop?

I pull at the clip and strands of my hair peel away, tumbling down my back. The dress snags on a thistle, and I stop by the oak tree and crouch down, trying to untangle it. When I straighten up, Jacob is there, staring not at the tree this time, but at me, and the look in his eyes is all-consuming.

I step towards him, but he's already there, the warmth of him surrounding me, smoothing away the goose bumps that have scattered across my arms. He pulls me behind the oak, away from prying eyes, and hidden behind the low boughs he bends his head and kisses first my lower lip, then my whole mouth, his earthy hands reaching up to tangle in my hair.

We break away and sink down on the damp grass, sitting close, our heads touching, and look out to sea. Jacob leans over and lifts something from beneath the roots of the tree. He opens his hands to reveal a huge black-brown beetle, as shiny as the sticky buds of a horse-chestnut tree.

'It's a stag beetle,' he says, and I think of the little deer that was taken down at the creek. 'See here?' He points to the horns that twist out from the beetle's head. 'They're meant to resemble a deer's antlers, but these are too long.'

The horns that the beetle is named for jut out at awkward angles. They're at least as long as the insect's body, and they twist towards each other like two trees growing close together, like two lovers intertwined. The poor animal can hardly move with the weight of them. It rotates its head endlessly, the antlers stabbing at the air like a fencer's sword. I put out my palm, and Jacob tips the beetle onto it. It's heavy, covering half my hand, and it feels its way across my skin with sharp, pricking feet. I should feel repulsed, but there's something bewitching in the way the horns entwine, like the curling vines that hide a fairy tale castle.

'Something terrible happened here,' Jacob says, looking out to sea, 'there's something sinister about the island's beauty, as if nature is trying to fight back but doesn't know how.'

The beetle drops onto my lap, and I feel its feet catch at the silk as it navigates its way over the sea of grey-green. It tips off my leg and into the grass, finding the cover of the tree's roots, and all at once I'm engulfed by the magnitude of what happened here. The mystery and the power of it swells over me, and I stand and pull Jacob to his feet, wanting only to escape it all.

'Come,' I say, leading him away from Dogger Bank, away from the dark windows of the house.

We walk north, out of the garden, until eventually the cliff begins a gentle descent to the shingle beach, and I register the cold sand of the dunes beneath my feet. I can see the salt pans from here, their pale white faces turned up towards the emerging moon.

We come to a spot where the dunes ripple and curve, creating a hollow just large enough for two, and I pull Jacob down into its soft embrace.

In the gathering dusk, I pull the dress over my head, the fabric slipping over me like liquid. I reach for Jacob's jumper and do the same, pulling it off and unbuttoning his shirt beneath, seeing the way his eyes gleam in the darkness.

The clothes pool on the sand, and in the dark they are the colour of pebbles, the colour of marram grass at night, and they twist and twine together like lovers. We lie back, and I am lost in the warmth of him, drunk on the bosky smell of his skin.

It is as if the world has disappeared, as if the sea has arced over us, sheltering us beneath the curve of its waves, and we two are an island, ancient and wise. In this soft hollow that has become the world, we explore with hands and mouths the very nature of our bodies, drinking in the patterns and intricacies, the similarities and the differences, while the sky and the sea and the world holds its breath and waits.

Afterwards we dress. The sky above us has changed, metamorphosing from green to a dark, velvet blue. Jacob sits, pulling me with him to gaze out over the sea, the bare skin of our arms touching, and I'm lost in the changing colours, my mind reeling with all that I have felt and all that I have read and all that I have seen.

'Look,' Jacob says, pointing to the north. Far away over the military base, a strange cloud is shifting and contorting. It reminds me of a shoal of fish, darting one way then another.

'What is it?'

'It's a murmuration. Hundreds of starlings, flying together before they go to roost. But it shouldn't be happening. Starlings only murmur in the winter.'

We watch the dark cloud as it seethes across the sky. Like clouds, I think I can see shapes in it, too: an animal, a spider's web, a tree, blurring and changing so sharply that they are lost before my mind can catch hold of them. And then it changes course and suddenly it's growing closer. I can hear the rush of the birds' wings as they pour towards us, as the black cloud takes on a new form, something majestic in its magnitude. It looks like a whale, undulating through the sky; as it rears above us, it opens its wide mouth and dives down, as if to swallow us whole. I throw my arm over my face, but with a screeching call, the starlings burst apart, scattering away, dissolving into the sky.

Jacob lets out a shaky breath. 'Bloody hell,' he says.

I can feel my heartbeat pulsing through me, the blood coursing through my veins. I turn and look at the moonlight, seeing how it has licked the beach clean. The last of the water is withdrawing from around the wells now. They tower over the rippled sand, their shadows broken, fragmented. There are five altogether, each of them in differing states of disrepair. Two have crumbled so much that they are barely more than a pile of rubble, but three stand straight and tall. The moon is reflected on the water that's held inside them, perfectly still now that it has no tidal urge.

Between the wells, thin curved structures reach up out of the sand like grasping fingers.

'Are those whale bones?' I ask.

Jacob shakes his head. 'I think they're shipwrecks,' he says, 'or boat wrecks, at least.'

I think of the *Zilver*, lost to the sea. Is it among the sad skeletons out there on the sand? I picture all of the sailors lost at sea over the years, fallen deep into the water along with their broken boats, drifting against the sea bed. I think of everything I've seen here: the butterfly with the human eyes, the phosphorescence and the intricate spider web. I picture the pearl I found, the way it swirled and shimmered bewitchingly. When I close my eyes, the impossible murmuration rushes towards me again, as if I'm an intruder, trespassing on its secret isle.

'There was an explosion,' I say, speaking to the sea, though I feel Jacob stir at my words. 'An experiment gone wrong. The bombs they tested here, after they requisitioned the island: Miss Stourbridge says they were nuclear. They thought there was no one here, but she was here. She witnessed it.'

'That's not possible,' he says. 'We would know about nuclear testing if it had happened here. It would be in all the history books.'

'But what if it was done in secret?'

'She can't have been here. They wouldn't have allowed it.'

'I don't think they knew. She ... Jacob, I think she was pregnant.' The brass scales in the study flash before my eyes again, the scrap of paper next to them, recording the weight of something, the vital signs written in little snatches: *pale today, breathing quickly.*

I risk a glance to my left. Jacob is sitting back, reeling from this information. I can see by his face he is slotting pieces of the puzzle into place.

'Could it have happened?' I ask, hearing the pleading in my voice. 'I'm so confused by everything I've seen here. It all points to what she's saying, but there's no tangible proof.'

Jacob is gazing out to sea, but his eyes are elsewhere, focused on what I'm saying.

'I've spent so much time with her,' I continue, 'and I really think she believes it, and it makes me want to believe it, too, because underneath the prickliness and the severity, she's a good person, Jacob. She's kind. And I think she cares about me,' I add, realising for the first time how important this is to me. 'I don't think she would lie.'

He is silent, watching the sea as the tide begins to turn.

'You've met her,' I persist. 'What do you think?'

His eyes are on the horizon. When he speaks, I can see he is choosing his words carefully, his voice monotone.

'I've been here for quite a few weeks now,' he says. 'I've seen the strangeness of the island. What she's told you: it *could* be possible, theoretically.' He turns to me, his eyes pulling at the thoughts that drift on the surface of my face, visible for anyone to see. 'But perhaps it has always been like this, Tartelin – its own genetic bubble in the North Sea.'

I nod, running my fingers across the dune and scooping up a handful of sand. It's as cold as sea water, and I let it trickle through my fingers.

'She's an extremely intelligent woman, Miss Stourbridge, I see that, but she's also very old.' He turns and looks at the sea again. There is doubt and confusion and intrigue etched into his face, and a softness in his expression that I want to wilt into, but I can't give myself up to him, not yet.

I get to my feet, brushing sand from my dress. 'I'll talk to her tomorrow,' I say, my throat constricting at the thought of broaching the subject with her, but I know I must do it, and with that thought comes a surge of pride: I am no longer the tentative, frightened person I was when I arrived. I have changed. Metamorphosed. I am strong enough now to confront her.

I look out over the sea. The water is closing over the tips of the boat wrecks now, dark and smooth and glittering, as if it's putting a finger to its lips, pretending that they were never there.

'I need to get to the bottom of what happened here,' I say, speaking to the sea. 'We've come so far, she and I. I just hope she knows she can trust me.'

Jacob stands and scoops my hair out of the silk dress. He doesn't say anything, only drops his head, his lips brushing mine in affirmation.

Chapter Twenty-Five

Tartelin

Summer 2018

That night my sleep is velvet blue, thick and dreamless, and when I wake in the morning, I forget for a moment where I am. I see the edge of the seaweed wallpaper, lifting away from the wall, and I run my finger under it, feeling the whisper of a breeze from the hole that lies beneath. For a moment I think I hear my mother whispering to me, but then I remember that she will never say my name again, and I lie still and hold in my mind instead the dunes that cradled Jacob and me a few hours ago, the basin of stars above us.

The day waits for me, unfurling across the window in drips of dew brightness that promise to be swept away by the sun. Whatever happens today, I know that — come the evening — I must ask Miss Stourbridge a difficult question.

I spend the day searching for butterflies, but nothing comes close enough for me to catch and, in all truthfulness, my heart is not in it. At the back of my mind are the revelations about Marianne's father and about Nan, and deep beneath that my nerves are like a rippling pool, coming to the surface every now and again to remind me of the questions I must ask of my employer.

I get back to Dogger Bank and go to my little washroom downstairs to clean myself up before preparing the evening meal.

Further down the corridor, I hear the keening of the wind, so human that it startles me. I remember the workroom down there, the smell of salted fish, the bolts of silk piled on the shelves, and an idea comes to me.

In the workroom, I rummage through the shelves. There is an ancient pot of what looks like glue here, long hardened into solidity, and behind it I find an old embroidery kit: needles and thread, and a good pair of scissors. I test them. The sound they make slicing through the air is like silver, raising the hairs on the back of my neck.

I cut swatches of Dohhalund silk, enjoying the feeling of it slipping through my fingers. As I gather the pieces together, I notice a wine-rack in a dark corner. I choose a bottle at random, wiping the slick of dust from its label. The words feel strange in my mouth, Dutch, I think. I take my new-found treasures to my room.

Upstairs, I cut and tear the silk, thinking of the bird I saw in the meadow: those gills, that gleaming, iridescent throat. I snip tiny cuts into each piece until they resemble the filaments of feathers, and then I layer the silk, one on top of the other, colour upon colour, sewing them together, thinking of all the birds I have ever made.

But I am done with making birds. I look over at Nan's sea-green dress, abandoned on the chair, its hem dusted with golden sand. It is beautiful, but it does not belong to me. I turn back to the fragile pieces of feathered silk, layered like scales, and my hand drifts up and touches my cheek as I think.

This piece, it will be for me. With this silk I will make my own dress. I will grow my own feathers, and then? Then, I will wrap them about myself, and I will fly.

At dinner, I bring in the bottle of wine I took from the storeroom. Miss Stourbridge looks at it in surprise. The cork comes out cracked, but the wine is good and sharp and only slightly vinegary. The first sip warms me as I sit at my end of the table, slowly stirring the clear soup in my bowl, my ribs constricting at the thought of starting a conversation about the blast.

'I had no idea there was still wine down there,' Miss Stourbridge says, sipping tentatively, her mouth puckered in nervous anticipation. 'Not bad,' she says, nodding. She takes up her spoon, and sips at her soup noisily. I can feel her eyes on me as I look down at my own bowl.

'It's good,' she says. 'Perhaps you should try it. You never know, it might taste better this time.' She smiles at me, smacking her lips with pleasure.

I level my spoon and wait for a piece of seaweed to float by, then I lift it to my lips. The taste is reminiscent of the salt that Nan gave me on my second day, a full, rounded flavour that belies the thinness of the soup. It is delicious, and I realise I'm starving.

From far away downstairs, that strange keening cry of the wind echoes up to us. Miss Stourbridge looks up.

'Did you hear that?' she says sharply.

'What?'

'It sounded like ...' She pauses, listening.

The sound comes again, distant, but clear, like the crying of a newborn. A strange expression crosses her face for a moment, as if the years have fallen away, but it's quickly replaced by her usual stern composure. She lifts her wine glass and takes a deep sip, her eyelashes fluttering as she swallows. My stomach twists in knots at the questions I need to ask her, and I take a gulp of wine to give me courage.

'I would like you to catch me something else,' Miss Stourbridge says suddenly, putting down her glass and wiping invisible crumbs from the table, as if she is wiping away whatever thoughts flitted across her mind.

'Another butterfly?' The killing jar containing yesterday's catch is still on her desk. The butterflies stopped moving hours ago, but she hasn't set them.

Miss Stourbridge shakes her head. 'No, a fish.'

I baulk at the idea. 'A fish? How—'

'It's easy. It just requires a different sort of net.'

'Can't you ask your fisherman to get one?'

'I need one alive, and I need one soon. There are buckets in the annexe. I only need something small, a sand eel or a sprat. To be honest, even a shrimp will do, but the more species, the better. I'm sure you can find them all at low tide, trapped in those little lagoons that form down near the chapel ruins.

'Have we finished with butterflies, then?' I ask, feeling a tinge of frustration.

'For the moment.'

I think of the strange butterfly with the human-looking eyes. 'I'm sorry if I didn't catch the right kind,' I say.

'No matter. Perhaps you will find catching fish less ... distressing,' she says.

I stir the spoon through my soup. 'What are you actually looking for?' I ask, spooning the last of the broth into my mouth and swallowing tightly, the mussels I still can't stomach settling on the bottom of the bowl like washed-up sailors. I wipe my lips with my napkin.

'I'm looking for changes in the animals, in the way they look and the way they behave. I'm looking for proof of what happened: you know that.'

'But what are you hoping you'll find?'

My question stops Miss Stourbridge mid-sip. Her eyes rest on the open door behind me, the window in the distance, the sea beyond.

'There's something important out there, isn't there?' I say, turning to share her gaze outside, thinking about the way she studies the water

277

obsessively through her telescope. 'There's something you haven't told me about. In the sea. That's why we're moving on to fish.'

'It doesn't concern you,' she says, taking another sip of her soup.

'But it does.'

She looks up sharply, unused to my answering back.

'What will you do with them?' I ask. 'The fish that I bring you?'

'I will observe them. The copper bath was built to store herring. I will keep them there and study them. If there are any aberrations among them, I will end their life and dissect them.'

'Do you kill every aberration you come across?' The words leave my mouth before I can check myself. Miss Stourbridge stiffens. She is looking at my cheek, I can feel her eyes glancing off the ruffled skin there.

I am sick of being looked at.

'You already know there's mutation on this island. You've shown it to me in the swallows outside your window, and the Chinese cabinet is filled with mutated butterflies. How many things will you need to kill before you have sufficient evidence? What happened here in 1955, Marianne? What are you really looking for?' I stop short. I have never called her by her first name before.

She is leaning back as if I've slapped her. She puts her spoon down quietly, her eyes fixed on it.

'I'm sorry,' I say, the words coming out like a sigh. 'I just need to know.'

She stays silent, her eyes sharp and black. I pick up my napkin, twisting it in my hands.

'You call me your assistant,' I start again, 'but in order to assist you, shouldn't you let me in on what we're searching for? You've been so good to me, giving me a home at a time in my life where I felt so at odds with the world, and I'm thankful for it, really I am. I've begun to heal here after everything that happened with my mum. I think – I hope – I've looked after you well enough. I've done as you've asked, at least most of the time.'

Here Miss Stourbridge's mouth lifts in a smile, and I'm bolstered by it.

'And yet there's this ... barrier ... between us. You say there was an explosion, that only you witnessed it, but you won't give me any details. You send me out there, onto what I now know is an extremely dangerous island, giving me only the barest hints of the danger I could put myself in.' I take a deep breath. 'It took your long-lost sister coming back into your life before you would tell me about your past. And even now, you're still holding back.'

The napkin is coiled tightly around my fingers now, cutting into the flesh so that it looks white.

'I've given up everything to be here, and I know it was my decision,' I say as she opens her mouth to object, 'but this place, it's become so special to me ... *you* have become so special to me, and I don't know how I can carry on here if you won't trust me with the truth.'

She's quiet for so long that I begin to feel stupid, sitting there, as if I've made a terrible judgement. I drop my head, waiting for the angry remonstrations to start, the stubborn denial.

'You're right,' she says finally, and I let out a breath I hadn't realised I was holding.

She brings her hands together at her chin, wringing them, rubbing at them.

'I haven't been completely honest with you,' she says. 'It takes time for me to trust. I told myself I would tell you everything once I knew I could trust you. I thought that once I had told you about my father and Nan, that it would be easier to tell you the rest. But it's hard, Tartelin.'

A trickle of excitement pricks at my cheeks. I can feel the heat of it rushing through my skin, spreading over my face. 'Why?'

'Because ... what happened is so terrible,' she says, and her voice is strangled with grief. A coldness sweeps over me.

'I am ashamed, Tartelin. I am deeply, basely ashamed. For years it has been all I have thought about. I am sickened with myself. I think that's why I decided to come back here: to try to understand why I did exactly what I did.

'I promise you that I will tell you everything, but not tonight. It is late and I am tired, and my mind is foggy from the wine.'

I wilt with frustration. So, this is how she is playing it, fobbing me off until tomorrow, when no doubt she will find some other excuse not to tell me.

The shrill, mewling sound of the wind comes again from downstairs, and Miss Stourbridge's head snaps towards the door.

'What was that?' she says, cocking her head as if to hear better.

'It's only the wind.'

'I thought for a moment ...' She trails off, shaking her head.

My heart begins to pulse inside me. 'You thought it was a baby,' I say. The words are out before I can stop them.

She looks up, meeting my gaze, and there is fear in her eyes.

'I thought the same thing the other day, but it's just the wind. There *was* a baby though, wasn't there, Miss Stourbridge? In 1955. When the blast happened.'

Her mouth is open in surprise, and her face is as white as the flesh of the fish we ate on my first night here.

'Was it your baby?' I whisper.

Silence fills the room. It is a calm, warm silence, as if everything is out in the open at last. I take a deep breath of air, waiting for as long as it takes for the truth to be told.

Miss Stourbridge's shoulders droop, as if she is sighing.

'Yes,' she says, 'yes it was.'

Chapter Twenty-Six

Marianne
July 1955

Marianne bent over the ragged remains of the butterfly's wing, her swollen stomach pressed against the edge of the desk. The wing was torn away almost down to the core. She had already snipped its frayed edges into a neat line, cauterising the tiny blood vessels as she did so. The insect held still, as if knowing that any movement might end its already short life.

She had found the cocoon hanging under a clump of nettles, and known immediately that it was a peacock butterfly. Years of lepidoptera study took over, and, unable to leave it behind, she brought it back to the house to pupate alongside the brimstones that were already hanging in the puparium.

And there the cocoon had stayed until, unknown to Marianne, the butterfly had begun to hatch, clawing its way out and landing awkwardly at the bottom of the puparium. She found it hours later, its wing stuck to the glass, the scales smeared like an impressionist painting. It had tried in vain to fly, pulling so hard that the wing had torn away, and it lay, limp and fragile, its one remaining wing pulsing.

Marianne had stood looking at it, her hand to her stomach as her baby stretched and turned deep inside her. She remembered another butterfly, many years ago, that had been saved with tissue paper and glue and the careful hands of a friend. And so, she set about construct-ing a new wing.

Now, she gripped the tweezers in her left hand and, with great care, lifted the silken waxed wing she had made from the petri dish, stopping to consider it in mid-air. It was a perfect match to the quaking butterfly's remaining wing, even down to the glittering dust that coated its surface.

She painted a fine dab of clear glue onto its edge and brought it fluidly in to the broken wing, holding it in place with motionless hands. Two shimmering blue eyes aligned and gazed up at her from the butterfly's hindwings, and she allowed herself a small smile.

Carefully, she opened the tweezers, and the butterfly lay pulsing on the desk, unaware it was free.

'Go,' she said, wishing it upwards.

Slowly, delicately, it lifted its wings, both the real and the manufac-tured, until they closed above it. Marianne frowned as the silk wing lagged slightly, but then, with sudden weightlessness, the butterfly took off. It flew around the great panelled room, and she took delight in its jagged, miraculous flight.

She turned back to her desk to clear away the remnants of her work.

From far away, a heavy thud cascaded across the island. Marianne barely heard it, dismissing it as the soft boom of controlled explosions that often echoed from the spit of land at the north. But a second or two later, the room was steeped in a wave. It tore through the space, a solid thing: not air or water, but something you could drown in nonetheless, and Marianne watched, paralysed with fear, as the walls bounced and bent and returned, and the butterfly dropped.

In the absence of sound that remained after the explosion, she stared around the room, feeling the weight of the blast in her ears still. Her eyes landed on the butterfly, fallen on the desk. With a shaking finger she touched the tip of its tongue, uncurled in death. Its man-made wing was intact, but its real wing was shrivelled and diaphanous, like the skeleton of a winter leaf.

At the same moment, the muscles in her abdomen drew tight like gripping fingers, and she doubled over, reaching for her stomach, where the curious life inside her was moving, recoiling, dancing in a way she had never felt before.

Chapter Twenty-Seven

Tartelin

Summer 2018

When I wake the next morning, my first thought is of Marianne, and the baby she had here, all those years ago. When we said goodnight last night, I had the feeling that Miss Stourbridge was trying to summon up the courage to tell me everything right there, but in the end her nerve failed her, and she only nodded at me and wheeled herself away, unable to carry on.

I stretch in the warmth of the bed, knowing that today I won't be going out in search of butterflies or fish. She has promised to tell me the rest of her story, and in the bedroom next to mine, I hear her chair creak as she pulls herself into it from her bed.

I tiptoe downstairs and make a pot of tea. Knocking on her door, I leave the tray on the floor. Then I go to my bedroom and sit on my bed, and I wait.

I watch the light on my bedroom wall begin to change as the sun creeps higher, the seaweed pattern of the wallpaper appearing to undulate at its touch. There is a soft knock on the door, and I jump.

'Miss Brown?' comes the voice. 'Can I see you in the sitting room for a moment?'

Miss Brown. She hasn't called me that for a long time. Why would she start now? I swallow down my fear. 'One minute.'

I dress slowly, taking my time. My mouth is dry; there are so many thoughts running through my mind. Did I overstep the mark last night? Perhaps she's sending me home. Perhaps the long night gave her time to realise that she doesn't want to give up any more of her secrets to me, that she doesn't need me any more.

And it's only now, as these thoughts come to me, that I realise I don't want to go; not yet. There is too much on this island that I don't want to give up: there is the clear, uncompromising light of the sea. There is Jacob and his blue-eyed dog. There is the taste of briny seaweed and the thrill of finding a pearl. There is the sight of a freshly caught fish, the sharing of photographs and the bright gleam of a butterfly's wing.

And then there is Miss Stourbridge, the closest thing, I realise now, that I have to a family.

Once I'm dressed, I stand in my room, and it feels like home. It feels right. I walk slowly to the panelled room, as if to my death. Everything around me is heightened: the butterflies on the walls, the nets and top hat hanging from hooks on the landing. They all look unreal, like props in a show or exhibits in a museum.

She is sitting in front of her telescope. When I come in, she doesn't turn from it as she usually does, but continues to look, her eye pressed against the eyepiece.

'The silk dress looked beautiful on you the other day,' she says, still turned away from me, still watching the sea. 'No wonder he loves you.'

'Love's a strong word,' I say, going over to the fireplace and winding the broken clock, my eyes tracking the second hand as it moves irregularly round the face.

'Isn't everything about love, really?' Miss Stourbridge turns. 'Love and hate, they're just two sides of the same coin.' She presses her fingers against the skin around her eye socket, smoothing away the telescope's mark. 'I loved my father. And I loved Nan. But I hated them both a little, too. Seeing you in that dress reminded me so much more vividly than any photographs of what I had; of what I lost. It was the first dress we produced for the Dohhalund Silk Company, the product of so many events that happened that fateful year.'

She pushes the telescope aside and wheels herself as close as possible to the window.

'I knew Nan would never wear it,' she says, her voice misting the glass, 'but I always held out hope that she would come back. She taught me how to nurture the silkworms, how to unwind the cocoons that went into making the silk. It felt right to make something in her honour. Especially after what I did to her.' She shakes her head sadly, still looking outside. 'I was so angry, and so full of grief. I just ... stopped speaking to her. I should have said so many things. But in the end, I just told her to go.' She presses her head against the cold glass.

'My sister,' she says, and the emotion of those two words is so deep that I can see she is drowning. She turns to look at me over her shoulder. 'You do remind me of her, Tartelin. You have the same glint in your eye, whatever hardships you have faced, however deep down it is buried.'

I'm taken aback by her words, by how kindly they are spoken.

She goes over to her desk. Next to it, the puparium is still open, the discarded cocoons abandoned inside. She closes the lid and looks at me.

'Are you sure you want to know?' she asks. 'About what happened in 1955? Are you sure?' There is regret and fear in her voice, and for the first time she sounds as feeble and old as she looks; but I nod, feeling the prickle in my scalp that has heralded every strange new thing that's happened to me on this island.

Her hand is still on the puparium lid, and she turns back to it, regarding the glass box silently.

'I suppose it all started with a butterfly,' she begins.

Chapter Twenty-Eight

Marianne

July 1955

Clutching at her stomach, Marianne scooped up the poor, mutilated butterfly, and pulled herself from the desk, gritting her teeth and mustering enough energy to stagger to the chaise. She sank down and lay her cheek against the cool silk, the baby inside her thrashing and churning.

The dead butterfly dropped from her hand to the floor, and she knew no more.

She awoke sometime later, dazed, disorientated, her skin hot to the touch. Time seemed to unfurl in pulses, her whole world the slow dance of the baby in her stomach, the emerging ache above her temple.

After days, or hours, or months, she pulled herself up and stood, trembling, at the window. It took her a moment to realise that it was night-time now, and instead of the garden and the sea outside, her own face stared back at her. Even in the darkened reflection, her skin was a deep crimson. She looked down at her hands and saw the colour had spread there too.

Scarlet fever? she thought. Meningitis? Blood poisoning? Her blood certainly felt poisoned. It was rushing round her body, dropping in waterfalls from her heart to her womb. Occasionally it would disappear from her head altogether and she found herself more than once crumpled in a heap on the floor with no idea how she had got there.

Marianne awoke from one of these episodes, stirring slowly, her cheek pressed to the rough wool of the rug. She pulled herself to her feet and sat on the chaise, looking at the clock on the mantelpiece. Eight o'clock. She put her hand to her stomach, pressing, assessing. Far away, she thought she could hear the alarm sirens from the military base, or was it just the memory of the clock, chiming in her head?

Hunger ravaged through her, and with it a strange craving for salt water. She pulled herself up and staggered to a side table where she chewed her way through what remained of the fruit in the bowl. Outside the window, it was constant twilight, as if a sea fog had drifted in and got caught on the barbed wire that was strung across the island. Her ears replayed the sound of the blast again and again, as if it had caught somewhere behind her eardrums and wouldn't let go.

The fog, or smoke, or whatever it was, began to clear in the morning. Marianne got shakily to her feet and approached the tall, thin window to the north that overlooked the military base in the distance, lifting her father's binoculars to her eyes. The base, built to withstand the most ferocious of explosions, had changed. Her breath caught sharply inwards: the furthest testing facility was no longer whole. The raised roof had collapsed down onto itself, and she turned away, not wanting to look any more.

Her eyes settled instead on the picture window that framed the easterly view of the sea. She gazed greedily out through the glass, craving the comforting sight of the chapel at the end of the garden.

But where the little building had stood, its bell tower summoning them to worship since before she was born, a sharp cliff edge had taken its place, and beyond it, a roiling mass of sea water churned angrily.

Marianne bent over to be sick.

She awoke sometime later in her bed, not knowing how she had got there. She could hear the mantel clock, its tick like the wormy heartbeat of something only half alive. She was sure it had just struck eight; that only an hour before, it had done the same. She lay in bed, listening. Beneath the clock's chimes, she had the peculiar feeling that Nan was stirring in the room next to her, her soft breath just audible through the hole in the wall. She pushed aside the flap of wallpaper, her mouth brushing the plaster, desperate to talk to her, to make amends for everything she had done, but then she shook her head. She was getting confused: Nan had not been there for years.

The next day her fever abated briefly, and she sat at the desk, trying to contain her rising fear by following her normal routine, checking the brimstone cocoons in the puparium for signs of hatching. There was a swallow's nest above the window, and she sat, staring out over the sea for hours, waiting for the mother swallow to return. In the evening, she turned on the radio. It hissed and crackled, settling at last on a voice reading the evening news bulletin. She twisted the knob, and it came into focus. Marianne listened intently, but there was no mention of Dohhalund. Nothing about a blast. Had she imagined the explosion in her fevered state? The shipping forecast began abruptly, and she flicked the radio off, turning to stare out of the thin window to the north of the island, where the two bomb-testing sites stood. She put her hand on her stomach, stretched tight against her smock like an island rearing from the sea, her brow furrowed, thinking.

There *had* been an explosion, but why, she didn't know. Could it be linked, this illness and the blast that had bent the walls for a brief moment? She looked down at her engorged stomach, and a word came to her, a word she had read about in one of her science books.

Radiation.

Fear spiralled through her. Was that why the military had told them to leave? Were they testing something more dangerous than just explosives? She remembered the way her baby had writhed and squirmed inside her when the blast had split through the room. Might it need medical treatment when it was born? The thought crossed her mind that she should try to leave. But how? She knew from her meticulous planning that the military had ordered a ban of vessels in Dohhalund's waters. She had had to pay the fisherman a princely sum to coax him to break the law and collect her and her newborn a few weeks from now.

No, there was nothing for it but to wait until the prearranged collection date. Nothing had changed, really, not on the face of it. Her eyes flicked to the window. If she was right, then whatever radiation that had been released in the blast could still be out there, even now. In here, at least, she and her baby were safe, for the moment.

Out of the shadows, a girl's voice whispered, *Try to save it. It deserves a chance.*

Marianne opened her eyes, staring around the empty room. She knew that voice; she remembered the cadence of it so well, even after all these years.

'Nan?' she said, wide-eyed, but the voice said no more.

The following day, a headache plagued her for so long that black commas flashed before her eyes. She watched from her bed as a skein of geese scissored across the window, the usual V formation staggered and broken. The mother swallow was still not back. She wondered how long its babies could survive without food.

That evening, she lit the lamps for the first time since she'd gone into hiding, blinking them on and off at the window in the vague hope that someone might see them and send help.

She began marking off the days on the calendar in the study, any hope that her malady was just severe morning sickness slowly leaking away. Her hands became red and itchy, the rash spreading across her whole body. It marbled her stomach, and she wondered if the baby inside her was covered in it too.

As she scraped out a can of tinned potatoes, trying to swallow their fuzzy softness without gagging, she thought longingly of sea water, craving the taste of Dohhalund salt on her tongue. She could feel the crunch of it between her teeth, and more than once she reached out to pinch a crystal of it from the floor, only to realise there was nothing there.

'Salt,' she whispered to her baby, as if speaking the word might conjure the taste of it in her mouth. 'Salt.'

The days stretched before her in a fevered haze. She lay on the chaise, her hands on her stomach, and recited the Latin names of butterflies to pass the time. At the sound of her voice, the baby stilled, as if it was listening.

'*Papilionidae*,' Marianne said, whispering the words like a strange magic spell. '*Nymphalidae, Pieridae, Lycaenidae.*'

Her thoughts, spiked with illness, drifted back to her life before. It was easier to live in memories, to think of her childhood and the years before Papa died – and sometimes the years afterward. Lying on the chaise, waiting for the darkness outside to enfold her, she thought of Papa's unmarked grave, hidden in the corner of the chapel's small cemetery. Did his bones go over the cliff along with the chapel? Was he, even now, lying on the beach below, or had the sea taken him for its own?

'The sea is made up of unspeakable sadness,' she whispered. It was an island saying, a soothing mantra her mother had taught her, encompassing the respect and fear they had for the water that shrouded their lives.

She thought of the last time she had seen her mother, a few days before, sitting tall and proud as her wheelchair was hoisted over the side of the boat. Mama was nearly eighty, skeletal and frail, but still grasping onto the brittle vestiges of beauty. Marianne hoped that she had arrived safely at the cottage they had rented in Lowestoft; that their maid would look after her well.

She closed her eyes, and her mother appeared to her. Not the frail woman in the wheelchair, but the tall, incandescently beautiful woman of her childhood. Despite – and possibly because of – her beauty, it had been easy to ignore Mama, but after Papa died, her mother had been released from the golden shackles that had bound her to the house. In the days after his death, she had rallied, showing a strength Marianne hadn't known was within her. The debtors came back. They took the *Schoonheid*. They collected up the precious antiques and the ornate rugs from the house and carried them away. Mama managed to hide a few things in a storeroom, but still they lost so much.

The workers began to drift away, hitching lifts on passing boats that had moved into their waters, leaving the Stourbridge women almost alone on the island, with nothing but the silkworms and the mulberry trees to call their own. Marianne, only a few months shy of sixteen, and feeling the weight of her responsibilities, threw everything into the silk business, teaching herself the process of turning silk thread into luxurious bolts of fabric. Each night she fell into bed exhausted, her mind comfortingly blank as she drifted into a dreamless sleep.

In the spring of 1928, as the last of the herring girls mournfully waved their handkerchiefs from the deck of the floating bridge, Marianne had stood with her mother and Nan on the quay, waving farewell.

When the ferry was out of sight, Marianne took a sharp breath of air to bolster her, then she took hold of Nan's elbow, steering her out of earshot of her mother. It was the first time she had spoken to her since before Papa had died.

'I need to hear your side of the story,' she said quietly to her, watching her mother out of the corner of her eye.

Nan's usually calm eyes widened with apprehension, and a seed of hope began to bloom deep inside Marianne.

'Tell me, Nan, do you know who you are?' she whispered, but even as the words left her lips, she saw the way Nan lowered her eyes to the ground, saw the small nod of her head, and she let go of Nan's elbow as if stung.

'I thought … I thought we were friends,' Marianne said, her voice cracking. 'I thought we could tell each other anything.'

'We are, Marianne. But how could I tell you I was his daughter? It would have destroyed what we have.'

'We have nothing,' Marianne hissed, blinking away the tears as her mother approached.

As the cruel spring wind caught at their clothes and hair, Mama took their hands in hers so that the three of them formed a broken triangle.

'We women must stick together,' she said, 'this is a woman's isle now.'

But Marianne snatched her hand away and started back to Dogger Bank alone, leaving her mother and Nan behind on the quay.

A quiet clicking brought her back to the sitting room. She lifted her head from the chaise, wiping at her sore, cracked mouth, and blinked in the dark. It was all so long ago, and yet somehow it felt just like yesterday.

The brimstones in the puparium were finally emerging. Marianne lit a gas lamp and crept over to the glass box where they were hanging. The first one was already creeping out of its chrysalis. It was rare for them to hatch in the dark, and she made a mental note to write down her findings.

The crackling of a second cocoon caught her attention as another butterfly began to pull its wings free. She sat and waited, watching as the cocoon went from being a part of the insect to an empty shell.

Sitting in the dark, listening to the tick of the broken clock on the mantel, she thought about the peacock butterfly she had released into the room just as the blast happened. She remembered the joyous feeling at seeing it alight into the air, its handmade wing weighing it down so that it spiralled lopsidedly up towards the ceiling.

Her intention had never been to save *any* of the butterflies from these cocoons. Their only purpose had been to give her another reason to stay behind after Mama went.

'Just until they hatch,' she had told her mother. 'The army won't know I'm here. I can pack up the last of our possessions while I wait for them to appear. What harm can it do?' Pregnancy, it seems, encouraged duplicity.

It was a simple plan: to stay on the island a few more weeks and have the baby. Afterwards, she would take it to an orphanage in Ipswich, and return to her mother in the cottage at Lowestoft. She had not made a contingency plan for a blast.

Now, she watched the first of the brimstones appear in the darkness with only a gas lamp to light their way into the world. She had laid the remains of the peacock butterfly on the desk, and she looked at it now, thinking again of the butterfly she and Nan had saved years ago. She sighed, trying to banish the thoughts. She was getting sentimental. What good was it to think of Nan now?

She had so little control over the path of her thoughts, the fever raging through her body in waves, making her mind jump back and forth through time. Tentatively, she gave in to her memories again. It was like trying to see through a thick fog in the dead of night: shapes reared up at her – people, pearls, moths – and she took a deep breath and exhaled, allowing her mind to travel back to the weeks immediately after her father's death.

She remembered the dimly lit chapel, the candles flickering over the stained-glass windows. The funeral service had been at midnight, organised secretly in whispered instructions from her mother, for island people do not mourn those who have taken their own lives.

At the service, Marianne gazed at the herrings carved into the pew in front of her, so consumed by her own grief that to her streaming eyes it seemed as if they had broken away from the pine and begun swimming through the air.

She sensed Nan enter the pew behind her, and she turned her head a fraction until she could see her, reflected in the gleam of a candlestick nearby. Her face was pale and downcast. They were so close that the hair at Marianne's neck stirred from Nan's trembling breaths, but she did not turn around. *It's because of you*, she wanted to say.

After the funeral, Marianne walked in the darkness on the beach alone, a stoppered bottle in her hand. Inside was a long letter to her father, mottled with so many tears that they shivered like condensation on the inside of the glass. She lifted her arm and hurled it into the sea, every cruel, vicious thought she had ever had fusing together in her mind and cementing itself there.

The adult Marianne stirred, licking her dry lips and realising she was still sitting at the desk. She rubbed at her temple to banish the memories.

The brimstones in the puparium were pumping blood into their unfurling wings now. She bent and peered closer, her stomach pressing against the edge of the desk, watching as their antennae twitched, the hair on their bodies drying. There was something not quite right about one of them. It appeared to have a slight rusty tinge to the edges of its wings. Marianne rubbed at her forehead again, running a hand over her tired eyes.

The first butterfly to hatch was dry now, its acid green wings uncurled and smooth. Marianne went to lift the lid.

Every living thing deserves a chance, doesn't it?

That whispered voice again, floating in the darkness behind her.

'Nan?' Marianne looked over her shoulder. The lamp was dim, the pool of light not reaching the corners of the room. She had the feeling that someone had stepped back just before she turned, standing out of sight in the shadows. She stared around the room, her eyes wide, trying to take in as much light as possible.

'Stupid girl,' she said to herself, shaking her head. 'Of course she's not here. It's a memory, that's all.' But still her heart pounded in her chest.

She turned back to the butterflies and lifted the lid, putting her hand into the puparium. Startled, they began to fly, their wings flapping against the glass to get away.

She paused. Why not let these ones go, too?

She could feel her sister behind her again, the faint breath stirring the hair on her neck. She had a feeling that if she turned this time, she would find her, just over her shoulder, just as she had been in the pew all those years ago. But she stayed facing the puparium, her eyes on the butterflies.

'I can't, Nan,' she whispered. 'I can't let them go. They're not right. I need to study them. I need to know what it means.'

Behind her, there was something like a sigh, and then Marianne leaned over the puparium, and caught the nearest butterfly, dropping it quickly into the waiting killing jar.

In the morning, she awoke to the stirrings of sunshine on her face. She was aware, for the first time, of a clearness to her head. She opened her eyes, and put her hand to her forehead, feeling cool skin where it had been hot the night before.

She sat up and looked out at the deep blue of the sky through the window. The island looked so inviting, the sun glancing off the pebbles, stroking its fingers over the yellow gorse. Far away, she could just make out the coast of England.

'I am sick of being indoors,' she whispered to the baby, and it kicked lazily in reply.

In the kitchen, she rooted through the remainder of the tinned food. She had planned her rations meticulously, but now nothing tasted right, the traces of fever still distorting her tastebuds. She stirred some porridge on the stove, adding powdered milk to it. But the smell of the milk was sour in her nose, and she stood at the closed back door instead, staring out through the frosted pane of glass at the brightness beyond. The sun poured through, warming her skin.

What if it was all in my head? she thought. *What if the blast never happened; if it was just the fever playing tricks on me, and now I'm getting better?*

She put a hand on the doorknob. She could almost taste the rush of the salt-wet breeze coming in off the sea. She squinted at the bright light shining in through the opaque glass, a darker patch at its centre that looked a little like the shape of a girl, beckoning to her.

Marianne twisted the knob.

She opened the door a crack. The world outside looked normal. It smelt normal, too, the fresh morning air cutting through the burnt smell of curdled porridge, and she pulled it wide and took a step outside, breathing in the coconut perfume of gorse, the whisper of salted air she had almost forgotten existed.

But there was something missing, too. Something *wrong*. She stood, trying to work out what it was, and then it hit her: there was no birdsong. No peacocks called raucously; no seagulls cried to each other. There were no sparrows chattering in the hedgerows, no skylarks singing above. The world was so still that it made her dizzy to look at it. The sky was a clear, hazy blue, as if something hung in the air, not quite visible to the naked eye.

She bent down, a hand awkwardly supporting her belly, and picked up a stone by the back door, dropping it immediately. Had she imagined a strange warmth to it?

It was then that the baby began to twist and turn inside her, just as it had when the blast happened. She could feel its powerful kicks thrusting into her muscles, knocking at her bones as if it were trying to flee, to push her back inside to safety. Quickly, she stepped back into the house and shut the door. Looking again through the panel of glass, the world outside felt changed, suddenly, metamorphosed into something alien, as if, like a chameleon, it had only been pretending to look like the island she knew.

Upstairs in the sitting room, she closed the door and sank down at the desk, wondering all the time, *What have I done? What have I done?*

She stayed shut in the room for the rest of the day, killing and setting the brimstones as they hatched one by one. It was menial work, requiring little thought, and the slow routine of it took her mind from what was happening both inside and outside the house, calming her whenever the edges of panic began to set in.

As she worked, she began to notice marked differences in the butterflies' appearance. They were all notably smaller than brimstones she had caught in previous years, the orange dot on their wings not quite central. She looked at the remaining pupae, hanging side by side, slowly maturing. She wanted to pull them down and tear them apart, to find out exactly what was forming beneath the shells, but she knew she must wait.

That evening, Marianne sat for some time, the latest specimen clinging to her finger. It had hatched an hour before. This one was female – smaller and paler than the large yellow-green males. One of its hind wings was so small that it would not be able to fly. She studied it as it crept down her hand, examining the useless, deformed wing, watching as the antennae weaved drunkenly about. Then she took the cork lid from the killing jar and dropped the butterfly in, watching as it became tipsy, then stilled.

'Mutation,' she whispered to herself, shaking her head at the implausibility of it all.

The changes to these creatures *must* be chance, they must be. She refused to believe they were anything else, for if she gave in to her belief – that these insects were mutating inside their cocoons as a direct result of the blast – then she would have to acknowledge that the baby growing inside her might be changing too.

And what would happen, when her own little butterfly hatched, pushed from her cocoon-like womb? What differences might there be then, in its tiny, delicate body, and, more importantly, what would that mean for its survival?

Chapter Twenty-Nine

/

Tartelin

Summer 2018

I sit back on the chaise, aghast at what Miss Stourbridge has told me — pregnant and alone in an abandoned house, far, far away from the rest of the world, not sure what is real or what is imagined. It feels as if I'm listening to one of my mother's stories; a fairy tale made up of fragments of reality.

By the time she stops talking, it's late afternoon. She's only briefly referred to the baby's father, a secret tryst with a fisherman who was long gone by the time she realised she was carrying his child. She must have been quite old when it happened; perhaps she'd thought she was too old to get pregnant.

Miss Stourbridge rouses, giving her head a little shake as if she's struggling to swim back to the present. It feels as if she's come to the end of her story. So often in the past she has begun to tell me something, and then her grief has stoppered it. Perhaps her baby did not survive. I don't push her to explain.

'Would you take me over to the window, please?' she asks quietly, and I push her wheelchair. As she approaches the telescope, her thin arms reach greedily out for it, and she puts her eye to it and goes still. I stare out to sea, letting the rush of the waves hypnotise me, thinking about all that she's told me: the illness that followed the blast, the worry over her unborn baby.

'Sometimes,' she says, startling me, 'I think I see something swimming out there, a pinniped or a porpoise. Up and down, up and down it goes, as if it is patrolling the water.' Her voice has a high, childlike quality as she clutches the telescope to her eye. 'Sometimes I see it basking in the sun. It never stays long, and it drops underwater for so long that I think it won't resurface, but then it appears again, sleek and fat.'

She breaks off, leaning back from the telescope. When she turns to me, her face has taken on the expression of a frightened child. She pulls something from the pocket of her smock. It's wrapped in thin tissue paper, and as she begins to peel away the layers, I see it's the oyster shell that Nan gave me.

'You asked me yesterday what I'm hoping to find,' she says, the shell glimmering in her shaking hands. She turns it so that the polished interior is visible, the strange creature baring its teeth at us both. 'This,' she says, 'I want to find this.'

'What is it, Miss Stourbridge?'

She stares down at the shell, her shrewd eyes clear of cloud.

'Months after it all happened, when I was well again, I began to suspect that my mind had made it all up,' she says. 'Not just the explosion, but the pregnancy; everything.' Her words are slurred, thick, distorted syllables rolling from her lips, as if she's struggling through the memories. 'There are people whose minds do that, you know. A chemical imbalance. Schizophrenia, bipolar disorder, high fever. So many conditions can do it if you give them the right foundations. But of course, things like that weren't talked about in the Fifties. Back then, I would have been labelled mad, so I stayed quiet.'

'But you would know if you'd had a baby, surely?'

'How, Tartelin? Tell me how?' Her voice is a quiet shriek, setting the glass lamps around us ringing.

I open my mouth to explain and close it again quickly, realising I don't actually know the answer. 'Do *you* think you had a baby?' I ask.

Miss Stourbridge looks down at the shell in her lap, and she sighs. 'I dream of her every night,' she whispers.

Chapter Thirty

Marianne

July 1955

She had been pacing the room since before the sun went down. Her stomach hung away from her as if it was not a part of her, and yet the pain she felt radiating from it wracked through her whole body in waves that mirrored the crashing tide outside. She wanted to saw at her skin, to slice away the appendage. It was pulling her down, onto her knees, onto the rug, and between moments of lucidity she could hear the lowing of a cow, the keening of a bird of prey, and was it her, this noise, this never-ending moan?

Her head was crashing with migraine. Where is my mother, she thought, where is Nan? Where is my dear papa? Why have they left me? Why aren't they here, cooling my brow? Why am I alone?

The clock on the mantel struck eight, and something small and white and slippery slithered between her legs and landed on the rug. Marianne bent round, not understanding, and there was her baby, sucking at the air like a fish. It was so tiny, and it was wet, like a newly emerged butterfly. It took two, three gulps, the skin at the base of its ribcage sucking into itself, and lay still.

Marianne didn't know how long she sat, crouched on the rug next to the little being, watching its chest for any sign of life. It was as still as a moth in laurel. She examined the minuscule fingernails, and stroked the downy hairs that covered its body like a newly hatched chick, and she saw that it was a girl. Carefully, she scooped it up and wrapped it in a blanket, cradling it to her. She watched its little face, hardly daring to breathe, waiting.

In the womb, she had thought of her baby as bonny and plump, but this creature was too fragile for this world to ever have had much of a chance at life.

Better not to name it, she thought, better not to call it anything, than to begin to love it now. She placed the little thing in an open desk drawer and staggered back to the chaise. Lying down, she folded her arms into the soft deflation of her belly, and waited, her eyes flickering from the drawer to the dark bloom of blood that stained the rug on the floor in front of her.

She dreamed she was in a Dogger boat, following the silver herring. The shoal was so vast below her that it *became* the sea, and as the Dogger cut swiftly through, she reached in and pulled out a fish, a thin, bony specimen, and it gasped in her hand, its gills pressing desperately against the sides of its neck, its eyes staring at her, willing her to put it back.

Marianne awoke. She could still hear gasping, like a fish out of water. She tumbled off the chaise and rushed to the drawer, and there was her baby, its little nostrils inflating, deflating, trying to suck in lungfuls of air.

She pulled it from the drawer, the blanket falling away. Its body was no longer white, but red, and it was working so hard to stay alive that its throat sucked flat against the cartilage there, creating a hollow each time it gasped inwards. It was staring, pleading with her to help. Then its eyelids closed, and the huge sucking, shuddering breaths slowed and stopped.

305

Marianne rubbed at the little body helplessly. Its chest was not moving at all now, no air puffed from the tiny nostrils, but from its throat came a strangled, mewling sound, like the keening of the wind, and she stared desperately around the room.

'Help,' she whispered to the house, to the walls around her, 'help me.'

She thought she saw a dark shadow as someone flitted towards the bathroom, and then her eyes fell on the copper bathtub beyond, and she rushed towards it and turned on the tap. The water spewed forth, tainted and briny, and she held the child under its stream. Like a fish, the tiny face puckered and gaped, and it screamed angrily, the sound shrill above the pouring of the tap, and Marianne slid down onto the bathroom floor, holding her soaking child, relief flooding through her.

'There now, little thing,' she whimpered, 'there now.'

Is this a dream? she thought. She felt the papery hot skin of her child against her own. They were both high with fever. A fever dream, then. Surely reality must be the calm of the Dogger boat she had been on, and this was only a nightmare.

I will wake soon, she pleaded with herself, I will wake, lulled by the rocking of the boat on the water, and all of this will be over.

That night, Marianne woke every time her baby mewled, her breasts aching at the noise, but the child would not suckle, and she took to painfully squeezing the thick yellow first-milk into its hungry little mouth.

She had steadfastly refused to name it thus far, thinking of it only as *the baby*. But sometimes, when she was half asleep, the names of fish swam into her head: *little sprat*, or *minnow*, the words latching onto her child with tentacled love.

In the dead of night, she stood at the window, holding her baby, listening to the ebb and flow of the sea outside, and her craving for salt crept back. She smacked her lips together, thinking of the crystals of Dohhalund salt in the kitchen downstairs, and only a spark of lucidity stopped her from leaving her baby and going in search of it.

Each morning she carried the child to the study, and placed it carefully in the brass bowl of Papa's old scales, but each day the scales gave her bad news: the baby was losing weight, however much she tried to feed it. There came a day when the child had lost ounces, and its head in the brass bowl seemed abnormally large against its shrunken body.

In the bathroom, she filled the copper tub with tepid water and lowered the child in, and it stretched and luxuriated in the warmth, twisting and turning, until all of a sudden its slippery skin was free of her hands, the water closing over its head. For a second that seemed to stretch over minutes, Marianne watched as her baby appeared to swim underwater, its tiny mouth gaping and swallowing. And then it opened its eyes and turned and stared up at her through the water, its pupils so large that the whole of its irises seemed black.

To Marianne, it was as if her baby was truly seeing for the first time, as if it could only bear to open its eyes in the dim light of the water, and she took a step back from the bath. *Just to see*, she told herself.

It seemed in that moment as if they were on two sides of a mirror, the baby below and Marianne above, their worlds divided. Panicking, she reached in and plucked it out, bringing it back to the world it was meant to be in.

At night, when the baby slept fitfully beside her, Marianne could not sleep. Once, in the early hours of the morning she thought she saw Nan, standing in the shadows in a corner of the room, silk moths in her hair, but when she got up to investigate, the shadows were empty.

She moved feverishly from one day to the next, a taste of salt always on her tongue, thinking only of the baby's thirst, the baby's needs, never her own. She was so tired that she fell asleep often without meaning to, snatching minutes of sleep throughout the day, sometimes when she was standing at the window with her baby, waking just as her arms began to loose their grip.

When she did sleep, she dreamed of the copper bathtub filled to the brim with sea water, clear and still. At the bottom, seaweed shifted and danced, hiding creatures of the deep. She dreamed her child swam down to the bottom, disappearing from sight in the green fronds at its depths.

In the daylight, she put her ear to the child's little mouth, to its chest, and all she could hear was a ragged, fluttery sound, as if something was caught in its throat. She imagined silk moths in there, hatching in the blood vessels, burrowing out and choking the baby from the inside. She could see its bones now – slivers of clavicle, knotted nubs of spine – running beneath the skin, thin as matchsticks. When she looked at them both in the mirror, they were two skeletons wrapped together, neither alive nor dead.

On a morning so cold and at odds with the time of year that her joints ached and her breath formed mist in the room, Marianne felt herself surfacing from a sleep that she had barely begun to embrace. The sun was barely risen, and she stirred uneasily, only wanting to dive back down, but something caught her consciousness, snagging at her thoughts like a line spooling out to catch a fish.

She could feel the little body of the baby next to her, limp and lifeless. Sleep left her quickly then, and she lifted it, cradling the head.

'Come on, little minnow, come on,' she whispered, rubbing at the child's skin, warming it, cooing words of encouragement into the white shell of its ear, but her baby would not move. 'Please,' she said, 'don't leave me, don't leave me alone.' Her voice cracked, loud in the silent room, and she stared at the child, unwrapping the blankets and studying it properly for the first time, counting the eyelashes splayed across its cheeks, touching the tiny creases in its elbows. It was so thin, the skin white but for a red tinge where the blood had collected, pooling along the back, at the nape of the neck, in the soft hubs of the heels. It was hardly human at all any more.

'My daughter,' she whispered, placing her lips on the baby's tiny stomach, 'my sweet daughter.'

It was the first time she had allowed herself to think of the child as anything other than 'it', and the rush of love that came with the word made her dizzy. It felt right to say it, to acknowledge her small life, and she said it again, the words spilling out of her, filling the house, 'my daughter, my daughter.'

She went to the copper bath and twisted, not the usual tap, but the large, salt-water one, filling the bath until it was high and cold and deep. She carried the child into the bathroom and lowered the little body into the water. The shock of the chilled salt liquid made her daughter come alive again, spinning and kicking as she had in the womb.

Marianne leant over the copper tub, her nails digging into the side, and watched this curious amphibian, part fish, part child, a seed of an idea forming in her mind, a raging thirst for salt building in her throat.

As the sun tipped over the sea's horizon, Marianne wrapped a scarf around her mouth and bundled the child up in blankets, and they made their way downstairs, and out through the front door.

Outside, the island didn't look any different, and Marianne wondered if, after all, the blast had only been in her head. Two swans flew over them, circling the oyster beds. A scrawny tabby cat darted from under a bush and dashed away.

Even then, she didn't really understand what she meant to do. As she reached the beach and her own tongue caught the taste of salt in the spray, her brain took over, and she laid the child down on the stones. Pulling her scarf away from her mouth, she knelt at the freezing cold water and scooped up handfuls of the sea, swallowing it, gulping it, relishing the pain of the salt as it slid down her throat.

The salt's sting cleared her mind, and she turned to her daughter, lifting the tiny creature in her arms, cooing to her, unwrapping the layers. The baby's pearl-white limbs startled outwards, stretching toward the sea as if in longing.

The tide was on the turn, lapping at the shore. Marianne waded deep into the water, ignoring the cold that knocked at her bones, holding her daughter close so that she could feel her heart. The child's black eyes were open and she watched her mother as the loving sea came between them. Little wisps of hair swayed like anemones; starfish fingers flexed.

Something in Marianne died that day as her child reached out for the sea. Something changed in her as the salt water submerged her baby. In the world beneath the water's surface, her daughter twisted and turned as if she had fins instead of hands and feet, and then all Marianne could see was a silhouette growing smaller and smaller, a dark shadow, diving far below.

A flurry of bubbles rose to the surface, and then the child was gone.

Chapter Thirty-One

Tartelin

Summer 2018

Miss Stourbridge's face is grey, the skin around her jaw slack from exhaustion, and for a brief moment her mouth takes on a silent, juddering scream. It mirrors my own thoughts so exactly, a horror that is not possible to put into words.

The clock strikes eight, though it must be nearer to midnight, and she wipes her hands over her eyes.

'I must sleep,' she says, and I can hear a faint click in her jaw, as if the muscles are groaning silently at the movement. She rolls the wheelchair slowly over to the door, and I stay in the panelled room, unable to tear my mind away from all that she's told me.

I get up at last and extinguish the lights, then I make my way to my own room, stopping outside her bedroom door for a brief moment, imagining her in there: the courage it has taken to relive what she went through. It strikes me that perhaps part of the reason she came back here was so that she could try to repent for her actions all those years ago.

In my bedroom, I pull back the quilt and get into bed, taking comfort from the little heart that sits above my pillow. I lie there, not intending to go to sleep, not yet. The wallpaper drifts gently against the wall, like seaweed on the ocean floor, and I think of Marianne, mere inches away. Is she lying awake too, going over again and again what she did?

My eyelids close.

I am alone in the panelled room. Above me, near the ceiling, a peacock butterfly dances. I tip my head back to follow its path, and the skin of my belly stretches taut, pulling against my body. I look down to find a sac of fluid and blood and bone protruding from me, bulbous and sod-heavy. And then my skin begins to crack and crisp, peeling away beneath my breasts like the shell of a cocoon, and a single wet wing unfolds from within, a bleary eye flickering upwards, looking straight at me.

I come up for air, keenly awake, feeling tears on my cheeks and sweat on my skin, my mouth parched. I pull myself up and sit on the edge of the bed, waiting for my breathing to return to normal, and I search through the gloom for the window, for reassurance of the room that I am in; the time that I am in. The moonlight outside is dappled, as if the house is surrounded by trees, their branches gesticulating, and I go to get out of bed, to see what's causing the movement.

My feet have barely touched the floor when it happens. A rumble, so deep and so loud that for a moment I think it is the blast, echoing to me across the years. The floor is shaking, and the wardrobe door swings open on its hinges.

It feels like the noise goes on for ever, and I'm anchored on the edge of the bed, holding the mattress for support, but then, just as quickly, it's over, and all I can hear is the patter of shale, heavy dust landing.

The sea is in my ears, the sound of the waves tumbling over the shore, as if they're just outside my door, knocking to be let in. I tiptoe across the room, and cautiously crook it open. It's dark in the hallway, and loud. A crack has appeared on the wall opposite. The sound of the sea roars here, belching and angry. I step out and pause outside Miss Stourbridge's door, listening, but the sound of the sea draws me onwards, and I continue on, walking cautiously along the hallway towards the panelled room. I push the door open, and the roar of the sea is violent in my ears.

Where the picture window stood, where Miss Stourbridge's desk, and the puparium and the countless killing jars were lined up, now there is nothing but dark, open sky and the smell of sea in the air. The whole of the back of the house has gone, fallen into the sea. Floorboards jut out into the air, and moonlight floods the room. It is the most beautiful and the most terrible view I have ever seen. Below the roar of the water is a creaking sound. I can feel it too, the house moving almost imperceptibly, shuddering like a great wounded beast. I turn and run back to Miss Stourbridge's room, lurching as if on a ship.

I fling open the door. Miss Stourbridge is fast asleep, wrapped up in blankets on the bed. For a moment, I am transfixed. Pinned to the walls are hundreds of drawings: sketches of seals and sea creatures, and picture after picture of a tiny newborn baby. But I have no time to look properly. I run to the bed and shake her awake.

'Miss Stourbridge, Marianne, wake up!'

She rouses sluggishly, and blinks, her eyes opening far too slowly. I keep looking back, listening for the roar that will precipitate the house beginning to crumble. Every sinew in my being commands me to flee, but I stay, pulling off the blankets.

It is then that I see her legs. They are thin and blackened, like dried lengths of seaweed, knobbled and gnarled.

She is alert all of a sudden, pushing herself up in bed.

I draw my eyes away from her legs. 'The house is falling into the sea,' I tell her. 'Half of it's gone already, we must get out. Now!'

Miss Stourbridge cocks her head, listening to the sea's roar as if it's a language she understands. 'Pass me my wheelchair, child,' she says.

I move the chair as close as possible, trying not to look at the way her emaciated legs follow her body, dragging behind, and Miss Stourbridge lowers herself into it. She pulls the blanket over her blackened legs, and I grip the handles of the chair and push, moving swiftly along the corridor. At the top of the stairs she lifts a hand.

'I must see this,' she says, taking hold of the wheels and turning towards the panelled room.

'Please, Marianne, we must go!'

She looks at me. 'You go,' she says, and she smiles, the wrinkles at the edge of her eyes fanning outwards like cockle shells. Then she turns the chair and pushes the door open.

I get a glimpse of the sea and sky and the moonlight, and I smell the wind as it comes hurtling across the water and into the room, consuming the space. And then the door closes, and it's as if the room exists in a different time. I turn to go, one hand on the banister, but my feet refuse to move, planted on the landing. I stand at the top of the stairs, trying to make myself descend, and then my legs make the decision for me. Heart racing, I swear quietly to myself as I turn swiftly and follow Miss Stourbridge into the panelled room.

She is silhouetted against the sky, close to the open edge of the house, her wheels within inches of the ends of the floorboards. Her hair, unleashed from its daytime pins, is flying about her face, and in the moonlight I can see her expression clearly. It is one of peace, of acceptance.

'Miss Stourbridge!' I shout over the wind, but she doesn't turn her head. I want to walk over to her and pull the chair back, but as I step closer, the whole room lists slightly, and I cannot do it.

I am angry with myself for coming in here. She is an old woman; she has every right to die like this. But still I stand there.

'Marianne,' I try one last time, but she doesn't show any sign of hearing me. There is a small, serene smile on her face.

I turn and pull the door open, struggling against the force of the wind. I'm halfway down the stairs before I hear it slam shut behind me.

Outside, I stop, breathless with terror, and stare at the house. It takes me a moment to realise that next to it, where the shells of two other houses should be, there is nothing but a vast patch of yawning black sky. I turn from the sight of it, trying to contain my panic.

There are two people on this island who could help me. I think of Jacob, his strength, his quiet courage, but then my mind shifts to the little brick building on the beach, the rusting bunk bed, the mussel shell in the shape of a moth.

I set out at a run along the path that will take me to the south beach, and the herring girls' quarters, hoping she is there.

It's late, but as I approach the old brick building, I see a thin spiral of smoke threading into the moonlight. Dogger Bank is not visible from here, shielded by the cliff. Nan is sitting cross-legged outside the little hut. She looks up in surprise as I approach.

'Tartelin!' she says as I come to a stop, bending over to get my breath back. The smile on her face vanishes as she sees my expression.

'Please help,' I say, 'it's Marianne.'

She draws herself to her feet like a ballerina, lithe for one so old, and matches my quick pace as we set off, jogging, back to the house. She doesn't ask what has happened. We approach Dogger Bank from the front. From here, it doesn't look any different, but as we skirt around the corner of the house, the full extent of what has happened is revealed. Nan stops, seeing the jagged edges of the exposed rooms, the copper bathtub hanging by a single pipe, the sheer drop to the water, far below. From here, it isn't possible to see Marianne, and I hope that she's moved away from the edge. I ignore the small voice that offers another explanation.

'She didn't want to leave,' I say, pointing up to what's left of the panelled room.

Nan nods. 'Of course,' she says, 'she wouldn't. Stubborn as a mule.'

We make our way back to the front of the house and enter via the main hall. It's hard to believe from here that anything untoward has happened. Together, we climb the stairs. The roar of the water gets louder as we ascend, and I push the door to the panelled room open.

Marianne is still there. A few more floorboards have fallen into the sea, and she has pulled her wheelchair back a little in response. I hold the door open, and Nan follows me in, her eyes round as she takes in the vast seascape in front of us. She reaches Marianne and kneels by her chair, placing a hand on hers. As if awoken by her touch, Marianne turns her head and sees Nan, and her mouth opens just a little in surprise. I cannot hear what they're saying over the wind, but I watch, seeing colour spread into my employer's cheeks.

Behind me, I hear footsteps, and I turn to see Jacob running up the stairs.

'You have to get out of here,' he shouts in my ear, and in answer, the house gives a great shudder, as if it's trying to evict us all.

'It's Marianne – she won't leave.'

'Please, go!' he implores, 'I'll meet you on the beach, near the salt pans.'

When I don't move, he puts his hands on my shoulders, and pulls me to him for an instant.

'I'll bring her down, I promise,' he shouts into my ear, then he looks at me with his conker-brown eyes, and I nod, the wind whipping my hair across my face. He smiles briefly, and then he edges into the room.

I turn and run, tearing down the steps and out into the cool of the night, and here I stop, stepping backwards slowly, looking up at the house in terror, watching, waiting.

Chapter Thirty-Two

Tartelin

Summer 2018

Eventually, in the midst of the adrenalin pumping around my body, I recall Jacob telling me to meet him near the salt pans. As my eyes get used to the dark, I see Gabbro, crouched on the ground nearby, her face staring intently at the house.

I wait for a moment more, and then I head north-east, taking a footpath that leads down to the sea. Every few moments I look back over my shoulder at the house.

When I get to the beach, I scan the sand all around me for their silhouettes, hoping they've found another way down here; that they are waiting for me, smiling with relief when they see that I'm safe. But the beach is deserted. In the distance to the south, there is enough light to see the dark form of Dogger Bank leaning out over the cliff, alone up there now, the remains of the other two houses disappeared into the sea. I sink down onto the sand, facing the house, and I wait.

In the dark, my ears have become my eyes. I listen desperately for any sound of approaching feet or faraway voices, anything to suggest Jacob and Nan have persuaded Marianne out of the house. After about twenty minutes, I hear a tearing sound, as if the world is ripping in two, and I jump to my feet. The house is trembling, teetering on the cliff edge, held by invisible strings. My heart drowns out the sound of the waves, banging in my ears like thunder. I picture the three of them inside, the floor tilting so steeply that they roll towards the sea like a string of broken pearls.

Helplessly, I watch as the house creaks and tips towards the sea. Miraculously it stays in one piece as it falls, and then, as it hits the waves, all I can see is a mushroom of dust erupting high into the air, surrounding the cliff and blotting out the moonlight.

I collapse on the ground, not wanting to look any more.

And then I hear a voice – a breathless, deep murmur – and I think, *Jacob*. I cannot discern the words, but the sound fills me with joy. The voice is followed by silhouettes, stumbling over the dunes: Jacob, carrying Marianne in his arms, Nan limping beside him, and Gabbro bringing up the rear as if she is herding them to safety.

When they reach the shore, Jacob lays Marianne down on the sand. Her eyes are open and fierce, but her face is grey, and her breathing shallow. She manages a smile when she sees me.

Nan tucks the blanket around Marianne's legs, clucking like a hen, and Jacob collapses down next to me on the sand and looks over to where the dust is settling. In the east, the sky is beginning to lighten to a strange, ethereal blue-green that reminds me of the silk dress, lost now to the sea. In the eerie gloom we can see the shape of the house, half submerged in the sea at the base of the cliffs, and I think of all the dresses, all the butterflies within, floating away on the next high tide.

Nan and Marianne are talking together in low whispers. I sit down next to Marianne, staring out to sea. The birds have not yet awoken, and I can hear the rattle of her breath below the rush of water on pebbles. Nan has arranged the blankets around her so that she's wrapped up tightly, cradled in the sand, and she is lying back, a look of contentment on her weary face, her eyes closed. I'm not sure if she's asleep.

'Thank you,' I say quietly.

'What for, child?' she says, her eyes still closed.

'For letting me come here. For helping me grieve.'

Marianne opens her eyes and smiles. Her face is still so pale. 'I think it's you that has helped me. It's a special place, this isle, isn't it?' she says, lifting a shaking hand and pointing. 'Look at that sky. It's the exact colour of a green hairstreak.'

'My mother would have called it *chartreuse*,' Nan says, sitting on Marianne's other side. 'We used to dye silk that colour when I lived in France.'

'We never did see eye to eye,' Marianne says quietly, raising her eyebrows. They share a smile, and she closes her eyes again. 'I'm glad you came back,' she says to Nan, her eyes still closed.

'This island pulls you back,' Nan says, looking out to sea.

I turn to follow her gaze. The sky over the sea is changing, metamorphosing in a thin line of bright green light just above the water. I listen to the sea's strange, hushed song, and I understand what she's talking about. I'm sure one day I will return here, too, and I feel sad at the thought, because knowing I will return means that first I have to leave.

Jacob is further down the shore, bending now and again to collect stones that shine in the moonlight.

'Go to him,' Marianne says. 'Talk to him. Let him in.' She reaches up and lays her hand over my heart. I clasp it briefly, and then I stand.

He greets me with a smile. His eyes look different: staring, as if the shock and fright of what he's just witnessed is still replaying somewhere in there. I wonder if he's imagining himself going down with it; how close he must have come.

I look down at the cascade of pebbles beneath our feet, seeing for the first time how they're made up of tiny segments, not just a solid, undulating mass. Jacob has taught me the names of some of the stones, and I recite them as I look. Chert and granite, schist and quartzite. Citrine, serpentine and gabbro.

'Pebbles look so different when they're wet,' Jacob says, interrupting my thoughts. He hands me a stone. It is golden yellow, almost translucent and slick with sea water.

'I used to take bagfuls back home when I was a kid,' he says. 'All the colours of the rainbow. But when they dried out, they just looked like stones again. I used to be so disappointed, but then I realised they're still special – it's just hidden inside.'

I look down at the stone, rolling it in my palm. It's already drying, frosted and rough, a plain pebble.

'I thought I'd lost you,' I whisper to him. My voice has taken on the roughness of the pebble's surface, but inside, just like the stone, I can feel myself glittering with relief.

Jacob doesn't reply. Instead, his fingers reach out briefly and find mine.

I walk back along the beach to Marianne, and she greets me with a smile tinged with sadness as I sit down next to her. Her brittle body is bundled up in blankets like the baby she brought to the shore all those years ago. The efforts of the story she told me have taken their toll. She lays her wizened hand on my knee, and I can see that she's going to try to explain her actions. In answer, I take her hand in mine, aware of how flimsy her bones are, and squeeze it gently.

I think of what it is to be a mother. My own mum did not bear me, but she was my mother in every possible way. She chose me as her daughter, and she loved me above all else. *Your mother may not have borne you*, a small voice inside me says, *but she is still your mother. Can't you choose your grandmother in the same way?*

I look over at Marianne, and my heart clutches in my ribcage. Can I bear the pain of loving and losing someone else? Her eyes are half closed, but still she's smiling at me, her face turned towards me as if I'm the sun, warming her on a chill day. I can hear the wheeze in her throat, the rattle of air failing to reach her lungs, and I think of her baby daughter all those years ago.

I think I'm beginning to understand what Marianne wants of me now: why she needed me to know the end of her story.

It is strange how life goes in circles, coming back to the same decision, the same place. She is looking at me under those tired eyelids, a pleading gleam in her eye that is simple to interpret now that I understand her story.

'You know I can't do it,' I whisper.

'Please,' she says, and I'm frightened by the pleading in her voice, as if the Miss Stourbridge I knew was abandoned like a sloughed cocoon in the house that slipped into the sea, and what is left is a vulnerable butterfly, newly hatched with hardly a day left to its name.

'Just … the edge. I want to be near her.' She's holding tightly to my hand now, grasping it with all of her failing strength.

I stand up and go over to Jacob, and I ask for his help. He doesn't question what I'm doing, but follows me back along the beach. Together, we carry Marianne to the edge of the water. Even though my eyes tell me how frail she is, I'm still surprised by the fragility of her body, the feeling that I may snap her birdlike bones at the softest touch. The tide is on its way in, and we place her on the soft sand, high enough so as not to get wet. As I go to stand, Marianne reaches out and touches my cheek. She's so frail that she can hardly speak, but she parts her dry lips and tries anyway.

'Everything is just … metamorphosis,' she says croakily.

I try to make sense of what she means. Is she talking about the island, about what has happened here since that fateful day? Or is it bigger than that? I put my hand briefly on hers, and we look out to sea together, marvelling at its calm beauty.

Tiredness overwhelms me as I go over to Nan and sit down. She has settled into the stones as if it is the comfiest bed in the world. She's constructing a little cairn of pebbles, balancing them precariously on top of one another, bright-eyed as a child.

'You understand her,' she says. 'Not many people did.'

'It's taken time,' I say.

Nan chuckles at the exhaustion in my voice. 'She has lived with many demons for a long time. And sea-people are by their very nature superstitious.' She leans into me, the touch of her shoulder against mine comforting.

'I can't imagine leaving this place,' I say. 'It gets under your skin, doesn't it?'

Nan sighs and sifts the sand from between the pebbles, letting it fall to the ground. 'I have been back on the island for months only, and in that time I have seen fish that pull themselves out of the water. I have seen birds with gills that dive in and never surface. Strange things happened here, Tartelin, even before the blast Marianne told me about, I think.' She nods her head wisely. Her voice is the sound of fairy tale, rich and full of the promise of untold stories. Somewhere in my mind it merges with that of my mother, and my eyelids begin to droop, the press of all that has happened overwhelming me.

I stifle a yawn, and push myself up off the ground, giving my head a little shake to keep myself from feeling sleepy. I look over to check on Marianne. She is still sitting by the sea, her eyes on an invisible horizon.

I go over to Jacob. He is crouched a little way away, Gabbro at his side, at ease in his own company. As I join him, he reaches behind us and pushes at the stones, moulding them as if they were made of clay. He indicates for me to climb into the space he's created, and he stretches out next to me. It is remarkably comfortable, sheltered from the breeze that comes off the sea, and I rest my head on his shoulder. My eyes are growing heavier, lulled by the sound of the waves and the verdure smell of him, and I try, oh I try, to keep them open.

Thoughts are drifting around my head like long, flimsy skeins of spider silk, floating in the air, separate and untouched. But as they fall, they cross over each other, twining and interlocking until they have formed a perfect web, and in it I can see Nan and Marianne and my mother and Jacob, and me.

As my eyes close, the last thing I see before I am asleep is Miss Stourbridge, sitting by the sea, the delicate white strands of her hair picked out by the fading moonlight.

When I wake, night has been replaced by the thin white light of early morning. While I have slept, the sea has shimmered up the sand, and it's close, mere feet away. I lift my head, trying not to wake Jacob or shift the bed of pebbles beneath me. Nan is curled up a little way away like a cat. Jacob doesn't stir as I climb carefully out of the bed he has made.

I am struck by the absence of something. And then I realise. Marianne is no longer on the sand. I stand up, the stones singing beneath me, and I step down to the shore. The water is calm, matching the silver sky above it. It's a strange light, reflecting off the still surface of the sea, a light that has the power to bend time. In the water by my feet, Marianne's discarded blanket sifts like a bank of seaweed on the tide.

I look out over the sea, thinking about her last words to me. Metamorphosis. I think about how the tides move in cycles, washing the sand clean, removing any trace that anything was ever there. But sometimes — after a storm, or a spring tide, or a blast — the sea can deliver unexpected surprises, reveal things that everyone believed to be gone for ever.

The sea is made up of unspeakable sadness. Never have I understood these words more clearly than I do now. However deeply our secrets are dropped into the ocean, there will always be an echo of them, coming back to haunt us.

I shade my eyes against the newly minted sun. In the distance, where the sea meets the sky, something swims. It is a creature born of this way of life in a way that we humans are not. It dances and plays in the water as if it knows I am there, communicating to me a joy and expectation of the world that belies anything I've seen before.

And then, as if it has shown me everything I need to know, it leaps into the air, its gleaming body twisting and turning, extolling the pleasure of living, of life, and it dives down, swallowed up by the waves. And it is gone.

Acknowledgements

I'm writing this in the middle of the pandemic, which is a bittersweet thing. It's a reminder of all the people I've met on the journey of writing this novel, of all the places I explored, all the brains I tapped before the world stilled. I was lucky enough to do it all before Covid-19 appeared and turned my wonderful, breathlessly beautiful world into the size of my house and garden.

My novel started with an obsession with Orford Ness, as it has for so many writers before me. One such writer is W. G. Sebald, whose book, *The Rings of Saturn*, hugely influenced my writing.

Thank you so much to David Mason, the lead ranger on the Ness, who took me on a tour of the strange, wild, flat spit of land. I lived near Orford Ness for years, and my dad spent many days there as a customs officer. It's a significant and fascinating place, now owned by the National Trust. Do visit it.

Thank you to Amy Nichols for her in-depth, kind and caring knowledge of babies that are born too early, and thank you to Vicky McKenzie for her wise words on ASD. Big thanks must also go to Emma Bamford for reading chunks of the novel, and spending hours WhatsApping me ideas for increasingly hilarious titles.

This novel began on the Creative Writing MA at the University of East Anglia, where I was awarded the Annabel Abbs Scholarship.

Thank you so much to Annabel for enabling me to spend time with so many brilliant, creative minds. Thank you to Jean McNeil for seeing something in this story when I had only just begun to peel back the layers, and thank you to my workshop class of the autumn term, who all helped shape this book into something I'm really proud of.

I have been lucky to have the insight of two editors on this book. Thank you to Kate Mills for such brilliant early thoughts on the sweep of the story, and to Cicely Aspinall for those little macro details that mean absolutely everything in a novel. My thanks also go out to Pen Isaac for the copyedits, and of course to the incredible team at HQ, who have turned my humble story into the most beautifully packaged book.

To my agent, Juliet Mushens: you are basically The Best Person in the World.

Writing at home in a pandemic has meant that I've often been accompanied by my husband and son, Matt and Seb, and I'm very thankful to say that it's been a pleasure to share this strange, never to be forgotten time with the two of you.

Finally, to Miss Pirrie, my English teacher who kindled my love of writing. I had tried to get in contact with her after publishing *The Illustrated Child*, and I managed to track her down, but alas, I missed her time on this earth by just a few days. In her honour, my thanks go to all teachers who ever dared us to dream.

Don't miss another captivating read from Polly Crosby

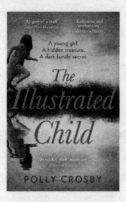

A young girl.
A hidden treasure.
A dark family secret.

Romilly Kemp has an idyllic childhood, roaming the wilderness that surrounds her father's ramshackle farmhouse. But when he makes her the star of his beautifully illustrated books, her carefree if somewhat lonely existence is threatened.

The books are thought to hold clues to an elaborate treasure hunt, and strangers turn up at their door, anxious to get a glimpse of the 'Kemp Treasure Girl'. But when her father falls ill, leaving Romilly more isolated and alone than ever, she begins to delve deeper into the books – and her past.

As she makes sense of the clues he has hidden, she finds a truth that is far darker and more devastating than any treasure hunt has a right to be. For not everything that is hidden is gold.

Available now in paperback, ebook and audio.

ONE PLACE. MANY STORIES

ONE PLACE. MANY STORIES

Bold, innovative and
empowering publishing.

FOLLOW US ON:

@HQStories